The Breath of Purpose

A novel by jrenee

The Breath Of Purpose

To God be the Glory for the great things He has done.
To Rich, Justin, Jacob, and Joshua, thank you so much for your support
To Mom and Lee ya'll are the best two musketeers a musketeer could have

© 2010 by jrenee. All rights reserved. No part of this book may be reproduced or transmitted in any form or by any means, electronic or mechanical, including photocopying, recording, or by any information storage and retrieval system, without permission in writing from the publisher.

Cover design by Warren Whitworth Jr. for Prodigal Designs

Author photograph by Lawrence Lightner for Essence of Light Photography

This book is a work of fiction. Any resemblance to real characters, locations, or settings is coincidental.

Unless otherwise noted, all references to biblical scripture are from the New International Version.

Printed in the United States of America.

ISBN-13: 978-1452815794

ISBN-10: 1452815798

Acknowledgements

    I first give honor and glory to the Almighty for His grace and mercy. I am thankful for His comfort and assurance through the process of hearing, believing, and then becoming a writer. This has been a journey of sacrifice, trials and triumphs. Thank you to my husband Rich for his prayers and encouragement. To my three sons, because I have you the bible says that I am a blessed woman. To my sister, author Lisa McNeill, you are always here "two" inspire me☺! I am grateful that God put us in the womb together because you are my spiritual advisor, my best girlfriend, and the best sister a girl could ever have. To my mom Pat Stokes, you have supported me through the good times and bad. You are always my champion, always wanting even greater for me. I thank you mom for being who you are, the best is yet to come. I know where you are if I need you☺. To my girls that knew me when Tanya, Lateea, Melinda, Selene you guys are special to me for so many reasons. To my good girlfriends, Ginaboo, Keysha (the bestest God-mommy on the planet), Natalie W., Stephanie G. and Veronica L., the shared tears, prayers, and good old-fashioned inside jokes help me make it through. I can't forget to say a special thank you to a woman that made me tap into my creative juices, and trusted what God had inside of me…Rev. Tracey you are the best! The first three *His Way Plays by jrenee* all started from one of your visions! To the Mt. Calvary AME Family under the leadership of the Fullers, I owe a lot of my spiritual growth to you. (Love ya AVP, EOS, and Soul II Soul). Thanks so much to Mr. Prodigal Designs himself, Warren Whitworth for taking my visions and making them reality. To my special family at The Maiden Choice School, it takes a remarkable person to do the things you do in the lives of God's most unique creations. And finally, if I've forgotten to mention you by name don't worry, I'll make sure to put you in the "thank you's" of the next novel coming your way very soon...

Chapter 1: Are You Talking To Me?

§

Ooh that felt…so…good. I know I shouldn't have done it, but it felt so absolutely good. Right in the middle of another lame excuse, I just jammed my finger as hard as I could on the little red end button. I'm sure it didn't take all that energy, but I was so completely tired. I wanted to punch something. I really wanted to break something. I wanted to bite something until it bled, but I just had to settle for the satisfaction of knowing that my husband was now continuing to talk to me and I'd just hung up on his black behind. Sure he'll be angry once he realizes what I did, but I'm grown. And he thinks that I'm just gonna sit here and let him talk to me any kind of way and continue to lie to me. Okay let me put this in perspective…two minutes earlier I flipped my cell phone open and he starts blah blah blahing about something.

Him: "You know what Renee…I'm not gonna keep answering the same question a million different ways. You asked if I was coming to the boys' game tonight and I told you no." Then me pulling the phone from my ear to look at it with attitude, like is this fool for real? Counting to ten, and then using the sweet voice.

"But this is like some championship thing. You know it means so much for him to have you there…hello? Anthony?"

Him: "Yeah…uh…remember I told you I got to go into work early, so I need my sleep. There will be other games. You blow everything out of proportion. The boys know I get to games when I can get to 'em. This is not the end of the world!"

Me trying to count to ten, but just barely making it to seven: "Who said anything about Armageddon, I'm just trying to get you to spend time with your children. The last time I checked I wasn't getting no child support check, so I know I'm not a single mother, right? Did I say that out loud? Apparently I did because now I don't even hear him breathing on the other line, so I continue my rant. "I work late…I work crazy hours, but I'm always there…they want their father." The old 'boys-need-their-dad' guilt trip…it works every time.

"They are not babies, for god's sake girl! You want to explain to my boss why I'm falling asleep on the job then I'll meet you at the game!"

"Never mind Anthony…just forget I asked. But this has got to stop. I can't do this anymore with you. Anthony?" I know this boy hears me.

"Yeah, I'm here, look I'll make it to the next one." He mumbled making sure to yawn loudly to emphasize how tired he was. Supposedly he worked late last night, but when I looked outside I could see him sleeping in his truck. Hmph probably didn't want me to smell whatever chick he was all laid up on. I mean he's been married to me for twenty years and he don't know I called up his job and found out he left work early? He must have forgotten who he was dealing with. So for now I'll let him think he got over on me. Okay back to me being pissed off…

"But I'm swamped. I have story deadlines a mile long. I can't make it. You could go for an inning or two." I begged looking at piles and piles of manila folders with red tags hanging from them.

Responding in his typical condescending monotone…"It's quarters Renee. The boy plays football, not baseball. And if you had your priorities straight, you'd be at that game. You don't seem to realize that what I do is hard work. I wish I could sit at a computer all day." He hissed, sucking his teeth.

So here I sit two minutes later with my thumb still smashed on the end button. Ooooh. My blood is boiling. I'm officially through. I never used to think of myself as a quitter, but at this point I'm done. I want to be in that life that I created in my dreams when I was ten. The perfect husband, the picket fence, five children…a dog. Can a sista just wake up for once from eight hours of sleep with her makeup and hair perfectly coifed and glide down the stairs like June Cleaver? Or better yet, why can't I come through the door of my fabulous brick Brownstone wearing a fierce outfit and engaging in an intellectual conversation with my brilliant doctor husband, named Heathcliff?

But I can't do that. I'm just existing right now. I'm existing in a life where my husband will not even think to call me back to find out if something happened to me since the phone abruptly disconnected. I'm existing on a job where a good day is multiple homicides, a fatal car crash, and a two year old found wandering around wearing only a pamper on the streets of Baltimore. I'm existing in a place where I am saved and claim to be in love with God, but I can't even stand to look in the mirror at myself. What is that all about? I have a job, a husband, children…the house, but I want…no I need more. I need to stand for something. I need to know why I'm here. Alright girl, get it together. You got work to do and less time to do it in now that you have a football game to get to in less than fifteen minutes. Drama…the subtitle of my life.

"Giirrll! Let me tell you about the latest and greatest…I heard that new girl they hired in accounting is supposed to be dating one of the Baltimore Ravens, he lives somewhere near you in Owings Mills. You ain't seen them together have you? I'mma try to see if she can hook a sista up with some VIP passes for the next game!" And speaking of drama.

"What I tell you about that office gossip girl? It will get you in trouble. The new girl, who happens to be named Natalie, might not want all ya'll in her business let alone up in no VIP suite with her and her people." Rumors ran wild up in this place…and most of the time it was loud-mouthed Marguerite, our front desk receptionist, at the root of it all.

"True…true, well speaking of triflin'…" she continued on, who was speaking of trifling? "What in the world was going on with that crime scene you covered this afternoon?" She pulled a chair up to my cluttered desk and started flipping through folders with her hideous five inch nails.

"I'm doing my best to put it out of my mind. Makes me wonder all the more, what this world is coming to?" I said quietly, shaking my head and moving the folders beyond her reach. I didn't like to indulge Marguerite, but ooh that last crime scene I just left, now that was some crazy stuff! Picture this…I'm walking up to this straight-out-of-Better-Homes-and-Gardens mansion, with a large wrought iron fence and a lush green lawn. I'm thinking they called me all the way out here for a tea party? But then I'm stopped by my buddy from the police department who fills me in on all the inside scoop for most of my stories. "Baby girl, you ain't gonna be ready for this one." He says to me lifting the caution tape for me to enter the house and make my way to the backyard. Still can't get the image out of my head. The red stiletto heels, the black fishnet stockings, the blonde wig, and the brown bloated body all swaying and bobbing together under the murky water of a swimming pool that was in desperate need of cleaning.

My original intention when I called Anthony was to tell him about it, and vent about having to work, when all he could do was complain about how tired and overworked he was. Well join the club.

"Renee I need to have that report on my desk in the next ten minutes, we want to go live with this as breaking news for the five-thirty lead in." And that annoying interruption officially ends the Renee Chase pity party. Alvin, my station manager had been working my next to last…and I mean I only got one more after this one, nerve. If he wasn't peeking his head in my cubicle asking me if I was done every two seconds, I'd have finished this ridiculous story thirty minutes ago. Not to mention Marguerite was still standing in my cubicle like she don't have nothing else to do, but be in my way. It's times like these that I wish I'd opted for the corner office with the door that could be locked from the inside.

After my telephone conversation or lack thereof with Anthony, I'm just not the one to be messing with. While Alvin is nagging me about the breaking news story, he must have forgot I did just hand him two of my most sensational stories about crime and corruption involving the police commissioner and the mayor not twenty minutes ago.

I was on my way out the door, thanking Jesus and giving Him glory for the end of another day about two hours ago, when a prominent business man…that's right I said man honey, decided to get himself found floating at the bottom of his pool, dressed in some questionable attire. I wouldn't have believed it, if I hadn't seen it with my own eyes, and now the image was burned in my brain. To top it all off, we'd honored him last year as our Man of the Year for his tireless work in the community with our youth. What is this world coming to? Renee, don't let them see you sweat girl. Press save on this report and let's get to steppin'. Besides I needed to get up because

Alvin and Marguerite were invading my personal space and it was getting a bit claustrophobic to me.

"Actually, I have your report right here." I said whipping the papers from the printer and handing them to him while they were still warm. Marguerite was doing her best to speed read what she could see so she could pass on the information to her gossip club. "Let me know if there are any changes. I need to input this into the teleprompt and run...Nick has a football game that I can't miss." The two Emmys sitting on my desk should be enough to let these people know I don't need a babysitter when it comes to news writing, but whenever we go live on a big story, Alvin likes to give the reports his once over. One hundred percent of the time he never changes anything, but at five-foot-three, he's got a complex, so I let the brotha think I care. I was going to just breathe and continue to pretend to wait patiently while he scanned the report.

"Fantastic! This will have those other fools scrambling around like chickens with their heads cut off! Ah...I love being on top. Nobody can stop me." Alvin was so excited; I thought he was going to kiss me. I mean his feet actually left the floor; he was literally jumping up and down. The man was starting his rendition of the Cabbage Patch dance right there in my cubicle.

"I made sure to send our condolences to his wife. This has got to be hard on the family." I hated to bust up his party, but I wanted to bring this all back into perspective, I mean we were talking about a dead body here.

"Yes...yes of course. Thanks Renee. Get that into the prompt and then I'll see you in the morning." He quickly excused himself from my cubicle and scurried about to see what some of the junior writers were working on. Some days I can't get out of here fast enough. I never imagined myself writing such graphic descriptions of crime scenes let alone getting first hand accounts of them while I was standing over actual dead bodies. Oh but that's right according to my husband, I sit at a computer all day.

"Yoo-hoo? Is anybody in there? Girl what you doin'? You prayin' for lost souls and criminals again?" Marguerite has once again interrupted my daydreams with her loud, high-pitched voice. Why was she still standing here? "I swear, you let that stuff get to you." She continued unmoved by my rolling eyes and loud sighs. "That guy they found in that pool wasn't nothing but a dog. I done already heard he was cheatin' on his wife and from what I hear, he must have been one of those down low brothas 'cuz he was wearing some women's clothes…" She was talking behind her hand like she was telling me a secret, but she was talking loud enough for everybody in the building to hear her.

"Marguerite…please. I don't need the extra details. I know the story, remember I went to the scene, I wrote the report for tonight. I don't want to pass judgment on nobody. We all need prayer, including you." I laughed trying to ease the tension I was feeling, while at the same time throwing my hand up in her face. Plus I needed a quick exit, and if there was anything that got Marguerite out of my face, it was mentioning anything about prayer or Jesus. The only time she's ever admitted being in a church was when she was waiting for the bus trip to Atlantic City a few months ago.

"You right about that Mrs. Renee. Well I'm going on break, if anybody is looking for me." See. Worked like a charm, thank you Lord, once again just the mention of prayer changes things! Keep on keeping on girl. And what I look like relaying messages about where Marguerite is going to be? I know she was in my mouth when I told Alvin I was leaving the building. If being nosy was a talent she could put on her resume, she'd have been promoted to general manager by now. And truth be told, she was always on break, so everybody always knew where to look for her, propped up in front of the television watching her stories, eating barbecue pork rinds, and drinking a pineapple soda.

"I'm going to my son's game, if anybody is looking for me. I have all of my reports done; call me on the cell if there's any trouble." I said as she was making her way to the break room. I really didn't mean that, but it sounded good. I was going to turn my cell phone off as soon as I got in the car.

****

"Get out of there! Throw it…throw it! Yes! Yes! Run…run!" That's my boy ya'll.

"Renee, your boy is going to take us all the way to state championship…you gotta tell me what you're feeding him." One of the parents of a boy that played on Nick's team said clapping me on the back.

"Hey, what can I say? It's God given talent. He sure didn't get it from me or his dad."

The man whose name I couldn't remember continued to come closer looking beyond me toward the car I'd just raced from.

"I thought my man was coming today, all the fathers are supposed to be getting together today after the game. We talked about it last week."

"Oh he had to…um…work. I'll let him know you asked about him." I won't, but it sounded good.

I made it to Nick's game right as they were going into half time. I managed to see him throw an excellent pass for a gain of thirty yards. That's why I was just screaming like a mad woman until the buzzer sounded. His team was up by two touchdowns.

"I'm going to grab a few sodas from the car, I'll bring one back for you. Here have a seat...there's plenty of room up here." He said pointing to a spot on the bleachers amongst other parents. Good. Now you can sit down and exhale Renee. Breathe slowly girlfriend. I hadn't had a panic attack in months, but I could feel one coming on. Sweat trickling, armpits itching, leg getting jittery, and heart beating a mile a minute. All the racing and running had gotten to me. I had football games, and tennis matches, and deadlines, and...I went on four ride along exclusives getting facts for stories this week alone. Each one of the crime scenes was more gruesome then the next. Every night it was becoming more and more difficult for me to fall asleep. The images were beginning to stay in my head. I tell you, it's getting hard to tell whether I am awake or still dreaming.

Last night, I went to an abandoned house, where police had gotten into a gun battle with some thugs, there was a woman and her child killed in the crossfire. As the vultures...I mean reporters began to gather at the scene, I heard a very distinct voice say to me... "Renee...be prepared, I have something for you to do." I froze. You better believe I ran home and got down on my knees. It wasn't just my usual ritual of praying for the loss souls and criminals as Marguerite had put it, but I needed some clarification from God. What did a dead woman and her child have to do with me? Lord? You talkin' to me?

"Hey ma, did you see me? The arm is just on fire like that...ya boy can't be stopped!" Nick said startling me out of my thoughts as his team ran past the stands and back out onto the field. He playfully kissed the right bicep on his throwing arm. He stopped long enough to ask where his dad was and see what I'd be cooking for dinner once he got home.

"I'm going to stop by the Food Lion on my way home. Dad said he'd be home when you got in, he worked late and needs to go in early tonight so he needs to sleep." I said covering for the fact that Anthony had missed yet another one of Nick's games.

"Cool. Enjoy the second-half; I got a little something for the other team." He sounded a little disappointed, but he still winked and rushed back into the huddle. I could see him whisper a quick prayer, tap his chest two times then raise his hand up to the sky. That was his routine before each play. God bless him, even though he got all the accolades for his spectacular plays, my son knew who the real quarterback was, and he should. He got raised in the church just like I did. Okay so I fall down a few times daily by thought word and deed. Case in point…hanging up on my husband, but God is not through with me yet. Now Nick on the other hand, at nine years old he walked up to that preacher all on his own and said he wanted to know more about Jesus and he hasn't been the same since. I'm not saying he wasn't a typical boy growing up and getting into everything he wasn't supposed to, but he was definitely a changed boy. Change is a word that I've been contemplating a lot lately. I want change, been praying for change. I even asked God the other night when my change was gonna come.

Chapter 2: It's On The Way

§

Guess what? You ask God a question…you gonna get an answer. My answer was definitely coming. As sure as I was standing at this checkout counter wondering why the man behind me kept bumping into my heels with his cart, I knew it was coming. Last night when I was praying and contemplating that horrible death scene I was covering with the news crew, I heard the word…*purpose*. Not just any old purpose…my purpose. The very reason I was created and formed in my mother's womb was near. It was absolutely coming and I was feeling like I was not prepared. I thought I would be overjoyed, praising God and speakin' in tongues, but at this very moment I was terrified. I don't know why I was so scared. My mother always told me 'don't be asking God for stuff if you don't what Him to give it to ya'. 'You gotta pray expectin' something', she'd often tell me. So here I stand, I couldn't pinpoint the day or the hour, but I knew it was very close.

"You come here often?" Cart man asked from way too close behind me.

"Whenever I need groceries." I answered sarcastically without looking in his direction. I'm busy feeling overwhelmed here brotha can you give me a break? You too close up on me.

And speaking of close…you ever get the feeling that the walls are closing in on you? I've felt it. It drives me absolutely crazy. From nowhere, I get this feeling of crushing closeness around me. It's suffocating. I know I sound a little paranoid…right? But I swear I can hear the theme music from Jaws in my head. Panic…you can't have me right now.

It took me years before I would admit that I had a problem with these attacks. You know a black Christian woman ain't supposed to be crazy! I mean for goodness sake, you got Jesus what you need to give all your money to a therapist for? But as Rev. Fowler said in church last Sunday, if you need a pill, then don't come up in that church if you haven't taken your medicine. Just when I thought I'd gotten past all of that confusion, then fear, doubt, and insecurity decided to rear it's ugly head. I went to praying more than I ever had in the past. But ever since I got up off my knees last night, every room I've walked into has suddenly gotten smaller. Lately the more I've prayed the more claustrophobic I feel. No, this is more than me being funny about my personal space; even though Cart Man is having a time waiting his turn behind me…this feels real. This feels like if I put my hand in front of me the air will be solid and thick enough to grab by the handful. I'm beginning to feel my world literally closing in on me. Breathe Renee. Smell the roses, blow out the candle…smell the roses, and blow out the candle. See, I'm talking to myself again, but it's a technique my therapist gave me and it helps me to calm down.

Why now Lord? Are you sure I'm the Renee Chase you want? This Renee is tired and fed up and not in a good mood at all. I'm not where I should be, or all I should be. This Renee has got a lot of wounds and worries that we need to talk about. Lord let me work on being the pulled together Renee, then we can discuss the future and destiny and all that good stuff.

"Ma'am? Ma'am. I said that comes to sixty dollars and fifty-two cents." Humph. Miss thing working at the counter is trying to be so pleasant. Isn't that nice, so…sweet. All I can make out in my haze of fear and tiredness while I try to bargain with God is those sparkling braces. Nametag says *Trisha*. Cute.

"Do you mind if I take a few things off? I only have forty dollars in cash on me. I left my card in the car…you know if I bring it in I go crazy." I'm lying again. Let me repent for that one right now. Why was I trying to fake the funk? Why do I always put on what my husband calls 'the voice'? You know, we all got one. I can break into mine without even realizing it, but I always know I've done it, because my cheeks start hurting from the strain of the fake smile.

"Uh…you can use my club card if you need it sweetheart." Cart man said from somewhere in the distance…I had totally tuned everybody out. I managed to cut my eyes at him and mouth 'no thank you'.

"Ma'am? Ma'am? I said what do you want me to take off?" I detected a bit of annoyance now. Trisha did not appreciate me interrupting her flow. Girlfriend had just turned her light off when I came over. I was the last customer she was going to check out before her smoke break. At least that's what I assumed when she flicked off her light and pulled a cigarette from her front pocket placing it above the ridge of her ear. Which is another reason I can't understand why Cart Man is still standing behind me with his cart grazing my tired heels? The girl turned the light off way before he got in this line. But he still wants to just smile and wink at me. My sons would say he's tryin' to 'push up' on me. Well he better back up if he don't want me to start pushing back.

"Forty-two thirty four." Uh. Oh. She's speaking in a tight monotone, with just a hint of exasperation. Did I also detect a loud sigh at the end of that last four boo, boo?

"O.k....um, let's see." Now the old me from back in the hood, could argue and say I thought this or that item was two for something, but I needed to save some of my tricks for the next shopping trip. Anyway I've decided Trisha's sudden attitude change is getting on my last nerve, and thanks to my boss, I do only have one left. Let me put this little girl out of her misery so she can take her little smoke break. With a dramatic flourish of my hand, and a you-wanna-back-up look on my face aimed at brother man behind me who was still trying to push is discount card in my direction, the box of lunch snacks was off the conveyor belt and dropped into one of those left over baskets under the counter.

"Outta forty…thirty three cents is your change." Trisha says ripping the receipt practically in half when she tore it away from the register to hand me my change. How she know I didn't want that coupon for Lean Cuisine that was on the back?

"Thank you. Have a good evening." Trisha was having a time bagging those groceries. Sorry girl I know that nicotine is calling. I should leave them items right there, but the least I can do is escort my precious Ben & Jerry's back to the freezer case. We will meet again Ben, give Jerry my best I guess ya'll are uninvited to my pity party. I could also help her bag the groceries, but I won't; I'm too busy trying hard to breath.

****

Thank God I made it outside. At least now I didn't feel like there were walls about to close in on me. I have been anticipating this season of purpose. I have always known that God had a great work for me to do. But I don't feel like my house is in order. I don't recognize my home or me. I just never thought He would pick me now. It's a straight up draught in my house…oh the faucets are working fine but after twenty years, my perfect Christian marriage feels like it's drying up. My babies are grown and so I feel like all my mommy juices are slowing down and turning to sludge. Let's not go into the literal drying up of our funds. It's getting to the point where I need to break out the dust buster every time I crack open my check book to pay a bill. And then there was the affair. I can't even get into that madness.

Do I sound bitter? I'm really not. I'm God's child honey, just desiring' some of that "exceedingly and abundantly" my bible talks about right about now. Even still, He has been so faithful to me, and I keep taking my broke self right on up to that tithing box. I know this is a season, an unusually, long season, but a season nonetheless.

It feels good though to know that I have made it through another day, and another tank of gas. It was getting a little sketchy there…the car has been running on fumes and God's great mercy for the last two days.

Chapter 3: Tryin' Hard To Breathe

§

The heavens are smiling on me, because I know this ain't my front door opening as I pull up my driveway. Is somebody coming to help a sista with the groceries? I'm gonna faint.

"Hey ma, what are we eating for dinner?" I knew it! Too good to be true. Is this child for real? Nick has a one-track mind…food, food, and more food. And he is always ravenous after a game. A game where my baby threw no less than four touch down passes!

"I'm good sweetie, and yes I will take some help with these bags, and the last time I checked we were having food for dinner." Lord, this tongue. I can't help it, this child knows better.

"Can we have pizza?" My six-foot-three-inch son says towering over me pleading for his favorite food group.

"No, I bought stuff for making the chicken and spinach thing." He gives me the silent treatment while he trudges toward the house with the lightest bags from my trunk.

My son Alex came running out of the house just as Nick made it to the door. "Hey ma…" His older brother stops him in his tracks.

"We're havin' the chicken thing, yo…so don't even bother askin'." See Nick is really trippin' now. Does he know he's not too big to get a beating? I don't like the attitude. Plus I got thirty-three cents to my name after working ten hours of overtime last week…I don't need a reason!

"Awwwww, maaaa!" Alex whines, "We just had the chicken thing."

"We didn't just have it, and I don't care if we ate it every day last week, that's what's for dinner. Now ya'll want something different then fix it yourselves." I huffed, dragging' my tired feet toward my door with three heavy bags in each hand. Trisha pulled the ultimate payback for my little stunt back at the store that chain-smoking fool didn't double bag my ghetto-sized detergent, and now the bag is ripping with each step I take. I'm desperately clutching it to these beanbags I call thighs. You'd think a grown man would come out of the house to help his wife, but not today. I know he heard me pull up because the brakes are squealing so bad it sounds like I'm running over Babe the pig every time I try to come to a stop. I've asked my man to get them checked but he's too busy making sure his baby, that would be the brand new '98 Lincoln Navigator parked next to my beat up '84 Maxima, is cleaned and shining.

Look, I know I'm blessed, there are women that wish they could have a saved black man that's working a nine to five, living in their house. And I even know woman at my church that are praying for children too, let alone two eatin'-you-outta-house-and-home healthy boys. They both can work a nerve though, since they so grown and don't need nobody no more.

My boys are rooted and grounded. They should be. I used some of the old 'spare the rod spoil the child' rules of parenting right from the good book. Nick likes to remind me that when he has children he's not going to spank them; he's just going to put them in 'time out'. I am still trying to think of a good comeback to that comment, but for some reason I can't get past laughing every time he says it. Yes…my boys turned out, or should I say are turning out to be some wonderful human beings.

All the stories I write about the status of young men in our community, make me all the more blessed that my children are who they are. If I've written about it once, I've written about it a thousand times…black males in jail, black males in gangs, black males unemployed. The only images they get to see are thugs with their pants down around there ankles grunting and moaning about ho's and money!

Well wouldn't you know…these thighs are good for something? I made it into the kitchen without dropping my detergent. I passed my dearly beloved reclining in front of the monstrosity he calls a television, sitting smack in the middle of my Shabby Chic French cottage-themed living room. Looking down into the sunken living room I gaze at my creamy white display shelf with the patina finish, the overstuffed pillows in shades of pastels and flowers, the matching antique sconces that flank the fire place, and then the silver and black seventy-two inch Sony television complete with internal-organ-shaking-surround-sound. It reminds me of one of the songs from the Sesame Street show the boys watched when they were little… 'One of these things is not like the others; one of these things does not belong.' Hmm. I wonder what that could be.

Anthony had the thing hauled in here two Saturdays ago. Its original destination was the basement, but since we live in a house made for normal-sized people, and not giants, the thing would not fit down the stairs, so there it sits.

Don't do it Renee. Jesus says just go on about your business…don't let your mouth get you in trouble. "I thought you said you had to go into work early? Isn't that why you didn't make it to Nick's game?" Sorry Jesus, extra time in the prayer closet, I promise. I know I sounded like I had an attitude, but what's up with that? I work too, I need sleep too, I want to watch television and have a few minutes to myself too.

"Yeah, they didn't need me to come in after all." He said with his mucky work boots still propped up on my creamy white ottoman. Now when we first got married, I thought my little roughneck was so cute. Coming in from a hard day working at McCormick's Spice Mill plant, smelling like garlic and covered in all kinds of secret ingredients. I'd let him plop down on the sofa and run and get my working man a huge plate of food. He could do no wrong. Right now every time I saw him he was wearing that uniform even when he wasn't working and I was sick of the way he smelled.

"And you found out…when?" I was trying to make a point here, to his son who worshipped the ground he walked on, but who right now was lounging right beside him without even a care. Now if I'd missed the game, it would have been me not getting my priorities straight between the kids and work. Believe me we've had that conversation more times than I care to mention.

"Hey babe, you need any help?" Tactic number two, change the subject when I'm beginning to make a point. Tactic number one is walk away. He's got a million of 'em. I've noticed over the past few years that the exchanges between my husband and I have slowly dwindled. This is not supposed to happen in a Christian marriage…right? But it is happening. The trustee and the steward of the church sitting up in their own house with a mess for a marriage. You could have never told me that we'd end up like this. We don't say anything ugly towards each other; we normally just don't say anything…period. As soon as the words left his lips I had a smart comment in my head. Right now in response to his question I want to say…'Sure now that I'm in the kitchen putting the groceries away', but I'm already up to about two hours in the prayer room so instead something a little nicer miraculously escapes my lips…

Releasing the death grip I had on the grocery bags I simply said, "I'm all set."

That wasn't nothing but the nails of Jesus keeping this tongue.

"Bro. Eric called from church, they changed ya'll trustee meeting to Thursday, and I'm gonna be at the church all day Saturday helping with the food pantry." See I'm bad because the whole time he was talking I had my eyes rolled up in my head and my lips pursed. When did the sound of my husband's voice become so annoying to me?

"Saturday Alex has a tennis match that you said you were taking him to and I'm going to be working so try to work that out somehow." And….nothing. He makes no comment. Not even a grunt or groan to let me know that he heard anything I just said. Help us Lord.

Just then the telephone rang.

"Phone!" Anthony yelled from his seat. I can hear. I know the phone is ringing. It can't be but one person, but maybe it's the publisher's clearinghouse saying that I won a million dollars. Before I can even get out a hello, the receiver starts squawking at me…

"Hey girl, what you doin'?" I have no one to blame but myself. I saw the caller I.D., but I had a momentary lapse in judgment and picked up the phone too quickly. Needless to say it was not Ed McMahon and I hadn't won a million dollars. It was my girl Shelita.

"What's up girl?" I said with my I-have-nothing-better-to-do-but-talk-to-you voice while I was rolling my eyes up in my head again. If I'm not careful they'll get stuck like that. "I'm just getting dinner together then I'm running some water and taking a hot bath so I can rest my weary, tired body." Oh you better believe I was talking loudly now for dearly beloved's benefit. Perhaps he'll overhear that a sista could use a break right now.

"Oh…well can I drop my kids over there for a few…I gotta make a run real quick?" She begged, probably already sitting outside my front door with the car running and the kids unbuckling their seatbelts.

O.K. let me explain my girl Shelita. She's my GGF. All my Caucasian co-workers at the television station have their BFF's (best friends forever) and I got my GGF (ghetto girlfriend). My good GGF is Shelita. We've known each other for at least twenty-five years. We go way back…before perms and weaves, before baby's daddies (hers) and husbands, before proper English and term papers (mine), and tongue rings with skin tight halter dresses to show off the tattoo you got at a house party (hers)! This girl is my ace, my home-slice, and my play sister. We share everything with each other.

Anyway enough of the stroll down memory lane…Shelita wants me to keep those off-the-hook kids again. Every time she asks, and even times she doesn't and just happens to be in the neighborhood, I agree to keep the rug rats. But I have to get my two cents in…

"I keep tellin' you about them runs. What are you doing Shelita? Those guys you're hanging with don't give a crap about you or your children. They have you running all hours of the night, doing God knows what. Now you know I love my little godchildren…every last one of 'em, but their mother is headed for trouble. I see it night after night on these streets. That ridiculousness you see on the news is very real." I'm sure she put the phone down when she realized I was getting on the soapbox, so she probably didn't hear most of what I said.

"Look. I'm grown. I don't need the lecture. You write about the stuff Renee, but I'm livin' it. I know what I'm doing, besides…Man-Man loves me and he ain't gonna have me out there in no junk that could get me locked up."

"I'm not worried about you getting locked up. As a matter of fact that's probably a safer place than those run-down houses up on Greenmount and Federal Street. Girl you know I seen Man-Man up on Biddle Street checking out his so-called boys. You tell me what business a thirty-eight year old man has with a bunch of wanna be teenage gangsters?" I shouted.

"Right. Right…I'm a poor excuse for a woman. Blah, blah, blah. Everybody can't be like you Renee. You so unhappy about everything, yet you got everything. You be preachin' to me about God gonna give me all kinds of joy, well where is yours, Mrs. saved and sanctified? Somebody like me would love to be where you are and have what you have. A house, a husband, two boys that's doin' good, ain't never been in jail. I gets what I can. O.k.? Man-Man buys me things, he be takin' care of my kids jest like they his own. One day he's gonna get me out of here. I might even move into one of them houses in your neighborhood!" She laughed to the point of coughing. Probably on whatever she was smoking in that car with those poor babies.

I didn't even catch the last part of the conversation. I was still back on the part where 'I'm unhappy about everything'. Am I really that obvious? I didn't realize I indicated anything other than pure bliss and contentment in my Christian middle-class existence. Believe me I know I'm blessed. But right now, I'm wondering why I have such a hard time just breathing?

"Yeah, I'll make sure to get you a housewarming gift. When are you dropping the kids off?" I answered her sarcastically.

"They walking up to the door now. I owe you one!" She said. At the same time I heard the doorbell ring.

"That's Shelita's kids; can somebody get the door please?" I yelled from the kitchen. Anthony got up and instead of answering the door, came in the kitchen.

"I think I'm going to go ahead and leave now to see if I can't get a few hours of overtime."

"That's convenient. Just in time for me to be here with five children by myself. The least you could do is stay through dinner. I know you don't have to be in for a few more hours. You know how Shelita's kids can get, and I just need a few minutes to unwind." I said tossing the dinner in the oven to finish cooking.

"Ain't nobody tell you to baby sit Shanay-nay's kids tonight." Anthony said purposefully mispronouncing Shelita's name.

"You just told me they didn't need you, now all of a sudden you have to go, but that's cool Anthony. Have a good night." The man broke all kinds of speed records leaving the house, no kiss, no hug, nothing like we used to do. He opened the door and walked out just as the kids raced in.

"We ain't eat yet!" They all chimed. Their momma had them trained.

"Take off your coats, dinner will be ready in twenty minutes." I said shaking my head.

Chapter 4: There is a Name

§

If it's true that names speak volumes about the individuals they describe, then give me the remote so I can turn down the volume on Shye. It's 1:30 in the morning and Shelita has not come back for her little angels. Shye is my seven year-old godson and he is everything but shy. He has two sisters, Goodness is ten and Punkin (I kid you not, the name is on the birth certificate) is eight. Shelita's first-born, my godson Twan is twenty-one years old and currently on his sixth year of a fifteen-year sentence in the state penitentiary for trying to be as the young folks say, "a big baller". I hate to remind his mother that he got locked up going on one of the 'quick runs' with her and her man of the week. To make matters worse he has a seven-year-old daughter. Yes, my dear Shelita is a granny and still has not grown up yet.

So check it out…I begged, begged and re-begged Shelita to give the children real people names that would translate in the business world, but I was promptly told to mind my business. She actually used some more colorful phrases, but I'm short on cash and if I said them I'd be indebted to the 'curse jar' that sits in the cabinet over the sink. Let me see how she put it, 'everybody don't wanna be bougie and white'.

First of all I'm anything but white; I'm one shade away from a really toasted almond with a mass of golden brown dreadlocks that hang past my shoulders. And my bank account reminds me that I ain't got enough money to be acting bougie. I'm set up with 401k and college funds for the kids, but the Chase's need to work on being better stewards over the 90% God gives to us each week. To Shelita, and a lot of the girls I hung around in the hood, the fact that I have a degree, and can string actual words found in the dictionary together to form a rational thought, makes me 'act white'.

I'll admit I wanted my children to have a level playing field. I didn't want them to be denied a job interview because they couldn't get a foot in the door of an employer putting them in the 'not suitable for interview' pile. So you know I wasn't gonna name them Crista'l Jenkins and Escalade Williams.

The names of my boys may be vanilla, but they are still strong chocolate brothers. If there was one thing their dad did right, it was to instill a rich heritage in them. Anthony used to make them do mini black history projects of strong black men. King, Ashe, X, Carver, Mr. Murray the black officer that lived down the street, Rev. Brooks the black minister that went into the prison to save souls, and Tyrone the black fireman that lives two doors down. You didn't have to be in the history books, just a strong, proud brotha. The reports were required to get privileges like playing outside, watching television, or getting allowance.

Anyway I digress. It's five whole minutes later and Shye is still jabbering on and on about some gansta rap video on BET Uncut. The child can't spell to save his life, but he can rap one of these songs word for word without missing a beat.

"Baby, quiet down, let's turn the television off and have some quiet time. You ain't sleepy yet?" I plead with him. I'm gonna need toothpicks to hold my eyes open soon, meanwhile Shye is ready to strap on a bass drum and give that Energizer bunny a run for his money. Shye is what my grandma and her people used to call *'special'*. He is a handful. I just had to pull about two dollars worth of change out of his mouth. You heard me. The boy just went about finding loose change in the sofa and started putting it in his mouth. He was running around jumping off of furniture, humming and having a good old time, like this is what a boy is supposed to do at this horrendous time in the morning.

"I said aren't you sleepy little one?" I had to repeat myself because he was really getting down to his favorite song and was oblivious to me.

"No, my mommy let me tay up wif her till it be morning time. tometimes I can help her and uncle Man-Man wif dey money countin'." O.k. besides my ears bleeding from the Ebonics… the poor child does not pronounce his 'es' sounds. I don't even want to know what this child has seen or heard on a daily basis.

"Shye lets turn the television off. You're in my house now and there's no money to be counted at this time in the morning. Go on in and lay down on my bed. I'm going to see what's keeping your mother." I said reaching over to grab the telephone from the side table.

"Can I go play playtation wif cousin Alex?" Where is the 'th' in this child's vocabulary? I've got to spend more time going over his letters and phonics. I'm the one that taught the boy how to spell his name and that "L-O-L-O-P" was actually "L-M-N-O-P". His poor mother just hasn't had enough time between having all her children, running errands for countless baby daddies/uncles, and trying to stay on a job longer than two weeks to get a full check. Not to mention, in addition to these three at my house, Shelita is a mom to a four year old and an eighteen-month old.

After four godchildren in a row, I told Shelita she was going to have to tap some other folks to take on the god parenting of any future kids. I take my duties seriously. I have birthdays memorized, go broke at Christmas, help purchase school uniforms and Easter outfits, and in the case of my dear Twan, some bail money on a few occasions. I probably went to more PTA meetings this year than Shelita has gone to in over ten years. I get the calls from the nurse; I get the progress reports from the teachers. I go on the fieldtrips. And for the most part my family has just fallen right into step with it all. Anthony just takes out extra blankets and sleeps on the sofa so I can have all of them in one room. I'm sure that has had some adverse affect on our relationship, but I can't remember the last time we had a serious conversation about us. I don't know how he feels about our own kids, how he feels about our finances, how he feels about the fact that we haven't been in the same bed with each other for about six months. So the train keeps chugging along on the same track, heading for the same destination day after day…with stops in misunderstanding, depression, and unhappiness, and a layover in the town of resentment.

*****

"Who dis?" some stranger has answered Shelita's cell phone after I've tried calling her for the past two hours. At 3:30 a.m. I am in no mood to deal with whoever has taken the liberty of answering her phone. God only knows where she is and what she's doing.

"I need to speak to Shelita." I say sternly, I really don't have time for games.

"Oh…Lita? She ain't here…she had to make a run, but I'll let her know you called." *Click.* I just got hung up on. O.k.….I don't have a good feeling about this. I'm calling back, I mean the person didn't even get my name, how will they give her the message?

"Renee...look ma... didn't I say I was gonna tell Lita you called?" Mr. Stranger has answered the phone and is calling me by my name? I'm getting a stabbing pain in my heart. Something is not quite right.

"Who is this? How did you know my name?" I said, angrily grilling the stranger.

"What? You ain't never heard of Calla I.D....you good? 'Cause if you are I'mma hang up."

"Wait! Where did Shelita go? She supposed to come pick her kids up from me, and I haven't heard from her, it's not like her to not call?" That wasn't exactly true. In fact it was very likely for her not to call or show up sometimes for days on end, but that was typically on a weekend. Shelita did have her limits and usually on a weeknight she'd be back in time for the children to get some rest before school. I hope this fool can't hear the worry that has crept into my voice. I'm trying to put on my I-ain't-afraid-of-no-ghost voice.

"Well it's pro'ly real hard to call you if she ain't got her phone, what you her mu'va or something?" He answers sarcastically.

Oh...he thinks he's so smart. Why doesn't she have her phone? Any other time you'd have to surgically remove it from her right breast where she keeps it most days and nights in her bra strap. Yeah my girl is something else. Anyway despite my misgivings I'm trying to stay civilized.

"Just a concerned friend, do you know when she's coming back?"

"Look, I don't be keepin' up with her like that, but if I see her and I'm still here, I'll let her know to call...a'ight Renee." *Click*.

Note to self; remind me to talk to that girl about putting my name in her phone. All this talk about names, there's only one name that I can think to call on right now. Don't get it twisted, you done heard me complain about a lot of stuff, but…I do know the Lord and I know Him in the pardoning of my sins. See with all that I do know ain't no reason for my life to be the way it is, for me to be so burdened. Renee Elizabeth Chase is a child of God. And as so I have this haunting feeling that He is preparing me for something. As I slowly drift to sleep I just keep repeating…Lord Jesus, please, please protect my friend wherever she may be.

Chapter 5: And He Will Answer By and By

§

I'm somewhere caught between a deep sleep and a dream. My purpose is about to take form and grow. There are images that are jumbled and suddenly I feel like I'm being tossed and turned. I must be dreaming about an earthquake, because everything around me is shaking. I'm so tired. Lord what are you trying to tell me this morning that can't wait for two more hours? *Bounce. Bounce. Bounce. CRASH!! CRYING!*

"What in the world is going on?" I mumbled to no one in particular while still in my sleep, slowly realizing it was 6:30 a.m. and Shye, who was practicing his trampoline skills on my bed, had just jumped himself right off the edge. He has got to be running on less than three hours of sleep. God only knows when he finally settled down and closed his eyes, I just couldn't hold out.

"OW! I HURTED MY HEAD! OW! I'M BLEEDIN'." Shye screamed at the top of his lungs.

"Be quiet boy; let me take a look at it. Dat's what you get for jumpin' on the bed. Didn't god-mommy tell you no jumpin' on the bed, dummy?!" That would be the mouth of my precious Punkin, doing what she does best…yelling at her brother.

"O.k. let's let god-mommy sleep. Come here Shye-Shye it's not that bad, let me kiss it." Ah…the soothing sounds of Goodness. I peeled one eyelid open just enough to watch her as she gathered the two little ones and pushed them out the door.

"Sorry we were so loud. He probably just got a little bump; can I get some ice to put on it?" She asked politely.

"Sure sweetie, it's some baggies in the top drawer beside the dishwasher. You want something to eat?" That girl is so different from her siblings in everyway. Polite, considerate…heck, literate.

"I'll just get them some cereal. Go back to sleep. I'll call you when mommy gets here."

"Did your mom tell you where she was going last night? I know as much as I don't want her to, she talks to you like ya'll best friends. So spill the beans." Ooohh, I was moving slow today, everything hurts when you're old and tired. Lately I just haven't been able to get enough rest, and each new day brings new aches and pains. On a serious note, I've been concerned about my health since my last physical. I haven't been sleeping well, I'm dealing with terrible headaches, but I'm just attributing it to stress.

"Well her and Mike were suppose to meet these guys that were selling all these clothes they lifted from this store in New York, but then mom was like real intent on getting 'lifted' herself if you know what I mean, and Mike said he knew somebody that had some stuff she could get high on if she did a little favor for him." Wow. A little bit too much information stated very matter-of-factly from a pre-teen child.

And Mike? That's Man-Man's real name, Goodness just refuses to call him that. It infuriates him. I overheard her arguing with her mother one time:

'Why you gotta be so ignorant and keep calling him Mike? E'ry body on the street call him Man-Man.' Shelita

screamed after Man-Man went to her with his feelings hurt that he couldn't get her daughter to give him his street props.

'Well I'm not everybody on the street, he's not taking care of his own children by all his other babies mothers like a real man so he doesn't deserve to be called a man let alone two.'

"Was Man-…I mean Mike going to go with your mom when she went to get 'lifted' as you say?"

"Most likely he'd just leave her there, go party with some other ho's and then come back and pick her up. And this is the guy she thinks is going to save her from her world…Well let me get them some food." Just as she turned to leave the telephone rang and Shelita's number showed up on the caller I.D. Goodness looked at the number and kept moving.

"You get it," She said. "I don't want to talk to her."

I yanked the phone off its base with a mouth full of two cents for my girl. I had all night to think about what an immature, irresponsible, inconsiderate mother Shelita had become, and I was about to let her know.

"It's about time you decided to call somebody!" I yelled into the receiver without saying hello.

"Is this Renee?" Wait. It was the voice of the stranger from last night. My heart began racing and my breath got caught in my throat. This can't be happening right now. My purpose.

"Who is this?" I managed to whisper.

"Who dis is ain't important, but I got something for you from your girl Lita."

"What? Where is she? Put her on the phone, I don't have time for games sir."

"No games ma…listen, it ain't too good about your girl. She messed with the wrong crew, that girl was on that old crazy stuff last night. Just in the wrong place at the wrong time." Wrong place? Wrong time? O.k. maybe she's in jail, I thought to myself, clinging to the hope that perhaps I'd heard God wrong this time. Maybe my moment hadn't quite come. I wrote about raids all the time. Shelita's been busted for possession and even a few soliciting charges in the past, let me get my self dressed and find out where to go to pick this girl up.

"Oh…a raid? I'll be darned." Remember I'm trying to keep my money in my pocket and not the curse jar. I could think of a whole lotta other things to say right about now! I threw my feet over the edge of the bed and hurriedly got dressed with the phone up to my ear. "Which precinct handled the bust?" I was starting to sound like that show my boy Roc produced a little while ago. Yeah this was exactly like an episode of The Corner.

"Dem boys from Downtown was on it…I think, but listen up sis…" This man keeps calling me 'Ma…sis', I'm quickly growing tired of the terms of endearment, this man don't know me like that. He continued. "Your girl ain't at the precinct, she in that freezer at the hospital shorty." I stopped. The freezer? The morgue?

"What kind of sick joke is this? Where's Mike?" I demanded.

"Shot's fired baby doll! Man-Man went down like a gansta! Them po-po's raided that house like some old Desert Storm warfare. Your girl was upstairs getting her groove on. Like I said…wrong place…wrong time. I'm out." *Click*. I had to will my fingers to stop shaking as I dialed the number back. This can't be happening.

"LOOK! I don't know why you called me, but I want some answers now!" I roared into the phone, nostrils flaring. I'm sure if I looked in a mirror there would be a vein popping out somewhere. I gotta watch it; my blood pressure was sky high at my last doctor visit.

"Oh, my bad ma…I called because we was going through some stuff Lita left here and there was this note to call Renee if something ever happened to her. You the only Renee in her phone, so you got called. I know the news is tough, Man-Man was my homey so I feel ya sis."

"I'm not your mother or your sister. Why were you going through her things?" I didn't realize a heart could beat so hard that it would cause your shirt to flutter in and out, but I swear that was happening to me, and my breath was beginning to come in quick short gasp. Roses…candles…roses…candles. Slow it down Renee.

"Where she at right now, she ain't gonna need none of this stuff. Now she do got some old paper in here with some picture of what must be you and her and a number so if you want it, it's yours."

"How can I get it? Where are you?" At this point, I was starting to talk slowly. I had the feeling like I was standing outside of my body because the realization was sinking in. It was here. My purpose was beginning to be birthed.

"I don't do cops Miss Renee so I'm not meetin' you, if that's what you thinking, so let me just leave this in the mailbox back at Lita's place. Then you figure it out." *Click.*

****

It could have easily been a full five minutes before I removed the hot receiver from my ear. As I pressed the phone into the cradle, the bedroom door slowly opened and in walked a solemn Goodness. We stared at each other for what seemed like an eternity.

"I felt bad about not wanting to talk to her so I picked up the phone in the kitchen to say hello." She said to me in a hushed tone.

"So you…" I began.

"Heard everything." She completed my sentence. I don't know what to do at this point.

"So she's dead, just like that huh?" she was speaking as if she was in a trance.

"Oh. Goodness. I'm so sorry." I approached her tentatively with my arms outstretched. I wanted to keep in mind that this is a young lady that is not used to hugs on a daily basis. At first she hesitated to step forward into my arms and then, she let me embrace her and she even squeezed back. A small whimper and a muffled cry followed. It was not the hysterical pleading for a loss mother I was expecting.

"I know about the number and the letter." She confided in me.

I attempted to break our embrace so I could look her in the eye and ask her to explain, but she refused to let go.

"What letter…a number?" My mind was starting to racing, not wanting this to be true. Not like this Lord, I thought to myself. I can't have the past come crashing back to the present, not like this. There were memories that were too painful, things I'd shut out, but now…now I am afraid this child will open the Pandora's box.

"Mommy always told me that if she got caught up, or something ever happened and she wasn't going to be able to come back home…that I should find you and ask you about the number sixteen. At the time she was talking about maybe things getting too hot on the block for her and Mike and maybe they might skip town for a while."

"She was going to skip town and leave you guys alone?" I asked incredulously.

"Come on now, she knows you'd never let that happen."

"Go on." I moved back to the bed to sit down for this…everything was going too fast.

"Anyway she just kept saying sixteen, sixteen, and that you'd know what she was talking about, but that she couldn't tell 'niggas because niggas can't be trusted'. Her words not mine." She knew she had to justify that because the rule in this house was we did not use the 'n' word.

"Goodness, baby you do understand that your mother is not coming back and we'll have to tell your brothers and sisters." I spoke in soft tones, gently brushing her thick braids behind her ears.

"God-mommy I'm not stupid. I know how my mom lived her life, and I know the consequences of that lifestyle. Every night I go to sleep I pray that God protects her and takes her away from all that mess. Well last night I guess He did." Her response was too profound for me. I wanted to make her feel cared for and she was comforting me. We both sat down on the bed facing each other. I was trying to find something in those eyes that told me how she was feeling and what she needed from me.

"So…how do you want to tell them? I'm letting you be a part of this decision making because you are the oldest."

"Why don't we just get our stuff and let Shye and Punkin go to school? I want to go with you to see my mom."

"At the morgue? Are you sure?"

"Yes." And with that she went about ironing her brother's and sister's clothes they'd thrown in the corner from the night before, helped them get their book bags together and walked them out to the truck so Anthony could take them to school. She explained that she wasn't feeling well to them and would be there when they got home.

"They still here? Where is their mother?" Anthony asked when I startled him by yanking open the door on the passenger side of the truck. When I got close to the truck, I could tell he was sound asleep. I heard him pull up about 4:30 am, but he never came in the house. He's been doing that a lot lately. When I questioned him about it, he said he was out there praying. I hope he was praying for a change to come over him and that I didn't find the address of whomever it was he was seeing instead of bringing his butt home. I called the plant early this morning and found out he left his shift early at 2:00 am; we live about thirty minutes from the plant, so there are about two hours unaccounted for in there.

"It's complicated; I'll explain it when I get back." I said buckling the children in their seats. Nick and Alex were on their way to school too. Goodness and I had an appointment with a dead woman.

Chapter 6: It's A Thin Line Between Love And Hate

§

We have been sitting here for one hour and twenty-three minutes. Who knew there would be a waiting list for folks to get into the morgue? For confidentiality and I guess respect they were only letting one family in at a time. When we raced in here this morning at 8:30 a.m. our names were eighth on the list. I could hear snatches of conversation from behind the Plexiglas enclosure of the receptionist's desk and gathered that somebody had passed in the night on one of the floors from the hospital. There had been a few fatalities in a massive motor vehicle accident, and then there was the bust on North Avenue. From all the news accounts it was pretty ugly. I know Alvin must have been ill with the fact that we weren't the first on the scene. After I turned my cell phone back on, I noticed I had more than ten missed calls from the station. The voice messages were pleading for me to call in to let them know if I could get to the scene of the bust.

The police had an undercover guy in the abandoned building they were using for the party that night. He was buying drugs and when he called for backup the thugs weren't so ready to go without a fight. They went busting through all the rooms and Shelita was shall we say 'taking care of business' with a man that decided to grab a gun from under the mattress and start shooting at whatever and whoever was coming through the door. The thought of all the confusion and noise, and bullets, makes me want to scream. To think of what her last moments must have been like, is tearing me up inside. I felt like if I hadn't kept the kids or insisted that she stay home...but that never worked before, so why am I even going there?

"You alright?" I glanced over at Goodness, who had not spoken to me since we left the house. This has to be at least the one-hundredth time I've asked her the same question. No conversation in the car. No 'god-mommy help me understand the meaning of life' questions. Nothing. I am totally at a loss as to how to even start a conversation with her at this point. Each time I think I have the nerve to mention something or offer a word of comfort, a hysterical family member bursts through the door from the viewing room shouting obscenities and vowing to kill the 'ema effas' that killed their loved one.

"NUMBER EIGHT!" I was startled again into reality as our number was being called. We walked up to the window, I showed some identification and we are taken back to see a woman I just spoke to yesterday about getting her life together.

"Wait..."Goodness paused and stepped behind me to bury her face in my coat. Here it comes I thought to myself. This is where she tells me she can't do this and it was a mistake to come. Instead she just peeks around my arm and asks... "Will her feet or her head be coming out first?" I have no response for that one, wasn't expecting that question. Good one Renee.

"Her feet dear, but she's covered up and you don't have to look if you're scared." The older man that was handling the 'unveiling' saved the day when he responded to her question, 'cause I sure was at a loss. I'd seen lots of dead bodies in my line of work, but none of them were being pulled out in front of me from a large drawer. He was compassionate though…he must see the fear in the one eye she has peeking out from behind my coat.

"O.k.….go…wait!" She hesitated again, and then stepped out from behind me.

"Goodness you don't have to do this sweetie. I can identify your mommy while you wait for me outside. I don't want you to be scared."

"I'm not scared…go" She motioned for the gentlemen to take the drawer out and uncover her mother.

Slowly the large metal drawer was pulled out and Shelita's body was now in front of us. With gloved hands the old man, whose nametag said *Clarence*, pulls the sheet down from her face to just below her shoulders. I began a quiet prayer:

Oh Father. I thank you for this life. I thank you for all you've done in protecting her these last thirty-five years. I am so saddened today, but I pray that you just watch over this woman's family, her children, Lord. And Lord if you could just…

"I love you mommy. Why didn't you listen to me? I knew something was going to happen." I hadn't realized with my eyes closed and my head bowed in prayer that Goodness had left my side and was now standing across from me looking into her mother's solid, cold face. Tears were leaking from her eyes and landing on Shelita's cheeks and sliding into her ears. It almost looked like she was crying herself.

Goodness continued, shaking her head from side to side.

"Well are you happy now? Did you get what you wanted? Was it worth this?! How could you care anything about me and go out and get yourself killed!"

I rushed to her side to comfort her but she pushed my hand away.

"NO! No god-mommy you can't hug this away! It's not going to be o.k. this time! She knew what she was doing and all of it was more important to her than me. Smokin' and snortin' and shootin' up every day. Every dag on day! I would beg her and plead with her to please stop. She was getting sick and losing weight, and not combing her hair or dressing like she cared about herself. She was getting used and she always picked those guys, those drugs, EVERYTHING over me!" She continued to scream, while Mr. Clarence just waited patiently and quietly on the side.

"Baby...please don't say that. Your mother loved you so much. She was sick, drugs make you sick. She wanted to stop, and she did a few times." I'm grasping at straws here.

"Oh yeah...Well then what happened? I'm not stupid; I know Shye got to be a crack baby with his ADHD self! And I know that last baby she had; the grandparents got custody because of her sorry life she was living. So please tell me how she loved me so much?" She said looking at me with her eyes wide, and arms crossed. You are on the spot now Renee. Give the girl an answer.

Before I made an attempt to answer I made a mental note to talk to this child about her tone with me, but right now I was giving her the benefit of the doubt because this whole situation is just difficult for anyone let alone a ten-year-old child.

"Honey, the life we grew up in, was a desperate one. There was little expected of us, nobody thought we could accomplish anything were we grew up. We were dirt poor and the way to succeed was get in with somebody on the street that had some credibility. Your mom made some bad decisions, but you all were her pride and joy. You don't know how many times she bragged about you to me."

"Why didn't you end up like her? Huh? Ya'll grew up together, life was so hard together, how did you end up like you are? My momma was pretty and she was smart. You should have seen her keeping track of all the money for these fools. Never had to write anything down…could multiply and divide in her head. One time one of my friends came over to study and she had brought a worksheet from her brother's college class, my mom finished in like two minutes, then went and shot some heroin."

"All I know is that I had a faith and determination to make it out. Shelita wants that for you. Don't be mad baby. I don't feel right telling you that because of all you have seen and gone through, but don't be mad. That mad will get you down and keep you down." O.k. that wasn't so bad. Lord just continue to give me the words to say.

"It's just that right now when I look at her I just get so angry! This did not have to happen. She left us! We don't have nothing! And for what…a few hours of being so high you don't even remember you were high!" Goodness turned back to her mother's body and was yelling with her mouth close to her ear as if she could hear her.

"Oh mommy, I want to say I love you and I'll miss you, but I can't right now! I hate you. I hate that you did this to me! I hate that I have to tell Shye and Punkin this crap about you! But you know what I won't miss though?…The endless nights wondering if you were coming home, the nights turning up my headphones so I couldn't hear you letting Mike smack you around to make himself feel stronger, the hours waiting outside the bathroom door for you to 'handle something right quick'! I won't miss it… or you one bit!" And with that said Goodness stormed out the door with me hot on her heels.

"Goodness! Goodness! Wait baby." I am old and this child has put on a Marian Jones marathon sprint out to the car. She opened the door, sat down and slammed it shut. I got in the driver's side and looked at her without a word, mainly because I was trying to catch my breath! I also realized I was just standing in a room with a dead woman and her child. Breathe Renee. God will show you.

"There is nothing you can say right now god-mommy. I am not mad at you, I know you love me, I just don't want to talk to anybody right now."

Chapter 7: The Queens of the Sixteen

§

    The mystery man has kept his promise. I looked in Shelita's mail slot and there was a tattered picture of Shelita and me in a b-girl stance rocking our 'tilt' style hair-dos stacked to perfection. As the older of the two of us, I was always a bit taller and thicker than Shelita. When we met she was fifteen and I was eighteen. I was the oldest, but Shelita set the trends. If she went and got a gold cap for her tooth with the dollar sign in it, then I went and got one. The big bamboo earrings with her name in them, the layers and layers of gold chain bracelets and necklaces…that's right, she was first and I would follow.
    When she moved into the neighborhood she was like a breath of fresh air. Don't get me wrong, she was loud and ghetto, but she was also beautiful and funny, and loving. I had never seen a black girl with one gray eye and one dark green eye that wasn't wearing contacts. Some of our girlfriends from the hood even wore purple ones. Her hair was dark and curly and most often worn in a huge ponytail wrapped in gold twine on the side of her head. All the boys liked her because she looked Puerto Rican. That was when light skinned was in. She loved all the attention, the boys would hoot and whistle as she walked by calling her Roxanne-Roxanne and professing to wanna to be her man.

Even at fifteen she was dressing like a much older woman. I could sense she was different. She came into my life because of 'the situation with her mom having to leave her dad for putting his hands on her in the wrong way' as she often described it to me. Shelita and Ms. Rose, her mom, didn't have money to move on up when she left her dad, so they moved on down to the projects on McCulloh Street and tried to make do with what little they had, just like everybody else.

We literally bumped into each other one day. I was leaving my apartment late, running toward the elevator; my head was down in my book trying to read the assignment for my current issues class. This was my senior year, and I was going to be the first in my family to graduate from high school. My brother dropped out when he was fifteen and my sister Gwen moved in with her boyfriend when she turned eighteen, two months shy of graduation. My mom wasn't taking any chances, she had me going clear across town, two buses and a half a mile walk to a lily-white country day school in the suburbs. I heard the ding of the elevator and was silently praising God that I wouldn't have to waste an additional ten seconds having to press the button for the door to open. So without looking up I kept up my fast pace and walked right into Shelita who was coming off the elevator.

"That book must be some kinda good." What? I thought to myself. Who was this stranger smiling at me, and even holding the elevator door open? I was expecting the usual rude 'watch where you're going!' that I got from all the triflin' neighbors in the building.

"Oh. I'm sorry, I'm late for the bus, and I didn't do this assignment, I really didn't mean to crash into you like that." I apologized, wanting to be nice, but realizing I needed to pick up the pace so I wouldn't miss the bus.

"Whoa, where you from? You sound like those white people on the news." She asked laughing. I didn't see anything funny; as a matter of fact I wanted to be angry. I heard that same line from my brother all the time. But the look on her face put me at ease. She wasn't making fun of me, it actually seemed like she was genuinely intrigued that I sounded so different.

"I'm from right here on McCulloh Street. I'm going to school, and I really need to catch the bus. You new around here?" I said shifting my weight back and forth trying hard not to seem rude.

"Yeah I just moved into 10-G a few days ago. I see you coming outta 10-J all the time, but you always in a rush, so I just leave you alone. You can tell that fine brotha of yours though that Shelita said hi." She said sashaying down the hallway without looking back.

I didn't have time to think too hard about this odd introduction, but something about this girl really staid with me all day. I wanted to know more about her. I already felt a connection for some reason.

Within a few short months we were like sisters. Shelita's mom actually let her drop out of school since she just didn't feel like going. In truth her mom was trying to do anything to stay on Shelita's good side. Let's just say Ms. Rose was running one of the oldest illegal businesses out of her apartment that a women could run on her own with just the tools God gave her and make a lot of money doing it.

Shelita told me she often threatened her mother with calling the police. To make matters worse, Ms. Rose was still secretly, or so she thought, seeing Shelita's dad. She only moved because the court said they'd put her in jail for exposing Shelita and her younger half-brother to a child molester. Ms. Rose agreed to give up custody of her son eventually to his birth father so she could spend more time going back and forth with her man.

Shelita spent a lot of time at our place; she said it felt like home. She respected my mom for being a hard worker, self-employed and doing it the legal way. She also had a huge crush on my older brother, who never wanted to give her the time of day. She was always quietly observing our interactions with one another. I would come to find out that Shelita spent a lot of time observing people and she was good. I remember one of her favorite pastimes was to just sit on the stoop of our building and analyze the folks in the neighborhood.

"See that girl over there? She just need to stop…"she started in one day.

"What's that?" I asked egging her on. I loved to hear her street-corner analyses.

"She been watchin' these hustlers around here playin' ball the same time everyday. Now she always got to do her clothes at the Laundromat the same time. She stands in that window pickin' up those nasty drawers of her, droppin' stuff and bending over. She lookin' for somebody to take care of her and she don't know how to go about it. I could show her a thing or two. Them jokers gonna let her keep making a fool of herself, then they gonna pass her around like she's a joint."

"Maybe the girl has a business bringing people's clothes to wash for them. She could be an entrepreneur." I said in the most serious tone I could muster.

"Girl puh-lease!" She said waving her hands wildly in the air, and we both broke out laughing. "There you go with your news lady talk. I swear one of these days I'mma look up and you gonna be on the channel eleven news."

"Yeah except I'll be reporting the news, not making it like your ghetto butt!" I screamed, laughing and holding my hand up.

"And you know that's right!" She howled with laughter and slapped me five.

It was so eerie to me how those comments made between friends in jest, had now come to pass. Once I graduated from college with my communications degree, I went on to my current job and became a writer for news Channel Two. I wasn't exactly reporting the news, but it was sure close. And as predicted so many years ago, Shelita's name was mentioned as one of the four 'suspects' killed in a police drug raid and shoot out. It was even Channel Eleven that I happened to be watching in the middle of the day while I was sitting in Shelita's living room, waiting for Goodness to come out of the bathroom. I was still respecting her wishes to be left alone. Yup, there we were standing in front of our stoop. The stoop at Sixteen McCulloh Street. On the back of the picture in faded pencil the words:

Lita and Nay, the Queens of the 16.

And finally, silent rivers of tears began to flow, because I knew what it all meant.

****

I must have fallen asleep, but the next thing I know I was awakened by a soft touch on my shoulder. The touch startled me and my hand immediately went to my heart. It was the last place I was holding the picture and it wasn't there now. I looked around to see where I misplaced it. Goodness was looking at the picture so closely as if she expected the women with her trademark eyes to begin speaking to her. After a few minutes she slowly looked up at me.
"God-mommy? Are you o.k.?"
"Oh. Yes, I didn't mean to fall asleep. I'm just tired. Listen Goodness I need to go somewhere and I want to do it alone. So can I take you back to the house to chill with

the boys until I get back? I think it would be good if you're there anyway when Shye and Punkin get home."

"That's cool. This place you have to go, does it have something to do with the sixteen mom kept telling me about…the sixteen on this building?" She said pointing to the picture.

"It does. But there are things I need to handle first before I can explain everything to you. You have to trust me on this." I said giving her a hug and a kiss on the forehead.

"You're about the only one I can trust. Let me get some clothes for us, and some of Shye's games. You've got to let the boy play some video games or he'll drive you crazy!"

Chapter 8: Confronting The Past

§

Crunch. Crack. Pop. The tires of my car rolled over broken glass and bottles and God only knows what as I pulled up in front of Sixteen McCulloh Street. It was only a fifteen-minute drive from where I lived now, but I hadn't been inside this building in over ten years. The building should be condemned. There were boarded up windows, dilapidated steps in the corridor, and even some apartments with doors hanging off the hinges. My nostrils were burning and my eyes were stinging from the smell of urine and the smoke of several peoples' highs. My heart was beating a mile a minute as I tentatively approached a familiar apartment door to knock. Well it was more like banging instead of knocking because I wanted the occupants to be able to hear me over the music that was blasting on the other side of the door. It wasn't until the door opened that I realized I'd been holding my breath. Partly because of the stench in the hallway and partly because I really didn't want to see the person who I knew was going to answer the door.

"Hey." My brother Antwan grunted and turned to head back into the apartment like we'd just seen each other yesterday instead of several years ago. I hadn't been back to this God forsaken place in ten years, but I'd had many opportunities to catch a glimpse of my brother standing on the street corners of Baltimore. Almost every story lead I followed about drugs and crime could be linked back to my brother. As much as I hated to admit it, he falls into the category of street hustler that you need to keep your young sons and daughters away from.

My brother used to be a force to be reckoned with when we were growing up. Nobody messed with "Big Ant's" money, his corners, or his ho's. That was until Big Ant got himself hooked on that poison he was selling. I've watched him literally wasting away each time I pass him on the corner. Sometimes I wave, sometimes I don't. I begged and pleaded, and had the brothers from my church doing interventions with him right there on the corner. It seemed like my prayers had been answered when he was finally arrested and served five years in jail. He came out drug-free and with a renewed sense of spirituality. I didn't see any harm then in letting him back into my life.

Anthony and I had been married for four years when I just brought my brother home to live with us, without even asking. There was a lot bottled up inside of me about our upbringing. There were secrets that I felt turned him into this hideous person. I was determined that I could change him. Boy when I think about the conflict that caused between my husband and me...but family...you're suppose to do all you can for family right?

The temptation of his former life proved too strong for Antwan, though. After a few months of living with us, Anthony's tools would come up missing, or my jewelry, or the microwave, even the loveseat in the basement just vanished one day. I would pray and plead for him to change and after so much time, I just got tired of the whole thing. I was pregnant with Alex at the time, and Nick was a little boy getting into everything, including a vial of white powder one day. I had a husband that I really did love and I knew we needed Antwan out of our lives. So we packed up his belongings, drove up to Sixteen McCulloh and dropped him off, with an admonishment from Anthony to 'never bring his crack-smokin', heroin-addicted black behind around our house again'. It was all I could do to contain myself sitting in the passenger side of the car, but I realized that Antwan didn't want anything different than what he woke up to every morning. I was not going to let myself be brought down by his circumstances, and so we left him and began rebuilding our lives.

"You gonna regret the day you ever turned your back on me." He said when I rolled down the window, to say goodbye. Antwan never called, never even tried to come by the house. It was as if we were dead to one another.

"Hey yourself." I answered just as coolly when I entered the apartment and closed the door behind me.

"You seen Shelita lately?" I probed to see if he'd been watching the news, or heard through the street-vine about what happened to her.

"Naw. Not lately. She was here about two weeks ago, staid for a few days and then was gone."

"Oh. You know she's dead right?"

"I heard." He answered quietly.

Without another word, I headed back to the last bedroom on the right. That was my room for eighteen years of my life. The things Shelita and I discussed in that room, and the plans we made there for our lives, our future. As I was walking I could feel Anthony stomping down the hall behind me, so I turned to face him. I may not have lived in the ghetto for a while, but a sista never forgets to watch her back, even if it is from family.

"Hey. Where you goin'? Don't come up in here tearin' stuff up! You don't live here no more. You ain't want me coming around your way; maybe I don't want you coming around mine!" He said jumping in my face.

"Watch your tone and your position when you talk to me…understand?" I kept moving toward the back and to my surprise there was a young lady in the room, sitting propped up against the headboard. Her hair, or should I say the hair she has purchased, is literally standing on end all over her head. I can't tell whether she just woke up, or that was actually the style she was going for…you never knew these days.

"Honey, I'm gonna need you to leave for a minute." I tried to be polite, pulling the covers back so she could get up and move to a different room.

"Ant…who dis woman? What you into old-heads now? Baby you ain't his type." She sneered crossing her arms over her barely there halter top like she owned the place.

"Girl be quiet dis my sista." He growled at her, and then turning to me he asked "What you need in here?"

I was searching his eyes to see if he really was that clueless or if he was playing dumb for the benefit of the flavor of the week sitting in the bed staring at us both.

"I need some time to myself. You know with all that has happened to Shelita, I just wanted to be in here again for old time's sake. See if there was maybe a trinket or something I could put in her casket. So…I need some space." I said, raising an eyebrow and looking directly at Miss I-think-I'm-all-that.

"Cool. We out. I gotta make a run anyway. Baby go out in the kitchen and get me some food." After she left he turned to me.

"Look I know you can't stand me for how everything went down wit Lita, and all the hell I put you and Anthony through, but that mess was a long time ago. Look how your life turned out, you got what you wanted right? You wanted to be somewhere with all them white people, and blend in, forget about us black folks trying to make it over on this side of town. And Lita…She got over it so you should have too."

"Get over it!" I fumed. "Is that what you've done Antwan? You've just forgotten about all the crap we went through when we were growing up! Oh I know you've just gotten over it so that's why you choose to stay here because everything was just so sunny and peachy. You couldn't think of a better place to live…right!? Well I had to get out. I am not going to let the past define who I am."

At this point I was so close to him I could smell whatever it was he drank for breakfast.

"Do I feel like I'm better than the Sixteen, you are darn right I do! I am not ashamed of having a college degree, and one or two white neighbors. That doesn't mean I have forgotten where I've come from. You think I don't know about 'the black folk strugglin', brotha I see a black woman struggling every time I look in the mirror!" I know I must look crazed standing in the middle of the disheveled bedroom. The site of the clothes in disarray and the dust and dirt reminds me of what my insides are feeling like at that very moment.

"Listen I ain't got the time or the energy to go through this with you. You take as much time as you need and leave me some kinda message 'bout Shelita's funeral." He said dismissing me with a wave.

"You plan on comin'?" I asked, placing a hand on my hip and giving him the black woman's head and neck slide. I know full well he won't show his face in any church.

"Naw, I don't do death…just let me know when everything gonna be, I'll send some flowers over."

"Oh boy…."I muttered sarcastically. "You're selling crack to middle school kids and that doesn't equal death to you?" He ignored me and walked out of the room.

Chapter 9: I Got What I Need

§

As soon as he left the room, I immediately dropped to my knees. I'd like to say it was for some reverent prayer, but I needed to take a look under the bed. Yes! There it was the floorboard slightly askew. Just enough that I knew what to look for, but not anything so out of the ordinary that anyone who wasn't a *Queen of the 16* would even notice. I pushed the bed over just an inch or two and pulled at the floorboard. The thing wouldn't move! O.k. it's not where I thought. Then my heart sank and I got an overwhelming feeling of nausea. Flat on my stomach looking under that bed with dust creeping up my nostrils and into my mouth, I really took the time to look at the old wooden floor and noticed that almost all of the boards looked askew. It was either because the place was falling apart or someone tore it apart looking for something. I pushed at a few more boards and then got up to sit on the bed, flustered and hot.

Just when I was in the middle of my *'please Lord help me figure this out'* prayer…it hit me! When I came in this room I was able to see little Miss sleeping beauty right in front of me. When I used to sleep in the room, the bed was on the other side behind the door. You'd have to come all the way in the room and make a tight turn to the right to see who was on the bed. That means my board was under that heavy looking dresser. I know Shelita didn't move that dresser to get to that board if she was in here two weeks ago.

"Miss...is you done? 'Cause I need to get my clothes and stuff to go to work." I was so deep in thought trying to figure out my next move, that I didn't notice the mistress of the night had returned.

"Oh...you got clothes here? You live with Ant or somethin'?" I had to turn on my 'round-the-way' attitude so this sista would not get it twisted. I might live in the county now, but I could still romp if I needed to.

"You could say dat. Me and him have an understandin', but I did move some of my stuff in here a coupla days ago."

"A few days ago?" He was just with Shelita two weeks ago; I see he has not changed at all.

"Yeah, he gonna let me decorate and everything. I'mma get things in here just like I like 'em. Anyway is you done?"

"Not really I need to move this dresser because I dropped my earring and when I tried to get it I pushed it further under here." Lord please forgive me for lying.

"I just moved this thing yesterday! You on your own sista, I just got my nails did." And with that she turned and walked back to the living room.

To my surprise the dresser was very easy to move. I guess when you're a size two your clothes don't weigh as much as when you're a twenty-two. I'd have a time moving my dresser by myself at home. I moved the dresser just enough to find my board...our board. I pulled at it and my breath caught in my throat. There was the blue velvety Crown Royal bag. I picked up the bag and reached inside of it. There were two letters, an official looking insurance paper, and a key. I unfolded the newest looking letter.

Nay,
Before you get mad at me…I didn't spend the money. What am I saying; you're probably mad at me because if you are reading this I'm probably dead. Let me get down to business. I ain't been feelin' real great lately. I just got a bad feeling. I'm too far-gone girl. But believe it or not, I been doing something for my kids. Remember how we used to take half of whatever money we had and put it in here? Girl whatever I got from hustlin' and odd jobs, I still put in here from time to time. All this time your brother thought I was still hot for him, but I needed somewhere to keep my stash. I don't really have no accurate count. I told the people at the bank I ain't even want one, because if I knew I'd probably smoke it up. Anyway take the key and go to the safe deposit box at the Wachovia on Reisterstown Road across from The Plaza. They already got your info so take some I.D. It's papers in there giving you all the rights over everything I own sis. And please, please, Nay don't let the kids get split up. I want you to have them. I know that's big but you got God on your side girl. Ain't you always tellin' me you can do all things through Him? Well start prayin'.
Lita

I don't know when it happened, but I started breathing again, and really slowly. Is there a word to describe complete confusion, and fear, and joy at the same time? Of course I was so confused and afraid about what this meant for my future, the future of the children, my marriage, my everything. But I was completely in awe, that all this time, the woman I thought was throwing her life away was actually making a way for a better life for her children. Lord you sure do work in mysterious ways.

After a few minutes the pounding of my heart slowed to a normal rhythm, which allowed me to come to my senses and fold up the papers, place them back in the bag and put the bag in my purse. Once I was confident that things were back the way they were, I backed out of the room with one last glance and a vow to never return.

"Find what you were looking for?" Antwan asked when I came down the hall.

"I thought you had somewhere to go?" Did I detect a smirk on his face?

"Don't take me long to do what I got to do." He said leaning against the kitchen counter eyeing me while he stuffed a huge wad of money in his pocket. Business must be picking back up, he's put a little meat on his bones since the last time I saw him.

"Oh, you just had to open the door and stick your hand out right? Exchange of goods and services, nothing like an honest two minutes of work." I said sarcastically.

"Look, did you find what you needed, 'cause I really gotta get in there." The diva of the apartment asked me as I walk right by her to the door.

"Yeah, I got exactly what I needed. It's all yours now. Hope I didn't make you late for work."

"Naw…I makes my own hours."

I bet you do…I thought to myself.

Chapter 10: Is It Well With My Soul?

§

Supposedly time flies when you're having fun, but what happens when you're just stuck in one place contemplating life and it's meaning? I've been sitting in my car outside of the Wachovia on Reisterstown Road, across from The Plaza with a letter in my hand that has changed the rest of my life. I want to go in, but I can't. There is so much in there I know I will have to explain to my family, my godchildren…heck myself! Anyway the kids will be home from school soon and I have decided to do what I do best, wait until another day. I know that whatever is in that bank is safe for the time being. I'll have to get home and do some heavy duty prayin' for God to order my steps up to and inside that bank.

I know God don't like it, but I'm always just using prayer as an excuse to procrastinate on things I know are tough, but need to be done. I ain't the only one though, every Sunday I go to church I hear one sista or another talking about 'I know I should leave him, but I'mma pray about it and wait to see what God say do', or 'Pastor keep askin' me to lead Praise and Worship, I told her I been prayin' about whether or not He want me to'. Oh Lord I'm going off on a tangent. I need to be home for my precious godchildren.

jrenee   The Breath Of Purpose

*****

    The girl never ceases to amaze me. Even though she missed school today, Goodness is doing extra assignments, she asked for from her teacher. She has gone over math homework with Punkin, reminding her about tens and hundreds, and carrying numbers 'til I thought the poor child was going to explode. And with her magic calm she's gotten Shye to quietly...yes quietly, sit still and play a video game. Now granted from where I'm sitting on this living room sofa, the boy done shot up two liquor stores and car jacked countless innocent people on this garbage they call entertainment, but the boy is quiet. And I need quiet right now. I'm going to need some of my very special extra virgin olive oil to break him away from them games and it might even take Pastor Fowler stopping by the house with a few of her prayer warriors.

    Not a word has been mentioned about Shelita. No one's asked "where's mommy?" or "when's mommy coming to get us?" These poor little ones are so used to having Shelita skip out on them and leave them for days at my house without so much as a pair of clean underwear. I'd long since given up on her leaving anything that was important to the growth and nourishment of a child anytime she dropped the kids off. Her idea of leaving them something to eat was a bag of candy, a sleeve of stale saltine crackers and a block of government cheese. After the first fifteen minutes the kids were in my house, there would always be candy wrappers strewn about and cracker crumbs stuck to anyone's backside that dared sit on the sofa. There was the one time she left a booklet of McDonald's coupons, but to Shelita that was the same as leaving $50.00.

    And always that infamous saying in parting as she was running to hop in the waiting car of some thug....

"Girl you know I owe you one!" No Shelita it's more like one million, but I never called her on it, or asked her to watch my kids. Mainly because I really didn't want my children anywhere around the madness she was living in, but also because despite her obvious flaws and careless lifestyle I absolutely loved the girl with all my heart.

"Hey ma. What's for dinner?"

"Nick...one of these days you are going to come through that door, and see me and ask me something different like 'how was your day' or 'can I get you anything', or you might just say 'I love you mom, you're the best mom'..." I started, with my eyes closed. I was rubbing my temples because of a fierce headache.

"O.k.... man... don't bite my head off! Yo...I just got home from practice, I'm hungry. I was gonna get a snack, but if dinner was ready I was gonna wait. I don't know what has you on edge, but get a grip. Yo I'm sorry; let me know when dinner is ready." He began to huff off in the direction of his basement bedroom I called The Dungeon, when I caught him by the shoulder pads sticking out haphazardly from his dirty football jersey. He had no choice but to turn in my direction. He was towering over me by at least eight inches, yet in a calm tone I looked him straight in the eyes (well really I have to tilt my head way back and look up at him) and said...

"Nick Brantley Chase...I am not your man or your yo. Mom is not one of the homeboys, so I suggest you adjust your attitude, take off this dirty uniform and put it in, *not around* your hamper and get cleaned up for dinner. Now you ain't the only one hungry so get it together. Now I am dealing with the death of a very close friend of mine so excuse me for needing to get a grip!" I released him and he began to make a loud sigh, but looked at me and thought better of it. With his helmet under his arm, he trudged down the steps.

During my exchange with Nick I hadn't noticed that Goodness had snuck into the kitchen and was stirring pots I'd left unattended while I was in a daze on the living room sofa thinking about what in the world was becoming of my life. The barrage of bullets coming from the street fighting game brought me back to the present surrounding.

"Shye, turn that mess down right now. Play something else. Don't you have a learning game for this machine?" I was really pleading more than asking at this point.

"Unh unh, dey only make the fightin' ones, I like to toot all the people." Mind you he hasn't batted a lash, or turned his attention away from the television screen.

"First of all young man…what did I tell you about using words that sound like animal sounds. You say 'No Ma'am' to a grown up o.k.? I'm going to the store with you to pick out some new games tomorrow. In the mean time, play the football one." He slowly paused the game and replaced the cartridge. At least the boy was listening to me.

It took a while to get to this point over the years. He hadn't learned respect or following directions at his house. Most of the time the only person that told him what to do and taught him right from wrong was Goodness. Speaking of which, I was on my way to relieve her from kitchen duty.

"Baby I got it. Why don't you set the table and help me get the kids rounded up to eat." I said taking the oven mitts out of her hands, so I could pull my buttery corn bread out of the oven. I don't care what kind of mood I'm in, or what drama is going on in my life, everything gets better with butter and cornbread.

"I don't mind helping. Things are going to get crazy around here pretty soon. I want to make sure we don't wear out our welcome until we can find someplace to stay." She said as she looked at me with sad eyes and left the kitchen. I could hear her in the living room talking to her brother and sister.

"Punkin and Shye come ya'll lets wash ya'lls hands...it's time for dinner."

"I already washed my hands when I came home from school! Why I gotta wash 'em again?" As I brought the first of the piping hot plates to the table, I noticed that Punkin had placed herself at the head of the table defiantly.

"Because since you been here you been messing in your hair, and playing with markers and your hands are dirty, now I'mma ask you one more time, then I'm telling god-mommy you don't need to eat." Goodness answered putting a little bass in her voice, just like she's heard me do a time or two with Nick and Alex.

"Aaaaaa-hhhhhaaaaa...Punkin can't eat...her bad...'cause her not wash her hands!" Shye began to sing loudly mocking his sister.

"Shut up! I am gonna eat...dummy! Don't make me give you a black eye!" She screamed jumping up from the table, knocking over her chair in the process of trying to get to her brother.

"Hey the only person that can change eye colors around here is me! Now everybody wash their hands and get to the dinner table in five minutes!" Anthony thundered out of nowhere. I know the ruckus must have woke him from his slumber. He goes in to work at six tonight until three in the morning so I know he was counting on at least one more hour of sleep.

"Yes sir!" everyone said and ran to the bathroom.

"I swear, I'm gonna have to rent a room to get some peace and quiet." He mumbled under his breath as he picked up the turned over chair and sat himself at the head of the table.

"Make sure you reserve a room for me too, I could use some peace." I said looking at him from my seat at the other end of the table. We used to sit right beside each other and embarrass the boys by looking into each other's eyes, and giggling about some of our private married moments.

"Humph. Peace. That's what you be at that church all day every day praying for right?" He remarked sarcastically. Before I could even dignify that remark with an answer Alex came bounding into the room with a pair of headphones still wrapped around his neck.

"Dag…it sounds like a gang war down here! What da deal?" Alex asked in his suburban-boy-trying-to-be-hood-voice.

"Boy get your silly self to the table, that's what da deal?" Anthony responded, he knows it's all jest. Joking or not he still held his hands out for Alex to give him the headphones. He knows better than to come to the table with them.

Alex is the comedian in addition to his other talents. It has lightened the mood and everyone sits down to a stick-to-your-ribs-meal of stuffed pork chops, rice, collards, and of course cornbread. I know it was the middle of the week, but when I stress out, I have to cook to relieve my stress. And when I got in this house from my day I was just cooking up a storm.

Nick has come to the table refreshed and clean without a hint of the exchange we'd had earlier. The boy is growing up and wanting his independence, but I ain't raise no fool. He knows he crossed the respect line with me, and leans in to kiss me on top of my head before he sits down.

"We good?" he asked reaching for the greens to pile them on his plate.

"We ah-ight!" I joked trying to sound hip. I can't stay mad at a star athlete, with grades like his, and who deep down in his heart would do anything for his momma.

Thankfully the rest of the night went well. Goodness got her brother and sister into the tub for me, while Alex helped to clean up the dishes and take the trash to cans on the back porch. Something is fishy because it's not his night, but I'll be hearing about a video game, or some stereo equipment he needs as a reward for doing these extra chores. For now I retired to the family room and put my feet back up on the sofa. I have a tension headache the size of Mt. Everest. I closed my eyes and squeezed my temples with my fingers, rubbing in a clockwise motion that was slowly making my mountain seem smaller and smaller. Shye startled me by sneaking up behind me on the sofa. His precious little lips were right beside my ear. With his most robust outside voice he pressed his lips to my ear and screamed…

"God-mommy is you gonna read me a 'tory for bed!"

Without opening my eyes, I took my finger from my temple and placed it at my lips to tell him to take it down a few notches.

"Ssshh baby, god-mommy has a headache, can you let uncle Anthony read to you? Go pick a book and take it to him, but ask him in your best little person voice or he'll say no. Got it?"

Just like that he was off in a new direction to bother someone else besides me; I knew I would have to make this up to Anthony. He called in to work right after dinner and placed himself on-call because he knew I had a rough day and wanted to give me a little break. I almost passed out when he said he was doing that, but God answers prayer so I didn't question him. And besides he does love the kids. He kinda got stuck in the role of godfather because he was married to me. Shelita didn't really know any strong male role models that could serve as godfathers. I mean she did pick some guy that goes by the name of "Murdah", who was 'boys' with her baby's father, but I told her I would never let her see Punkin again if she made me share the duties with that man.

    For now all was well.

Chapter 11: Where Is The Love?

§

"You want to tell me what's going on? What happened today when you went to the morgue?" Anthony asked as I slowly crept into bed.

The whole time I was downstairs on the sofa, I was hoping he'd be asleep when I got up here, because I was not in the explaining mood. It's one of the few times that Anthony and I were actually lying in bed together. Typically he fell asleep on the floor in the living room, hypnotized by the billion-inch television, and I would carry my tired bones on up the steps and fall fast asleep often times without a prayer crossing my lips. He didn't get called in tonight, so he's enjoying a rare night home I suppose. This is probably his attempt at intimacy, because he's cozied up and put his arm over my shoulder. I had to admit it did feel nice when he began rubbing my tired achy back, so I relaxed and began to fill him in on the events of the day.

"Well, Goodness got pretty upset with her mom, just frustrated I guess…I can't really imagine the life these poor children have had to live."

"Yeah, our boys don't even know how blessed they are sometimes." He said thoughtfully, still kneading that knot in my lower back.

"Say that!" I squealed as if he was preachin' real good. "I know we try to instill values and try to keep them from all this mess, but it scares me to death, now that they are really growing into men and can make decisions on their own."

"Now we just trust that what we taught them, and what God tells them will help them make those decisions." My husband said comforting me.

"You better preach it! How come you don't talk with me like this all the time? I miss the way we used to talk, and the way we used to pray together. We live separate lives and it does not feel good Anthony." I said turning over to face him.

"I don't know what to tell you. You're a lot different than the woman I met twenty years ago."

"Well yeah...Anthony I'm twenty years older." I remarked sarcastically rolling my eyes toward the ceiling.

"No I mean the Renee I used to know was vibrant, and carefree, and funny...now you're just so...so..." He began fumbling for words. The brotha is good, he knows he don't wanna mess this up.

"What? ...So what?" I can't wait to hear what he comes up with. I want to hear what the man who refuses to admit that he's balding, gained fifty pounds, and has changed a lot himself over the last twenty years has to say about me.

"You are so negative. You don't complain a lot about other stuff, but you sure are hard on yourself. You don't like you, so we all have to suffer." He said sweeping his arm in a large arc as if to include the whole world in his last statement.

"O.k. suffer? Now that's just taking it a bit too far don't you think? Really Anthony...you think I don't like myself. Baby I'm a child of God, created in His image, fearfully and wonderfully made..." I said boldly throwing his arm off of me, and sitting up in the middle of the bed.

"Yeah, Nay you say that, but you don't believe it. You are constantly looking for validation. Wanting to know that you look good enough. You are constantly saying yes to this one and that one because you want everybody else to need you. But I need you. My co-worker Latonya says you care more about what everyone else thinks, than you do about what I think."

"Latonya! Oh is that you're little girlfriend's name? Is she the one telling you to leave work early and roam around the streets instead of coming home to your wife? Do me a favor and keep my name out of your mouth when you're at work talking to Latonya!" At this point I was up out of the bed and stomping over to our chaise lounge.

"Here we go again! For the umpteenth time, I'm not cheating on you ok? And when I say that at least you know my word is my bond."

"Oh so you want to go there. I don't need you throwing anything from the past up in my face, not right now." I said, sitting in the chaise lounge at the foot of the bed. I was completely covered in my chenille throw, and getting settled because I had no intention of sleeping with the enemy.

"You think I don't see you walking around covering up when you get out of the shower, turning the lights out when you undress in here. I'm your husband. You don't want me to touch you, you don't want to go out, you don't want me to buy you clothes, because you don't want me to know your actual size…you all up in the scriptures why don't you re-read the part about the marriage bed!"

The brotha must really be feeling himself, 'cause he done sat up too and is looking me right in the eyes. This is quite the departure from the I'm-going-to-run-away-from-this-conversation Anthony that I'm used to. But if he wants to jump bad then I'm gonna take my go!

"You know what; you don't have to come at me like that! Like always you turn a good conversation into all the things that I'm not doing to keep our marriage strong. What about you Anthony? Huh? You love yourself so much right? Why you gotta have a truck like Desmond and his wife drive? Why'd you have to bring that huge television in here right after you went to the football party at Trevor's house? You know we can't afford that TV, but if one of them knucklehead friends got one, then Anthony gotta have one too! Ever since I've known you…you been trying to keep up with the Jones's, meanwhile the Chase's is strugglin'!" Another point for Renee, I thought as I crossed my arms and looked at him with my lips turned up on the side and neck slid to the other side.

"You call four bedrooms and a two car garage strugglin'!" He screamed incredulously.

"No I call it material things! Anthony I was happy when we had Nick and we were living in a one-bedroom apartment. Sure I love having a den, I love having nice things, but you and I are working day and night. We co-exist; we pass each other literally in the night, between my call-Renee-whenever-you-need-her-job and your night shift hours. You don't look at the bank accounts, you spend and spend because you know how much you make and it looks fantastic, but you don't see how much goes out. We are barely making bills, Anthony." I was trying to soften my voice because I was sure Alex was listening, his room was right next door to ours.

"Well tell me these things; I can pick up more shifts Renee." He sighed heavily, an expression of relief filling his face. This poor man thought extra hours would solve our problems.

"That's not going to help us…me and you." I said calmly, surprising myself. I got up to approach the bed, placing a finger on my chest and then his. "We are disconnected. You work so much as it is. You fill every available time you do have with activities with your boys.

I'm glad you help the men out at church on the weekend, but you don't come to church hardly anymore. And hey I'll even admit I can be down on my body, and I ain't gonna lie, the sex drive has dwindled. I'll give you that, but I need to feel comfort. I need to feel protected and provided for. That's what makes me want to be close and be intimate."

"So I'm not a good provider? Is that what it has been all this time? I haven't provided for you and my children so I don't get none!" Anthony said getting out the bed a bit too fast for me. The brother was on the razor edge of being that close to pushing a sista off the side of the bed and on the floor, which in my book constitutes domestic violence and gives me a pass to start whaling on his head.

"Oh…now we're getting somewhere! Is that why you don't come home on time? Is there somebody else giving you what you claim you don't get here Anthony? You need to call…what's her name…Latonya!"

"No…Because I take my vows very seriously. I wasn't just up there for show Renee. I'd rather not be here pretending instead of coming in here listening to you accuse me night after night. Are you guilty about something!?" He said pounding his chest with his fist and getting up in my face. The veins were popping out on the side of his neck. That was a low, insensitive blow.

"O.k. you know what, we are not seeing eye to eye. Before I say something that I will regret, I'm going to sleep in the guest room." I said grabbing a pillow from the bed and snatching the throw off of the chaise.

"Let me save you a trip." Anthony said and stormed out of the room to make his pilgrimage to his seventy-two inch Mecca. Just like the Muslims, he already had a pallet made up down there to lie down on right in front of the thing.

Wow, that didn't go as planned.

Chapter 12: Taking Care Of Business

§

God is a good God. Right about now I'm thankful for the brand new mercies this morning. Even in my disobedience my Father, God is looking out for me. Not only did I neglect to say a word of prayer last night before falling to sleep, I went to bed angry at my husband, I'd lied, cursed, and did all kinda other sins by thought, word and deed. But here it was another morning and my feet were on the floor slowly limping toward the bathroom.

In the last two years I've put on so much weight, my knees, feet, and back are so stiff in the morning, I literally look like the walking dead for the first twenty minutes of the day. I'm past complaining about it though. Just keep trudging along. I'm sure the thud of my aching feet was rocking the chandelier over the dining room table downstairs. Since it was still bright and early the house was completely quiet.

The scalding hot shower relaxed me, and opened a floodgate of emotions. Before I knew it there were tears silently running down my face and blending into the water flowing over my body and down the drain. At this point I couldn't even tell what the tears were from. Was it the memory of my dear friend? Could it have been the conversation with Antwan and the hurt it brought back to my memory? Was it the fight with Anthony? Whatever it was the tears kept blending, flowing, and draining…blending, flowing, and draining. I stood in the shower so long the water was beginning to run in lukewarm rivers over the rocky mountains, through the hills and valleys and down the large tree trunks otherwise know as my legs. I sure do hate to admit when my husband is right. Especially about how ashamed I've become of this temple that God has given me. This ain't the temple I had a few years ago, and I'm sure God don't even recognize it now. I'm officially obese according to my primary care physician, and borderline diabetic. When Anthony met me I was a working-my-diva-curves size fourteen, and now I was a–hide-it-under-a-tunic sized twenty-two. At this point I'm supposed to be controlling my sugar levels with my diet. What diet? Anyway, dimples in all the wrong places, here I stood behind the frosted (thankfully) glass enclosure of the shower, not wanting to step out into what my world had become. I began a quiet prayer, while I air dried…

Lord please guide my feet today. I know you don't give folk more than they can handle, but this does seem like a bit much. I am going to need your help here. The last funeral I planned was moms, and that was over fifteen years ago. I won't know what to put on the girl, what kind of casket, who could do the eulogy? I have so many questions. Am I really supposed to raise these young children? And these ain't easy kids might I point out. I know the bible says that I need not fear because the battle is not mine, but I definitely feel some wounds forming. I was just getting used to the idea of having one in college and one on the way out the door. I know…stop with the questions right? Where's my faith? I do trust you Lord. Help me to step aside and let you take control of this situation. I love you Lord, thank you for this day.

As I stepped out of the shower I glanced quickly at my reflection in the mirror. This was the first time I've stopped to look at myself naked in at least a month. I've got to do better. After quickly dressing, I stopped by the guest room to wake up the little one's only to find them wide-awake reading bible verses with their uncle Anthony. Will wonders ever cease?
"Good morning." I mumbled barely able to make eye contact.
"Hey, I thought you'd need some extra time to sleep in, so I rounded the kids up." He said quietly. Don't do that; don't try to be nice to me this morning when I'm still a little salty about last night.
"Thanks. Are Nick and Alex up yet?"
"Nick may be, but Alex is dead to the world as usual." He replied turning his attention back to his captive audience of three.
He's not exaggerating. I think I pulled a muscle last week, literally dragging Alex down the hall to the bathroom, while he was still comatose so he wouldn't be late for school.
"Alright little one, rise and shine! Time to make the donuts!" I yelled, after flipping on the lights and jumping onto the foot of Alex's bed. How anyone can find enough space in this room to lie down and go to sleep is beyond me. It's a wonder I didn't break my neck on the electric cords, DJ equipment, tennis racquets, balls, and notebooks strewn about. There are too many posters of Destiny's Child to even count, and so many DVD's and CD's they stood in wobbly waist high stacks in the corners of his room. He swears he needs two or three copies of everything. It's a waste of allowance if you ask me.
"Come on Alex Graham Chase, up and at 'em Alex Ant!" I sang loudly, while pulling the blanket off of him, and attempting to turn him over. We started calling him

'*lil an*t', not as a tribute to my brother, as he liked to claim, but because when he was born he looked so much like his dad, and because he was the teeniest tiniest little thing you ever wanted to see. His brother weighed in at nine pounds and eleven ounces and was born two weeks after he was supposed to arrive. My little Ant came two months prematurely.

The memory was so vivid because it was around the most emotionally draining time of my life. I'd just buried my mother. Despite having a sister and a brother that lived in close proximity, the task of planning the funeral fell solely on my shoulders. My brother who 'doesn't do death' didn't even bother to come to his own mother's funeral. It wasn't just because his street life made coming into a church a low priority…no he'd long before become estranged from our mother because he blamed her for some of the darkest years of his young childhood.

Added to that stress, was the pressure of how to divide her estate amongst her greedy brothers and sisters that came crawling out of the woodwork from nowhere. Ten in all and not a one could even tell you what her favorite color, or favorite song was. She'd been the only one to leave her small town and set out on her own, starting her own house cleaning business. Sure folks had laughed at her, heading to the big city just to 'clean some white folks houses', but that money put me through private school, college and graduate school.

I would often ask her:

"Momma, how can you keep giving and giving to them, when they don't appreciate what you give? They don't pick up the phone, or stop by, or even send you a card for your birthday."

Every time one of my aunts or uncles had a birthday, she'd send them a card with money, or a package with food and clothes, knowing that she would not get a phone call or even a thank you in return.

Her constant reply:

"Sweet pea," she'd start, looking me in the eyes. "I don't give to them to hear a 'thank you' or to get something in return. I give because it's what God has said I should do. I'm not worried about their accolades. I just want the Father to say 'well done'. God has blessed me to be a blessing. They think they are hurting me, by not acknowledging what I do, but it ain't about me. It ain't even about them. But they are getting blessed so that my grandson and that little bean you got in your belly will be blessed. I'm doing good because I want to sow a seed for future generations. You think I don't know that some of that birthday money be going toward light bills, and car notes, and rent? Most times I send that money is so all they children can eat."

"But momma" I would protest. "You know they probably using that money for liquor and partying, and God knows what else."

"You right, God does know what else. He also know the spirit with which I gave it. I can't worry too much 'bout what they doing and you don't either. God got my back"

Then she'd just go on about her business. I admired her strength of character. My mother retired at the age of fifty-five, sold her business and bought a new home in a gated community. She enjoyed her retirement to the fullest, traveling and spending time with her grandchildren. The day of her funeral, I stood looking at her casket realizing that my mentor, role model…my mommy was gone, and well…it just overwhelmed me.

It was during the reading of the thank-you cards, when I looked up from my program and caught a glimpse of my Uncle Butch that I got this sharp pain in my belly. I ignored it, and him…thinking it was just because I'd been on my feet all night preparing the repast for after the funeral. You know black folks will come to eat at a funeral even if they don't know the person that died! But then the pains kept coming, and by the time we left the plot at Kings Park Memorial Gardens, I'd begun to feel a slow trickle of fluid sliding down my inner thighs. We went straight to the hospital from the cemetery and three hours later, I had me a little bug of a boy.

    I know it was my mom's doing, trying to give me something else to think about instead of her. And it worked, I was so busy traveling back and forth to the hospital over that next month that I didn't have time to dwell on my loss. I was only focused on getting that baby to gain weight, and breathe without a machine so I could take him home. Exactly four weeks to the day he was born he came home. Too tiny to even fit in any of the outfits I'd just gotten at the baby shower a week before I brought him home.

    My bug began to gain weight, and has steadily gained weight over the last fifteen years. You'd never know that this tall, muscular tennis ace came into this world barely clinging to life, but God is just that awesome. And in my heart I knew that God had set him apart for a special work.

    "Alright Anty-poo, last call or I'm getting dad in here to get you out of bed!"

    "I'm up." I heard from under the pillow he placed over his head to drown out the sound of his nagging mother.

    "You have twenty minutes to be showered, dressed, and in the car."

    "I'm going with Nick, he said he would drop me off." He said, barely audible.

    "Oh…so ya'll best buddies now? Well don't make him late, you know how your brother is, he likes to get to school early to work-out before homeroom."

    When Nick first got the car he left his poor brother all alone. I mean what sixteen year old with wheels wanted to hang out with his thirteen year old brother? He would purposefully get up early and make a mad dash out the door, meanwhile I was still driving Alex to school, which in case you didn't know…is so not cool.

Now that Alex is the hottest DJ in town, with hordes of desperate females hanging around him, Nick has suddenly decided he needs to spend quality time with his brother. The boys are practically connected at the hip now. Oh they fight like animals every chance they get, but they have each other's back and love each other unconditionally.

"Come on little boy, I'm not waitin' all day!" I heard Nick yelling from outside. When I looked out my bedroom window I saw him sitting with his head hanging out of the driver's side. Alex was bringing the trashcans from around the back of the house. I know he wants something now because it's not his day to do trash…God bless his little soul. Can't blame him for trying. He finally got in the car and they sped off. The rest of the morning was surprisingly uneventful. Goodness, Shye, and Punkin, all got their breakfast of frosted flakes, put their bag lunches in their back packs, and piled into Anthony's truck to start their day.

To start my day, I was going to be calling out sick. Heck, I was due some time off. The novelty of my job had long ago worn off. The first day I stepped into that place. I was an intern with a master's degree in communications and a desire to change the world one news broadcast at a time. I was going to single handedly research, write, and produce news stories and programs about positive black men, women and children in our community. I quickly found out that my stories were being reduced to 1-2 minute blurbs, far less important than the daily murder toll in the city and even less important than the lotto numbers. It seemed that stories about positive leaders and gifted and talented teens just weren't cutting edge enough to be interesting to viewers. So I was now officially part of the media machine. It's gotten to the point where a story about a thirteen year old girl beating her classmate to death while being cheered on by her mother is no longer shocking. My co-workers can just laugh and eat donuts while we review the story of a toddler being killed while caught in the cross fire of a gang war, over turf that no one is paying a mortgage on.

As a Christian, I struggle with this job daily. I find myself praying for the victims and the criminals. Who am I to judge? We have all sinned and come short of the glory of God.

Anyway my brain was working overtime and I've really got to get out of here. Bottom line is regardless of the events of the last few days a sista has been so super stressed that I need to get away from work for a while. It's going to make some people upset, but I need this time to get over to Shelita's apartment. I want to find something decent…if that is possible, for her to wear on her way to her final resting place. As much as it hurts, I have to begin the process of helping my friend have a proper home going ceremony. I also need to do some digging and find out if she's left any more information for me and what I need to do with her children.

Chapter 13: The Making of a Queen

§

I spent five hours digging through memories in Shelita's apartment. And at the end of those five hours I looked like I did that one time I used my free employee pass to Gold's Gym. My heart was pounding, sweat was soaked through my blouse and I was literally in tears. Only this time I wasn't crying from some size zero trainer in spandex trying to kill me. I was overwhelmed with emotion because I was being forced to face a reality that I'd long ago, decided to deny. It was so overwhelming to be here, to see what I saw, to read and feel and touch all of the things that I wanted to forget about all these years. You think you know someone and then they die, and you really find out who they were.

In Shelita's closet I hauled out boxes and boxes of poems, she had written. Some of the writing dated back to the days when we were teenagers. She had written about the typical boys, and jewelry, and cars...but then she'd also written about the dark things in her past. The nights when she would be awaken by her dad coming into her room to kiss her and touch her in ways no young child should be touched. I was confused at first when I began reading the letters because they seemed to be written by someone other than Shelita. But they were all in her distinct swirly handwriting and all of them were in her private journals. Journals that she only shared with me on a few very rare occasions. I knew this was a complete invasion of privacy, but the more I read the more I couldn't stop reading. It was becoming evident to me that she wrote in the voices of two or three different people she'd imagined she could be while all the abuse was going on. The tears flowed when I read one passage she signed as *Rosa*. I recognized Rosa as the compassionate part of Shelita, the fragile young girl that was not ready to grow up so fast:

> *Why do you let him hurt us? I can see him when I'm floating above you. I can feel myself escape you and go high into the sky away from the pain. I hear those words he says to you, they are not nice, but up here the words float away and sound like sweet music. Up here it doesn't hurt, you just float. Come on Lita, be a big girl like me...take us away from this, make it stop...*

The tough talking alter ego she called *Roxy*, was not so nice. Roxy seemed to chastise Shelita and blame her for the awful abuse that happened night after night:

> *I can't stand you! You're so weak. You must like it Lita, why on earth do you let this monster keep coming back to me? I'm better than this, I'm a queen. Can't you get that in your stupid little head? I want this to stop right now! If you don't tell your mother I will and then that monster will be in jail! Do it now Lita or I swear I don't know what I'll do to you!...*

There were stacks and stacks of these letters, year's worth of hurt and anger scrawled on each page. I couldn't

jrenee   The Breath Of Purpose

stop reading, I wanted to, but I was being pulled in deeper and deeper the more I read. I knew if she'd written about all this hurt, then she would have written about October 20, 1976. With each new notebook, the dates kept getting closer and closer to a time that was embedded in my brain. My head was pounding, a rushing roaring river was overtaking my ears as my eyes ran over the pages. The memory of the day came rolling through my consciousness destroying all the peace and calm in it's path.

****

    My mind unwillingly goes back to twenty years earlier…I was coming home late because I missed my bus as usual. Thursdays were group study day and my mother would rather I walk home late, then miss an opportunity to study with my peers and increase my chances of passing every test. I didn't mind the walk from the bus stop it's just that on this particular day it was getting dark earlier.
    My brother had been in some major altercations with some rival street gangs, and a sista just wasn't feeling safe leisurely strolling around outside. So when I hit my block I went into full sprint mode to get up the front steps and in the door before anybody decided they wanted to jump Big Ant's sister to show him a lesson. I made it through the lobby downstairs and up ten flights of stairs in record time and got to the door breathless, but in one piece. I wasn't going to chance being stuck between floors in the elevator for almost two hours like the week before. As I approached the door to our apartment, I could hear all this screaming and commotion coming from the inside. If I didn't know any better I would have thought someone was getting killed in there. Going against my gut feeling to run, I placed my key in the door and twisted the knob. The door squeaked open as usual, but the chain and the

broom handle that was stuck in the hole my mother whittled out on the other side of the door, immediately stopped me. My mom liked to call it the ' original poor man's brinks security system'.

"Antwan, open this door! Let me in! What's going on in there?" No one answered and the screams inside where getting louder. I could tell it was a female voice, but it didn't sound familiar to me. My first agonizing thought was that the voice belonged to my mother. Was it mom? God please don't let some gang member be in there hurting my mother. My mind was racing, my heart was pounding out of my chest.

"Antwan! Mom! Somebody let me in!" I screamed throwing my body against the door hoping my weight would force the chain to break. And then I saw her through the crack in the door and the bottom dropped out of my stomach. I felt like I was being hurled off a bridge. She was running toward the door completely naked from the waste up and her clothes where ripped and torn from the waist down. My adrenaline went into overdrive as I began to attack the door, kicking and slamming my body into it until the locks broke free. By this time my brother has charged out of the room and was on top of her with his knees pinning her to the sofa.

"Don't you dare, try to run from me! You can't come in here and play grown if you not ready to act grown. I swear I will kill you if you tell anybody about this." He was literally growling, I could see spit flying from the sides of his mouth. His eyes were bulging out of his head.

"Antwan stop it right now! How could you do this? What in God's name are you doing to her? Stop you're choking her!" I was trying desperately to pull him up because all I could hear were gargles and gasps coming from underneath of him.

"I'm calling the cops on your black behind, right now! Stop it." In that instant he whirled around on me and smacked me right in the face. The blow stunned me for a second, but then I came charging back at him. He grabbed me by the shoulders and began to shake me violently. I mean I was starting to see bright little circles floating in my eyes and my teeth where clacking together.

"You ain't callin' nobody, you hear me little girl! I ain't the one to be messed with. My name is Big Ant and don't you ever forget it." By the grace of God he let me go and stormed out the door. He wasn't wearing a shirt, revealing scratches and gashes across his chest inflicted on him, by my friend who was sitting and struggling to regain her breath.

"Shelita? Are you o.k.? What in the world is going on here?" I slowly sat down beside her and took my jacket off to cover her exposed body.

"Nothing."

"Nothing? What did he do to you? Shelita, I don't care if he's my brother. I want to know what he did to you."

"I'm tellin' you he ain't mean no harm, girl we was just jokin' and it got a little outta hand." She had the nerve to try and smile, as she dabbed at her bloody lip with her fingers.

"I don't believe you. Why did he hurt you Shelita?" I was at the kitchen sink now, wetting paper towels to clean up her face and all the scratches on her chest.

"I was askin' for it…you know I been teasin' your brother all this time. I got the biggest crush on him and sometime I take it a little too far."

I guess the confused look on my face was making her feel like she needed to give me details. She explained that she'd come over to see me, forgetting the fact that I would be late from study group. Antwan was home alone so she invited herself to stay until I came home. She began to ask him why he never tried to get with her like all his other boys and he explained she was too young for him, he wasn't into playing games with little girls, he wanted a real woman. Shelita's feelings got hurt, she was used to men giving her attention because of her looks regardless of her age.

Without knowing what she was doing, Shelita said the worse thing she could have to my brother. Very innocently she implied that since he wasn't interested in her he must be 'a sissy'. As soon as the words left her mouth, she said Antwan turned into a monster immediately pushing her down on his bed, since she'd followed him to his bedroom. He was too strong for her, ripping at her top and forcing himself on her. She was totally confused as to why he kept screaming at her.

"He just kept saying, 'I'm not no sissy', 'He didn't make me a sissy', 'I'm a real man'!" She had no way of knowing that with those words she opened a dam of emotions that had been pent up inside of my brother. Shelita continued with the bizarre story of how my brother kept saying 'you're paying for this uncle Butch, I'm going to make you pay…I hate you uncle Butch.' She didn't know what it all meant.

As I sat there still boiling from the anger of what my brother had obviously done, I felt obligated to explain his doctor Jekyll, Mr. Hyde moment. It hurt me to tell the secret, but it had bubbled its way to the surface, and was now oozing out into the open in need of explaining. I shared with Shelita that for four years from the time Antwan was ten until he was fourteen, our Uncle Butch molested him.

It started off innocently enough, mom needed somebody to watch over us at night after she picked up a night contract cleaning office buildings. Uncle Butch came out of nowhere, he was recently split from his old lady and needed a place to stay. At the time, we didn't know he had a court order to stay away from her and her children. My mother always wanting to do good, thought it would be a blessing to all involved if she let him stay rent free in exchange for babysitting us when she worked nights. In our tiny apartment, Butch had to share the cramped room with Antwan.

I started to suspect something when my boisterous prankster of a big brother turned into this quiet, cowering kid every time Butch came into his presence. He started complaining of stomach cramps, he lost his appetite, he was always getting called to the principal's office. He began acting out when mom would call to say she would be later than expected, or if she made him stay home with Uncle Butch alone on days I went to help her clean.

Antwan turned to the streets as a way to escape. He wanted to turn into the biggest baddest thug on the block to make himself feel like a strong man. He was hurt physically and emotionally by what my uncle did. My mother never knew the true terror because without reason one day Butch left and never came back.

When he left my brother came to me and told me what I already knew. We told our mom, and she did everything in her power to try to get him put in jail. The only thing was Antwan didn't want to have to see him again, or testify about any of the horror. The trial and the things he did seemed to just fade into the background. As the days and years went on, Antwan dug himself deeper and deeper into his street life. My mother absolutely forbade him from living under her roof. She prayed day and night for him, fasted…the whole nine yards. She never gave up the hope that he would change his life. She knew she had poured into him the things that God had given to her and it was in His hands. But even with all of that said…his actions did not justify the abuse Shelita just endured.

"Wow. I didn't know. Why did I open my big mouth? I shoulda just left him alone." She said continuing to blame herself.

"Don't blame yourself, you are the victim here. Remember? We need to tell somebody."

"I don't want to…promise you won't tell. I'm gonna go and get cleaned up and just forget this whole thing even happened. I'm used to this kind of thing…with my dad and all."

"That doesn't make a bit of sense. You're used to abuse, so when it happens to you it's not as significant as if it happened to someone else? What kind of talk is that?" I said angrily.

"Girl, don't go getting news anchor on me. I'm a big girl. I can take care of myself. Promise you won't say anything Nay. Promise me." She begged pulling my coat tighter around her body.

And so I made a promise, that I regretted everyday of my life since then. I kept the incident from my mother, friends, everybody. That night after Shelita had gone home and changed, she came back to my apartment and we went into my room. While we were huddled together on my bed, tears streaming down our faces, we made our queen pact. We promised to always have each other's back, to always be friends in good times and bad no matter where we lived. We promised to take care of each other's children in the event that anything happened to either one of us, and we promised we were going to start a queen empire. We had dreams of owning a business together. We didn't know what it would be, but we dug in our pockets and pooled our money together that night. It was $11.30 to be exact. All we had was a crown royal bag to put the money in and then we hid it under the bed and swore that we would keep adding to this money and it would be our future.

"Wait…we need to put something down on paper. If we gonna be queens we need us a real pact, give me some paper." Shelita said reaching for my one of my notebooks.

jrenee   The Breath Of Purpose

We promise to be friends forever, we promise to love no matter the weather. Storms and clouds, or sun and blue skies, no one can hurt us even if they try. We will win in the end. We are strong, not weak. We have goals and dreams. Don't try to mess with the Queens of the 16.

We both signed the paper, folded it and put it with the money. Nine months later Shelita gave birth to my first godchild, my nephew Twan. Over the years our friendship went through many ups and downs. I was frustrated when it seemed to me Shelita gave up on our dream to get out of our dead-end existence. She dropped out of beauty school; she started hanging out with dealers and lowlifes, leaving her baby at home with her mother or me. She would ignore my attempts to help her fill out job applications, or even follow through with getting her GED. She never wanted to hear about what I was doing in college, and stopped talking about our goal to own a business. The one thing she was successful at, was making babies. I'd held her hand through two abortions, a miscarriage, and the births of her next three children.

*****

Well I have run out of Kleenex and I need to get moving. I found a beautiful coral colored suit and a teal shell in Shelita's closet. I'm going to give her my pearl earrings and necklace and a pair of laced gloves. She was always telling me she wanted to dress like a real church lady one day. The only thing missing was the big hat, but that wouldn't fit in the casket. After neatly packing up the letters and placing them in a large suitcase along with some items I want to share with my god-babies, I stood and took one last look at the room. I've only taken the few pictures and memories of the good times they had with their mom for them to cherish. Everything else about the past will be given to God. I want to try to instill in them a hope for their future. The bible says to put away old things and become a new creation in Christ.

As I headed home, I passed the bank again. You heard me…I went right past it. I've had enough of old memories to last me a few days, I'll get through the funeral and try to establish some order in my house, and then I'll march myself right in there.

Chapter 14: What Next?

§

Whoever said the freaks come out at night obviously ain't never been to a funeral in the 'hood before noon. I mean the people that came strolling up that aisle to pay their last respects to Shelita looked like they were dressed for the club. Now I know Lord I should not be passing judgment, but really do we not know that a leopard print cat suit just ain't the proper attire for a home-going ceremony? I was almost afraid one of them friends of hers would get up there and pour some liquor out on the floor. I declare, I never saw so many brown paper bags in my life. Goodness was so strong for her brother and sister. She wrapped her arms around each one of them and nestled them to her side.

The night before we'd sat down in one of our Chase Family meetings to explain to the children that their mom had passed away and her spirit had moved on to another place. Punkin wanted to know if her mother was going to heaven because she heard her say 'cussin words' and she knew that God didn't like them. I simply explained that everyone had used words in their life that God did not like and all we had to do was say we were sorry and ask Him to forgive us. I explained that on the inside her mom was a good person that prayed, and I know God loved her and protected her while she was alive. That seemed to be a good enough answer.

Shye was unusually quiet, but seemed to accept that his mom was not going to be coming back to get them. So with Anthony, my boys and my godchildren in a prayer circle, I asked God to give us all peace and strength for the road ahead. I prayed for guidance for the family and comfort for the children in the days to come. The next morning we all got dressed and waited for the limo to arrive that was taking us to March Funeral home.

Keeping his word, Antwan sent a huge, gaudy arrangement of flowers, but never showed up. This woman was the mother of his first-born son, which let's be real, was the product of a rape. I don't care how you look at it. And over the last 20 years, despite my adamant disapproval, Shelita was his on-again, off again girlfriend. She just couldn't get it in her head that she was worth more than what my brother could offer her.

Do I even have to say the funeral started late and dragged on as people went up to the microphone one by one in hysterics to scream and cry about how she didn't deserve to die, and somebody would pay for this…

When Christ is not in your life, you can't accept death as that natural part of living. You don't have peace of mind, you want to take revenge, and you can't morn with dignity. The humble minister stood just as another gansta was heading toward the microphone. In soft comforting tones he addressed the crowd.

"Loved ones, we are not here to condemn, or to speak revenge. God knows everything, and knows who is responsible for the tragedy that took your dear friend, sister and mother from you. It is our responsibility today, to honor this woman's life by not wasting another breath on hate and despair. We should be excited about the plans that He has for those of you that are still here. You have an opportunity to change your life." He continued with his sermon speaking from Romans 12: 1-2 emphasizing the need to be transformed by the renewing of your mind. The preacher talked about having the inner change be so complete, that the world would not even recognize you on the outside. When the invitation was extended to accept Christ, a young pregnant girl came to the altar. I silently thanked the Lord for saving two lives, and prayed that she would be steadfast. Shelita girl if it's only these two that you save, then your living was not in vain.

****

It was easily almost two in the morning before the last of Shelita's crew left my house. Anthony begged me not to have the repast at our house, but I couldn't think of anywhere else to have it. There was a wedding at the church so the fellowship hall was being used. The children had long since been put to bed and I was alone with my husband cleaning up the kitchen. It had come to the point where the tension in the kitchen was killing me, it actually felt like it was stifling the air. There is a storm brewing because not only did we have all element of street people in our house 'til all hours of the morning, but our son Alex decided to mess up and miss his midnight curfew.

I knew he wanted something when he started doing all those extra chores the other day. He asked his dad and I about DJing a party for one of his friends' 21st birthday. Up until now we had a strict non-alcoholic rule and would only let him spin for parties that we knew were for teens that had parents present. Alex assured us he would have one of his boys close the party for him since we absolutely would not budge on the curfew. Anthony and I did have reservations because this was a club party with alcohol, but we also trusted our son who was a good boy. We knew that our oldest son had gone to parties and was able to resist all kinds of temptation so we decided to give Alex this opportunity. Right now we were beginning to regret our decision.

"Now you know this don't make no sense." Anthony started, roughly towel drying the dishes as I handed them to him. "It's after 1:00 in the morning and that boy of yours is asking for it. This is just plain disrespect. He won't answer his cell phone, hasn't called to say he was going to be late…I can't wait to hear this excuse."

"He's just right down the street, if you're really worried you can drive by." I tried to offer to calm him down.

"Oh he don't want me driving by there. He better be home in ten minutes or else!"

"He'll be here. He's probably wrapping up right now. You know how Alex is with his equipment. Did you really think he would let somebody else handle his stuff? My guess is he's also trying to avoid all those fools we had up in here from Shelita's funeral. It was kind of wild in here." I said trying to give Alex the benefit of the doubt.

"Wild ain't the word. What did they think they were in the club or something? I thought we was gonna have to start pulling out stuff to make for breakfast." Anthony said slamming cupboard doors closed as he helped me put away dishes.

"I know…I'm sorry. Look, you go to bed, I can clean this up." I apologized. 'I'm sorry' was starting to be a familiar phrase whenever I opened my mouth to speak.

"Can't it wait 'til morning? Why don't you join me upstairs, I'll rub your back." He said with a mischievous smile, raising his eyebrows up and down.

"I really want to get this done. And besides I have to be up when Alex gets home. Go on up and I'll be up in a few minutes."

"Whatever." Anthony said as he threw a dishtowel a little too close in my direction and huffed off, obviously upset.

"Wait…whatever what? I am stressed Anthony and I don't need you to be mad at me right now."

"I'm stressed too. Once again, my wife is getting pulled in every direction except mine. I am really trying to be understanding, but if it's not work, it's the kids, if it's not our kids, it's somebody else's kids. When we do get time we argue, when we're not arguing you try to start one just for the sake of having one. Don't think I'm stupid Renee. I know you just don't want to spend time with me. I'm starting to wonder if…"

"It's not that Anthony…" I said interrupting him in mid-sentence. I didn't need him starting into anything about the past. "I can't do this right now. I have so many emotions going on inside of me. All the mess that I read about in those letters at Shelita's house, the funeral, the fact that she wants me to take care of her children permanently…"

"Wait…what is this about taking the children permanently?" He asked, coming to stand directly in front of me. I am so not liking this in-your-face-Anthony.

"Before Shelita died, she wrote a letter and asked me to keep her children together and raise them with our family."

"So when was I going to be a part of this decision? She's not just asking you to take her children, I live here too. This is my house. I do have some say right or wrong?" He said firmly, pointing around the kitchen to all the stuff I guess he was saying belonged to him too.

"You do. It's just that I haven't gotten a chance to find out all of the information. There has been too much going on in the last few days and weeks. I was going to tell you." My husband was not buying the I-need-more-time excuse, he wanted answers now. When I could not give him anymore, he sucked his teeth and stormed out of the kitchen. I was following him and got hit in the stomach by the swinging doors. That did it!

"O.k. I was wondering when the real Anthony would show up!" I screamed a little too loudly, we really hadn't gotten to the heat of the argument yet, I should really take it down a notch and wait to pull out my good argument voice a little later on, but that didn't stop me from barreling on.

"I knew you'd walk away from me at some point. But you know what that's fine, because I'm not in the mood to have this conversation with you!" I stomped up the first few stairs toward our bedroom. He ignored me, going to the closet in the foyer, to pull out the good old blanket and pillow so he could camp out on the sofa. Just for spite, I turned back around and headed to the kitchen so I could make as much noise as possible as I finished cleaning up. When I was done making whatever point I was trying to make, I purposefully walked close enough to the sofa to knock the pillow out from under his head as he was dozing off. I pretended not to notice as I headed up the stairs. He mumbled at me.

"I'm starting to think therapy is a good idea. It worked for you a little bit a few years ago didn't it? We need to talk to somebody before one of us ends up leaving." I was frozen in my spot. Tactic number three…the I'm leaving trick. This wasn't the first time we'd had this discussion about separation. We'd each used that one far too many times to even be taken seriously.

"You thinking about leaving me?" I asked, trying to sound calm. Something sounded a little too real, about this time when he said it.

"I don't feel like talking about it right now, you were the one nagging me about therapy a while back, and I'm just saying I think it's time. We've been through hell the past few years and I'm getting to the point where I can't take this anymore. I'll talk to Rev. Fowler at church this week and see if she has anybody she can recommend. Good night."

"Hey, I'm all for it, if you think it's even worth it." I said calling his bluff. He'd never gone so far as to saying he was going to look into counseling.

"Maybe it is, maybe it isn't." He said as he pulled the covers up over his head and turned off the coffee table lamp. End of discussion.

****

Of course all I did for the next two hours was replay the last words Anthony said to me over and over in my head. That mixed with the uneasy feeling of having not heard from Alex at three in the morning was killing me. My thoughts were rudely interrupted by the very obnoxious sound of wheels squealing to a halt outside my window, followed by the unmistakable sound of my son's voice.

"A-ight yo! I catch you later. Thanks for the ride; I'll get the rest of the equipment tomorrow. I gotta crash, my head is killing me."

I looked out just in time to see my obviously drunk son stumbling to the door fumbling for his keys. I immediately jumped out of bed and ran down the stairs to try and intercept him before his dad got to him. I was praying: *Lord please don't let Anthony be awake, Lord please let him be slee…*

"Boy get your behind in this house right now!" Too late…I thought to myself as Anthony yanked open the front door and pulled Alex in by his jacket.

"What in God's name do you think you are doing? Are you trying to wake everybody up so they can see what an idiot you are!?" He screamed.

"Anthony…calm down." I whispered as lights were coming on in the house across the street.

"I will not calm down! This boy has lost his mind. The nerve to miss your curfew by almost three hours! Comin' in this house smelling like a liquor store, can't barely stand up, I should knock you into next week!" Anthony was still screaming, and holding Alex up to his face by the collar on his jacket. I don't even think the poor child's feet were touching the floor anymore.

"Dad, man can you take it down, my head is pounding. I know I'm punished for probably the rest of my life right." Alex said, slurring his words and laughing as if he was insane.

"Alex, please…this is not a laughing matter. You have seriously disobeyed the rules of this house. And you've been drinking, why didn't you leave the party when you said you were going to? What happened to honesty and respect?" I was getting a little nervous here. Anthony was looking like he could kill this boy and after the fight we had, I know he just wasn't up for nonsense.

"Ma…come on you look so serious, I'm home, I didn't die in a fiery crash like I'm sure you thought I did. Chill I'm going to my room and sleep off this headache." Alex continued to smirk as if he'd been doing more than drinking alcohol. Anthony picked up on it too as he turned on the living room lights and came eye to blood shot red eye with his son.

"Have you been smoking weed?" Anthony asked standing with his nose almost touching Alex's nose. We both knew all too well the distinct smell of marijuana. Anthony admitted when we were dating that he'd puffed on his fair share of joints back in the day, and I knew the smell from the smoke that permeated my brother's clothes each night he came in off of the streets.

"What you think?" Alex remarked. I was sure he was high on something at this point the way he was challenging his father and refusing to back down. Before Anthony could grab him and I'm sure beat the black off of him, I lunged between the two of them and pushed Alex toward the steps.

"Just go to your room right now young man. You better not ever let me hear you talking to your father that way. You betrayed the trust of your father and me. Now if you know what is good for you, you will not say another word, go upstairs and get out of those stinky clothes and take your butt to bed…right now!"

It must have been the absolute hurt in my eyes that finally made him move, but he obeyed and trudged up the stairs holding onto the banister for dear life to steady himself. When he hit the top of the stairs, I could hear him running toward the bathroom. Let's just say he needed to empty the contents of his stomach.

"What next?" Anthony said more to himself than to me. While he stood there just shaking his head, I quietly walked upstairs and back to our room. The devil is a liar. I can't have this happening to my family.

Chapter 15: Let Some Healing Begin

§

True to his word, Anthony got a referral for us to attend couples therapy. Exactly one month to the day he first mentioned it, we began meeting on a weekly basis with Dr's. Michael and Sheila Branch. They were an African-American couple that specialized in Christian-based marriage counseling. Each session was an hour and a half. The first half hour we would meet separately to discuss individual needs and concerns. I know poor Sheila got an earful from me, and I couldn't imagine what Anthony was talking to Michael about. Honey just filling out the background information made me realize my family put the funk in dysfunctional.

We never discussed our private sessions, only continued to pray for one another that we would find some individual peace. After the private sessions all four of us would sit down in the cozy living room area complete with warm fireplace and drink hot tea or coco and discuss ways to strengthen a God-centered marriage.

Baby, I thought childbirth was painful, but nothing prepared me for the pain and hurt that would come as a result of truly opening up about what was going on inside of my home. Yeah we had all the folks at church fooled, but God wasn't laughing, we had work to do.

Initially I found myself being very defensive. I was surprised how comfortable Anthony was. You would have thought it had been his idea all along.

"Do you all pray?" Dr. Michael inquired at one of our first meetings.

"Of course! We know prayer changes things. Prayer is a daily part of our lives." I answered defensively. I gasped as if the answer should have been obvious. I mean we were seeking Christian counseling…hello?

"No…I mean together Mrs. Chase." He clarified.

"We used to, but I have to admit…I can't remember when the last time was that we actually prayed together. I mean we used to kneel together with the kids and the whole nine." Anthony smoothly replied.

"Why is that?" Dr. Sheila asked.

"We can't find time. Our hours are different, the children need us in one way or another, we have church responsibilities, we just get pulled in so many different directions." I answered. Didn't they read our questionnaire we filled out, don't they know we're busy! And we're paying for this?

"Directions that you choose to go in of your own free will." The good 'Mrs. Doctor' said coolly.

"Excuse me?" Get the neck slide inline Renee, this is a woman trained to read body language…un-purse the lips.

"You choose to work extra hours, and take on the task of helping out friends and family, and church ministries. You need to choose each other and make time to pray." Dr. Sheila said.

"Where do you propose we get the time, there are only so many hours in the day." I commented folding my arms, and then unfolding them because I know all about body language and I don't want them reading me right now.

"Well you say you argue with each other all the time. You argue about finances, and the children, and communication. Instead of arguing I suggest you use that time to pray. Pray about finances, pray about the children, pray that God would control your tongue, or allow you to receive what your spouse is saying. Don't choose outside activity that will pull you in so many different directions, regardless of whether you think it's the Christian thing to do." Dr. Michael was making me feel a bit small right now, I know he's not intending to, but a sista was getting a little convicted here.

"But doesn't God want us to clothe and feed the needy? Doesn't the word say to use our gifts and talents for the up building of the Kingdom?"

I turned to Anthony who was still quiet and relaxed, intently listening.

"Anthony when we got married, didn't we agree we wanted to be positive role models in our community? You were the one that encouraged me to join the Pastor's aide, and then you get mad when I'm busy with church and there is no dinner on the table." Before Anthony could answer, Dr. Michael interjected.

"The bible says, 'forsaking all others.' Your parents, friends, your children, and even the church do not come before your spouse in the eyes of God."

"Yeah…what he said." Anthony smiled and pointed to his new buddy. I was starting to think I should have picked the place we got counseling, but I know God will show Himself and we will make some steps towards being whole again in marriage.

*****

We'd been attending our sessions pretty regularly for about a month and both of us were making some individual progress but during our couple's sessions, there was still somewhat of a strain and I knew what it was about. It was time to deal with the elephant in the room, the huge topic that Anthony and I were dancing around ever so cautiously…the affair.

About four years ago our lives were literally turned upside down and inside out. I cheated on my husband. Close your mouth. O.k. so it wasn't one of those steamy-hotel-liaison-too-hot-to-handle type of affairs, but it was an affair nonetheless. The conservative old-school-Christian Renee tried to convince myself and my husband that it wasn't like really cheating because I never really consummated the relationship in the biblical way, and weren't other people cheating because they'd had sex outside of marriage? After all this was a married man at my church. A deacon, if you really want to get technical.

The attraction began innocently enough…we started out sharing an interest in the bible, and scripture to support each other as we were going through our 'tough times' with our spouses. And then scripture turned to dinner, and walks in the park, and holding hands. I allowed myself to fall emotionally in love with someone that was saying all the right things, and promising a greener grass on the other side of the fence than what I was living. I'm ashamed to admit that we shared kisses on more than one occasion and if I'm goin' on the way with Jesus I might as well just admit that we pretty much rounded third base on our way to home! It had actually gotten to the point were we made reservations to spend a weekend together.

We both got to the airport terminal and right up to the gate and couldn't go through with it. God totally just pulled me back. It had to be God because I had just emotionally checked out of my marriage, and had it not been for that still small voice, who knows what might have been. We must have been the most pitiful looking people with tickets to Jamaica anyone had ever seen. We both just sat in the waiting area and cried, and knew we had to go to God and repent for our sins and ask Him to forgive us. I can't tell you what ever happened to Deacon Matthew Redmond because we went our separate ways and never spoke again. The Redmond's relocated to another city, left the church and started their lives over again.

It was a full year before I actually confessed to Anthony. To say that he did not take it well would be putting it lightly. But what can you expect? I really thought at that point it would be the end of our marriage. There is not a good explanation as to the timing of the confession, but I felt like if things kept going the way they were and I kept losing my faith and respect in my husband and his decisions for our family that I could very easily fall into that same desire to be with someone else. So in the middle of one of our heated debates I just blurted it out. For the next year or so it was like that was his wakeup call. He was like night and day. He became this ultra-husband. Saying, doing, being all the right things, and then we stopped working on it, and it began to slide and here we are.

"That was the worst day of my life. No man on this earth ever wants to hear that his wife cheated on him. I felt like somebody just shot me in the heart." Anthony said quietly as if he was talking to himself.

"I knew that it hurt him, I really didn't mean for it to come out the way it did, but I felt like we were drifting further and further apart, and we were just roommates instead of spouses. I wanted him to know that he wasn't in as much control as he thought, that if he wasn't careful I would be gone." As I sat there finally saying the words out loud, it didn't really make any sense to me, but I had convinced myself that I had every right to do the things I had done with Matthew.

"And still after all this time, Renee I still gotta know why didn't you tell me? Why couldn't you just say change this or that, Anthony I'm not happy?" Yikes! The lower lip is quivering, I will lose it, if my husband starts to cry ya'll. Stay tough girl, don't let this be about everything you did wrong.

"Because you knew. How could you not know that it wasn't working? We were literally sinking in debt, there was no conversation, no intimacy, every comment laced with sarcasm. I know you could not have been happy during that time. And it's not up to me to be the one to say change this or that, if you can't see it."

"But your spouse can not read your mind. You have to think first that if he's not changing or doing something you don't like perhaps you have not communicated to him what it is that would make you happy." Dr. Michael in his calm voice interjects.

"I don't expect a mind reader, but at the time we'd been married for fifteen years, I would expect that I don't have to keep spelling things out." Come on people, I'm trying to keep my cool here, but I'm feeling a little dumped on.

"Are we to assume that you were doing everything the way I wanted you to? You don't think I wished for more intimacy, more home-cooked meals like I used to get when we first got married, less of you taking care of Shelita's kids all hours of the night, less of you calling about deadlines at the station…" Anthony was getting hyped at this point.

"I get it." I interrupted him, holding my hand up to stop the barrage of all the things I was doing wrong.

Chapter 16: You Need Jesus!

§

I've been sitting at my desk staring at the screensaver for the last ten minutes. It's not like I don't have a six-foot high pile of stories to finish up and get cued, but I can't keep my mind from wandering to those therapy sessions. It just feels like gang up on Renee every time we sit down to talk. Don't get me wrong, I'm appreciating that God obviously has some things to say to me about my role in the unraveling of my marriage, but can a sista get a break?

"It can't be that bad." Harold said as he walked past my cubicle. It's like he was reading my mind. Harold was an excellent writer. We both got jobs at the station at the same time and so had been working together for over fifteen years.

"Oh it is that bad, and I'm the reason why." I snapped out of my pity party long enough to click open a few files and start typing.

"Anything you care to talk about? You look like you just lost your best friend."

"Nothing to say really. Between you and me, Anthony and I are going to therapy. What can I say, marriage is a lot of work and we stopped working on ours a few years ago."

"Listen, you're preachin' to the choir. I'm not quite sure what's going on with Cynthia and me, but situations at home are definitely strained." This was the first time he'd confided in me about trouble at home. I better be careful with this, the last man I talked to about my marriage being in trouble tried to get me on a plane to Jamaica.

"I'm sorry to hear that, I had no idea. You guys seem so…so…" I was at a lost for words.

"Perfect. I know everybody says that. But believe me, we are far from perfect. I've been trying to get Cynthia to go to church with me, but she's still stuck on the Harold that she met back in the day. I still want to have a good time, but I want to do it for Jesus and baby girl is not trying to hear that. She thinks I'm soft now."

"What! Do you know how many women at my church would be throwing themselves at you right now? She doesn't know what she has. If it's any help to you, I can give you the contact for the couple we are seeing. Even though it hasn't been pretty, I can honestly say they know what they are doing, and they are Christians."

"Thanks Renee. I'll take that number. I'm gonna pray that you and Anthony keep working on this thing. I know you two love each other." I was passing the Branch's card to him around the side of the cubicle when Marguerite decided to bounce her way back to the break room. Her hip knocked the card out of my hand and onto the floor before Harold could grab it. I'm sure she was deliberately bending over very slowly in her too tight, too short, too low-cut outfit to pick up the card just for Harold's benefit.

"Ooh. What do we have here? Ya'll passin' love notes back and forth to each other? Don't let me tell you alls spouses. It's about time we had us a good old fashioned office romance around here." She said picking up the card and turning it over. "Marriage counseling?

What? Harold, don't tell me you and your woman ain't getting' along. If you need somebody to talk to then you know I'm here for you." She said as she handed him the card.

"I think I'll stick with the professionals for this one sweetie, but thanks." He said taking the card as he turned his back to her.

"Suit yourself, but if you ask me, Cynthia doesn't deserve you…I know somebody that could make you a whole lot happier." She was still lingering in the doorway to his cubicle playing with the tight curls in the fiery auburn weave that went down to her behind.

"I know somebody too. As a matter of fact I've been spending a lot of time with them already. It's been keeping me sane." He was tormenting her and I was absolutely enjoying it. The look on her face was priceless.

"Oh." She said flatly, all the smile gone out of her voice. "You already found somebody? You sure do work quick. Do I know 'em?" At this point she was talking with so much attitude you would have thought Harold was cheating on her. Had the hand on the hip and everything.

"Not sure, but you need to if you don't, His name is Jesus." That shut Ms. Thing right up. She realized Harold had just dissed her. She sucked her teeth and continued on down to the break room.

"You are a fool." I laughed. I definitely needed that after the way I'd been feeling.

"I might be, but the girl does need Jesus."

"Amen!" I shouted.

****

Two months into our sessions, it was Anthony's turn to experience a rude awakening about his role as the head of the household.

"What do you see as your role being head of the household?" Dr. Sheila asked him.

"Well, I take the role seriously. I am the primary breadwinner. Even though we are a two family income, the bulk of the bills are paid with my check." He answered confidently, dare I say the man had his chest poked out.

"Being the bread-winner does not make you the head of the household." Dr. Sheila replied.

"Hello up in here!" I exclaimed. I wished I could slap her five, but she didn't strike me as the up high, down low, too slow, kind of sista.

"Anthony is always trying to point out that we have this wonderful four bedroom home, a two car garage, children decked out in all the nicest gear, and I keep trying to say we are struggling to keep up with that. To me it doesn't cut it to just be working and paying bills, with no other input regarding the spiritual, mental well-being of your family." There you go girl, you said it. Let him try to explain that one.

"Look Renee, I read the bible, and I know that it says the man should be the provider. I feel like I've provided us with a home, nice cars, food to nourish our bodies."

"And for the soul? What do you do to ensure the souls of the family are nourished? God gave Adam the power to name the animals of the earth and the fowl of the air. The only power he gave him was the power to speak over things, he didn't get lightning bolts coming out of the fingertips, or the ability to morph into some mythic creature, but he was given the power of the tongue. You must speak perfecting into your wife, your children, your family, it is your responsibility as head of household." Dr. Michael joined in on the conversation.

The two of us were just convicted right there in those plush chairs by the fireplace. What ever happened to the weekly bible study we required the children to participate in? What ever happened to the space Anthony set aside in the loft area of the second floor that was to be dedicated as a prayer and meditation space? I know there are a pile of clean clothes there I brought upstairs from the laundry room that I haven't had time to fold. I know I saw Shye and Punkin wrestling each other on the pillows Anthony had placed in the corner to be used when we were on our face before God. The sacredness, the peace, the purpose of the place had been literally trampled on. And in so many ways this was what had happened, or should I say was and is happening to our marriage.

We've let so many other things come in and interrupt the very place God had designated as holy, our union. If it wasn't his younger sister staying with us because she fell on hard times, it was us taking families in from the church. If it wasn't me trying desperately to change a drug-addicted brother, it was Anthony dedicating all of his days off, and free time to ministering at drug treatment centers. We both worked crazy hours of overtime. Much of that overtime money was going toward hefty car payments for trucks, and televisions, and designer clothes and gadgets for ourselves and our children.

Yes even our children had taken up the personal time we spent with one another. Their needs became more important than our needs. And while not all the things we were doing were bad, in fact we were a blessing to many…we let it consume us. We needed to return back to our first true love, the way God wants us to turn back to Him when we have sinned. So on that night with soaked tissues, and throats sore from crying, we made the commitment to put God first and then to keep each other next. We knew this was not going to be an easy task with five other people in the house besides us, but God can do all things.

For twelve weeks total, we dedicated ourselves to the commitment of strengthening our marriage, and never missed a meeting with the Branch's. That newfound commitment allowed me to feel steadied for the road ahead. I decided that now was as good a time as any to take that next step and finally put to rest whatever part of my past was in that safe deposit box in Wachovia. God knows it was trifling, but it had been four months since Shelita's death and I have been avoiding the bank long enough. I knew the night she was killed that my purpose and calling was near. I had been called to raise my godchildren, and not only raise them, but help them to be elevated. Whatever was in that bank God intended to be used for the purpose of those children's future. He was going to do a miraculous thing. I just didn't know how miraculous until I got to the bank the next day.

Chapter 17: The Show Down/ No Weapon Formed

§

"Are you sure?" I asked sitting in the Plexiglas cubicle of the branch manager's office at the Wachovia on Reisterstown road. The news he'd just given me, coupled with the look of distrust on his face, had me at the edge of losing my religion.

"Yes Mrs. Chase, the contents of the safe deposit box under this name you have given me were taken nearly three months ago."

"That's impossible. Shelita specifically left instructions in the letter for me to use the key and get to this box." I said checking and rechecking the number of the box I'd written on a piece of paper.

"You say she left the letter two weeks before she died nearly four months ago?" Yes I said that…do you have any more questions Colombo? I thought to myself.

"Yes, actually it's almost been five months. Here's the letter to prove it." I said unfolding the tattered letter I'd been carrying around with me since the day I pulled it out of the floor over at The Sixteen.

"If you don't mind me asking, why have you waited so long to claim the contents?" He asked, squinting his eyes and raising one eyebrow.

"I can't tell you that. I don't know. Life has just been a whirlwind since she died. There were so many things happening at one time. This just doesn't make sense. Regardless of how long it took to come in, the contents of that box were to only be released to the legal parent or guardian of Shelita's children. I am their guardian. I have a signed legal document." I shoved the papers in his face. Take that Inspector Gadget.

"I understand that. Let me get some more information. Can you tell me how much money was in the box?"

"I don't know. You read the letter, Shelita mentions in there she didn't even know. You must have some record of who came and took the contents, without a key mind you."

"Oh, he had a key, as a matter of fact Mrs. Chase, he had a birth certificate and proof that he had fathered at least one of Ms. Graham's children." I guess my head snapping up in surprise let him know he'd said too much, because he immediately stopped talking and turned bright red.

"Did you say he came with a birth certificate and a key?" My head was beginning to pound again. I was about to go off up in there!

"I've already said too much." He answered, gathering the papers on his desk and shoving them into a folder.

"I want to see the signature." I demanded. I was causing a scene and not ashamed of it. At this point I was confident he'd already hit that silent alarm to alert security to the crazy black woman acting ghetto in his cubicle. I could care less, bring on whoever you can, I'm ready.

"I'm not allowed to give you that information." He said, now holding the folder up to his chest in a very protective manner.

"I want to see the signature right now!...O.k.... let me do one better. Was is Antwan Billows?" The blank stare on his face let me know that I hit the nail on the head. My brother. Why? Why didn't I go to the bank as soon as I found the letter? How could I fail at something so big Lord? Didn't you tell me in all those visions that you had something for those children, and you let Antwan take it? I don't get it.

"Did you even do a background check! You just gave away her children's future to a street criminal!" I screamed accusing him of wrongdoing. I wanted to blame anyone else beside myself for not obeying God's direct order to me.

"Mrs. Chase, I know this is alarming, but we can only go by the information presented to us, and he had all the documentation. Now if you don't mind, I'm going to have to ask you to leave, unless there is another banking issue I can help you with." The bank manager sounded as if he was beginning to feel sorry for me.

"Well first you can ask your security guard over there to stand down, because I will put a hurtin' on him. I'm on my way out of here. Now I know this is against company policy, but can you at least tell me how much was in the account?"

"$28,000.00." He said very quietly, avoiding eye contact. And so the weapon was formed.

****

It seemed Antwan wasted no time moving on up to a deluxe apartment in the sky. Every one on the block knew Big Ant had come into some money. I soon found this out when I went looking for him back at The Sixteen. I found out he moved, with that hussy I met in the bedroom the day I went there after Shelita died. So now I had to be buzzed in, with some fancy security door to gain entrance to a luxury condo overlooking the Inner Harbor in downtown Baltimore. He answered the door wearing an all white linen leisure suit and a pair of really dark sunglasses, somebody's' been watching too much *Belly* on DVD.

"Well. Well. Well." He said, taking a puff on a cigar and purposefully blowing the smoke in my face. "Took you long enough. I thought you were smart." As we settled down on his brand new white leather sofa set from Value City, I caught a glimpse of the new 'Killah' tattoo he had emblazoned on his right forearm. You can take the man out the ghetto, but …well you know how it goes.

"Killah, huh? You just so big and bad. Antwan I don't understand why you just don't leave this life alone. You're getting too old for this mess."

"I might be old, but I got new tricks. Look around Renee, I'm living big time just like you, off of Shelita's dime." He said making a sweeping motion around the condo and starting to cackle like a hen.

"You knew all along. Why didn't you just say something? I might have given you some money."

"No you wouldn't Renee. I don't exist to you…remember? You let me go way back, to be with your man and your children. The church says drop people that pull you down, right?" He laughed sarcastically.

Meanwhile a woman came gliding out of the bedroom with nothing on but a pair of heels and stockings. She handed Antwan some money and turned back around toward the way she came without even acknowledging the fact that I was sitting there.

"I see old habits die hard. You right back into pimpin' women. I knew it when I saw that chick at your place." I said disgusted.

"That's how much you know, she's my main woman, I don't have her working the streets. She helps me recruit…yeah, she's my recruitment manager. The streets are rough out here, we just doing our part to help these young girls get back on their feet and earn some cash.

You forgot all about them mean streets over there in the county, ain't you Renee?" He said laughing while he counted the money he just got from one of his employees.

"I don't have time for games with you. I tried to love you unconditionally. I know what you been through, remember I was there. I saw what you did to Shelita and I was never the same. I had nightmares. And even after that, risked my marriage to try and get your strung out self off the street."

"Yeah, Renee... little Miss good Samaritan. Well your plan backfired. See the good guy doesn't always win. It was so hard not to laugh at you crawling around in that bedroom looking for the money." He was cackling like a hen again, mouth wide open laughing. From my vantage point I got a clear view of the new gold and diamond fronts he had covering his teeth.

"How long did you know?" I was using all of God's power to stay in my seat and not just smack the mess out of him.

"'Bout as long and you knew what was happening to me in our apartment with uncle Butch...yeah, you claim to know that something was up, but you didn't say anything to anybody."

"Antwan, I was young and confused. I was scared. What you don't know is that I confronted uncle Butch, yeah, told him that I knew he was doing something he wasn't supposed to do. You know what he did? He said he would kill you and hurt momma if I said anything. I didn't know any better. I have tried to make things right with you Antwan, but I can't take the blame. When you had a chance to put him in jail, you refused to testify. You were so worried about your image that you let him go and he probably did it again to somebody else."

"I don't have time for this, I want you to leave. I got what I deserve now, this is my payback for all the years of hell."

"Boy you better be happy that God hasn't really given you what you deserved. I want to know how in the world you could take Shelita's money when her body wasn't even cold in the ground yet. I know she didn't tell you where the money was hidden, how did you find out?"

"Man, Shelita was falling off. She would come to the crib so high, babbling out of her mind, trying to keep what she was doing a secret. I hooked her up a few times with some good rock, so she kept coming back for more. I found her passed out under the bed one night so I did some investigating and found your little stash and love letter to each other about being queens! Yeah right!" He began laughing so hard I thought he was going to choke.

"I'm glad this is so funny to you. But trust me when I say that no weapon formed against me and those kids is gonna prosper."

"Baby I got $28,000.00 not to mention thousands more I helped myself to before she even got a chance to put it in the bank, that sounds pretty prosperous to me! But I tell you what, since I'm in the giving mood, I'll give you half of what I got left. Here." He said between laughing and puffs on his cigar. While he was talking he'd opened a small drawer on his new coffee table and threw a wad of twenties at me.

"That's $1000.00, see how much college you can get for three kids with that!"

"You should know me enough, to know that I believe that God will make provision for these children. He would not have me be their mother if he did not already have a way for them." I said taking the crisp bills, and folding them into my hand.

"Blah, Blah, Blah. I'm done Renee. You and I don't have any reason to see each other." He said turning his back on me to look at out of the huge floor to ceiling window. *He must feel like he's on top of the world*, I thought to myself.

"I pray that before it is too late, you repent and seek Gods face. That you ask for forgiveness for all the wrong you have done. You can't keep hiding behind your hurt and your past. God wants to heal and deliver you Antwan and you just keep turning your back."

"Enough with the Sunday school lesson. It's time for you to bounce. My old lady will be home from her spa appointment soon and she wasn't feeling you the last time she saw you. Said you was looking down on her, like she wasn't good enough."

"That's not even in my nature, so whatever she felt was her own opinion of herself. I'm out of here."

And with that I took the seed that God was going to multiply and went on my way. I can't keep beating myself up about my brother. The bible says that some seeds fall on stony ground and some land in good soil. I can't determine whether the seed will bring forth fruit, all I can do is go about spreading the news. I am believing God that one day Antwan will turn his life around.

****

Although I had taken the confrontation with my brother fairly well, Anthony went ballistic. He was livid when I recounted the details of the day, from the bank to the show down with Antwan.

"Why didn't you call me Renee?" He asked, pacing the floor in our bedroom.

"For what? So you could come and ya'll two could fight to the death? That is playing into the enemies hands Anthony. Trust me when I say that I am going to take this money and it will grow to beyond what Shelita could have ever imagined for her children. God will do it."

"All I can say is you are better than me. And I know we've been surviving these last months without knowing about the money, but it's the principle of it all."

"You can't let that consume you. Let's just move forward. Focus on our future with our family." I wrapped my arms around my husband and gave him a warm kiss. Since counseling I've been getting and giving a lot more hugs and kisses, Hershey's ain't got nothing on me.

Chapter 18: New Love Leads To New Hurt

§

The seasons were changing outside my window and by the grace of God in my home also. The past three months have been amazing to me. If I never knew that God loved Renee Chase, I sure did know it now. My beautiful children, all five of them, were getting used to their routines.

After our sessions ended with the Branch's, Anthony and I continued to follow their advice. We started datin' each other all over again. We went on our first date to the movies and dinner trying to rekindle our flame about two weeks ago. It was funny and awkward to be so clumsy and out of touch with each other as we made an effort to return to the intimacy we once enjoyed. It was still taking time for me to come to terms with my middle aged body, that love-making was still a lights out, covers up to the chin, type of ordeal for me.

Imagine my shock when I came home one day and heard soft music and smelled delicious cinnamon candles. I saw a note on the banister leading upstairs:

Hello my lovely lady,
Take the stairs for an evening of relaxation and pampering.

Hardly able to contain my joy and curiosity, I ran up the stairs even though I was dog-tired. I followed rose petals to the bedroom door and slowly pushed it open. There was yet another note left in the middle of the bed, which was now covered in red satin sheets.

A warm bath awaits, soak your tired body and be prepared for a surprise.

As I sat in the absolutely soothing hot tub filled with bubbles, I was munching on the cheese, fruit, and crackers left for me. While I was wondering where in the world my husband was and what he was up to, I could hear him moving around in our room. I got out of the tub and threw on the silk robe he draped over the terry-clothed ottoman, and stepped out of the bathroom. Anthony had set up a massage table and was waiting patiently for me to lie down on it.

"Aren't you filled with surprises? Where are the kids?" This was too good to be true. At any moment I was sure someone under the age of eighteen would burst into the room and spoil the mood.

"Alex is at a friends', and the rest of 'em are at Ty and Gina's having a game night. So we have the house to ourselves for the next three hours." He was so proud of the fact that he'd gotten every little detail down to the childcare taken care of. I was impressed.

"This is so special. What's the occasion?" I asked eyeing him suspiciously. I didn't want this to be one of those Maury Povich moments…like I brought you all the way here to tell you that I'm datin' your best friend kinda things.

"I love my wife. God has given me a gift and I am just cherishing my gift a little tonight if that's all right with you." He said kissing me gently on the forehead, as he pulled the sheets back for me.

"Well then brotha, don't let me stop you…get to cherishin'." I said laughing as I got comfortable on the table. Anthony delicately began kneading and massaging away all the stress and tension of the day. *Thank you Lord! What a blessing this i*s I thought to myself when suddenly the air in the room changed. Anthony had been concentrating on one area of the body and while initially it felt great, I could tell the touch of his hands were somehow different.

"What's this?" He asked, kneading deeper.

I opened my eyes and saw his look of concern, and then immediately closed them.

"Come on now I think you're a little too old for the talk about boy parts and girl parts, child. It may not be in the same place it was twenty years ago, but it's the same thing." I joked nervously, trying to clear the tension in the room.

"No babe. Something doesn't feel right. Put your hand here." He said, placing my right and on the outer edge of my left breast.

"It's a lump." We both said together. We were both silent for what was probably five seconds, but seemed like an eternity.

"Well!" I jumped up. "It's probably one of those fat globs. You know I have gained so much weight." I continued frantically looking around for some clothes to put on my body.

"Wait. Renee, slow down…was the lump there last week? Last month? Has it changed in size?" Anthony began rattling off questions.

"I don't know." I mumbled. My mind was reeling. I thought I felt something weird in the shower the other day, but because I never really did a self-exam before I wasn't quite sure of what I was feeling. In my typical manner, I just decided I would wait a few days and inspect the area again hoping that it would just be gone.

"Does it feel like the other one? Is the right one lumpy too?"

"I said I don't know! Anthony it's no big deal. Just…"

"It is a big deal! How can you not know? Don't you check that kind of stuff every once in a while? Aren't women supposed to do self-exams in the shower? I remember you were doing a story on it for the station. Renee your mother had breast cancer, for goodness sake why weren't you checking?"

"Don't yell at me! You are over reacting."

"Am I? Help me out here then. You're telling me you wouldn't be as upset if I had some weird lump growing somewhere? Why does this always happen? We need to pray. The devil is a liar. I have not come this far and made sacrifices to lose you."

"Anthony!" I wanted to slap some sense into him, but I was probably the one that needed to be slapped. "You just went from zero to sixty in five seconds! You act like I'm dead, already Anthony. Calm down. You are right…We need prayer. Let's just calm down and breathe here. God has a plan for me and I know that it entails me raising some brand new kids so I ain't going nowhere no time soon. We know someone who can handle all things even when we can't. Hold me, let's go to God together on this." And we did.

I have never in my life heard my husband pray with such passion and sincerity for healing. This was before we even knew whether or not the lump was even something to be concerned about. Here we were together in each other's arms crying and laying ourselves open, not just about my health, but about our marriage, our children, our finances. I know it may sound strange to someone that is not in a personal relationship with God, but we were thankful for the events of the evening. If my husband and I had not been obedient about strengthening our marriage, if we had not been obedient about finding time for one another, we may not have been spending this night together and by the time the lump was discovered, it may have been too late. What the devil meant for evil, God will turn it around and use it for good.

Chapter 19: Not Just Another Chase Family Meeting

§

I have it. I have cancer. *Aggressive cell-type* was the word the doctor used. Let me see what other glorious adjectives did he throw at me in his office that day…? Oh yeah… *"invasive, life-threatening, carcinoma in-situ"*. My oncology team, headed by Dr. Gordon Grander, were recommending some rigorous, radical treatment to attack this poison in my body. It was time for another Chase family meeting. Anthony and I decided to wait until we had all the facts before we gathered the children together to tell them about my life changing diagnosis. So after several doctors' visits, blood tests, and biopsies the time had come to get the family together on one accord. As usual we opened in prayer with my baby Shye taking the lead. He had gotten so much more confident with his speaking that he didn't mind praying aloud without the fear of someone making fun of how he spoke.

Now Punkin that was a different story. She was never one to mince words, and as a matter of fact we were working hard on helping her know when to keep her mouth shut. When she was growing up around Shelita, she was hanging with people old enough to be her parents, yet she was able to take part in every conversation about every and any topic from drugs to sex. So before we even got the *amen's* out, she was talking over everyone.

"Alright, so what did big head do now? Any time we have these meetings lately it's because Shye is wildin' out in school."

"Young lady you will watch that tone. If I have to speak to you again you will be on punishment. Now mom has something to tell you about, so listen up." Anthony reprimanded her. He disciplined her the same way he did Nick and Alex, no preferential treatment up in this house.

"Yes sir." She softened up and gave me her full attention.

"Well really it's not that big. I have not been feeling well lately so I went to the doctor and turns out I need to have surgery to make it all better."

"Why are you talking to us like we're two? What's the surgery mom? You wouldn't be having a family meeting for a minor surgery. I mean, you had a root canal a while ago and didn't nobody call a Chase family meeting." Alex has always been attuned to me more than anybody in this house. He'd been eyeing me very curiously the past few months, constantly asking me if I was o.k.

"Well, Alex if you must know…I have been diagnosed with breast cancer."

"Mom! Tell me how that's not a big deal? Didn't Grammy have breast cancer?" He yelled almost standing up from his seat.

"Sweetie, there are different kinds. Daddy and I have talked to the doctors and we know what is best and what will work. So I don't want to see any sad faces around here. You know that we believe that God is a healer. He has given our doctors and our team clarity as to what will cure me and make me feel better." I said patting his hand the way I used to do when he fell and had a boo-boo.

"Do you have to get it removed?" Goodness asked. She knew so much more than I did at her age.

"Yes. That is the surgery. Then I will have some chemotherapy, and radiation to be sure all of the bad cells are gone, and we move on from there." I looked to Anthony to interject something, because I was starting to feel uncomfortable with the children's questioning eyes on me.

"Most likely your mom may be tired and need some help around the house. She will need to rest and can't be bothered with loud noise and fights between brothers and sisters understood." Anthony said sternly looking each child in the eye. Everyone was there for the meeting except my big boy Nick. He was away on a campus visit to Ohio State University, meeting with the coaches and the Athletic department. I didn't see any point in interrupting his weekend. He was the star there for the next three days with plenty of luncheons and information groups to attend all before he even graduated from high school!

"Yes sir!" They all said in unison.

"Alright! Let's get back to homework and chores. Punkin I need to have a talk with you about what sweeping means. You can't just leave piles all around the kitchen for me to step in, use the dust pan baby."

And with that the Chases were back to business as usual. I jumped up and began doing my normal routine. Getting dinner on the table, sitting with Shye to review his speech exercises, checking my manuscripts for the stories I'd been given, taking a shower, and saying my prayers with Anthony before laying my tired butt in the bed.

In two weeks I would be a woman with one breast.

Chapter 20: The Race Is Not Given To The Swift

§

Some of the most frustrating times in my life have been when God has given me a direct answer to my prayers. That's because the answer was "*not yet, my child*". Renee Chase does not like "*not yet*". I want either a clear yes or no. Not yet means I have more work to do. It means I need to practice more patience with these frazzled nerves of mine. It means that 'it' is for me, whatever "it" is, but…not yet.

So my reply to God lately has been not *'Why Lord?'*, which was my anthem a few years ago, but *'When'*. Not that accusatory when like:

"When you gonna give me my stuff?"

But more like well… "When I am ready Lord so many lives will be changed. When you do bless me and elevate me my children will bear the fruit of the labor. When you do take me where it is you are preparing me to go right now, I will be utterly ridiculous in my praise!" I was all ready to step in, rip my blouse open to reveal my superwoman symbol and start being a mom to Goodness, Shye, and Punkin. I was ready to start my new life over with my husband, and be 'wonder wife'. Just when I was praising God for finally making it to my purpose, He said *"not yet"*, and I get the "C" bomb, right in the chest.

So I'm frustrated, but I'm also anticipating the move of God, and that has got me all tingly inside. Of course that strange sensation could be coming from the port-a-cath that is delivering the chemo to some very unlucky cancers cells right about now. When I'm all hooked up to the machine, in my ugly blue recliner at the hospital, I like to close my eyes and imagine those cells just trying to run and having nowhere to hide. It feels like I can feel every drop of the drug coursing through each vessel. I know they think I just about lost my mind in here. As each hair has fallen from my head, and the list of foods I can tolerate dwindles, and my skin gets more and more sensitive to every detergent I buy, I just keep on smiling and thanking God. I mean a sista coulda been dead! Hello up in here!

"Mrs. Renee can I get you some more ice chips?" Shelly asked. She was the oncology nurse assigned to the chemo room today.

"No darling, I'm just about done, I'll get something at home…Listen is the group still on for tomorrow?"

"We are going to be here, but I expect that since Miss Sylvia passed away a lot of her friends won't much feel up to being here." She sighed heavily as she was unhooking me from the lines. This was just as much a loss for her as it was for the group.

As soon as I got my diagnosis I immediately looked for a support group for African-American women living with and surviving breast cancer. It took me two months to find a group of real sista's that would open up about the good, the bad, and the ugly. I was invited to join a group of ladies one day after talking to Deanna, a young woman who had made the decision to have a double mastectomy at the age of twenty-five. I was blown away at her courage and was excited to hear for myself the crazy stories she would relay to me second-hand while we both waited our turn to be hooked to the chemo drip.

The experience was better than I could have ever imagined. I have seen those girls faithfully for the last six months, laughing, crying and sharing wacky stories about our families. I got to brag about my oldest boy graduating from high school with honors and being accepted to college on a football scholarship. I shared stories of Shye's success with writing, and winning his class spelling bee. Alex was winning his way to a spot on the Maryland Youth Tennis League to represent the state at the national championship, even though at home he was acting a pure fool.

In all that time, even knowing what we all shared in common, it never dawned on me that someone in the group would die. Miss Sylvia was the most outspoken woman in the group. A no-nonsense-tell-cancer-to-kiss-my-you-know-what kind of lady. She told us two months ago that her cancer had returned and that it was inoperable, and Dr. Grander wasn't giving her much time. She laughed as we cried.

"What ya'll so sad fo'? This mean I ain't gotta pay no more taxes!" Miss Sylvia said with her hands on her hips just smiling.

"God done gave me so much time here on this earth. I can't complain about none of it. The things I done did in my life, wasn't nothing but God's will. So how I'm gonna be mad at Him for wantin' me up there to share some of my stories with them angels?" She reminded me so much of my mom and her words of wisdom to me about truly valuing each day because we don't know when it will be our last. And so she was laid to rest in a beautiful home-going ceremony yesterday. When I tell you it was a party up in there, I'm talking 'bout, Shelita's crew didn't have nothing on these people, and they were doing it all in the name of Jesus! Ain't no party like a Holy Ghost Party, 'cause a Holy Ghost party don't stop!

jrenee   The Breath Of Purpose

****

    As we stood in a circle grasping hands tightly, there was a silence that was deafening. Ms. Sylvia was our designated chaplain and typically started and ended each meeting with a get-straight-into-heaven, and shame-the-devil, soul stirring prayer. It seemed like nobody wanted to step up and take the place of our departed sister.
    "Thank you Lord." I whispered into the air. Then more echoes of *'thank you's'* followed from every woman standing in that circle.
    "Thank you for our lives, thank you for our pain and our hurt, thank you for unexpected days and joys we never knew we would see. Father we miss our sister, we wish for complete healing for each person, but know that it is ultimately your will. The healing may come in the form of peace of mind, the healing may be pleasure in the small things in life, and the healing may be a stronger prayer life. Father as we stand here today united in this circle, let us be on one accord in the spirit. Let sadness and confusion be taken away and replaced by a courage, that we will all make it to see glory. That we will all be in a place one day of your choosing where there will be no more pain, no more suffering, no cancer or illness. We rejoice today that our sister has gone on up. Amen." I hadn't intended to say all of that, but I felt God speaking those words to me. Deanna pulled me close to her and hugged me so hard, with tears running down her beautiful young face.
    "Mrs. Renee, that was so beautiful…I really needed that today. I loved Ms. Sylvia like my own grandmother. I remember when I was getting ready for my wedding and I was so nervous about my honeymoon and the fact that I hadn't received any lingerie I thought fit me properly in my chest area, she said '*child, if you think that boy is interested in what the lingerie look like you more naïve*

than I thought'." She laughed and we all joined in, because we knew her to be a straight talker.

"That's not as bad as the time she came outside with the wig on backwards!" Another group member Charlene joined in.

"Right! The red one! The front part was in the back and the tag was in the front! She said she'd worn it like that all day and had hit the mid-day number so she was gonna wear that wig just like that any time she played her lotto!" Deanna remembered wiping tears from her eyes as she laughed.

"Ya'll know what's crazy?...I think it actually worked a few times." I said laughing until my eyes were filled with tears.

"Look what Ms. Sylvia gave me the week before she passed away." Tanya pulled a piece of paper from her purse and unfolded it. There was a list of twenty items and fifteen of them had been checked off.

"These were the things she wanted to do before she died. She was almost done. She made me promise that we'd finish her list for her, and warned me that she'd be watching to make sure we did."

Tanya who was the closest to Sylvia had such a serious look on her face. She'd been caring for Ms. Sylvia in her own home, instead of putting her in hospice care. We all huddled together and looked at the list. Some of the things were simple, some were adventurous. She had checked off things like, walking barefoot on the beach, going to Vegas for a weekend, riding a roller coaster. Of course she left all the insanely crazy things on the list for us to do! She probably did it on purpose knowing Ms. Sylvia.

"Well she didn't say anything about we all had to do each one of these. I say we write them down on a piece of paper and pull them randomly." I suggested when it looked like we were going to all just chicken out right there after reading the words on the paper. There were ten of us, so we paired up and pulled a challenge from a hat. I was paired with Deanna, and together we were going to…drum roll please…

"Run a marathon!" We both shouted. Deanna seemed excited, but of course if I was twenty-five and built like Flo Jo, I might be jumping up and down with excitement too. I on the other hand was in shock. I half wanted to pull out the paper that said, bungee jump because I figured it would be a quick death in the event that anything went wrong. This marathon was going to be a slow painful journey of training, and trying hard to make it to the finish line.

Chapter 21: I Don't Have All The Answers

§

    Somewhere there was a disconnect. The sun and the moon must be out of alignment. The earth must be off it axis! Someone has lost their mind in my house because it is 6:30 am on a Saturday and I can hear every kick, punch, and back-flip on that darn play-station game in Alex's room that he has so graciously been sharing with Shye. Now I had a little talk with Jesus and promised Him that I would be even-toned and cool in matters when addressing issues like why I only get three and a half hours of sleep on the weekend. A sista is draggin'. I worked a double at the station, the cancer treatment is wiping me out, not to mention I've been training for The Race For a Cure half-marathon! I gotta pee, but I need to talk to my child first. He needs some good old-fashioned nurturing. My illness has really taken a toll on Alex. My symptoms seem to affect him, more than they affect me. I'm running myself ragged putting on appearances and trying to keep up the same routine so that nobody in the family will feel the wrath I'm feeling from this cancer.

    "Something wrong?" I asked standing in his doorway, looking into his heavy sleepy eyes. And is that a whisker on his upper lip? When did my baby grow up?

"Unh, Uhn." This means '*no beautiful mother*' in teenage boy language. I've mastered the translation in the last few years.

"So turn the game down then…why are you up so early? Where is Shye-Shye?"

"He's in with Punkin watchin' cartoons. I ain't been to sleep because I got a lot on my mind."

So much for all the private school education, Alex also known as 'DJ Chase' is going to always try to represent, so he must sound hood even at the crack of dawn. Over the last few months it's like he's developed an alter ego that is intent on smoking and drinking and doing everything completely opposite of how he was raised. He thinks he's hiding it from us, but we daily pray for him. His father has punished him more times in the last month than I can even count on both hands and feet.

"Anything a very intelligent mother who is worried can help you with?" I saw lots of rapid thumb movement on the controls of the game, and a few yawns, but not even a glance in my direction. So I kissed his forehead and turned toward the door to leave.

"It's just that you never talk about what's happening to you. And I know I'm suppose to believe that God will heal you and just go on believin' and recievin', but I can't. I had a dream I was at your funeral." He still wasn't looking at me, and somehow didn't miss a bit of action on that game. I was absolutely frozen. He was right. I hadn't talked about the cancer or the treatment since the family meeting almost eight months ago. I kind of just brushed it off as 'just a little thing' that would pass. I expected everyone to watch me sleep for days after chemo, walk around with stylish wigs and painted on eyebrows and just act like nothing was different.

"O.k." I said sitting next to him on the bed and clicking the television off. "What do you want me to say? What will comfort you sweetie? I want you to be ok with all of this." I was rubbing his back without even realizing it. I could feel the raised outline of the new tattoo he'd gotten and been trying to hide under t-shirts for the last two weeks.

"See that makes it worse ma. You the sick one and you wanna know how to make me feel better." He tossed the controller and pushed himself off of the bed.

"I wanna know what will make you feel better. I wanna know what you think about my dream? What do you think about when you're hooked up to the machine for the chemo or lying under the radiation? Does it hurt? Are you scared? Why don't you tell us how we should deal because right now I can't! I don't want you to die!"

My stomach felt nauseous and I couldn't tell if it was the medicine, the fact that I hadn't eaten, or the fact that I'd been trying to keep my eyes on my son as he's paced back and forth in front of me.

Wow. My eighteen year old has just pulled a Renee Chase, on me. I know now why he always gives me the *'which-question-do-you-want-me-to-answer'* look when I go off on him for missing curfew and start firing questions at him all in one breath before he can answer.

"Hey everything alright in here? Sounds like Ike and Tina up in here, can a brotha get some rest?" Anthony had peeked his head in the room as he passed on his way to our bedroom. Saved by the cranky husband, I owe you Lord.

"Sorry babe, Alex had a bad dream so I was just talking about it with him…I need to get going anyway. I'm going to an appointment in an hour." I ran out the door and down the hall, literally bumping into Goodness as she wiped sleep from her eyes and paused with a puzzled look.

"You o.k. mommy Nay?" She asked.

"Yes." I answered still running to my bathroom to have another talk with my Lord, why is everyone up in my business so early in the morning? I made it to the door right as the first hot tear slid down my cheek. There are no eyelashes for the plump drop of water to get caught in so it ran like a leaky faucet over my nose and into my mouth. With the door closed behind me to support my weight, I sank down to the floor.

What was that Lord? My son wants answers. You could have prepared me in a vision or something. What do I tell him? Do I say *"hell yeah I'm scared of this…crap."* I know Lord, I'm working on the cursing, but situations got me stressed out.

Do I tell him that it burns and hurts to get radiation aimed at my chest that is designed to kill and destroy every cell it comes in contact with? Do I pull down the collar of my shirt and show him the icky bruised skin around this thing called a port-a-cath that feels more like a porthole in my chest? Can I say that the netting on these ridiculous wigs itches so bad I want to scratch my scalp until it bleeds? Will it make him feel better to hear that I'm scared and I don't want to die, that I want to live forever and ever? I would love to be 120 years old with my picture on a Smuckers jar telling everybody about my secrets for longevity. I don't want to die, but you gave me this strange unexplained thing. You did this, not me. I am for some reason calm and at peace or maybe I'm insane and this is the calm before the storm. Lord please bring peace to my baby's mind until I can get up enough courage to answer all of his hard questions…now…I gotta go.

I looked in the mirror, yes me looking in the mirror…I dried my eyes, put on the I'm-feeling-casually-fly-in-my-velour-track-suit-wig and got to steppin'. I've got some bras to buy. The night we discovered the lump was supposed to be the night we re-ignited the love life. Since then, we have been intimate, but the truth is I know my fatigue has put a damper on the creativity and spontaneity. I'm doing my duty as a wife and trying to bring back a little spice. Watch out now!

Chapter 22: Getting Back In Stride Again

§

Humiliating. That's all I've got to say. This had to have been the most humiliating experience of my life. I was standing there with my right breast in this white woman's hand. You heard me. I was getting fitted for my fake boob until the new one was ready. I'm preparing my body to have the flap surgery to rebuild my left breast with my own skin and tissue. I even get a tummy tuck out of the deal!

"This is gonna be hard to match, hon." Irma my breast expert said while holding my right breast out away from my body. She handled it the same way normal people toss luggage around. Well I'm about to take my oversized carry-on and get the heck out of dodge. Why am I doing this? Why am I standing here with this little Jewish woman who's eye to eye with my nipple (which isn't saying much for her since my nipple is six inches below where it should be. I'd give her 4'5" on a good day with heels).

"Oh, that's fine, this is just a temporary fix sweetie, I'm getting the flap augmentation on the left side once I'm all healed." My face hurt, because I was doing my best to smile real hard.

"You should get them to lift this and take some of the fat out of it" she stated still holding my breast hostage. "They can make it smaller, you know it would make you look like you lost twenty pounds, easy." I get it lady, I thought to myself. Now give me my fat breast back and go find my thing-a-ma-bob, so I can get out of here and get my fat butt a Big-Mac.

"I'll talk to the surgeon…anyway I have another appointment so can we, you know…get me fitted?" I said shooing her toward the dressing room door. I'm ready to be out of here. She left me standing there in the small fitting room with the curtain wide open and after a few seconds she barged back in without warning.

"We don't have your color, but this is the biggest one I got. It fits inside a 44 triple E. Raise your arms." She ordered as she pulled my arms up for me, fastened the bra, and twisted it and me around. It looked like it took all of her strength to hoist me into the empty cup. The left side had a hidden pocket that held a firm, peach colored silicone mound with a small perky pink nipple molded onto the front of it. Irma explained that the life-like color was:

"Just incase you wanted to wear one of those lacey numbers the girls wear now a days for their fellas. He sees this through the lace and doesn't know the difference."

"Well…that's great…um I'll take it." What is happening to me? My eyes are watering. I am seriously about to lose it. I just want to get far away from here. Where is the tub filled with Calgon when you need it? This wall, this steel exterior that I've developed is about to crumble. I can't do this anymore. The façade, the superwoman has lost her powers.

I want my own brown mound, not some lifeless hard brick filler. Why the left one Lord? Why Lord? The left one was life. The left breast produced more milk when I was feeding the boys. The left one was more sensitive, always more aware of the soft kisses and whispers from my husband's lips. The left one let me know when it was that time of the month. It supported tired little heads of boys that crawled into my bed to seek comfort from nightmares or rest snuggling in the crook of my left arm. It was the perfect pillow for listening to bedtime stories.

Aaarrrrgh! I'm mad, I'm mad, I'm mad and I want it back! I'm mad, my throat hurts, it throbs, because I want to scream and cry and take this thing off of me. It's not me. It's not me…Wait…Irma looks concerned. The features on her face are starting to blur, she's floating in front of me, because my eyes are overflowing with tears. Great. I'm crying about buying a bra.

"Hon listen, if it means that much to you, I can order a dark one, it'll take two weeks tops." Irma offered, cautiously backing away from me in the tiny dressing room.

"No this is only temporary." I said while wiping tears from my eyes. After breaking all speed records to get dressed and pay for my new bra, I left and sat paralyzed in my car. I couldn't believe I just had a break down in front of a complete stranger and while I was half nude! Lord you got some sense of humor. After digging down in my shirt and pulling out the new insert, I place it on the seat next to me. We have to get to know one another; it just felt like it covered too many memories. It just felt so heavy on my chest. I can't replace what I lost, but I can create a new memory for this body. I trust you God. If you didn't want that on this temple then it had to go. Wait 'til I tell the girls in the group about this I chuckled to myself as I drove away.

*****

It had been one week since my little meltdown at the bra store, and I still hadn't talked to Anthony about it. I've worn the bra but not the insert. I know I could just use one of my bras for that matter, but I'm taking baby steps here. I was wearing the dumb thing today. Somehow it doesn't feel as heavy as it did a week ago. Lord please don't let my husband say anything to make me upset about this thing. Deep breaths Renee, that's it. Smell the roses...blow out the candles...you know the routine. Slowly now one foot in front of the other, open the bathroom door and walk out there girl. Your public awaits you.

My heart was beating so hard, like the night I found out about Shelita's death. I saw the insert beating, twitching to the rapid rate of the pounding in my chest. Beads of sweat were popping up on my lips and nose and my underarms were itching. I was so nervous about Anthony seeing me. You would think this was our honeymoon night and not the evening of our 22nd Wedding Anniversary.

We had a romantic candlelit dinner made by yours truly and now my husband was pouring some sparkling cider into two of our best wine glasses, and waiting in anticipation to see my '*let-me-slip-into-something-more-comfortable*' outfit. After things go a little hot and heavy on the living room sofa, I promised him I had a sexy outfit for him to see. Yeah, we're acting like teenagers, but it really feels good to be reconnecting.

Alright. I've stalled enough. Teddy Pendergrass was out there warning my husband to *Turn off the lights, and light a candle.* And just as he did that I stepped out of the bathroom.

"Va-va-voom! Lady, what did you do with my wife, you look absolutely gorgeous." Anthony said looking me up and down.

"You like." I said with a twirl and a little boost of confidence. I sauntered over to Anthony who was sitting on the chaise at the foot of the bed.

"I love. I can't believe you went through all this trouble for me tonight, the dinner, the beautiful watch you gave me, this sexy outfit…you really outdid yourself."

"It was no trouble at all, now kiss me you fool." And with that my cuddly bear of a husband took me into his arms and smothered me with warm kisses. The evening ended perfectly. It was the most passionate night we ever had together. No words can describe the incredible heights that we soared to together.

The night was not without drama though. I had a wardrobe malfunction when the insert fell out right in the middle of our passion-filled evening. Anthony never said a word, he just helped me put it back in, all the while telling me how beautiful I was. There were more tender words from my husband and tears of joy and relief from me. We talked into the wee hours of the morning about how blessed we were to have each other. Anthony described how grateful he was that God was back in the center of our relationship, and he knew that meant we could not fail. He even had the nerve to start singing that Frankie Beverly and Maze song with the lyrics, *"I'm so happy to see you and me…back in stride again…"*

The next morning, full of joy and happiness and a bit of a pep in my step, I put my new stride to the test. Going up to the registration desk for the race I felt so calm, but once I got my number and stuck it to my shirt the nerves started to kick in. Not right now, doubt. You can't have me right now. Breathe in through your nose and out through your mouth girlfriend. I jumped around a bit and shook my limbs to get the juices flowing. Deanna ran up to me in her matching running pants and halter top with enhanced padding on the top. She looked gorgeous. I looked like a middle-aged woman that was running on a dare.

"Alright Mrs. Renee, lets say a little prayer and remember to just keep a steady pace. We are just trying to finish, we ain't aiming to break no records." She joked and held my hands while we said a prayer.

And you know prayer changes things. Not just little things, I'm talking about big things. I kept up with that girl for the first half of the race! I'm not saying a shin wasn't achin' a time or two. And I did catch a cramp in the side that nearly knocked the wind out of me, but I kept pressing on. I had time to think on how God had truly blessed my life. And as if I needed confirmation, every few miles I would look up and there was a different member of my family cheering me on. Poor Shye practically ran the whole race with me, jostling through the crowd on the sidewalk.

"You can do it mommy! Keep going!" He yelled.

Nick had come back into town for the occasion and brought a young lady named Laurie who he claimed was the love of his life. He was there to hand me a drink of water when I was about half way through.

Goodness and Punkin handed me cold towels about five miles from the finish line.

"Looking good momma, you are the best runner out here!" Punkin said, waving the sign she'd made with glitter and rhinestones the night before that read *My Mom's Already # 1*. Of course the only place I was number one, was in the eyes of my family, and that was just enough for me.

I finished, yes that's right…finished the race in five hours. Deanna, who I encouraged to go on ahead of me was there to greet me fresh-faced as if she'd just walked to the mailbox and back. Anthony and the kids were all there with roses and homemade ribbons that said I won the race. Yeah, at this point I was feeling like the enemy couldn't throw anything my way. Just like Anthony had said the night before, we just could not fail.

Chapter 23: Letting Him Go To Let Him Grow

§

Knowing you can't fail does not mean the devil won't try his best to make you. Anthony had to break two of our date nights, two weeks in a row because he got called into work. I had been getting pressure to meet some pretty crazy deadlines for stories at the station. I mean can folk just stop shooting each other and setting stuff on fire so I can spend some quality time with my man?

To make matters worse, Alex continued to show his behind, as my mother would say. He was deliberately disobeying his curfew and the rules of the house. One particular night, which in actuality was really an ungodly time in the morning, I over heard him and his father. They were getting into it because Alex got caught missing his curfew by two hours. Anthony, who typically had been getting home at three in the morning, beat him home on this particular morning. I hated to admit that most nights I was so exhausted, I didn't know if he made it in before curfew or was taking advantage of the fact that he knew I'd be sound asleep.

"You want to tell me why it's 2:30 a.m. and your butt is just getting home?" Anthony said right after I heard the door close. I'm sure Alex was startled to hear his dad's voice in the darkness.

"I fell asleep at Troy's house playin' video games." He answered, not sounding too sure of himself.

"Don't lie to me. Alex, how many nights you been lying to your mother and sneaking in here before I get home in the morning?"

"Dad I'm serious, I overslept. It was a mistake." He insisted.

"Did you call your mother to tell her you were going to be late?"

"I was asleep, remember?" Alex answered sarcastically.

"Boy don't make me go upside your head. I wasn't born yesterday. Man I was your age once. I know all the tricks. Now I have come in here three times in the last week and felt the hood of that car and it was still warm at 3:00 in the morning. How do you explain a car that stays warm three hours after it's turned off?" Alex was now driving Nick's car since he was away at college, the poor car has gone through yet another set of transformations. DJ Chase added these ridiculous speakers that are so big nobody can sit in the back seat now, and they glow in the dark!

Alex had no response, which made Anthony even more upset.

"I asked you a question! Now since you don't have any answers, I'll take those keys. No car for you for a month."

"How am I supposed to get to school and work? I got two parties to DJ this weekend dad."

"You should have thought about that at 11:59 when you realized you weren't standing at the threshold of that door."

"I promise it won't happen again. Please dad, you can't take the car keys."

"Give me the keys before I go take the battery out of the car!" Anthony yelled.

"I swear. I can't wait to get out of here! I must be the only eighteen year old with a curfew. I'm a grown man and I gotta be in the house at midnight! I hate this place." Alex was getting all his feelings out as he walked away from his dad and up the stairs. He knew better than to say those things to his face. He knew his father's philosophy that no matter how old you were if you were living under his roof and eating his food, you were going to obey his rules. So man, woman, cat or dog nobody was coming or going out of that house after midnight, everybody did chores, nobody was to get phone calls after 8:00 pm, and nobody was having anybody of the opposite sex in their bedroom.

****

It took Anthony a few minutes to complete his routine of shedding his work uniform in the laundry room, getting the plate of food I left in the microwave for him, and climbing the stairs to quietly peek in on me.

"I'm up." I whispered as he entered the room on his tiptoes trying not to disturb me.

"I know…I'm sorry I got loud down there, but your son is up to no good. It don't make sense. He knows you don't hear him come in after curfew."

"Maybe he really did fall asleep. You know how glazed over you can get after playing those games. Sometimes Shye falls fast asleep with the controller still in his hand." I laughed, trying to lighten the mood.

"Yeah, but he ain't getting much sleeping done with these." He said while at the same time throwing a pack of condoms on the bed between us.

My hand moved to pick them up. My mouth was moving, but nothing was coming out. I knew what I was looking at, but I didn't want to believe what I was seeing.

"In the glove compartment, in case you are wondering where I found them."

I was still speechless

"There's three there, it was a pack of twelve." He said shaking his head.

"So you think he's…" I can't even complete the sentence.

"Renee, come on. Think about what we were doing when we were his age."

"I'd rather not." I said closing my eyes and squeezing them shut so I could get the image out of my mind, of my son doing something I was doing at his age. My momma raised me right, but I did stray a time or two let's just be real and shame the devil up in here.

"Don't worry, I'mma talk to his grown butt tomorrow. He wants to disobey, come in late, and have sex, then he can move out." Anthony said angrily stabbing at the food on his plate.

"Anthony. Don't get carried away. He made a mistake. I know if you talk to him…"

"Renee…I been talking. We talked when he got caught with the weed, we talked when he came in here drunk not once, but twice! We talked when he took your car and went joy riding with his hoodlum friends and got pulled over by the cops. I am done talking."

"I can understand, this is so frustrating, but…" I sat up in the bed to plead on Alex's behalf.

"And not only that…"He said cutting me off in mid-sentence. "He has three younger siblings that are watching his every move. You want Goodness and Punkin to start being fast in the pants? You know they startin' younger and younger these days? Both them girls got stuff buddin' out all over the place. And Shye,

Renee…Shye looks up to Alex. Every word that comes out of his mouth, that boy repeats. He's even trying to dress like him now with those stupid long t-shirts halfway down his knees look like he's wearin' a dress."

"Where would he go? You can't just put him out on the street."

"That's where he spends most of his time anyway. He wanna be in the streets, I'm about to give him an open invitation."

"That's our baby. Can we just think about this a little more?" I begged.

"Renee, that's our grown son. Alex is not a baby. Let him try life on his own for a while and see if he don't realize how blessed he was while he was living under this roof."

The next morning, after what seemed like an eternity of prayer the night before, we sat down with Alex and discussed his moving out. Really there wasn't much discussion. Anthony was surprisingly very calm in relaying his concerns that Alex had become increasingly disrespectful, was deliberately disobeying the rules of the house, and it was not going to be tolerated any longer. Alex sat staring at his dad with his mouth wide open. He looked to me for some sign that this was all a joke, but I could not offer him that comfort.

"Are you serious?" He said looking from one of us to the other. He stood up slowly.

"I'm getting thrown out because I made some mistakes, like everybody else in this world? Wow…o.k. That's cool because I was getting sick of being treated like a baby around here anyway! Let me just go, so ya'll can go on pretending like ya'll are just Mr. And Mrs. Perfect. I'm sorry I didn't live up to your little standards. Forgive me for not being the star athlete with the football scholarship and the 4.0 like Nick. You know what?

Maybe I can crash with Uncle Antwan…I'm sure he's got plenty of space at his crib."

"Alex, you better not even go within ten miles of that place. I mean it! That man does not have your best interest in mind." I warned, desperate to cling on to the illusion that I could still keep my baby safe.

"Oh…and kicking me out on the street is in my best interest ma?" He said a bit too loudly, and a bit too close to my face.

"Smoking weed, drinking, having sex…is that in your best interest son?" Anthony questioned, stepping in between Alex and I.

"It worked for you didn't it?" Before he could even get the whole sarcastic remark out, Alex was thrown to the floor by the tremendous slap across his face from his father.

"Anthony! Please! Don't do this. Get it together you two, right now! Alex…you have got to get your things sweetie, and do as your father has asked."

Alex scrambled to his feet, dazed and probably scared out of his mind. I pushed Anthony out the door to get some more distance between them, hoping he'd take the hint and get in his truck to go for a ride to cool down. Then, I ran up the stairs as fast as a middle-aged, slightly less over-weight woman could go.

"What is all the noise about? I had like five more minutes on my alarm momma, dang!"

"Punkin, girl don't mess with me this morning, get yourself dressed and downstairs, you got breakfast duty."

"Momma it's Alex's turn for breakfast, remember I got dinner dishes this week?"

"I said you got breakfast, so scoot!" I countered, pushing her in the direction of the bathroom she shared with Goodness. I made it to Alex's room just in time to see him frantically stuffing clothes into a large duffle bag.

All the while Shye was firing questions at him as only he can do.

"But why you gotta go? What daddy say? Why you crying? Can I go wif, I mean *with* you?" He was practically on his brother's back, he'd gotten so close to him.

"Look boy, I ain't got time for all these questions. I just gotta get up out of here. So now you can be a big boy and have your own room." Alex said putting the duffle down to begin jamming clothes and CD's into a large trash bag.

"I don't want my own room. I'm scared of the dark. I like when you be tellin' me stories. What if monsters come out of the closet?" Shye was pitifully pleading to his brother.

"Look, I told you there aren't any monsters. Just say that prayer I told you to say and you'll be safe. Alright peace bro." Alex hugged Shye who had worked himself into a cry and was now silently trying to recover complete with hiccups and all.

"Alex, I am so sorry it had to come to this." I said quietly, wanting to give him a hug.

"Yeah, me too." He pushed passed me to leave.

"Wait! Where are you staying? Make sure you get breakfast before you leave for school."

"I might skip school today, I have to do a little something called trying to find a place to stay." He said sarcastically. He stopped and came back to give me a hug.

"Look ma, I know I messed up. I didn't mean to hurt you, but I can't take it here anyway. Too many rules. I'll probably stay with my girl and her people. I'll call you later…ah-ight!" He laughed and gave me a kiss on the forehead. It was almost as if his dad had just set him free. Lord God in Heaven! Please watch over my baby!

Chapter 24: Breathing Out Fear

§

It had been one week since Alex went to stay with 'his girl' as he put it. I didn't even know the child had a girl. And what kind of parents let a girl bring a guy home to spend the night anyway? I've never met the girl, but Punkin was able to fill me in on a bit of information one night as we were washing the dishes.

"Momma, I know that hoochie girl Alex live with." She stated matter-of-factly.

"First of all, watch your language. How do you know the girl?"

"My friend Latavia at school said her big sister got a nigga livin' with her in the basement, and his name Alex."

"Punkin Marie Chase! Did I not tell you a thousand times we don't use the "N" word in this house? If I hear it one more time, you will be on punishment." I said sternly.

"Momma, I'm just repeatin' what the girl said. I'm sorry…so anyway she said her big sister boyfriend just moved in and they was gonna be married."

"What is this girl's name?"

"Traniece. But e'erybody call her Niecey. She was in the eleventh grade, but she dropped out of school so she could be a dancer, and I don't mean no ballerina momma. She got two babies...that's all I know."

"Alright, I'm done with you...upstairs." I said shooing her away from her chores and out of my face.

"Momma you not mad at me are you? I'm just telling the truth from what I heard people say."

"I'm not mad, just please go to your room, I need some time to myself."

This is what you told me to do right? I mean I'm saving Shelita's children from a life of desperation on the street, and my own child is out there doing God knows what. Lord I'm confused. You gonna have to seriously help me out with this one. My flesh and blood, my child that grew up here in this loving home, with two parents is out in the street? I'm trying hard here to live by the whatever-your-will credo, but I'm struggling. I want to hear from my baby. To know that he's alright. Do it Lord.

****

Later that night Anthony and I prayed together for Alex, that he would be safe and return home. I was just hoping that I would be able to hear from him. Just as the thought crossed my mind, the telephone rang. Thank you Lord for pitying my groan.

"Hello." I answered with my heart pounding.

"Hey ma, it's Alex. Just wanted to check in."

"Oh my 'lil Anty-poo! Baby I have been worried sick. Where are you? Are you eating? Who are you staying with?" I knew I was rattling of questions a mile a minute, but I needed to know my child was o.k.

"I'm staying with Niecey and some of her people." That's all I get? I thought to myself. Didn't I just ask you a whole bunch of questions? Uh uh. I don't care how grown you think you are, you don't get to just answer me any old kind of way. Do you?

"How many of her people are you staying with and where are you sleeping?" I said sitting straight up in the bed.

"Ma, I ain't getting into all of that, I was just calling to let you know I was safe. You can call me on my cell if you need me for anything. Peace." And then I heard a dial tone. My child just hung up on me. Somebody help me pick my jaw up off my lap. This is absolutely unbelievable.

"I hope you are happy Anthony, your son is living in a house full of God only knows what, with some exotic dancer and 'her people' as he puts it." I fumed after I finally was able to close my mouth.

"Renee, Alex will be alright. We just got finished praying for him, I'm not going to worry if I've just prayed."

"This is not the life God intended for Alex." I argued. I could feel tears trying to form, there was definitely a lump in my throat.

"But Alex has got to realize that. It's not going to mean anything coming from you. That boy has got to hear it from God himself. Alex has got to pray for himself, Alex has got to get to a point where he knows that momma and daddy can't do nothing for him, but God can do everything for him."

I know my husband was doing everything he could to comfort me, but something told me this was only the beginning of a terrible storm. I was starting to get that close, stifling, suffocating feeling I had before Shelita was murdered. I was having a hard time breathing again. I started trying to practice something I learned in my individual therapy sessions with Rev. Sheila. I began to calmly try to breathe in God's peace and purpose, and exhale confusion, anxiety, and doubt. Oh yeah. I didn't need those old silly roses and candles anymore. That's it Renee…I thought to myself…breathe in purpose, breathe out fear. As I fell into a rhythm of breathing, I could feel the deep furrow in my brow relax and disappear. Anthony snuggled close and placed his hand over my heart. He slowly began to assume the same breathing pattern, and we both drifted off to sleep.

Chapter 25: Getting In The Right Place For The Test

§

It had been three months since Alex moved out. I could count the number of times he called me on one hand. Shye just started feeling comfortable sleeping without a night light, but still held his brother's pillow tightly in his arms each night. The change initially caused a regression in all the wonderful progress he'd made with his speech and his behavioral issues at school. I was called to the school no less than twenty times in the last three months. If I had to sit in one more IEP team meeting and hear from one more counselor about how changes at home can affect students like Shye, I was going to scream. Did they not know that I was getting double the acting out they were seeing in school? Just when I thought the worse was over, last night, Shye wanted to have himself a tantrum about his bedtime, a routine that has remained unchanged since he and his sisters began living here.

"Shye why is your light still on? It is bedtime young man." I remember saying. I was annoyed because this was the third time I'd come in his room to remind him to go to sleep.

"I not tired." He said defiantly, sitting on the edge of the bed with his arms folded, eyebrows knitted together and lips poked way out.

"Shye, it's *I'm*, not I. And I don't want to have to come back in here tonight. The next person you see will be dad." I warned through clenched teeth, thinking that just the thought of Anthony getting up out the bed, would make him dive under the covers. Well not on this particular night.

"He not my dad. You not my mommy. I not tired! Leave me alone!" He screamed forgetting all of his rules about possessives, and sticking his tongue out at me to boot.

"Little boy, I'm not playing with you, now get your behind under those covers." I went to put my hands on his shoulders to make him lie down and that boy hauled off and bit me. I mean he sunk those teeth deep into my forearm. It was all I could do not to smack the living daylights out of him. We spent the next five minutes in a battle of wills. I was trying to hold him at arms length while he grabbed whatever he could and threw it across the room. All of the commotion brought Goodness to the room, still groggy with sleep.

"What in the world is going on in here mommy Nay?" She didn't wait for me to answer before she jumped in and grabbed Shye from behind, holding him in a bear hug.

"Sshh. Shye-Shye it's alright. I'm here, calm down little brother." She began to rock him from side to side.

"I want Alex. Mommy bad, her make him go away. Her don't love him no more." He stopped fighting and collapsed in his sister's arms, crying. She continued to hold him tight. All I could do was stand there and begin to pray silently for this child that was so hurt, who had only experienced loss and neglect in his life.

"Shye, mommy Nay loves Alex. He is a big boy and needs to learn how to be a grown up in the world. Remember when we have family prayer we talk about God giving us tests like we have at school and the only way we can do better is if we study?" She said referring to our weekly ritual, where we gather the entire family in the living room for bible study and prayer.

"I 'member." He softly replied.

"Well Alex can only study for his test if he has a chance to live someplace where he can't cheat and have his mommy and daddy give him all the answers. Understand?"

I heard myself saying yes at the same time Shye did. Goodness had no idea that God had just used her to confirm that we'd made the right decision with Alex.

"Maybe we need to go away so we can pass the test too." Shye concluded.

"No baby. You are right where God wants you right now." I interjected. He even let me pull him close to me so that he was leaning against my right side. "I have just begun a new lesson plan with you and your sisters. Some of the old notes you were given when you were younger, were from the wrong book."

"So is you…I mean, *are* you going to teach us from the right book?" He asked, looking at me with a renewed excitement.

"Honey, I'm going to teach you from the only book I know, and that's the bible." I gave him a kiss on the forehead.

"And I think somewhere in that book, it says you owe mommy Nay an apology because you did something hurtful to her, boy." Goodness piped in, looking at her brother with her arms crossed.

"Oh…I…I'm sorry mommy." He said with his eyes downcast.

"Apology accepted. Now let's get those cinnamon buns in the bed. Mommy loves ya'll." I hugged my babies and we all said our goodnights.

Chapter 26: Keepin' It Real Gansta

§

As if on cue, the devil took it upon himself the very next day, to cast doubt on the confirmation that God gave me last night. And of course, the very person that spoke the words of encouragement last night, would be the one to deliver the blow to my spirit today. As Goodness walked through the door I could tell something was on her mind. She wasn't her usual cheerful self. She didn't even yell at her brother and sister to get started on their homework. I was heading back out to the station to finish a write up about yet another gang involved shooting in a typically 'quiet family-oriented' neighborhood in Baltimore county when she stopped me.

"Are you on your way out mommy Nay?" She was wringing her hands together, and was having a hard time looking me in my eyes.

"Yes Goodness, but I have a few minutes for my baby. What's up with you? You look like I feel right about now. And I could use about three more hours of sleep!" I joked, but it did nothing to lighten the mood.

"I don't know how to say this, so I'm just going to tell it straight up. I saw Alex today and he look like he is tore up."

"Where did you see Alex?" My heart was doing this dreadful thumping that began to hurt in my chest.

"I've been hearing some rumors around school, that Alex be on the corner running for Uncle Ant and he's got that girl running with him. I had to see for myself so I took the Metro downtown and got off on North and Pennsylvania. Sure enough there he was. Mommy he looks bad. I almost didn't recognize him. He was drinking something. Looked a mess to me with his pants all hanging down." She filled me in, with a look of disgust on her face.

"First of all missy, you know better than to take the Metro anywhere but home after school! What if something had happened? You earned yourself two days without telephone or T.V. privileges for that stunt, understood? Now, Goodness, are you sure it was your brother? If you didn't recognize him, maybe you just thought you saw him."

"Naw mommy. I called his name and he looked at me. Right at me, then came to me and said he better not ever see me down there again if I knew what was good for me." Tears began to slide down her cheeks. "Mommy I'm scared, Alex is gonna be just like…you know who…" Goodness had gotten to the point where she didn't even want to mention her birth mother's name.

"Oh my God! Where did you say he was?" I was frantic now, racing around to find my cell phone to call out of work. I had every intention of going to find Alex and bring his tail home.

"Mommy you can't go out there. You don't feel good, this will only make you feel worse." She said pulling on my arm.

"Hush! Make sure dad gets up in two hours for work, I'm going to just ride around that area until I see him. Don't you say a word about where I'm going do you hear me?"

I knew as the words were coming out of my mouth, it was the wrong thing to teach this girl. I knew and actually half-hoped, she wouldn't listen to me. I was thinking it might do Alex some good to get a good old-fashioned whuppin' from his father.

"Mommy...wait!" Goodness tried to block my access to the front door.

"Girl, I love you, but I don't want to have to go off. My patience is wearing thin. Let me out this door!" I demanded.

"I will...I just wanted you to know one more thing before you go."

"What child?"

"Alex's girl, she looked like to me her stomach was real big." My world collapsed right there at the door. Alex...expecting a child? Alex ...selling drugs? Alex so far out there, that his own sister couldn't recognize him? It didn't seem real. But as I would soon find out, it was all too real.

****

This was a real street corner I was slowly pulling my car up to. All I could hear was some real loud obnoxious music booming from a real gaudy truck that had shiny wheels, and could hop up and down with the rhythm of the music. There were real prostitutes that looked like they were under the age of sixteen lined up in a group of four. They were leaning against the side of a real abandoned building. So many filthy words scrawled on the boarded up windows in spray paint. So many makeshift memorials written on buildings with R.I.P. messages to gangsters with names like Pookie, 'Lil Man, and Big Dawg. And now out of nowhere came a real brotha holding his real baggy pants up by the waistband as he stepped up to my window. He was real high because he didn't even know who I was until he leaned in to ask me what I was in the mood to buy.

"What can I get for…oh sh.." I cut him off before he could even utter a vile curse word in my face, grabbing him hard by the collar and pulling his upper body inside the car with me.

"Alex get your black behind in this car right now!" Flashes of me trying to get my brother off the street at this age flew in and out of my mind.

"Ma, go home! I knew Goodness couldn't keep her mouth shut!" He pulled away from me a little too forcefully, so that it felt like the nails were being ripped from my fingers.

"Alex, get in the car, I'm taking you home right now!" I demanded, attempting to push my door open and get out so I could drag his butt into the car. He blocked me, pushing against the door, so that I couldn't move.

"That's not my home no more, remember! I'm good, ma you need to bounce right now, if you know what's good for you." At this point several young men came up to him, asking if he was alright, like I'm the one that's putting him in danger. At the same time a black Lexus truck with pitch black tinted windows rolled up and stopped behind where we were making a scene.

"Ma, I gotta make a run real quick. I'mma holla at you later." And just as if he had just told me he was going to get a gallon of milk, he opened the door to the truck and left me there. I immediately jumped out of the car running after the truck. I screamed and screamed for him to come back to no avail.

"Don't worry 'lil momma, if you want some stuff that bad, I got something for you." An old-school fool just showed up out of nowhere with a vial of something waving it in my face.

"I don't need a thing from you!" I growled and got back in my car. While I sat crying with the windows up and the doors locked, one of the girls came over and knocked on the window. Just one look at her swollen belly in her tight fitting outfit made me nauseous. I knew this had to be Alex's girl Traniece. She pulled on the door a few times and signaled for me to unlock it. Instead I just rolled down my window, shooting daggers at her with my bloodshot, tear-filled eyes.

"You must be G's mother. I'm Niecey his soon-to-be baby's mother." She said proudly with a ridiculous grin on her face rubbing her stomach.

"Excuse me, what did you call Alex,…G?"

"Oh, my bad, I meant Big G 'cause my baby be bringin' in big time money! It ain't nothing for him to make a few g's 'round here in a less than an hour! That's more than I can make in tips in a week dancing." I held my hand up to stop her from talking.

"What makes you think I want to hear this nonsense? Little girl, what you and my son are doing is leading to nothing but trouble. I want you to get yourself off of this street and tell me where I can find Alex right now!" I finally unlocked the door and reached over to push the passenger side open so she could get in. Instead she closed the door and just leaned as far in as her stomach would allow.

"I ain't gonna be able to do that. He just left with Big Ant, and it ain't no telling where they gonna end up tonight, but I'll tell him to call you when he comes home." She says popping gum between every word.

"That was Antwan Billows in that black truck?" I asked. My breath was coming in short gasps again. I could feel the well of tears getting ready to erupt. My own brother was continuing to seek, kill and destroy me, through my son now.

"You betta believe it was. My baby only hangs with the biggest ballers! The boss himself, so you know we gets paid and nobody can touch us. He knows how to keep it real gansta." And with that she stepped away from the window, flagged down a car that had been circling the block and got into the passenger side.

Chapter 27: He'll Never Let Go

§

Believe it or not Alex actually called me later that night. I was sitting with Anthony explaining the whole ordeal to him when the phone rang. It was some unidentified number so Anthony picked up the phone. The look on his face told me who it was before he even mouthed the words "it's Alex" to me.

"Boy, let me tell you. You better be glad it was your mother that saw you standing on that corner and not me. I think you have lost your mind! This is absolutely unacceptable. We did not raise you to be a street thug and a criminal. Now you got your mother, crying and worried about whether she'll be planning your funeral just like Shelita's. And another thing…" Anthony pulled the phone away from his ear with a surprised jolt. He turned to me with a look I'd never seen on his face before.

"That Negro just hung up on me! Renee…that's it, I'm going to find that boy right now!" Just as he threw the covers off to jump out the bed, the same unidentified number showed up again. I threw myself on the phone to block him from picking it up.

"Let me get it! Anthony, just calm down and let me answer the phone." I picked up the receiver and attempted to stay in control of my breathing.

"Hello? Alex."

"Ma you better get your husband. He can't talk to me like that. I am not some little boy he can threaten! I'm Big G! He don't wanna mess with me. I got a lot of people that got my back on these streets. And if you know what's good for you, you betta not ever try to put your hands on me like you did today." His voice was so strange. I couldn't even recognize it.

"Why are you doing this? Who are you? Baby why don't you just come home? I love you and it's not too late to turn this around. I know you have a baby on the way, but momma will help you. Baby you need to pray and…"

"Mom, I didn't call for a sermon. I knew you were pretty upset when I saw you today, so I just wanted to let you know I was good." He rudely cut me off. This was not the child I birthed almost nineteen years ago.

"You're not good Alex. You are selling drugs on the corner. And I know you're using. Do you have any idea what you look like? And that girl of yours that is so proud about being your 'baby's mother', ain't doing nothing but trickin' on that same corner. I saw her getting into a car when I pulled off and I know she wasn't giving out directions. This is the kind of person you want to have a child with?"

"Look I ain't gonna let you talk about her like that. She's hustlin' so we can stay on top. You can't even imagine the kind of money she brings in. When the baby comes, my girl won't have to want for anything because I'll be all set up. I know you can't see it from where you are, but what I'm doin' right now…the work I'm puttin' in…I ain't gonna never be broke."

"Just stop it! I can't take this anymore. Alex you are being tricked by the devil. Antwan is trying to kill you. It might not feel like a literal death but he is killing you inside. He doesn't care about you, he wants to hurt me. Honey that money, and those cars, and all the hustlin' in the world is not going to amount to anything but death and destruction. Please Alex…please come home." I begged. Anthony suddenly wrestled the phone from my hands and roared into the mouth piece, without even putting the phone up to his ear.

"I will not have you treating my wife this way! Now I don't know who you are, Alex…Big G…God knows who else. But the devil is a liar. You were not raised this way. You lived a blessed life. We can't bring you back, you gotta want it for yourself. But until you do, you will not ever call this house and make your mother sick like this again. Alex, you look deep in your heart and listen to what God is speaking to you."

And with that he hung up on his son. I could not talk. I could not breath. I was trying to think *breath out purpose and breath in fear…or was it breath in purpose, out fear*? I'm getting confused here…I felt like I was getting light headed. I needed to just lie back for a while. The air felt strange, the room began to spin. I could hear Anthony, but he sounded like he was so far away.

"Renee…Renee…baby what's wrong?" And then everything faded to black.

****

The black slowly lightened to gray, and the gray turned to white, then bright white. Why was everything so white? Uh. Oh. Lord? Is this what I think it is? It's so quiet and peaceful. Everything I thought it would be except for that annoying beeping sound every ten seconds, and the vice grip pressure on my right bicep every so often.

"Renee?…Renee?…" I could hear Anthony's voice. Whoa. Anthony's here too? That man always said he'd follow me to the end of time, but this is a bit ridiculous.

"Mrs. Chase, can you squeeze my hand?" Dr. Grander? Now that's more than a coincidence. I know me, Anthony, and Dr. Grander ain't all in Heaven at the same time.

"Renee, baby open your eyes." Oh, my boo sounds so worried. He don't know I'm struggling to open these lids, they seem so heavy though.

"Mr. Chase, I think we have her stabilized. She's probably just very tired right now. We are going to keep her tonight. She's definitely dehydrated and her blood pressure is not quite where I want it yet. We want to get some more IV fluids on board, and increase her blood pressure medicine overnight. I want to run some more labs and get a check on her white-blood cells while she's here."

"Is it alright to have the kids come in?" I could barely hear Anthony, he still sounded so far away.

"Of course, but she'll need some rest, so don't overdo it." I turned my head and opened my eyes in time to see Anthony and Dr. Grander leaving the room. So I'm at the hospital. Thank you Lord for protecting me and getting me here. I thought I was a goner. Guess I still got some more work to do down here.

"Hey beautiful. You gave me a scare." Anthony said with a look of relief on his face as he entered the room with my three youngest in tow. He bent down to kiss my cheek.

"Sorry about that. You know I've been talking about needing a few days off of work." I joked, struggling to sit up and maneuver all the tubes and lines going into my arms.

"Renee, the doc says you haven't been eating enough, or getting enough fluid. Now of course I thought he must not be talking about my wife, the woman who yells at me if I don't drink a gallon of water a day. I knew it wasn't the Renee I live with that knows that after her last round of chemo a few months ago, her doctor told her to continue to eat healthy and drink plenty of fluids. I know…"

"O.k.…guilty as charged. I'm a do-as-I-say kind of person. You know that. Now if I don't get some hugs and kisses pretty soon from my munchkins then I don't know what I'll do." After I said that Shye practically jumped on the bed with me and smothered me with hugs and kisses, followed by Punkin, who we were now calling by her middle name Marie, and Goodness.

"Mom, you can't leave me, I got too much stuff you need to help me with. Dad don't know nothing about how to do hair and makeup." Goodness joked.

"Yeah and looked what he picked out for me to wear today. I had to let all my friends know my momma was sick, that's why I looked this way." Marie said opening her jacket to reveal her mismatched outfit.

"Thanks a lot!" Anthony laughed, playfully grabbing her in a bear hug.

God I thank you for sending them to me for a little while, to nurture and to love. My faith in my purpose is renewed. I don't know what the future holds, but I know You'll be holding my hand. And Lord even though Alex has let go of your hand, grab him by the wrist for me and don't let go.

Chapter 28: God Said It, I Believe It

§

It's been a few weeks since my blackout episode. Anthony has been watching my fluid intake like a hawk. I swear sometimes he tries to pour liquid in my mouth while I'm sleeping. I know my baby loves me, so I have to just take it, he means well. He wasn't too happy about how quickly I returned to work, but I needed to immerse myself in something to take my mind off of Alex. Of course my work ended up doing nothing but putting Alex right in the forefront of my mind.

You'd think that with all the shocking news I write about each week, nothing would surprise me. But today I got some disturbing news. I'm not so sure whether it was the news or just how I found out that was bothering me.

I was officially a grandmother. I hadn't gotten invited to a baby shower, or received a birth announcement in the mail. I wasn't in the delivery room hyperventilating along side a drugged-out exotic dancer, but I was actually gathering details on a story I was writing up about babies born to drug addicted mothers. The NICU nurse was taking me around, giving me all the medical jargon about side effects and statistics when I happened to be looking in the incubator of one tiny baby. Because of the baby's extremely small size and delicate fragile state, I assumed she was premature.

In actuality Morgan Beautiful Chase was born full-term exactly four weeks prior. At this time she was struggling for her life because her mother was knowingly exposing her to alcohol, marijuana, and the occasional line of cocaine during her entire pregnancy. Her heart and lungs where not functioning properly, her brain waves were sporadic, and she was grossly underweight. Not to mention she was having withdraw symptoms that wracked her tiny body with pain.

"If you ask me, these mothers should be put in jail and never allowed to have any more babies. Take this little one for example. Her mother has two other kids, by two different men. And the father of this one is a no-good drug dealer. You should see the way he comes in here with his expensive clothes, always on his cell phone. He doesn't even care about his daughter." The nurse had no idea who she was talking to, let alone my relationship to that no good drug dealer. Everything she was saying was true, but the words were cutting me like a knife.

"Is she going to be alright?" I asked her placing my pen and pad under my arm so I could lean in and get a better look at my one-month-old grandchild.

"Oh, this little one is a fighter. We took her off of the ventilator last night and she's done pretty good, even took some formula from a dropper today. I've been praying for her." She answered, smiling. *God thank you for placing this praying woman in my grandbaby's path.*

"Thank you. You keep praying for her and for her parents. Are they letting her mother take her home? I mean this is strictly off the records."

"Yeah, this court system is crazy. We know Traniece Hopkins all too well around here. She took some parenting classes, and the father claimed he would be the primary caregiver, so they are letting her go home with them. I'm sure she'll end up being raised by whoever is taking care of her half brother and sister."

I wanted to drop everything and roll that incubator right out of that hospital. God knows there was plenty of room at my house and in my heart for another child. And this was no ordinary child, this was my grandbaby. But just then a voice came to me. *"I've got this one Renee, you don't have to worry."* Now I know the voice was coming from God because the nurse had walked off to take care of other little ones, and there wasn't anyone standing in my vicinity. Besides me and God have been having some very personal conversations and I've come to know the sound of His voice.

"I hear you Lord." I whispered. I then gathered my notepad and voice recorder to leave, but before I did, I bent down to look at the baby face to face. I blew her a little kiss. I wanted to breathe a little life into her spirit.

"Bye-Bye sweet baby. You hold on, because God has got something in store for your life. No matter what it looks like, you will have a blessed life, just like your dad had. You will be blessed more than you can even imagine. Ya'll are going to make it out of this together. I know one day we'll meet again. Nana loves ya."

****

As soon as I left the hospital and turned in my story, I raced home. I was on a mission. The bible says to speak those things that are not as though they are, and that was just what I was doing in a kind of round about way.

"What in the world are you doing down here momma?" Marie asked.

"Well if it isn't the artist formerly known as Punkin." I joked, throwing one of the t-shirts I was folding in her direction.

"Stop it momma. I don't want to ever be called Punkin again. That is so ghetto." She said rolling her eyes with her hands on her hips. The same hips that had begun to spread so that her twelve-year-old body was looking more like a twenty-year-old body. Much to Anthony's horror we had to sit down and have a fact's of life discussion with her when she began maturing right before our eyes. Living the lifestyle she used to live, the girl actually could have taught us a thing or two, I mean she's seen some things! But we needed to go a bit more into the changes her body was going through, and the effects of hormones. I actually had to hang real size C cup bras on the line to dry for this girl. Even after my augmentation surgery I wasn't holdin' it down like she was.

"I know you better take those hands off of what you think you got. Come help me get these clothes up, and after that we're cleaning out the Dungeon."

"The Dungeon? I'm not going in there. Every time Nick comes home from college it smells like Doritos and animals in there. Let him clean his own room." Nick was in his senior year at Ohio State University.

The boy went there on a football scholarship and messed around and got himself accepted to the college's Moritz law school. Nick was the evidence of my faith. When I tell you no eye has seen, or ear heard what is in store for this boy! He left for college and did all that he set out to achieve. Dean's list, star athlete, internship at one of the prestigious law firms in Ohio. He's developed a very serious relationship with Laurie that I think will lead to a walk down the aisle. And he continued to pray. Many nights he'd call me saying that he just wanted to pray for me, because he knew I was tormenting over Alex. My own son became my prayer partner! And yes, I…even I have to admit those games looked great on that big screen television. We had college game night parties at our house all the time. Anthony even flew out to Ohio for a few home games. It would take a few days for him to come down from the clouds whenever he returned home.

"That room is not going to be Nick's room when he comes home. Alex and Morgan will be living down here." I stated.

"Momma! Alex is coming back to live with us? When!" Marie was jumping up and down as if I told her she was getting that cell phone she's been begging me for…not gonna happen.

"I'm not quite sure. Alex doesn't even know he's coming back home yet." I said smiling at the confused look on her face.

"So you tellin' me Alex is coming home, bringing his newborn baby and he don't even know he's coming yet? Is that dumb girl coming with all her other babies?" She asked, with her arms crossed.

"God didn't tell me that. I just know that in His time, He will send Alex home."

"Well momma, I can't argue. You said God told you that you'd be taking care of me, Goodness, and big-head Shye and you did. You said God told you that you would be healed from the cancer and you were…so If God told you this, then I believe it."

"Good then, hand me that box over there, we got to empty this dresser so we can take it in the room and start getting things organized."

Chapter 29: It's In The Making

§

I was absolutely loving the new Yolanda Adams CD that was streaming over the internet as I listened to Heaven 600 on my computer. If I couldn't make it to church some Sundays when I was really behind deadline, that woman and her voice just took me right on to the altar.

"Hey. You look like you are having a blessed morning." The smooth voice of my co-worker made me look up from my mountain of work.

"Harold, every morning I wake up on this side is a blessed morning. Now what about you? I thought I was gonna have to pick your chin up off the ground the way you were moping around here yesterday. Is everything alright with you?"

"I'd like to say it is, but the night before last, Cynthia came home from happy hour with her girls and she had two numbers in her cell phone that I didn't recognize."

"Wow. Really? What made her show you the cell phone?"

"I hate to admit it, but I was looking through her things after she stumbled up the stairs to bed without even saying hello to me. It was well after ten o'clock. Let's just say that one hour turned into a happy four or five hours for Cynthia and her crew." He said mumbling under his breath. This was a good man, and I hated seeing him this way. I considered him a friend and a brother in Christ. I'm going to make a note to have Anthony give him a call.

"Are you suspicious that she may be…you know…seeing someone else?" I was trying to tread lightly on this delicate subject.

"She can see as many people as she wants, it's the sleeping with 'em that I'm worried about." I knew he was trying to joke to ease the discomfort he was feeling.

"Did you try the Branch's yet?"

"We did. She went for two meetings and gave it up. Said she wasn't ready for people to be all up in her business. But I'm not giving up that easily. I love my wife and I want to work this out. I'm just gonna pray that God will open up another opportunity for us to get couples' therapy, but in the meantime, I'm going to talk to Rev. Branch man to man. He really has given me a lot of word that has gone toward making me stronger."

"How can you stay with Cynthia when you have so much distrust? I mean when you saw those numbers what did it do to you inside? You don't have to answer…I'm just wondering. You know just thinking that I probably wouldn't be as calm about it as you are, but that's just the human side of me." I was really looking for a man's perspective, but if we were being real, I'm sure Anthony had been in his shoes when the whole Deacon Redmond thing happened.

"Man. It's hard. A few years ago, I would have went up those stairs, pulled her butt out that bed and made her call those numbers in front of me so I could talk to those dudes! Then I would have gone to each of their houses and had me a good old-fashioned street brawl! But that's just not who God says I am now. He says that He will work everything out in the end, that He's already fought the battle. Look, I'm gonna be realistic…Cynthia may not be the woman for me, but until God says so, I'm going to do what He tells me to do."

"I like the way that sounds. I'm still on this kick about Alex coming home and it's driving everybody insane in my house. They can't see him there because of how stupid he's acting right now. But as Rev. Fowler always says… 'you gotta see it, before you can see it'. And that's just what I'm doing. Harold, you are a good guy, and I totally see you happily married to a good woman."

"Renee. I accept that. And listen for what it's worth…I believe Alex is coming home to you soon. It's already in the making."

Chapter 30: God's Time Is Not Our Time

§

"Goodness can you take this lamp down to Alex's room? I tried to get a neutral color because I probably have so much pink down there now for Morgan, Alex will have a fit." I handed the lamp to Goodness and she silently took it toward the basement door.

"What's gotten into you? You look grumpy."

"Not grumpy…just a little worried about you mommy Nay." She said looking at me with her hand on the doorknob.

"What do you have to be worried about me for? I have had a clean bill of health for almost two years. I know you're not worried about this swelling in my arm, Goodness we talked about this, and it's just lymph drainage. It happens to lots of women who've had mastectomies." I said trying to reassure her.

"No mommy, I'm not worried about your arm, or your fluid, or any of that stuff. I'm worried about your heart."

"My heart? Sweetie, what on earth are you talking about?" I asked, patting the sofa cushion next to me to encourage her to come over to where I was sitting, while I was unloading more things for the room downstairs. She walked toward me still carrying the lamp and sat on the sofa.

"Mommy...you were so convinced that Alex was going to be coming back home with Morgan, but that was more than six months ago. He hasn't called. You haven't even seen him on the street, but you still buying things for his room and making everybody call that Alex's room. I don't want you to get your heart broken if he never comes back." She said sadly as she kneaded my swollen arm subconsciously.

"Alex will be back...God told me. Now all I can do is be obedient and be sure there is a place prepared for him. God's time is not our time, so I can't tell you when it will be or how it will even come about. Until it does though, you can't worry about me. Just continue to pray that God's will be done in our lives."

"But don't you get tired of waiting?" She asked, sighing loudly.

"A few years ago, I might have. But look what He's brought me through. I trust God, baby. He has never failed me yet. Now, take the lamp downstairs and do it believing that Alex will be there to turn it on and off." I said giving her a nudge on her chin. I wanted her to keep her head up. The devil can't see that any one part of the whole is defeated, because then he thinks he has room to come in.

"Yes Ma'am." She said, forcing a smile.

Later that night she came to me while I was in the middle of my third set of over-the-door arm pulleys my PT gave me for home exercise, to apologize for her fear and doubt.

"I didn't mean to question your faith in what God told you mommy Nay."

"I know darling. My strong faith comes from life experience. You keep on living and you'll be the same way." I was breathing heavily now because my poor arm was getting tired, but I was able to lift it a few degrees more than I did in therapy yesterday.

"Well I've experienced enough to know that God loved me enough to put me here with you." Goodness said, taking the towel I had wrapped around my neck and dabbing my dripping forehead.

"He has a sense of humor don't you think? I mean I'm a crazy momma aren't I?" I said making funny faces at her.

"Well you look silly doing these exercises, but no you're not crazy." She kissed me on my forehead and went up to bed. I continued my last set of pulleys and went upstairs to have Anthony wrap my left arm.

I'd been in physical therapy for the past few weeks to help reduce some of the swelling that had slowly accumulated in my arm. I began to notice the swelling when I couldn't get my wedding band off to clean it. I'd also had a tough time trying on dresses for one of the most important days of my life. Nick was getting married! He and Laurie shared the big news when they were here for the Christmas holiday last year. The two planned the whole thing themselves, and would be getting hitched in two weeks. Don't ask me why I waited until the last minute to try and find a dress. I'm glad I did though, since Christmas I've lost fifteen pounds, which brings my total weight lost since my diagnosis up to forty-five pounds. And all I've been doing is just walking and eating healthier and of course drinking plenty of fluids. But this summer has been unusually hot and it just triggered my lymph edema, so I've had to change the style of dress I'm wearing so my arm will be more comfortable. But not to worry a sista is still looking sexy.

Thinking back on the day we went hunting for my dress, I thought it was funny that Nick was feeling a bit uncomfortable with my new figure:

"Mom, don't you think that shows a bit too many curves. Don't forget my boys from Ohio are coming in for this wedding. I don't want to have to go to blows with nobody for tryin' to holla at my momma!" He said with a very serious look on his face the day we went to try on my dress. He insisted on coming with me.

"Oh hush! Ain't no twenty-something boy gonna be interested in me." I said turning around in the mirror. I had to admit the dress was making me look just like I did when I was his age.

"They better not be! Look you finish trying things on, I have to make a call to Laurie and ask her what color she wanted you to get again." He was so cute. The boy absolutely loved Laurie and respected her in so many ways. He was doing all he could to make this day so special for her. On the other hand, we all were a bit disappointed that Alex wouldn't be at the wedding. Nick wanted nothing more than to have his brother be his best man, but Alex just refused to associate himself with us. He was so captivated by Antwan and his life of luxury.

"She said mauve. What in the world is mauve?" Nick had returned to the store with a confused look on his face.

"Don't worry, momma's got this one. Go grab something from the food court because I know you're dying to get something to eat, and I'll meet you at the car."

"You're the best." He said making a mad dash out the door.

Chapter 31: The Devil Ain't Nothin' But Mad

§

I couldn't believe I was standing here wishing any man in my life traveling mercies as they were on their way to a bachelor party, but the time had come and the words were coming out of my mouth.

"Ya'll betta know how to act. That's all I got to say." I joked with Nick and Anthony. He was so proud that his son asked him to be a part of the festivities that I thought he would explode at any minute. He was trying to be so cool, dressing like Nick's young college buddies that had come into town for the wedding. Nick warned his buddies that he didn't want an obnoxious bachelor party with drinking and strippers, he wanted a more mature low-key gathering.

The day started with a round of golf with the guys including Laurie's dad. Anthony and Laurie's dad, Melvin where like long lost brothers despite the almost twenty year age difference. The men then spent the afternoon getting pampered, shaved and massaged at Jazzmine's Salon and Spa in Towson, and tonight they were going out for a nice dinner and some jazz. All of Nick's friends knew the kind of lifestyle he chose to live, so they knew there would be no drinking, smoking or cursing. He'd done a good job of surrounding himself with like-minded friends, so everyone was having a wonderful time.

"We should be saying the same thing to ya'll. I ain't never seen Marla so gussied up since our wedding day." Mr. Melvin Chadwick said looking at Laurie's mom who was standing beside me with her hair and makeup done to perfection.

"Oh Melvin, you just have yourself a good time with the boys, and don't you worry about what us gorgeous ladies are doing tonight." She joked, giving him a peck on the cheek. The two have been married for over forty years. Laurie is their youngest, she was a 'surprise blessing' as Mrs. Chadwick put it.

"Well momma Chadwick, don't have my bride-to-be out too late, she's got a very important date in the morning." Nick said giving his future mother-in-law a hug.

We all gave each other well wishes and went our separate ways. I don't know how the boys were fairing, but us girls were having a lovely time. It started off with a wonderful prayer led by Laurie while we were still in the stretch limousine we'd rented for the evening. A daughter-in-law that can pray, Lord you are just outdoing yourself!

"Renee I just love your hair! It is so thick and beautiful. Did you notice a change in the texture after the chemo?" Marla asked. I was lost in the laughter and chatter of the young girls in the limo that I almost didn't hear what she said.

"It has been a blessing, the way the hair has grown back. I had been growing my locs for over twelve years when they began to fall out. It's grown back in fuller and thicker than before, but with lots of gray. I'm embracing it though. I think it makes me look smarter" I laughed patting my full head of hair. I'd just gone to the salon and had it twisted into double strand twist that I planned on releasing tomorrow so my head could be crowned with a mass of silvery grey crinkles.

"Baby, you are working it. And I can tell by the way your husband looks at you, that he loves it too." She beamed and gave me a high five. I liked this lady. Yes, Marla was going to be a great addition to the family.

We continued to share stories throughout the night that thoroughly embarrassed Laurie and I'm sure Nick would be blushing as well. At the end of the night Laurie and her girlfriends went back to the hotel to rest up for the big day. Marla decided to stay with us since Melvin would be coming back with Nick and Anthony. She said they hadn't spent a night apart since they'd been married, and they weren't going to start anytime soon. I did not blame the woman. I only continued to pray that Anthony and I could know the type of love these two shared. We continued bonding over a cup of tea and decided to wait up for our men. Our peaceful waiting was interrupted by the loud very distinct sound of my son Alex, arguing with Nick outside.

"What in the world is all that ruckus?" Marla asked jumping up to peak out of the curtain. As soon as I stood up the front door swung open and Mr. Chadwick charged in with a fretful look on his face.

"Marla you might want to get on upstairs, this ain't gonna be too pretty." He grabbed her by the hands to pull her up from the sofa. The two hurried as fast as their sixty-something legs could take them.

"What is going on here?" I asked stepping out onto the porch. I could see Nick as he turned toward me with a swollen lip. His shirt, torn right down the middle, was full of blood.

"Mom go back in the house, this is between me and Alex." He said turning back toward his brother, who was leaning out of the passenger side of what had become his favorite black truck to ride in. I didn't even need to ask who was in the driver's side.

"Sis…you betta call your boy on in the house, he don't want none of this." Antwan said leaning across the seat so that I could see his face.

"If you know what's good for you, you'll get this truck from in front my house! I thought I told you not to ever come around here the last time I threw you out of here. That goes for both of you!" Anthony yelled, standing his ground beside Nick. I could tell the two had been in some altercation, but I was very confused as to what or why.

"Ma, I was just trying to give my brother a gift for his wedding. But it seems like he's too holy to take money from me. He calls himself trying to set me straight. He's gonna mess around and get hurt." Alex said laughing in his brother's face. He looked completely different. He'd gained a bit of weight, I guess living a life of excess included food. He had a large sparkling diamond in his ear and a gaudy ring on his right pinky. Not to mention enough chains around his neck to make a chain link fence a mile long.

"I don't want nothing from this criminal. Alex you know you don't have to live like this. You should have been my best man…we should have been together tonight, not you and him. Man you are killing yourself and you don't even know it. I know you think you bad and everything but you're dead man…you're dead!" Nick was getting so emotional I could hear his voice cracking.

"Oh…what you 'bout to cry now? Man I don't need this…Don't say I never gave you anything." Alex said laughing hysterically and throwing a wad of money in the air that burst into separate pieces looking like leaves falling to the ground. He rolled up his window and was off again into the night. Nick and his dad turned and stalked up to the house, leaving the cash right where it fell. Once they were inside and everybody had counted to ten, I decided to get to the bottom of what had just happened.

"Sweetie, how in the world did you two end up going at each other?" I asked Nick, placing a bag of frozen peas on his upper lip.

"We just happened to be at the same club. Everything was going fine until the waitress brought this round of liquor to the table. Now you know I'm not drinking and everybody at the table is not drinking, so I looked around to see who had sent it over. Meanwhile she points to a guy at the bar." Nick begins to recount the story, taking breaks between every few words to touch his swollen lip with his tongue.

"Turns out Alex's girl Traniece was in the area and spotted us. She must have let him know we were there. We politely refused the drinks, but asked him to come over to join us…so we could celebrate like a family." Anthony had picked up the story, so Nick could continue icing his lip. It was not going to look good to have a busted lip in his wedding portraits.

"But you know he came over and immediately started acting a fool, ma. He was using foul language and was so wasted he was spilling his drink on my boys. Then he made a rude comment about a certain body part on Laurie and I just lost it…Oh my goodness…Mr. Chadwick, he must think I'm crazy!" Nick said remembering that he just went off in front of his future father-in-law.

"Son, you don't have to worry about me. I heard you tryin' to talk some sense into your brother." Mr. and Mrs. Chadwick had come back downstairs quietly and were standing in the living room. None of us had even noticed.

"Yeah, baby we can't pass no kind of judgment. We lost our oldest boy to that AIDS virus. He got himself hooked on them drugs, was using dirty needles." Mrs.

Chadwick said, going over to Nick to pat him on the shoulder.

"I know Laurie don't talk about it much, 'cause she was so young when we was battlin' with him out there on them streets. But don't you worry none…I seen that boy softening up when you was talking to him. He know he not supposed to be out there. He'll come around." Mr. Chadwick said giving Nick some encouragement.

"Thank you so much for your understanding spirit." I said to both of them.

"Come on…it's the night before one of the biggest days in our children's lives. We are about to blend two God-fearing families together and the devil ain't nothing but mad. Let's do him one better and say us a prayer. We can't worry 'bout all this turmoil. The bible says 'in this life you will suffer trials and tribulations, but fear not because I've already overcome the world'." Mrs. Chadwick said holding her hands out for us to join her and make a circle.

"Amen." Anthony finally said. We stood in a tight circle each of us taking turns until we were speaking in tongues and Nick ended up in the center of the circle on his face crying. God you are awesome. I can't wait until tomorrow.

****

The wedding day was bittersweet. I was so blessed to have my child married to such a virtuous woman, and become part of a magnificent family like the Chadwick's. I cried all day and into the night from sheer joy. It was going to be hard for me to see him go back to Ohio, but that is where Laurie was from, and he wanted her to be close to her family. After meeting the Chadwick's, though, I knew they'd treat him just as good as we would have. He called me when they were settled into their new single family home and he was overjoyed to find out that one month after they were married, they were expecting their first child. Nick called me each week with progress reports and sent grainy, black and white sonogram pictures each time Laurie had one taken. I'd done enough stories about fertility, and had seen my fair share of sonograms fooling around with Shelita that I could tell from the shots he was having a boy. Nick and Laurie wanted to be surprised so I kept it to myself. Another Chase man, Lord you are good.

Chapter 32: Too Precious To Be Pressed

§

With both of his older boys out of the house, I thought it would be a great idea for Anthony to spend some time bonding with the girls. He'd told me on a few occasions that since they were older and interested in boys, and girl things, he felt like he couldn't relate. I thought I had the remedy for that and was excited to see how my plan worked. I was waiting like a child on Christmas day to see them return from my little experiment. Wait a minute…something must have happened. The two people walking up to the front door definitely don't look happy with one another.

"I told you this was a bad idea." Anthony said to me when I greeted him at the front door.

"What? No bags? Where's the infamous prom dress?" I asked. My baby Goodness was going to her junior prom. My how time flies!

"I spent three hours in the mall with that girl, and there is not a thing in there for her. Renee everything has got skin showing all over the place. I'm not having my daughter looking like a street walker."

"Mommy it wasn't even that bad. Everything I tried on that I liked, he hated. Daddy wasn't even giving it a chance. I saw the dress I wanted, but he refused to buy it. All the girls are wearing dresses that show a little skin." She said putting on her best little pout.

"If I'm spending my money on something, there better be enough material on the thing for me to get my money's worth. Now I'm done…ya'll can go back out tomorrow." Anthony said defeated, throwing his hands in the air.

"Daddy the prom is in three days! I have to get a dress right now. Mario has to know what color corsage to get me. I have to find shoes…ugh!" Goodness was fifteen now, that's all I can say about that. Everything was life or death to a fifteen year old. And this was junior prom, so her dad was really not on her list of favorite people right now.

"Sweetie, lets get some dinner, and you and me will go back out in an hour. Sound good? Now thank your father for agreeing to spend time with you and to pay for this dress." I said turning her around to face her father, and giving her my now familiar nudge on the chin.

"Thanks daddy." She mumbled and went up to her room.

"So the bonding idea was a bad one, huh?" I said as I snuggled up to Anthony who was sitting with his head in his hands on the sofa.

"Babe, I had no idea. There were teenaged girls all over that mall, just giggling and screaming and talking so fast. We ran into some of her friends, I swear they were talking about me right in front of my face, and I don't even know what they were saying." He laughed, able to admit that he was no match for a group of teenaged girls.

"Don't worry, I'm sure she talks about me too. But isn't it good to see her with friends, and going to the prom, and doing so well in school? I mean the girl is on track to graduate at sixteen." I said in awe of God.

"I couldn't be more blessed. I know you take on so much, and I have to admit that a few years ago I didn't know if adopting Shelita's kids was a good idea. Only because I knew it meant you'd be stressed. Now who would have thought it was gonna be our own flesh and blood actin' a pure fool?" Anthony said, shaking his head.

"I sure didn't see it. But I'm sure if it had been revealed to me I might not have been obedient and taken the children, thinking I could save Alex from what he is doing. Then who is to say where they would be or Alex would be? We don't know."

"Amen. I'm going to see if I can get a little sleep before I go into work tonight. I'm gonna say a pray that God keeps you sane while you're out there looking for that prom dress." He joked and then headed up the stairs.

And fifteen minutes before the mall was closing, I was saying a prayer myself. I had walked what had to be ten miles in a circle around three different malls with Goodness trying on at least thirty different dresses.

"Girlfriend, I'm telling you right now. If it ain't in this store, then you just not going to the…"

"Mommy this is it! This is it! I love it!" I could hear Goodness jumping up and down in the fitting room. She slowly opened the door and walked out in front of me. What can I say? She was absolutely radiant. A lump formed in my throat. She stood there wearing a full-length pastel purple gown with a beaded bodice. There was a silky beaded overlay that wrapped around the waist and fell away from the sides to reveal a skirt that went straight to the floor in a shimmering column.

"Well?" She asked twirling around to look at herself in the large mirror.

"You look fabulous. If Shelita could see you now…Baby you are just gorgeous. And dad's going to love it, because the only thing showing are your shoulders."

"Are you kidding? He'll probably say that's too much skin." We both laughed, because we knew it was true. At that point she quickly changed so we could pay for the dress and get her home so she could get on that phone and tell everybody she knew about it.

****

Three days later we were snapping pictures and pinning on boutonnieres. Anthony had arranged for a limousine to pick up Goodness and Mario with three other couples. She was not too happy that he would also be following them down to the Hyatt and taking pictures as they got out of the limousine. Goodness knows her dad very well, and was worried he would stick around until the end, checking up on her.

"Mommy, are you sure we need to take more pictures when we get there? I mean I'm getting the professional one's from Essence of Light done, and we can get limousine shots here." She hinted, hoping I could talk her father out of embarrassing her.

"The person that paid for everything, gets to decide how many pictures get taken, and where they get taken." Anthony piped in before I could answer. The man truly was paying for just about everything. He paid for the dress, the shoes, the day at the spa getting the hair and nails done, and some fabulous earrings. He was also footing the bill for the most expensive package of prom pictures. The last time we got to make such a big fuss, was for Nick's prom. Alex had missed both of his proms. I guess it's not gangsta to wear a tux and a corsage.

"Yes sir." She mumbled.

"Now let's go over some rules." He started, taking the four boys who were escorting the girls to the prom over to the dining room area.

"Dad, please…we know the rules." Goodness said with exasperation.

"You might as well calm down, because you know how dad is." Her sister chimed in.

"I don't need your two cents Marie, thank you very much. Make yourself useful, go get the purse I left upstairs, please." She playfully tapped her sister on the head.

"Yes Sir!" All of the boys said in unison after Anthony released them from the huddle in the dining room area. Mario had started to sweat already, poor boy…he's been getting the talk about rules ever since he started calling Goodness at the beginning of the school year.

Mario's parents were just as strict as we were, they only allowed the two on group dates, he had an 11:00 o'clock curfew, and he was not allowed to have Goodness over unless one of his parents was home. His parents even limited the number of times they could talk to each other a day on the telephone. I liked the Conways a whole lot! They were raising a gentleman that was God-fearing. Of course I thought I had done that too in Alex's case. That's enough Renee, you've got to stop comparing everything and everybody to Alex. God has got this one under control.

According to Anthony's spy report, the evening went well. He drove around for thirty minutes after the limousine dropped off the couples and snuck back into the event to see how things were going. It was exactly midnight when Mario escorted Goodness to the door. Her father and I were waiting for her. It was all I could do to pin Anthony down so he wouldn't scare the two of them by opening the door.

"Give them a chance to say their good-bye's." I said throwing my leg over his.

"He can wave 'bye' from the car. He's probably out there trying to get his last feel in, you know these young guys that work down at the plant are just full of stories of how they hooked up with some teenager that looked twenty-something. And incase you don't know, hooked up got a whole new meaning from when me and you was that age." Anthony said trying to get out from under my leg.

"You act like you talking to somebody that hasn't written a million stories on teenage pregnancy and the rising rate of black people under the age of thirty that are dying from AIDS and HIV. You need to just calm down Anthony…besides a little hug never hurt nobody." I teased, trying to get him to relax a little.

He half laughed, half gasped at my comment. "Remember our first time on your grandma's back porch? It was the summer you turned fourteen and was all up in my face talking about 'my granny's out doin' her shoppin' if you want to come over and talk'…" He sounded pathetic trying to mimic a teenage girl's voice.

"First of all I ain't never sound that country. I was just trying to put on the charm 'cause I knew you was a big old country bumpkin. And if I recall correctly, you invited yourself in after you saw my granny get in her car and drive up the road past your house." I laughed, but my stomach did start to do a little flip, because as I recalled…things did get a little hot and heavy that day. Before I could even get the image into my head, Anthony felt obligated to continue the story.

"Yeah…I see that look on your face now. You remember…when we hugged and one thing led to another…" It was all coming back to me now. We did do some things that I'm not proud to say I did, but that was then and this is now. It was a good thing my granny came roaring into the front yard in her loud hoopty, giving us enough warning or else we would have literally been caught with our pants down!

"O.k. get the door, what are you waiting for?" I said jumping up and pulling him up to break up whatever was happening on my porch. Our darling daughter beat us to the punch. She opened the door just as Anthony was reaching for the knob.

"Gotcha! Ya'll are a trip." She laughed. "What did you think we were doing? I am too precious to be pressed for some boy. I had a great time, and we had a little kiss, but that was all." She was smiling the kind of smile that says there's something more, but you'll never know.

"Dad in the room. I don't need to hear about any kisses." Anthony said playfully covering his ears. My heart slowed down to a normal pace and I was able to breath again.

"Well I love you guys, and thanks for everything. It was perfect. I never imagined I'd have an opportunity to feel like such a princess. I'm going up to bed. I'll tell you all about it in the morning."

"And when you say all…do you mean you'll tell us about whatever it is that is keeping that silly grin on your face." I said giving Goodness a hug as she was slowly walking up the steps to her bedroom.

She sighed loudly.

 "Mario is just the cutest guy I've ever met. Didn't you think he looked so cute in his tux mom?"

"I got to get out of here…I'm late as it is, go get in that bed and make sure you hang that dress up so it don't get wrinkled."

Did I detect a hint of jealousy there? Anthony was starting to see that those long sighs and batting eyelashes were no longer just reserved for him alone. He looked at me and shook his head after Goodness finally made it to the top of the stairs, humming softly to herself. Anthony left for work, he took comp time just so he could be here when Goodness got home. I kissed him goodnight and went on up for what I hoped would be a restful night of sleep.

Chapter 33: All Is Well

§

It's 3:30 in the morning. I don't like 3:30 in the morning. The telephone is ringing. I really don't like it when the telephone rings at 3:30 in the morning. Nothing good happens at this hour in the morning. *Pick up the receiver Renee, it could be Anthony just calling to say he's working a double.*

I growled in a low voice as I snatched the phone off of the base.

"Hello." I tried to sound as annoyed and inconvenienced as I felt.

"Rise and shine Renee! You have to come meet me, we are trying to scoop a story that is in progress right now!"

No this woman did not call me at this ungodly hour talking about some news story. As much as I admired Julia Tambor for being the top-rated black female news anchor on the East Coast, the girl was a bit obsessive. Most of the other anchors just enjoyed the luxury of having a great story delivered to them while they sat behind the desk and made it look good. Julia wanted to be out there on the front lines. I really was biased and did my best writing and producing for her stories, but tonight she done went a bit too far.

"Julia? Girl...I love you like a sister, but even my family knows they can't call me at this hour. Besides Harold is writing for you this week, I'm taking some time off."

With weddings and proms and working three breaking stories in a row last week, I'd decided to take a little me time. For some reason God had told me to fast and I liked to have quiet and time for study when I was fasting so I called in for a few days. Last night when I was in my prayer closet, I was still enough to hear that God wanted the fast to be seven days.
Seven...interesting. That was the longest I'd ever fasted on my own. Anthony and I had gone on forty-day fasts together during the Lenten season, or when we were asking God to reveal something to us along this journey that has been filled with my medical issues, and with Alex's self-destruction. I even had to fast to ask God to help me with my tongue the first few years Shye was here, honey the child just makes you want to cuss sometimes.

This fast was very different because as I prayed, God just spoke it to me, other times I would decide I needed to fast and then I would ask God to reveal to me what, when and for how long. I was having a time of it though. I was only on day number two and feigning for some Ben and Jerry's Butter Pecan. I was not in the mood for this foolishness so early in the morning.

"Renee, I need you girl. I want this exclusive. My contact with the Chief of police says we can have full access, interviews...everything if we get our guys down there ASAP! I need this to blow everybody out of the water! I got a tip from law enforcement that they are doing a huge raid, and they are bringing down Big Ant."

Now I was a little interested. Nobody at the station knew I was any relation to him and I wanted to keep it that way. I could almost feel Julia's energy through the telephone as she continued trying to convince me to leave my warm bed.

"The word is they are not only getting him for the drugs and the guns, but also running a huge prostitution ring out of that fancy condo he's living in!" The woman was just too excited by crime. I had to admit though, I wanted to see the look on Antwan's face when he was brought out of the building in handcuffs.

"I'll meet you in fifteen minutes outside of police headquarters." I agreed and got ready in a hurry. I would need to quickly call Anthony to let him know I'd be out for about an hour or two and to look in on the kids when he got home at 4:00 am.

"Thanks girl, I owe you one." Julia said with excitement. That was the last thing Shelita said to me the night she left the children with me. I just had this overwhelming feeling that something was about to go down.

As we pulled up to the dark parking lot where the officers where setting up their stake out, I was tempted to give Julia a brown paper bag to breathe in because she was so jazzed up about the fact, that there were no other news vans in sight, she was literally hyperventilating.

"Are you going to be alright? I can't have you passing out the minute we go live." I joked with her putting my hand on her wrist pretending to take her pulse.

"Stop Renee! You know I live for this, don't even joke like that. I have been following this thug and his run-ins with law enforcement for the last year. It's amazing how he avoids getting charged with any serious crimes. If you ask me, we need to be investigating these cops, something is a little fishy. I almost hate to admit it but, Big Ant is a bit charming with those sexy hazel eyes. I can see how any woman could get turned on by his game." Her voice sounded as if she were talking about her first true love. I was getting more and more nauseated

as she kept going on about how captivated she was by my brother.
"Listen to you. You sound like you're in love with the guy. He's a menace, a sick person whose goal in life is to destroy innocent people. He deserves whatever he gets tonight." I said, leaving her with her mouth wide open. I was always pretty impartial when it came to the stories we covered. Of course as soon as I got home I'd be up in the prayer closet, but this time I could not hide my disgust. I almost took the car door off the hinges as I pushed it open. I got out and gathered some key tidbits for the story cards I was going to write up and give to her for the live feed and for the broadcast on the 6:00 a.m. Early Edition. We were feeling pretty confident that the bust would go according to plan, so we settled back in the van and waited for the cops to come out of the building with a line of heathens in shackles. Just another day at the office.
After a few minutes of awkward silence, Julia looked up from the story cards she was pretending to read.
"Hey listen, I didn't mean to upset you. I know you are a Christian and I'm pretty sure that all this craziness we cover must get to you. I really don't know how you do it. I mean how can you spend a night out with us looking into the eyes of someone whose just been murdered and then go to church and praise the Lord the next day?"
"Well first of all He deserves that praise because I wasn't the one murdered, and my household was covered so all of my family was safe. Even with all that's going on with my son Alex out in these streets, God has a greater purpose and is protecting him. I praise Him because He sacrificed so much and there was no news story about Him and His sacrifice. He did it not for recognition but just because He loves me. So I can't do nothing but praise him."

"You sound like some of the preachers I hear on the radio. I'm thinking I need to go to church with you one of these days so I can get some sleep at night, and be able to give thanks in spite of how things look. Well listen…I didn't mean to ramble. We've got about thirty minutes before this thing goes down and I know I woke you up so why don't you just chill and I'll give you a heads up when the officers signal me."

"Bless you girl, I need about fifteen minutes and I'll be good as new." Just as I was putting my head back to rest on the seat and catch a few minutes of sleep, a familiar black Lexus truck pulled up in front of the building with jet black tinted windows. This is not good Lord. When the door opened Alex jumped out of the driver's side! At the same time Antwan came running out of the building screaming.

"5-O! 5-O! They tryin' to bust up in there yo…get out of here!" Alex began to turn and run toward the direction of the van I was sitting in, when all of sudden there were monstrous, loud bursts, erupting from everywhere. I looked to see Antwan waving a gun and firing shots at the police officers that where approaching the building on the right.

Alex? Where was Alex? Wasn't he running toward me? I jumped out of the car and headed toward the building.

"Alex! Alex! That's my baby! Stop shooting! Stop shooting!" I was screaming and waving my arms like a mad woman.

"Get down!" A police officer grabbed me and threw me to the ground to protect me from the bullets that were flying. I wasn't even thinking about getting shot. I laid there for what seemed like an eternity. Then there was absolute silence. No voices, no sirens blaring, and no sound from the frantic feet I saw running in every direction. Just silence. Everything was moving in slow motion, the red and blue lights from the police cars where swirling around distorting the faces of all the people that had gathered at the scene. I could see people moving, but there was no noise. I looked over to where I last saw Alex and could see the bright gaudy light of the video camera spotlight hovering over him. Julia and the camera man where setting up the tripod to mount the camera. Slowly I began to hear her voice above all the commotion as the soundtrack to my nightmare returned.

"In five, four, three, two, one…We are live at the scene of a massive police raid and shoot out. It appears that two suspects have been fatally wounded, their names and identities have not yet been released."

Suspects? Fatally wounded? Not my son. God please, don't take Alex from me. I know you have something for him. Please God.

"Somebody help! Somebody…help my baby!" I knew I was screaming but I could not hear myself. I ran to his lifeless body lying face-down in the parking lot. There was blood everywhere. He wasn't moving. His face was a grotesque mangle of white bone, and pink jagged flesh where a gaping hole replaced the smooth brown skin of his right cheek. His leg was twisted at an awkward angle with a growing dark pool of red blooming over the tan pants that covered his thigh. His eyes were wide open, but where not looking at anything. *God! Please! If it is your will…*

"Get that camera out of here. Somebody get an ambulance!" I knew I must have looked like a wild woman, my head still tied in the scarf I was sleeping in to protect my newly growing locs. Since I wasn't going to be in front of the camera I just threw on a coat and headed out the door. And now, here I was on the news…

****

Alex lay in a drug-induced coma for almost two weeks. He had been shot seven times. Now if you know me by now, you know I believe in a little something called faith. Seven days of fasting. That was given to me directly from above. One day for each of those bullets he took. Seven is the number of completion. Those seven shots did some damage to my baby's body, but they did not touch his soul.

Seven shots. One through is right hand, one passed through his cheek and out of his mouth, one entered his side and missed all vital organs to exit out of the other side. There was a bullet still lodged in his pelvis. One grazed his left ear, still another shattered the femur on his right leg. The last one was lodged near his spinal cord. Yet he did not die. It was nothing but the blood of Jesus.

Antwan had not been as blessed. He was killed at the scene. I mourned for a life that could have been…should have been, but I could not mourn for the evil that he created in my life. The God in me helped me to put together a simple ceremony for him after his body was released by the state medical examiner. In fact the medical examiner also confirmed that many of the bullet fragments found in Alex's body were not from the police officers, but from Antwan's gun. He was trying to kill Alex. As Antwan lay dying, Julia reported his last words where:

"I hope I got him…She'll regret the day she turned on me." It was over now.

Alex was stable now the doctors would be operating tomorrow. There was a whole team of doctors and surgical specialists that we were praying for in that operating room. The way it was described was almost like they'd be taking turns in carefully mapped out shifts. Plastic surgeons, neurologist, orthopedic surgeons…He needed some plastic surgery to his face, orthopedic surgery to repair his broken leg, and would need surgery to remove the two bullets still in his body and repair damage to his spinal cord and lumbar discs. The chief of the surgical team very grimly told us the prognosis for Alex to regain his ability to walk was not good. I wasn't worried about that at all. My baby would be coming back home, and more importantly returning to God. I know it will take some time, but it will happen.

"He's got a big day tomorrow." The nurse said to me as she changed the bag of IV fluid that was dripping slowly into his arm.

"He'll be just fine. God's working with this one." I said in hushed tones, all the while rubbing his arm. I read quietly from the bible to him every night. He might not have been able to talk, but I knew he could hear me.

"I hear that. It's a whole lot of other one's that come through here that God needs to work on. You have a good night Mrs. Chase, the shift is changing so I'll be leaving."

"Thanks for all your help Lisa." Lisa was Alex's nurse on the 3-11 pm shift every day since he'd gotten here. She was a compassionate person, and never once passed judgment on him, despite the fact that there was a police officer stationed outside his door. I'm sure she knew who he was, and why the officer was outside, but she showed him tenderness and care. I actually heard her whisper a small prayer one night when I was entering the room. She turned the small radio on his bedside table to a gospel station, and chastised the morning shift nurses when they turned it to secular music. She took good care of him and I appreciated that God placed her there for that specific time.

"Officer Shaw, can I get you any coffee?" I offered as I passed him on my way to the cafeteria. He'd been stationed outside of Alex's door because he was after all still a suspect in a major drug raid. I saw it more as protection…not only was the officer keeping Alex under arrest, but he was keeping the thugs he used to hang around away from him. Just because Antwan was dead, did not mean there weren't other people from his past that wanted to get in here and make sure he was coming back to them.

Many of his boys saw this as a badge of honor that he'd been shot so many times and survived. Everybody trying to be Tupac and 50-Cent. Goodness said all the boys at her school were boasting about how they wanted to be like her brother Alex when they got older. These boys were actually excited about the prospect of being able to join a gang and get involved in street violence.

"Naw Mrs. Chase I'm good. How's our boy doing in there? Sounds like he's stable enough for the surgery in the morning." Officer Shaw had taken an interest in Alex's well being. He told me one night that he'd seen so many people from the church coming in and praying for Alex that he knew he would be on the right path after he got out of the hospital.

"All is well, Officer Shaw…all is well." I said smiling.

Chapter 34: I'll Be Walking Into My Purpose

§

After almost six hours of surgery, Alex was taken to intensive care to recover for a few days. He was excited to be getting a chance to have his first meal of solid food. For the time being his tray was lying on the bedside table, because just as he was about to eat, yet another doctor from the surgical team came to visit.

"Alex can you feel me touching you here?" Dr. Kanzer the neurosurgeon was giving Alex a battery of post-surgical examinations. He had Alex lying flat in the bed and was poking his big toe on his left foot with a pretty sharp looking instrument, and Alex wasn't budging. His legs where just laying limply in the same position the last doctor placed them in, he hadn't budged. He was just as frustrated by this doctor's exam as he was with the last visit when he wasn't able to hold his knee in the flexed position the way the orthopedic doctor asked him to. I tried to hide any concern in my eyes because Alex was staring right at me.

"I can't feel it…are you touching me doc? Mom should I be feeling something right now?" He was looking back and forth between the two of us. If he could muster up enough strength I'm sure he'd try to sit up to look down at his toe, but the spinal brace around his torso was restricting him.

"Alex, just relax, and try to concentrate on what the doctor is asking you." I said in my calmest tone.

"But I can't see it, is he touching my toe?" He asked with concern.

"Dr. Kanzer, I'm going to step out so you can finish the exam." I said excusing myself so I could go to the waiting room and cry. I didn't want to upset Alex.

"Momma, what's wrong?" Shye came over to hug me, he was becoming such a big boy.

"I'm o.k. just a bit anxious about Alex getting the feeling back in his legs. The doctor was giving him a test just now, and he really wasn't doing so good." I admitted.

"Momma, didn't you say the bible says to be anxious for nothing." He said very matter-of-factly.

"That it does, deacon Shye. So you have been listening to me." I responded, laughing as I pulled him into an embrace. Just as I released him, I looked up to see Dr. Kanzer.

"It's really too early to tell how Alex will do as far as recovering full motor and sensory input from his spine. After talking with some of my colleagues about their findings it seems that he's gained some sensation in a pattern that is consistent with the location of the gunshot wound to the spinal cord, but very little muscle function."

Uh…can you say that in English? I think to myself. I guess my blank stare made the doctor feel like he had to clarify all that jargon.

"I imagine that after some swelling from surgery has gone down, and we begin some physical therapy we can better make a determination. I'm putting the order in to have him transferred to the rehabilitation floor to begin vigorous therapy three times a day." He said with a weak smile.

"That sounds great. What can we do to help him?" I asked perking up a bit. I didn't think rehabilitation could start so soon after surgery.

"Pray Mrs. Chase…just pray." He said and extended his hand toward me as he got up to leave. Now I like a doctor that knows the worth of prayer.

"Hey big-head." Alex called to Shye as we entered the room.

"Come here and give me a hug." Even though he was just about Alex's size now, Shye still longed to be the little brother and was tickled to have Alex back in his life.

"The doctor said you are going to be working hard, bro. You have to get better so we can play basketball together. I'll even let you win." Shye said laughing with his brother.

"What…let me win? Boy don't let me get back on my feet, I'll show you how to really ball. You don't know I taught Shaq everything he knows." Alex joined in the joking. He was trying his best to show a strong front for his brother.

"Tomorrow you'll be transferred upstairs babe, and the real work begins. Are you ready?" I asked sitting in the bedside chair, opening containers so he could finally get a chance to eat, what was now probably a cold brick of meatloaf surprise.

"Mom, I am as ready as I'll ever be. I had a dream last night that I was preparing a long speech for some event. I have no idea what that's all about, but whatever it was for, there where a lot of steps to get up to the platform where I was suppose to be speaking. I plan on being able to walk up those steps. Now pass me whatever that brown stuff is on that tray a brotha is hungry!"

"It is so, sweetie. It is so!" I kissed him on the forehead and dragged Shye out of the room reluctantly so his brother could finish eating and get some rest. Alex was on the way to his purpose and it began with a gunshot, just like the shots that brought my youngest babies into my life.

God this next part of the journey is going to be tough. It's easy to spiral down into a valley, but it's hard work climbing your way up out of that thing. Thank you for bringing him through thus far.

****

"I'll be right there."

This was the third time the clinical coordinator from the hospital had called my cell phone. I wasn't trying to get a speeding ticket, but apparently I was taking too long to get to the emergency meeting she'd called. I had to drop the stories I was working on for Julia on Harold's desk for him to complete. One of these days they were going to recognize that man for his awesome writing ability and stop passing him over for promotions. He was a lifesaver. I raced passed Marguerite who was on her way to the break room and was just itching to ask me about the story we were working on about a very popular football player caught in a betting scandal. Apparently a cousin of hers had dated the guy. At this point I could care less, so I kept trucking almost knocking her over.

"Not now Marguerite." I said giving her the hand. I had more important things on my mind. The hospital was threatening to throw Alex out of the rehabilitation program because he was being less than cooperative.

The first week was great, he was excited about the possibility of regaining his ability to walk, and then the pain and reality kicked in. He had a major setback when he developed an infection from a bedsore and wasn't able to have therapy for a few days.

Alex had been there for almost a month and could barely stand for more than five minutes. He could take awkward steps using a rolling walker and needed the support of the occupational and physical therapist on either side of him. He was still on spinal precautions, which meant he needed to be very careful about twisting his body when he moved. He's grown tired of asking for help to go to the bathroom or having to wait to get bathed. He is a miserable person and is taking it out on the staff. He's refused therapy at least one time every day this week. I decided to drop in and check on him before I went into the conference room. I opened the door to his room and ducked just in time to narrowly miss the pink bedpan that Alex had just flung in that direction.

"What on earth is your problem little boy!" I yelled bending down to pick up the bedpan. The way I was feeling right now, I wanted to fling the thing right back at him. So much for the calm I'd breathed in and out in the car in preparation for the meeting.

"I can't stand this place! Everybody is an idiot. I've been ringing this bell for almost an hour! I need to go to the bathroom and I'm not using that dumb thing. I want to go into the bathroom like a grown man. Look ma they got a freakin' diaper on me…this thing is for old people. They got this stupid alarm on the bed so I can't get up and go myself because everybody is so afraid I'm going to fall down! I just want to be out of here. I hate this place!"

"Are you done? Alex…You have got the bedpan so you can go to the bathroom when you feel you need to without putting yourself in harms way. You are not the only patient they have in here. Now what's this I hear about you refusing therapy? Do you know I'm here because they want to kick your behind out of this place?" I said loudly…I was really trying hard not to yell.

"Good, let me go home then!" He yelled, grabbing the telephone and pulling it out of the wall so he could hurl it across the room. His endurance was such an issue that after the bed pan throwing he was so weak the phone landed a few inches from his bed with a loud clang.

"And do what? Sit on the sofa? I'm not going to be running around doing things for you. Your brother and sisters are in school and me and dad are working. Alex you need to get better so that you can be independent. Isn't that what you want?" I said approaching the bed to wrestle the ceramic cup out of his hand that he was preparing to throw.

"Mom, this is too hard. I can't do it. I been trying for a month to walk. I can't make it from here to there without feeling like I'm about to pass out." He said pointing from his bed to the bathroom door a few short steps away. His voice began to tremble. I placed the cup back on the table out of his reach.

"But one month ago, nobody even knew if you'd be able to walk at all. Alex you couldn't even sit on the edge of the bed, let alone stand. You can stand up and take steps now. Believe in yourself…no better yet believe in what God is going to do for you. Now you have a choice. I can go into that meeting and sign the papers for you to leave so you can just wallow in pity on the sofa at home, or I can go in there and boldly ask them to let you stay because you will make a commitment to work your hardest so you can walk up those steps you dreamed about. So which is it?" I was out of breath as if I'd just run a race.

"Mom, I want to do it, but I'm scared. Besides, what is walking going to do for me? I have to go to court as soon as I get out of here, I'll probably do time for all the stuff they found that linked me to Uncle Ant. So I get back to walking so I can walk into a cell?" He answered.

His voice was angry now. After Alex was stable enough, the district attorney's office sent officers over to interrogate him about his involvement with Antwan. The night of the raid he was not in possession of any drugs or weapons, which wasn't nothing but protection from above, because typically Alex handled large sums of money and drugs for his uncle on a daily basis. He was actually on his way to make a pick-up so that he could begin distributing that weekend. It was after all prom season and plenty of young people out past curfew looking for something dangerous to get into. Since he cooperated with police and was not seen as an immediate risk, the officer was no longer stationed outside his door and he began to enjoy a little bit of freedom. Freedom, which it seemed like, he was trying hard not to lose.

"Is that what this is all about? Alex, I wish I could say that you wouldn't have to pay the consequences for that raid, but you can't delay and delay thinking that you can put off any punishment that you have coming to you. We can just pray for favor as far as the courts are concerned, but there are always repercussions. You very well might have to walk into a cell, but God will be walking with you. And when you walk out, you'll be walking into the life of your daughter, you'll be walking into the purpose that God has for you." I don't know where all that was coming from, but I felt like I needed to speak this into Alex's life. Just as he was about to answer, his nurse cautiously peeked into the room.

"Mrs. Chase they are waiting for you to start the meeting."

"I'm on my way in two minutes, let them know I'll be right there." I never took my eyes off of Alex, he knew I was waiting for him to make a decision.

"Tell them I want to walk." He said with a tear rolling down his cheek.

Chapter 35: Free To Be Who God Wants Me To Be

§

And walk he did. Alex spent the next four weeks in a battle with his muscles and bones. He literally had to will them to move the way he wanted them to go. When I went back for his discharge planning meeting I got reports from the therapists that Alex was making them join him in a little prayer before each session. His nurses said he'd be in the room doing pushups and leg exercises in the bed. He'd gotten to the point where he no longer needed the bed alarm. In fact, he graduated to a green plastic ID bracelet which meant he was able to take his cane and do laps around the nurses station whenever the feeling hit him. He tried to walk at least three laps before every meal and after each therapy session. The day he was able to pull his socks on without using the plastic sock grabber you would have thought he'd just graduated from college! We both were shouting in there. Today I was bringing him some clothes because he was ready to get out of hospital gowns. Let me see how did he put it…he was tired of 'wearing a dress'.

"Wait Ma! Stay right there…let me show you something." Alex said rising from his bed as soon as I came into his room loaded down with bags full of new clothes, underwear and shoes that all my church family wanted to give to him. Of course there were gossipers and nay-sayers at the church that wanted to shake their heads and scandalize the Chase family name for what Alex had done, but there were a select few that rallied around us, praying day and night. They were encouraged by the weekly reports I gave them each Sunday.

"Hold on sweetie let me put these bags down…your cane is all the way over here by the door." I warned.

"No…leave it right there. I want to show you something." He insisted. I stopped in my tracks and watched him get up from the bed and walk over to me. He was still favoring his right leg. It had been mended together with an external fixator, so he looked like a robot with the black metal frame being held together by large pins and screws that went into his leg at all angles. He had been given permission to bear as much weight on it as he could tolerate, but it was still painful which caused him to limp. Despite all of that my child just walked by himself. When he got over to me, he gave me the biggest, tightest, hug he'd ever given me and I exhaled.

"Oh…Alex! When did the doctor say you could walk without the cane?"

"He didn't. But ma ever since I've been walking more, that cane's been slowing me down. So I started trying to walk without it just in my room. Today I went back and forth from the door to my bed about five times. I did it ma, all by myself." He said practically jumping up and down.

"See…I told you. Alex baby this is wonderful. It looks like you'll be getting out of here sooner than we expected."

"That's right. I got work to do. Niecey's mom bought Morgan by to see me today. That girl is getting so big. I can't believe she's gonna be two years old in a matter of months. She jumped in my arms and was kissing me. Saying 'daddy…daddy'. It sounded so good." I wished I had a camera so I could snap a picture of the huge smile on his face.

"Baby that is wonderful. It's nothing like getting love from your own child."

I wanted to say more, but I didn't want my voice to give away the fact that I was seriously concerned about Morgan and her well-being. I hated to see her in that household with so much confusion, but God wasn't telling me it was time to move on it yet.

"What's that look all about?" Lord this child and his intuition. Like mother like son.

"Niecey's mom has been by the house a few times since you've been in here. I didn't want to upset you with all that was going on."

"I already know. Troy came by and told me that Traniece escaped that night of the raid, but got arrested a few weeks later for possession and solicitation. Man…how could I have put my child in so much danger?"

I was not too thrilled to hear that Troy had been in to see him. He and Alex got in a lot of trouble drinking and drugging even before we put him out of the house. I hadn't heard Alex mention his name for a while.

"Look at you. I can see those wheels turning. Don't worry ma, Troy didn't stay long. He only got in here because he works in patient transport and was bringing somebody up to this floor. I happened to see him when I was on one of my trips around the nurses' station." He laughed.

"I know, but he was always up to no good. I don't want anything to turn you away from where you are going." Stop it Renee…you are starting that worrying thing again. Alex is in God's hands. End of story, nothing Troy can do to him now.

"Troy never held a gun to my head when we were smoking or drinking ma, I did that all by myself. Besides he wasn't the one that had his child living up in a building with dealers and whores. Now my daughter has a mother in jail and probably a father that's on his way too." Alex said sadly. The joy of the great accomplishment he just showed me was all but forgotten.

"It's not time to blame yourself. Traniece is a grown up and made her own decisions. She'll be in jail for at least a year or more on these last charges. Her mother told me she is so burdened right now with taking care of all her grandchildren. I can understand her frustration. You have children and they mess up then you get stuck trying to clean up the mess."

"I can't have Morgan living in so much confusion. Ma…I don't want you to feel like Ms. Carla, so swamped with my mess, but…"

"But what sweetie?" I asked taking him by the arm to lead him back over to the bed. He'd been standing for a while and was shifting his weight from side to side. I didn't want him to overdo it.

"I was just wondering…and I understand if you say no." He said lifting his hands in surrender.

"Just say what you want to say Alex." My heart was fluttering because I already knew what he wanted to ask.

"Can you take Morgan for me? I mean I have every intention of being a good parent for her. I won't know my fate until after my court date, but I want full custody and I'll need a stable home for her until I can get back on my feet." He said sitting on the edge of the bed and using his arms to lift him self and slide back into a reclined position. He was grimacing with every move, so I knew he was in pain, despite his strong front.

"Alex, you and Morgan already have a room at the house. God showed me more than a year ago, that you two would be coming back home together. We will work out the logistics, but just know that it is done." As soon as I said that he gave me a big hug. The door opened and in walked a very attractive, olive-skinned, young woman dressed in scrubs. She had jet black curly hair that hung in a large pony tail to her mid-back.

"Good afternoon, you must be Alex's mom. I'm Monica, his physical therapist." She said extending her hand to me. No wonder he wanted to wear his own clothes. Alex was trying to impress his therapist.

"Well don't let me get in the way. Make him work hard, I want to see tears." I joked.

"You just might, we are doing stairs today. And I think the occupational therapist said she wanted to work on tub transfers with you." She laughed and grabbed his cane that was leaning against the wall.

"Monica you can leave that cane, I've been walking without. And I'm not afraid of no stairs." He said confidently.

"You go Alex. I told you I thought you were ready to get rid of that thing. We can start working on walking on outdoor surfaces too today." She said. She sounded so excited.

"Well let me put some clothes on then baby. I want to look good if we're going to be outside together." Alex remarked, giving her a wink.

"Oh brother…stop flirting with Monica and get your butt ready for therapy. I'll see you tomorrow with dad and the kids. You'll get a chance to show off for them." I said gathering my things to leave.

****

It was a good thing Alex had worked so hard with Monica on those stairs, because a few days after he was discharged from the hospital he was walking up the courthouse steps to stand trial.

"I made it." He paused and turned towards the direction he'd just come from.

"Twenty-five steps. The most I ever did at one time without a break." Alex said when we got to the top of the wide cement staircase.

"Well let's just keep right on climbing son. You can only go up to the next level from here. Whatever that judge says is going to be ordained by God. He's not gonna give you any more or any less than you can handle. Remember you got your whole family here to support you. Nick will be waiting by the telephone to hear the verdict." Anthony said wrapping his arms around Alex's shoulders.

"Dad, I'm not worried. We've prayed about this and I'm just ready to do my time so I can move on."

"Alex, I'm proud of you and I'm glad you're not out on the streets anymore. I love the thought that you'll be with us again." Marie beamed giving her brother a hug.

"Yeah big bro, we are claiming the victory. You know how the Chase's do it! So let's go in there and handle this." Shye said giving his brother a high-five.

We all walked in the building, Alex was immediately taken from us to meet with his lawyer before the proceedings started. We settled into our seats directly behind the defendant's table. The trial went smoothly. Alex was cooperative, telling the truth and confessing to his part in the events of the night in question. When I say God showed him favor I mean, that despite what he was involved with, because he never had a criminal record, he was given a light sentence and a stern warning from the judge.

"Will the defendant please stand?" The bailiff shouted. Alex and his lawyer stood as directed.

"Young man, unlike many of the defendants I see coming into this courtroom, you are *not* a statistic." The judge started looking directly into Alex's eyes.

"You come from a stable home, a loving family, you are an intelligent individual. It is obvious that the people sitting behind you love you very much. The choices you made were completely irresponsible. You have no one to blame but yourself. And to make matters worse, you put the life of your child in jeopardy. There are so many young people that wish they had what you had. Not the money and the excess, but just pure love from a mother and father. I don't want to ever see you back in my court room again…is that understood?"

"Yes sir." He answered quietly, never taking his eyes off of the judge.

"Now as for sentencing, I am going against the court recommendation of mandatory incarceration and placing you on house arrest for six months to be followed by eighteen months of probation. That is the decision of this court…court adjourned!"

And with the loud bang of the gavel, Alex was free to go. Well not exactly free, he had to get fitted with a black ankle monitor, but my baby would be coming home. What can I say? We were so excited we were getting our dance on right there in the courtroom. I thought they were going to throw us out.

Chapter 36: The Pieces Are Falling Into Place

§

"Let me tell you something woman…If God ever tells you anything about me that has to do with doom and gloom, let me know beforehand. It seems like you got a direct line." Anthony said with a little laugh as we settled into bed. It was only 9:30 but we'd spent all day out with the kids, including Morgan and we were pooped. We went to the Maryland State fair, hit Forman Mills and did some school shopping for the upcoming school year, and went out to dinner at The Olive Branch. The kids wanted to keep going, but Alex begged us to be sure we brought Morgan home in time for him to read her a story before she went to bed.

"What are you talking about?" I asked him, easing onto my right side. I was aching from all the walking we'd done, and the sweltering heat was not doing me any good as far as the swelling in my left arm.

"I'm talking 'bout everything. You just claim stuff and it happens, you don't accept stuff and it don't happen."

"Honey didn't you hear that scripture that Rev. Fowler used in her sermon Sunday that said 'whatever you bind on earth shall be bound in heaven and whatever you release on earth shall be released in heaven'? I can live by that rule because I love the Lord and I trust Him. He knows it so He gives me that authority." I said boldly kissing him on the cheek when I was done talking.

"I am in awe. Alex is back here with Morgan, Shye is a dynamo on the debate team, Goodness at sixteen in her last year of high school and already killin' it on them SAT test. What can't God do?" He said, using his fingers to count off all the blessings our family had received from God

"Nothing is impossible with Him. I mean look at Alex. He is becoming the best dad. Nick called him the other night to ask him something about the baby crying because he was teething. Can you believe it? Nick...calling to ask Alex for advice? He's got that girl down there learning her prayers and scriptures, teaching her the apostle's creed and she can't even say but ten words." I laughed.

"She knows how to say *'amen'*, *'thank you Jesus'*, and *'please daddy'*! That's the way it's supposed to be. I'm just impressed with the brotha corn-rowing that child's hair. I wouldn't have a clue what to do with all that hair, and all them beads!" Anthony continued in his praise for his son, shaking his head.

"He's doing what a parent should do. I heard him praying for Traniece last night too."

"He's a better man than me." Anthony said quietly.

"No, he's just as good as you. I know you Anthony Chase and you would do the same thing. You're a softy. Now go to bed." I clicked off the light and went to bed. I had a peaceful rest. All was falling into place.

The next morning I was greeted with the smell of bacon and fresh coffee as I came down the stairs.

"Hey you...what are you doing up so early?" I questioned Alex as he moved around in the kitchen preparing one of his big breakfasts. I think since he's been home, we've all gained about twenty pounds. He's spent all of his free time reading cookbooks, watching cooking shows, and trying out new recipes. His dad is overjoyed at having a gourmet meal prepared for him every night.

"Couldn't sleep…I had another dream about speaking in front of a large crowd again. I'm thinking it might have something to do with the fact that I used to be a DJ, maybe I should look into getting back into the entertainment business?" He said dumping fresh fruit into the blender.

"God will reveal what those dreams are about. I have my own ideas, but I'll wait for God to let you know." I smiled taking a seat at the table in the breakfast nook.

"I know what you're thinking ma, and I just can't see me preachin' to nobody." He said flipping some fluffy pancakes onto a plate and sliding it toward me at the table. He garnished the side of the plate with some fresh raspberries and a sprig of mint, Emeril ain't got nothing on my baby.

"It wouldn't be you preachin', it would be God preaching through you. You're just the vessel baby. And if that doesn't work out you can always be a chef." I joked biting into my pancakes and washing it down with the drink that Alex mixed for me. He was always trying to get me to try one energy drink after another. Today's smoothie had a fresh strawberry and banana taste to it. I'd been dragging lately and my little boy was becoming concerned.

"Well I've been listening to this pastor from the church Monica goes to, and he is always preachin' about people running from their true gifts. I'm doing my best not to run from anything God would have for me. As soon as I get this thing off my ankle I'm going to visit her church." He said raising his pants leg to reveal the monitor.

"Oh...do I detect a little something between you and Monica? She was a pretty girl, very exotic looking." I said with a wink. I was being nosy, but the girl did give off a good first impression, and she's been dropping by the house every week to give Alex taped sermons from her church services. She was the type of female I wanted in my son's life, not to mention she would be a great influence on Morgan. *O.k....Just stop Renee, you are getting carried away.*

"She's Egyptian, her people are actually from Cairo. But you can just slow down on going shopping for any mother-of-the-groom dresses ma. Monica is just a really good friend. She is somebody that God placed in my life to help me during a tough time. Besides she's engaged to be married. She's doing it right though ma...she told me that her and her man are practicing celibacy. I told her, that you'd be in love with her."

"Now just how did ya'll happen to get on the subject of celibacy?" I wanted to know because folk don't just start bragging about being celibate.

"Well you know, I still got a little playa' up in me...so I was trying to put some smooth moves on Monica and she promptly set me straight. I thought all these rippling muscles would have her falling all over me." He joked.

He was pretending to do the same body builder poses he used to do when he and his brother were little boys watching the Mr. Universe competitions.

"She was always about business though, told me about her relationship and asked me if I was saved. I'm just getting back into the word, but that shut a brotha down cold." He said laughing.

"See...young people are getting the idea that it's cool to wait until marriage. It's never too late to choose that lifestyle and honor your temple." I said between bites.

"I can't believe I'm having this conversation with my mother, but just so you know…I'm going to give this celibacy thing a try. I mean it's kind of difficult to not be celibate when you live in your parents basement with a house arrest monitor around your ankle, but once it comes off…you know…then I'll give it a try." He said sitting down with his plate of whole-wheat toast, veggie sausage and orange juice.

"You are so funny. You'll be out there dating soon enough. And these girls out here are fast, honey. Now I've got to get going. Thanks for the breakfast." I said grabbing a piece of bacon and running out the door. Alex had purposefully left the pork off of my plate. He'd given up eating pork and red meat when he was in the hospital and was trying to set me on the same path. Anthony, however was not having that, so Alex always relented and cooked a few pieces for his old stubborn dad.

Chapter 37: Time To Move On

§

It never fails. Whenever I actually leave the house on time, there is a stalled vehicle on the side of interstate 695 that every driver in front of me has to slow down to gawk at. Maryland has got to be the rubbernecking capital of the world. Have we never seen a person change a tire before people? I have to admit though, the bumper to bumper traffic in the morning was usually where I got my best praise on. Pumpin' my gospel CD's...oh yes!... I gets my sho' nuff praise on.

Can you blame me? I've had to prepare myself and put on the full armor of God each and every time I enter that station now that Marguerite has been given the title of administrative assistant. Oh she's sitting in the same front desk receptionist spot, but her title has changed. I think she and Alvin are having a little affair because there is no way in the world he promoted her based on her work performance. Now she feels like she can tell everybody what is and is not in her job description. The girl actually had the nerve to print out a list and put it in everybody's mail slot. First of all who knew she could type, because I never saw the woman do anything but talk on the telephone. It was a two-paged single spaced document, but some of the highlights were...She wasn't going out for coffee runs anymore, she wasn't taking hand written messages, from here on out everybody's going straight to voicemail, and she wasn't working over time. Among the few things she was going to do, the number one thing was she was going to be extending her lunch from a half hour to an hour. As I walked into the front door, I was so grateful that God answered prayer because old girl was not at her desk to annoy me first thing in the morning. I might actually get some work done. As soon as I made it to my cubicle all of my joy quickly faded.

"Can I help you?" No this girl was not standing at my desk looking through my papers.

"Oh. Hey Renee…I was just checking to make sure I put a folder on your desk about some leads Alvin wanted you to follow up on. He's going to need completed assignments from you in a more timely manner." She said giving me a stern look with her arms folded over her fully running over cups.

"Excuse you. Who are you talking to? I complete all my assignments on time and before time, not that I need to clarify that with you." I said gently pushing her to the side so I could sit down.

"It seems like your taking your time with that Antwan Billows story. You know Alvin has wanted you to write an expose' about all the major police officers, and city leaders he did business with. That raid was months ago, and the file is still sitting on your desk." She tapped the file with the orange label that used to be hidden under a mound of work, but was now lying on the top of the stack. So she'd been rifling through my things?

"I'm sorry, I thought you were a receptionist, I didn't realize you were a private investigator." I said looking up at her with my eyes narrowed.

"Administrative Assistant." She hissed through clenched teeth.

"And I have this stations' interest at heart. If anybody else caught wind of all the information you have,

Alvin would be devastated, so write the story already." She said with a major attitude.

"Only a select few people know the information, so if anything got out, I'd know who leaked it. So if you want to go spreading information be my guest, but it might hurt your boyfriend's feelings." I said standing up to face her. I didn't like the feeling I was getting sitting at my desk with her looking down on me.

"I don't know what you are trying to imply, but I wouldn't be so bold with the accusations. I think it's more than a coincidence that you seemed to be able to dig up all this personal information about Antwan that nobody else could find, and that you share the same last name. I mean you were Renee Billows before you got married right?" With each word she was inching closer and closer to me.

"Maybe the bigger story might be why you let those officers kill your brother. Word around the station is that you were pretty psyched to see him…let me see…what did you say?… *'get what he deserves'*? Why didn't you call him and let him know they were after him? Little perfect Renee…can't make this go away can you?" She said standing so close I could see the glue on her fake eyelashes.

Well it's obvious that Julia let a little bit of our conversation in the van spill, I'll have to deal with her later. Right now Renee from the hood is taking issue with the attitude that is being thrown her way.

"I don't have anything to hide. You want to play this game and threaten to tell somebody that Antwan was my brother, then go ahead. But just know that your idle chatter means nothing to me. You can scandalize me. You might as well, because you've done it to just about everybody else. I don't know who hurt you, but you have to resolve that sista. As for me, I bless the Lord for showing me who I work with. Now if you don't mind, I have work to do." I said turning her around and pushing her out of my space.

"You alright over there?" Harold called over the fabric wall we shared on the front side of my cubicle.

"Honey I ain't got time to worry about that woman. I guess you heard what she was saying." I said walking around to sit in the chair beside his desk.

His space was crowded with pictures of his family. Even ones of him and Cynthia, despite the trouble they were going through. That's the kind of loyalty to family Harold possessed. I've had to ask the Lord on numerous occasions to forgive me for the tinge of jealousy I felt every time I looked at these pictures, or listened to him telling me a story about his close knit family. He was the oldest of five children. There were pictures of his whole family at reunions, on vacation, at graduations. Everybody looked so happy. There wasn't enough room on his tiny desk space so he had pictures pinned to all four sides of his cubicle, and on magnets that stuck to the cabinets above his desk. Some late nights when he wasn't working I would come and sit at his desk and just imagine that I had this kind of life with my brother and sister.

"It was hard not to hear. Marguerite just has one of those voices, even when she calls herself whispering." He chuckled a little. "If you want to talk, I am here, but you don't have to."

"What can I say? When I was growing up I had a brother and a sister. Life isn't always fair, my sister moved away with a man that abused her, and my brother got turned into a monster. I wish that he never got molested. I wish that he never felt like he had to prove himself. I wish that he knew I loved him so much. I would pray so many nights that he would acknowledge that I tried everything that I knew to do, to try and change his life. But he hated me…he absolutely hated me. I wish sometimes that God hadn't blessed me with so much instead of him." I started to cry. Harold handed me some tissues and opened the pocket bible that always sat on his desk.

"Now Renee, you know that we always talk about how God's favor isn't fair. You are where you are supposed to be because that is the will of God. It hasn't been all roses and rainbows for you, so don't start blaming God for blessing you. From what it sounds like your brother was not able to forgive. The bible says here that in order for your sins to be forgiven by God you must first forgive others that have wronged you. Now I know you think you did your brother wrong, but I know you Renee and if you say you loved him and tried to treat him with dignity then you've done your part. The bible says that God will treat you the way you've treated others. So boo on Marguerite and her triflin' self." He said closing the book and patting me on the back with a smile.

"Thank you, Harold. I really needed that. I have let this thing fester for too long. I've got a story to write that's been sitting on my desk." I said rising to stand.

"But listen, if you want me to do the story I can. I promise to be as respectful to your family as possible." He offered, and I'm confident he would have been capable of writing a wonderful story.

"No, I think the writing will be cathartic. It will help me to heal some old wounds to get this all out on paper. I'll let you read it before it goes to air."

"I would be honored." He said giving me a quick hug.

"Aren't you two cozy…and you have the nerve to talk about me and Alvin?" Marguerite sneered as she passed us on her way to the break room. I started to follow her so I could just get my beat down on…this girl don't know the Renee Billows from the hood. Harold put a hand on my shoulder to stop me.

"Girl, I'm gonna have to beat you over the head with this bible. That is a trick. Don't let her get the best of you." Harold said picking up his word. I know. I know. Love your enemies. I'm working on it Lord.

Chapter 38: Time Is On Our Side

§

If there was one time that our daughter Marie's bold mouth came it handy, it was during the night when one unsuspecting girl was waiting for Alex to put Morgan to bed. It was his custom that no matter where he was, or whom he happened to be with, he needed to make it home to read Morgan a bedtime story and tuck her into her pink princess bed. Alex had practically taken over the entire basement level, creating two bedroom spaces for both he and Morgan, a play area complete with miniature kitchen, a lounge area with a bookshelf and television for watching Veggie Tales and Barney, and a small area was set aside for prayer.

True to his word, Alex had indeed begun dating again as soon as the ankle monitor came off. He literally went out with the female officer that took the thing off of him at the probation office. She was sweet but he told me he dropped her after just two dates because she cursed too much and she smelled like smoke. He'd also begun going to Faith Tabernacle, the church his therapist Monica belonged to. You know ain't nothing like a single black man walking into a church, and the man claims to be saved. That's like wearing a "fresh meat" sign on your back. It was no wonder his next succession of dates came from the ladies in the singles ministry at the church. Both of his sisters and I feared he was going back to his womanizing ways.

"Alex, you need to stop going through all the ladies at church. People are going to think you're just a dog." Marie said chastising her brother as her and I sat on the bed with Morgan waiting for her dad to pick out a story from the overstuffed shelf.

"Everybody knows I'm not a dog. Now I can't help it if the ladies are hypnotized by my good looks." He joked pulling Morgan close to him so she could nestle in the crook of his arm.

"You've got to be kidding. Ain't nobody hypnotized. They probably talking about you trying to see which one of them can be your 'baby's momma'. You know how desperate these girls are. I should go upstairs and tell that chick waiting for you that she's wasting her time." She said making a move to get up from the bed.

"Now why would a saved woman, want to be my baby's momma? The young ladies at this church are working on being virtuous Marie, that's a word you need to look up in the dictionary." He joked.

"Wow…you really have been in the house too long. Those young girls at church are triflin' as momma says. You're just a trophy to them…and with the way you're acting you're playing right into their hands." She said pointing her finger at her brother.

"Marie, don't be rude to your brother. Now Alex, she does have a point. Be careful about how you're choosing who to date. These ladies all know each other, you don't want to look like the church pimp. There's nothing wrong with dating, but be mindful of these girls' feelings. Plus you don't want Morgan to be confused by the fact there are so many young ladies coming in and out of her dad's life." I said getting up from the bed to give him some daddy time with Morgan and to get Marie out of his space.

When we got upstairs I saw the young lady fixing her hair and adding some lipstick to her already too red lips. My mother would have said she looked like she fell and busted her mouth.

"See momma, that girl is just not right. Look at that tight sweater. She wouldn't wear that to church would she? I remember you told me I need to dress like I would if Jesus could see me wherever I was." Marie said, shaking her head like one of the church mothers at Calvary Zion Baptist where we worshipped every Sunday. She was a youth leader and the girl was just on fire for Christ.

"If you remember that, then why did I need to put back two of those little barely there mini-skirts you picked out when we went school shopping?" I asked.

"Momma I was gonna wear pants underneath of them, that's the style. Look I been living here long enough to know the rules about clothes. I know I look good, so I don't need to flaunt everything God gave me." She said, emphasizing that last sentence a little too loudly and directing it right into the living room.

"Well everybody doesn't have that same mentality. Go offer the young lady something to drink." I said pushing her toward the living room. I was trying to keep an eye on her because I could tell by the way she walked over to the girl, there was going to be trouble.

"You want something to drink?" She asked, with her hands on her hips.

"No…is Alex almost done?" The young lady asked, spritzing some perfume behind her ear, and dabbing a bit on her cleavage. The nerve of some people…It was all I could do not to go out there and take one of my chenille throw blankets to cover her up.

"Alex is spending time with his daughter right now. You got a problem with that?" Marie said getting a bit too close to the woman's face.

"I just wanted to know because we are on a date. I mean...he didn't say anything about how long he'd be, and I want to know if I need to go home or wait. I'm not tryin' to be here all night." She answered looking at her watch and matching Marie's attitude.

"Well it sounds like you need to just go on home." Marie said with her lips twisted and head sliding every which way on the top of her neck. I had to intervene before this turned ugly. Marie didn't want us using her former 'ghetto' name, but she sure could pull that former persona up at the drop of a dime.

"Excuse us..." I said grabbing Marie by the arm and pulling her back into the kitchen.

"Why must you pick a fight with every woman your brother brings home?"

"She's not right. I can tell it's burning her up that she has to wait for him. A good Christian lady would be like... *'I'll wait as long as it takes'*." She said putting on a super sweet voice and batting her eyelashes at me.

"Baby, this is a person Alex chose to date. He will make the decision if she's right or wrong. Go in there and apologize and then take yourself to bed." Just as she was preparing to go back in the room, Alex emerged from the basement.

"She's out like a light. I'll be taking Tiffany home in about an hour mom, is that alright?" Alex was well aware that since he was back under our roof he needed to abide by the curfew rules as well as the opposite sex rule. His dad and I still expected his company, no matter how old he was to be out of this house by 11:00 pm. And he knew he was expected to be back in this house by midnight.

"You might want to take her home now, she sounded like she was getting a little impatient a minute ago." Marie said through clenched teeth.

"Marie, girl...you are too much. Don't worry about Tiffany, she's great to talk too, but I know she's not the one for me. I hate to admit, but I was thinking about what you said while I was saying my prayers with Morgan. You might have been a little bit right. She's been dropping hints all night, and let's just say she really isn't leaving much to the imagination with that outfit." He said quietly enough not to hurt the poor girls feelings. She was still eagerly awaiting him, having pulled the hem of her skirt up a bit when she crossed her legs. Lord help. Alex playfully tapped his sister on the arm and gave her a hug, then went into the living room.

"Tiffany, thank you for your patience. My little girl is such a blessing to me, that I can't let her go to bed without giving thanks to God and treating her to one of her favorite stories, which on some nights seems to be all of the stories she's heard so far. She's the number one lady in my life."

"No problem, I was just enjoying talking to your sister." She said smiling so hard her cheeks had to be hurting.

"See now I know you lyin'...Marie? Having an enjoyable conversation?" He joked, just as Marie came and stood beside him. She nudged him in his back hard enough for him to loose his footing.

"Watch it boy! Anyway...Tanya...I mean Tiffany, I keep getting Alex's girlfriends mixed up! It was nice meeting you. Sorry if I said anything that made you feel uncomfortable. Ya'll have a good night." She said with the fakest smile on her face.

That Marie is something else. Had to get that last little dig in. What am I gonna do with her?

"I'm going to say good night as well, help yourselves to some of that pound cake in the fridge. Alex made it and it's fabulous." I said and followed Marie up to bed.

"Momma, you're not supposed to be telling her all the good things about Alex. Once she finds out he cooks, then she'll be expecting him to do that too."

"Oh hush and take yourself on to bed. I want to see what you've laid out to wear before you turn those lights out." I called after her as she hurried to her room.

"Yes, ma'am." She grumbled.

Satisfied with what, both my girls put out to wear…oh yes even the sixteen year old had to pass inspection…I climbed into bed.

Alex was falling right into the routine of things, I had to smile to myself when I heard him quietly open the front door and set the alarm downstairs. It was exactly 11:59. He climbed the stairs and peeked into my room.

"I know you're up. Just wanted to say I love you ma." And without waiting for me to reply he closed the door and headed downstairs. If I knew Alex, he'd be up half the night with the reading light on pouring over the bible his dad gave him the day he was released from the hospital. Look what a little time and faith in God has done for the Chase family. Thank you Lord, I thought to myself and drifted back to sleep.

Chapter 39: And It Does Not Yet Appear

§

"Now faith is the substance of things hoped for and the evidence of things not seen. I'm right in the bible for all my Sunday school folk and sanctified saints. Turn to Hebrews chapter eleven and verse one. Now watch me here…because too many of ya'll know the whole verse, but only operatin' on half the verse."

I had to agree with Rev. Bantum as I sat listening intently beside Alex and Morgan. The whole family was visiting Faith Tabernacle today because Alex and Morgan were going to be baptized. I knew a whole lot about acting on faith and this was just the word tailor made for me and my family.

"Amen…you sayin' something right there brother." Anthony piped in, waving his bible in the air.

"Yeah…it's a whole lot of ya'll hoping for God to answer your prayers, and hoping for a breakthrough, but where's the evidence that you believe it will come to pass?" He paused to wipe his brow with his handkerchief and take a sip of water.

"Hope without evidence is just a wish…and God ain't in the wishin' business. True faith means Lord I don't see no water, but I'm gonna go 'head and build this ark. True faith means Lord I'm too old to have me a baby, but I'm gonna go 'head and put this nursery together because you said it was so. Do I have anybody that can testify?" He paused as the congregation shouted *'amen'* and *'you preachin' pastor'*.

"True faith means I don't have the money for that brand new home you told me I was gonna get Lord, but let me start cleaning this house out I got right now, and start packing up for when you gonna move me!" He was using the cordless microphone now and had come to the front row of seats in the congregation.

"You betta say that!" I said, jumping up from my seat. All I could think of was how my faith had me preparing that room for Alex even when no one else could see it. I could see why Alex had grown so much in his spiritual walk under this man, he was able to teach as well as preach from the word of God.

"So it's time out for getting on your knees and hoping for things in 2002. God wants to see evidence that you believe in His promises, in His power. Our motto at Faith Tabernacle will be 'It's time for me to do in 2002'…be faithful over a few things so God can make you ruler over many! Somebody say amen!" He thundered into the microphone amidst shouts of amen's and hallelujah's.

I looked over to see Alex just as enthusiastic about the sermon as his father and I. He was able to finish scriptures the pastor quoted, and knew where to turn in the bible without looking at the table of contents whenever a scripture was interjected into the sermon. That's what I call a prayer answered. Thank you Lord. I think the whole Chase family, Shye and Marie included stood for the rest of the time Rev. Bantum was speaking. It was nothing like enjoying the word with my whole family. Across the aisle, Goodness was sitting with Mario and his family, who wanted to be here with us to celebrate this blessing.

The Conway's had been there for us through prayer, and even to sit with the children when we both were at the hospital with Alex. They knew the battle we had waged to get our son back and where just as proud as we were. Besides they were practically family...Goodness and Mario spent a lot of time together between our two houses. The two were officially boyfriend and girlfriend.

The time had come for the baptism. Alex was the only adult of the ten new members to be baptized. He told me that he knew he'd been baptized as a young boy at our church, but felt in order for him to truly be reborn into the person that God wanted him to be he needed to be baptized again.

Both he and Morgan received an African-inspired baptism. They wore matching white and gold kente cloth attire. We stood proudly by as Alex held up his daughter to be presented to the church as a new sister in Christ. He cried and smothered her with kisses. I cried so much it was nearly impossible for me to tell if the camera was in focus because of all my tears. Anthony had to take the camera so we'd have some memories of our son re-dedicating his life to Christ. After the ceremony Rev. Bantum made his way over to where we stood.

"Mr. and Mrs. Chase, it is indeed a pleasure to finally meet you. You've raised a fine boy. I've had counsel with this young man in my office and he's told me so much about you." He said patting Alex on the shoulder.

"Uh. Oh...none of it was true." Anthony joked.

"You have nothing to worry about Mr. Chase. He's done nothing but sing your praises. He knows that prayin' parents brought his butt in off those streets." Rev. Bantum said with his booming voice, giving Alex a stern look.

"Now I've got to get back to my office to prepare for second service, but all I've got to say is your patience and faith in the Almighty is paying off. The bible teaches us that if you train up a child...no matter if they stray, they will come back. He's a wonderful father to this little one here, and he's been a blessing to the young boys here as a mentor. And it does not yet appear…He won't hear of it, but I know God has a great work for Alex in this church." He said putting his arm around Alex's shoulder and giving him a hearty shake.

"Yeah, Alex knows it too, and once he gets tired enough, he'll stop running from it. God bless you Rev. Bantum we'll definitely visit again." I said giving him a hug.

"Please do and give your pastor Rev. Fowler my condolences on the passing of her mother."

"We certainly will." Anthony said giving him a firm handshake.

"Well…looks like you better start preparing some sermons young man." He said turning back to Alex.

"Dad…you are real funny. Just because I got work to do, doesn't mean I'll be preaching." Alex said scooping up Morgan and busying himself getting her dolls and coloring books together. He always began to fidget whenever we mentioned him becoming a preacher.

"Look, I don't care what he does…I'm hungry. Can we go get something to eat already?" Marie asked.

"That sounds like a good idea. Morgan sweetie what do you want to eat?" Alex sounded relieved now that the subject had changed to food.

"I want some chicken." She said cheerfully. Just like her dad, she could eat chicken a million different ways.

We headed out the door, stopping every few feet for Alex to say hello, or get congratulations and well wishes from all the single young women at the church. There were even a few church mothers clamoring to kiss him on the cheek. He took it all in stride. This was not the same man that walked into this church this morning, and I was grateful for the change.

Chapter 40: Look At God

§

"Well, well, well…if it isn't Rev. Gansta!" Nick said giving his brother a hard time. We were all standing at the baggage claim area when he came up behind us, grabbing his brother in a tight embrace and rubbing his knuckles on the top of his head, like they used to do when they were younger. Although Anthony and I had been able to visit Nick and Laurie from time to time, the kids had never been able to come to Ohio. We decided to take a family trip to let them see where the oldest Chase boy called home. Nick was delighted to have us all. He said he had a big surprise to tell us and wouldn't give up anything the whole ride from the airport.

"Are we there yet?" Marie called from the back of the huge SUV Nick was driving. As one of the top young, black, corporate lawyers in Ohio, God had blessed his family with three vehicles, a spacious home, and a membership to an exclusive golf club. Anthony couldn't wait to go out with his boys tomorrow morning. They had a 7:30 am tee time.

"Girl, hold your horses. We'll be there soon. Laurie has prepared a fantastic lunch for you guys…she's trying out new recipes she wants to include on her menu list." Nick said proudly.

Laurie was a fantastic cook. After she had the baby her career path took a completely different turn. While she was home with the baby she began baking, which turned into her selling cookies as a fundraiser for her church, which turned into her taking orders for special occasions, which turned into Heavenly Creations Bakery.

In the last year she'd begun to branch out into light fare, then full course meals. She and Nick became business partners and opened another location called Heavenly Creations Eatery that was listed in the local papers as having 'the best soul-food served with a classy touch'. My guess was Nick's big surprise would involve us getting a chance to dine at this new restaurant. He described it to me the last time he called home and I was able to look at elegant shots taken of the interior that he had posted on the restaurant's website.

"For real though, I'm not trying to be jumping on the bandwagon with Marie, but we do need to be getting to your house very quickly or at least stopping at a bathroom. I'm working on having this girl completely potty trained and we haven't seen a potty in about two hours." Alex said with a squirming Morgan sitting beside him.

"Daddy, I got to go pee pee." She said as if on cue.

"Hold on Morgan…Uncle Nick's house is just a few minutes away." Nick said putting the pedal to the metal. I'm sure he didn't want any accidents in his spanking new truck. We made it to the house in record time. Alex and Morgan were the first out…he was holding her under his arm like a football and racing toward the door with her legs and arms bouncing every which way. He nearly bowled over a very pregnant Laurie.

"What is this? Nick you didn't say anything about Laurie expecting again!" I shouted running to her and giving her a big hug.

"Surprise!" They both shouted together.

"How could you keep this from us? How far along are you?" I asked rubbing her stomach gently.

"Well I've really had a tough time of it momma Renee. We weren't so sure the babies would do well so we just wanted to keep it to ourselves." She said smiling.

"Wait! Did you say babies? Are ya'll having twins?" Goodness asked. I hadn't even picked up on the fact that she'd said babies instead of baby.

"That's really the surprise mom! Laurie and I are having twins. And if she knows what's good for her she'll go back in and put her feet up." Nick said turning his wife back toward the door and guiding her into the house. After the truck was unloaded and Alex made it out of the bathroom with a dry Morgan, the kids went to the back yard to enjoy the swimming pool and basketball court. Anthony and I settled on the sofa to listen to Nick and Laurie tell us about the struggles they'd been having with the pregnancy.

"Of course at first we were so excited. We both talked about wanting to try again after Nicky turned one. It took a little longer to get pregnant this time. We visited the doctor and she said everything was fine and we should just be patient." Laurie was speaking so softly while she told us the story.

"Ma, you know we just started praying. I took some time off of work, the Chadwick's kept Nicky for us for a week so we could just relax and concentrate on each other. With in a little time Laurie took a test and it was positive. But then she had so much pain and started to bleed so we went to the hospital and found out there was a problem with her becoming dilated too early." Nick said squeezing his wife's hand.

"Oh no…I'm so sorry you had to go through that." I said

"Well after that I was put on strict bed rest." Laurie said rubbing her stomach in slow circles.

"Which if you ask me, she's not doing a good job at." Nick piped in.

"Well it's kind of hard when you have a two year old running around. Plus I've been busy trying to get new ideas for the business, and don't forget that dinner party. Ya'll we had a request to host a huge birthday party for one of the Cincinnati Bengals players!"

"But we have staff for that…Mrs. Chadwick even offered to stay with us to help out, but Laurie wouldn't have it. I married my mother, a woman that tries to be everything to everybody. She was on her feet for more than ten hours that night. I finally made her sit down, and she made one of the waiters get her the office chair with wheels on it so she could still wheel around the kitchen making sure every plate was just right before it went out." Nick said shaking his head.

"It's a disease that you have got to get a cure for Laurie…trust me. You only do harm to yourself." Anthony said looking right at me.

"I think my mom passed the disease on to me." Laurie joked.

"Well, now that we know…you better believe we will keep those little ones' and you in our prayers. Now tell me how I can help you get lunch together, I don't want you on your feet for the rest of the time we are here." Just as I said that I could hear my little grandson Nick Jr. who we called Nicky, jabbering through the baby monitor.

"Well…if you don't mind getting the baby for me…that would be a great help." I made my way up the winding staircase to the second floor and opened the door to Nicky's room. He had the most pleasant smile on his face as he stood up in the crib to greet me. No matter how much time passed in between my visits, he always seemed happy to see me and his granddaddy. He raised his arms for me to lift him up. As soon as I placed him on the floor he was running to his toy box to get a ball to throw. The boy loved all kinds of balls and you had to be on your p's and q's because whether you liked it or not, he was gonna throw one at you and fully expected for it to be thrown back.

"How's my favorite little Nicky boy!?" I said getting down on my knees to play with him. We tossed the ball back and forth a few times and then he was off running in another direction. As soon as he hit the hallway he got to the stairs and tried to maneuver the latch on the safety gate. The boy was too much.

"Come on ya'll it's time to eat!" Anthony yelled outside and up the stairs. There was a mad stampede to the table with Marie in the lead. Laurie had outdone herself with a spread of Creole shrimp and cheese grits, fried and baked fish, sweet potato casserole with marshmallows, and fresh turnip greens with cornbread. She even made spicy grilled chicken and fresh vegetables for Alex who was putting us all to shame with his healthy lifestyle. He did have to give in though when we brought out the peach cobbler and vanilla ice cream. For the rest of the night we played games around the sofa so Laurie could join in. Being the protective husband he was, Nick carried her up the stairs to bed when she started dozing off right in the middle of all the noise.

"She's been wiped out lately." He said once he returned back to the living room.

"Between all of the tests she's had to have and going back and forth to the hospital…she just hasn't had a break. After her last stay about two weeks ago, she left the hospital and went right to the restaurant. I didn't find out she'd left against medical advice until I was at the nurse's station asking why she wasn't in her room! I really worry about her."

"Like I told your mom so many nights when she was up worrying about Alex, if you pray…you've got to stop worrying." Anthony said giving Nick a pat on the back.

"I hear you dad." Nick said solemnly.

"Well I know one thing ya'll need to be worried about..." Alex started to say as he got up with a sleeping Morgan in his arms.

"What?" Nick and Anthony said together with confused looks on their faces.

"How bad ya'll gonna get beat on that golf course by yours truly tomorrow." Alex answered laughing.

"Boy take that child to bed and get some sleep yourself because I think you're starting to hallucinate!" Nick said.

"In all honesty we are all probably a little jet lagged. It's been a long day, so kids let's call it a night. Get yourselves in the bed so we can get up and out early tomorrow." I said amidst groans and pleas to stay up a little later. There was so much space in this house that Alex and Shye had their own guest room with a bathroom attached and a video game unit already hooked up to the television. The girls shared a room with a walk-in closet the size of each of their rooms back home, Morgan was sleeping in a big kid bed that was in her cousin Nicky's room, and Anthony and I had a spacious suite all to ourselves complete with sun deck and a steam shower.

"Look at God." He whispered into my ear as we lay snuggling with each other.

"Ain't He just alright? All that He continues to bless Nick and Laurie with, it's just beyond anything you'd ever imagine. And now two more little babies!" I turned to look Anthony in the eyes.

"I know...two more children for you to spoil and go overboard at the store buying clothes for." He laughed kissing me on the lips.

"I spoil you and you love it." I teased.

"Well you my woman, that's what you supposed to do." He joked trying to sound like a cave man.

"But in all seriousness, I'm more than blessed by all that God is doing for our son. I know they've had a tough time with this pregnancy, but I also know that God is working it out even as we pray."

"He is doing something. We just have to wait and see what his plans are for those babies. Now good night babe."

Chapter 41: God Is With Us

§

For the next ten days, all we could do was look at God and all He'd done for Nick and his little family. Laurie was doing her best to keep her feet up, and if we went anywhere outside of the house, Nick made her get in a wheelchair so he could push her around. We had planned on being in town for four more days and had a lot more family activities we wanted to do, but Laurie had begun to feel fatigued and had increased pain so we decided to stay close to home for the remainder of the stay. The Chadwick's were over on this particular night and Melvin and Nick were paired against me and Anthony in a fierce Spades competition.

"I learned a long time ago, if I wanted to stay married to that man, we couldn't play no card games together." Marla said as she watched the game from a seat beside her husband.

"Oh go on Marla, it wasn't that bad. You just didn't like always loosing to me." Melvin joked, giving her a peck on the cheek.

"No, I didn't like always letting you win." She laughed raising her hand for me to give her a high-five.

"Nick how many books you think you got there son?" Melvin said looking very serious.

"Better make it good, because I know I got at least six or more." I said bluffing. Anthony looked at me so he could pick up any signals. We were great partners when we put our minds to it. Right before Nick could answer we heard a loud crash come from upstairs.

"Help me! Nick please come up here! Please…Oh God no!" Laurie was screaming and crying at the top of the staircase. We all jumped up as soon as we heard her and followed Nick to the stairs. The breath left my body when I got to the large entryway and looked up at her leaning against the banister. She was standing in her nightgown that was stained with blood.

"I felt something…a sharp pain. Oh Nick! I feel like the babies are coming! Please God no!" She was crying and collapsed into Nick's arms as soon as he made it to where she was standing.

"Mommy, what's going on?" Goodness and Marie had come out of their room when they heard all the commotion.

"Girls, go back into the room, take Morgan and Nicky. We need to get Laurie to the hospital." I said pushing them toward the room before the younger children came out to see what was happening.

"Baby, calm down now. You just lay down. Get her to the bed Nick, I'm calling 911." Melvin said as he went to the telephone on the bedside table in the master bedroom. Nick picked Laurie up and carried her to the bed, which had also been stained with blood.

"Laurie, listen to me…Just breath slowly. Slow your breathing and concentrate on relaxing. Help is on the way." I heard myself saying. I was at the bedside holding her hand and didn't even know how I'd gotten there.

"Father in heaven please have mercy on my baby. Lord help her right now, Father. We don't know what's happening right now Lord, but we gonna put it all in your

hands." Marla had begun to pray on her knees right at Laurie's bedside.

Even though it seemed like an eternity, the ambulance arrived in less than five minutes. Laurie was loaded onto the stretcher and whisked away with sirens blaring. After leaving instructions for Goodness and Marie to watch the younger ones, Nick, Anthony, Alex and I got into Nick's truck and raced to the hospital. Alex was going to stay behind, but his brother begged him to come.

"I need you man. I can't do this without you." Nick said with tears welling in his eyes. We got to the hospital just as she was being taken to the back surrounded by nurses and emergency room staff. It was just like an episode of ER with doctors and nurses shouting in frantic voices. Nick was allowed to go back to be by her side. Alex asked where the chapel was and went off by himself to pray. Anthony and I just held each other in the waiting room.

"I can't even imagine what she's going through right now." I thought out loud.

The Chadwick's ran in a little after we got there. All the commotion had made Nicky very upset so they wanted to stay and reassure him that mommy would be o.k. before they left for the hospital.

"Any word?" They both said in unison.

"Not yet. Nick is back there now." Anthony said getting up so Marla could have a seat.

The ER waiting room was crowded. Some folks were stretched across two or three seats sound asleep, so seating was scarce. I was getting up to offer Melvin my seat as well. Just out of respect since my momma always told me to respect my elders.

"No Renee you keep that seat warm for me, I'm gonna go to the chapel for a bit." He said and walked off in the direction we'd seen Alex going in not a few minutes before.

"You wish you could just take all the pain for 'em don't you?" Marla said after a long silence.

"I mean, this is my baby…I wouldn't wish this kind of thing on nobody, but this is my baby. What can a mother do when something like this happens?" She said shaking her head. I didn't know if she wanted a response. At this moment I was really at a loss for words. I just wanted to see Nick come out of that door and tell us something about what was going on.

****

It had been a few hours since they'd gone back there. Anthony and Melvin had been to the cafeteria and back. Alex had checked on Morgan at least five times and we were all getting a little concerned. Just when I was prepared to ask the nurses if I could go in the back, Nick emerged though the double doors that led back into the patient care area. I could tell his eyes were red and swollen.

"Honey?" I walked over to him. He looked like he was about to collapse, he was staggering over to us.

"We lost one." He cried. And we all gathered around him to hold him up.

"They tried everything they could, but it was too late. He just wasn't able to hold on."

"But look at God, that means one little one is yet holding on…What's going to happen to the other baby?" Melvin asked always able to see the praise through the pain.

"They are going to try to keep Laurie here until its safe for that baby to be born. They are arranging a room for her now on the high-risk floor. Momma Chadwick she was asking for you. Let me take you back to her right now. She needs her momma." He said turning to Marla.

"Thank you for bein' such a strong man for my little girl. Ya'll gonna get through this. You mark my words. Now let me get to my baby girl." The two disappeared behind the doors together, with in a few brief moments Nick returned. He walked up to his brother and whispered something in his ear.

"Mom, I'm going to the chapel with Nick for a little while. If ya'll want to go home we can get a ride back with the Chadwick's." This was a scene I'd prayed about many nights. To see both my boys locked in a brotherly embrace headed off to pray, but I never thought it would be after an event like this. We just don't know.

****

"We just don't know." I found myself repeating to Shye and Marie after we got back to the house. We always wanted the children to feel open to ask us any questions, which at times left Anthony and I in some very uncomfortable conversations, but the children trusted that we would be honest with them. Right now they were both wanting to know how this could have happened to their sister-in-law.

"Mama, why would God let something so horrible happen to Laurie? She is such a good person, she's a good woman. I mean you are always saying that." Marie asked.

"Honey, just because you are a good person, does not mean that painful things won't happen to you. This is not a punishment for something that Laurie did. Death is a part of life. Everything that lives must die." That sounded pretty good Renee, thank you Lord for those words.

"But I thought you said because we accept Jesus that we have eternal life, so we don't really die right?" Shye asked joining in the conversation.

"Well the body that we have dies, but our spirit does live on eternally if we've accepted Christ. God has a plan for every life and we just don't know what that plan is until He reveals it."

"So His plan could be for somebody to live a very short life?" Marie asked sounding more confused.

"Lifetimes are measured in different ways. Some of us will live very long and others will not, as I said we just don't know. But what I do know is that God has kept one little baby in Laurie's stomach for a reason. So we have to thank God for that miracle and continue to give Him glory for what He will do in that little life." I said giving each one a kiss on the forehead, this was my unspoken signal that mama didn't have any more answers so the conversation was over.

"I guess I'll understand it better when I'm as old as you are." Marie said laughing.

"Thanks a lot!" I laughed.

The Chadwick's brought Alex home a few hours later. Nick had already called to say he'd be staying overnight with Laurie at the hospital.

For the next three days we were there, we visited Laurie and brought her lots of goodies to snack on. I made sure all of the laundry was folded and made an attempt at cooking something in her state-of-the-art kitchen, so Nick would have some meals for a while. As a family we decided it would be a good idea for Laurie's parents to keep Nicky while she was in the hospital. This way Nick could go to work and stay at the hospital as much as he wanted. We packed up our things and left on our way back to Baltimore.

"I'm sorry we all have to say good bye this way." Nick said sadly.

"Darling we had a wonderful time. God is still in the healing and blessing business. He'll continue to comfort you through all of this. Just keep your eyes on Him." I said, and we all hugged and went our separate ways, Nick back to the hospital to sit with Laurie, and the rest of the Chase's to the terminal to board the plane.

After we left, Laurie remained in the hospital with her bed angled so that her feet were higher than her head for almost six weeks. Despite her loss, she was in good spirits. In a video, Nick sent to us…She laughed and smiled and made fun of her awkward positioning saying she felt like the blood was rushing to her head. Two days after we got the video, Nick called to say that Emmanuel Jordan Chase (EJ for short) had been born. He was a healthy five pounds and eleven ounces and was eating like a champ. Emmanuel…God with us…what an awesome name.

Chapter 42: Rejoice In The Lord Always

§

Yes I had become that grandparent. You know the one that whips out the mile long sheet of wallet-sized pictures of their grandchildren taken every two weeks since birth. I was sitting with my sister-friends at another one of my cancer group meetings and I just couldn't resist. We'd renamed ourselves The Soulful Sister Survivors. Today we were meeting at Tanya's house to give her a pep talk. She was trying to back out of her challenge. She and Charlene were the last pair to complete one of Ms. Sylvia's adventures. With all of our hectic schedules and just the basic chaos of life, it had taken us almost two years to coordinate time for all of us to do what we picked. It took Deanna and I a few months to even train for our race before we completed it, and we were going right down the list in order. So here we were at the final challenge and Tanya's feet were getting cold.

"I don't care what nobody says, black folk was not meant to bungee jump." Tanya protested munching on chips and salsa.

"Look girl, you were the one that promised Ms. Sylvia we were going to finish her list. Now I don't want to jump to my death either, but we pulled it so we gotta do it." Charlene said.

"O.k. that whole death part is not helping me none." Tanya whined.

"You guys have been taking practice jumps. You know the crew has taken all the precautions...I'd do it for you, but I already did my challenge." Sherrie piped in to offer support.

"Oh...yeah, some challenge, rock climbing. If you ask me, you and Tammy got the easiest one." Tanya said

"You try climbing a wall with a fresh manicure honey, now that's a challenge." Sherrie said holding up a newly French-manicured hand.

"Yeah, ya'll remember she had to get hoisted back down because she thought she broke a nail, it is always drama with you girl." Tammy said.

"Drama is my life, don't hate on a diva." She said laughing.

"O.k. so back to me and my last will and testament." Tanya started. "I don't have no money in the bank, but ya'll can have my Earth Wind and Fire collection if something happens to me." We all busted out laughing.

"Everything is going to be fine. Monique and Stephanie made it through hang gliding, Joyce and Madison entered the amateur horse racing competition and finished in one piece." I said trying to ease her nerves. We'd all been pretty skeptical about completing each of the challenges, but it wasn't nothing that prayer and faith couldn't fix.

"Dead last...and hanging onto the reigns for dear life, but it's the effort that counts!" Madison interjected slapping five to her partner in the race, Joyce.

"Ya'll are fools. But let me just say that God has not given us a spirit of fear. I'm sure this is easy for me to say because I'm not jumping off a bridge tomorrow, but girls I know it's gonna be o.k. Besides...you have to live so you can have you some grandbabies like these cutie pies. Did I show ya'll this one? It's the first time Emmanuel held his bottle by himself. Oooh…and this was when Nicky made a basket on the big-boy basketball court, and this is my Morgan girl all dressed up for Sunday…"

"Lord, stop her before we be here all night." Tanya joked. We spent the rest of the time eating and getting caught up on our latest lab results, whose turn it was to get a mammogram, and what we'd be wearing tomorrow at the big event.

"Well I'm going to be wearing this." Deanna said, unzipping the jacket to the warm-up suit she was wearing. Underneath she had on a pink tee. We initially thought it was one of the symbolic pink shirts that practically every store was carrying in honor of breast cancer awareness. It wasn't until she stood up that we realized the shirt had a large fuchsia pink arrow pointing down with a caption that said *"My Mommy's A Survivor"*. Everybody screamed.

"Oh my goodness! How far along are you?" This was becoming a familiar phrase to me.

"I am still in my first trimester, but everything is going very well. Michael and I are thrilled. Can you believe it… me? Having a baby?" Deanna said beaming.

"Of course I can believe it. And this baby will have some brothers and sisters too. Congratulations girlfriend." I said giving her a hug. We all joined in the group hug followed by almost an hour of prayer for our sisters that were preparing to jump, and for our sister that was going to become a mother.

The next day, wearing our matching pink tees and jeans, we stood looking up as Tanya and Charlene stepped up to the edge of the platform designed for them to jump from. They were part of a group of thirty people the girls' rounded up to take donations and Jump For a Cure.

There were hundreds of well wishers standing with us. When it was Tanya's turn we all held hands and our breaths. We had to double over in laughter though, because she screamed the whole way down. Charlene did her jump like a pro, we didn't hear a peep from her until she was safely lowered in the boat that awaited them.

"We did it!" She shouted, with her arms raised above her head. "We did it…Thank you Lord!" She hugged Tanya as they waited for the last few people to jump. They raised over $10,000.00 for the cause.

****

"Surprise!" We all yelled when Deanna came through the front door. She thought she was coming to my house for another Soulful Survivor meeting six months after her announcement, but she walked…well more like waddled, the girl had put on fifty pounds and was absolutely glowing, right into her baby shower.

"You guys are sneaky…but I love you!" She said wiping tears from her eyes. She was even more surprised when she looked around the room and realized her husband and his family were there and so was her mother and sisters from North Carolina.

"How did ya'll keep this a secret? Momma when did you get here?" She went around hugging everyone and getting pats on the belly. Anthony took Michael and all of the men outside in the backyard to play volleyball and keep an eye on the grill. He'd set up horseshoes so Deanna's southern relatives would feel at home. From the loud shouts and cheers I heard coming from the backyard; he'd succeeded.

Her family pulled out all the stops. The child got more gifts than one baby could ever need in a lifetime. I had to marvel at how so much had changed since I was raising infants. Who knew babies needed warm wipes to clean their poopy behinds? Bottles looked different and so did car seats. And every big name designer was making miniature clothes for infants. This baby was going to be dressed honey. Alex gave Deanna and Michael a baby's first bible, and a gospel lullaby CD.

"This has been such a blessing to me and Mike. We can't say thank you enough for all the support and well wishes, and the wonderful gifts. When I was diagnosed, and knew I needed to have my breasts removed, I didn't think that I'd be a desirable woman, let alone a wife and mother. But that is because I didn't see myself the way that God saw me. Today when I look around and see my husband and all of these things, which are the tangible evidence of His vision for my life I am so overwhelmed. I will rejoice in the Lord always. That He would choose me to bless this way." There was not a dry eye in the house. Of course Anthony claimed he had smoke in his eye from the grill, but I knew he was feeling something, because everything Deanna said, could have come out of our mouths as well.

Chapter 43: Feel The FIRE!

§

There was no denying the real tears that streamed down Anthony's face as Goodness stood at the podium giving the senior speech at her high school graduation. She was class valedictorian with a perfect 4.0 GPA. At sixteen going on seventeen she was the youngest member of her graduating class and she was headed to Spelman College as a Biology Pre-Med major. She looked so confident standing at that podium. A far cry from the young lady that was sitting with her head in her hands many a night preparing for this day. It was all I could do to keep myself from reaching into the waste paper basket and reading one of the crumpled up pages she'd discarded with an exasperated sigh.

"Ugh! I can't do this. Why did I have to be valedictorian? I think I'm just going to get up and say 'way to go everybody…congratulations' and then just sit down." She said ripping another piece of paper to shreds. We were going to have quite the bag ready for recycling this week. Alex, who not only changed his eating habits, his praying habits, and his dating habits, also became more aware of the environment and had everybody on a recycling kick. He was just changing all the way around and I was not going to complain.

"What's wrong, you got writers block?" I asked.

"No, I actually have so much to say, I can't figure out what to cut out. Mommy I would have never thought I'd be here in this space, doing this right now. I knew I was gonna get good grades. I really didn't have anything else to do, but throw myself into school before we came to live here. But to have the opportunity to go to college…I'm so grateful for what you've done. And now I can't even figure out how to give you thanks, and say the wonderful things about my teachers, and my friends, and Rev. Fowler, and Rev. Tracey…who was always telling me my latter would be greater…." Her voice was beginning to tremble.

"I get the picture baby, you don't have to include me in your speech. I don't need accolades. Baby, I was being obedient. Just put down all those words, and then try to cut out what you think you won't need."

"There are more words than I can write, there is just no way to cut it down, but I have so much pressure to do so. Plus in addition to only having ten minutes to speak, they said I can't mention anything about God because they don't want to alienate anybody. My guidance counselor warned me that they'd turn off the microphone if I started talking about religion too much." She sighed and threw up her hands.

"Are you serious?" Now that one had me stumped. If the President can say God bless America in a speech, then my child should be able to give Him a shout out too.

"Yeah, they know how I am…the prayer group in the mornings, saying my grace at lunch, not cursing and acting a fool, they know I'm different than most of the kids at that school. And I don't bite my tongue, telling them the difference is Jesus. It makes a few people squirm, and I get funny looks, but so what!"

"I know that's right! I wish I had your confidence when I was your age. I'm not one to say go against the rules, but if you want to give some honor and praise to God, then you go right on ahead baby." I got up and picked up all the paper around her chair to dump in the recycling bin and went on about my business.

We hadn't talked about the speech anymore because she wanted it to be a surprise. So far I was impressed. She mentioned that I inspired her to want to be the first person to find a cure for breast cancer. She encouraged her class that this was going to be a year of new beginnings for them. So far so good, no microphones being adjusted one way or the other.

"And in closing, I challenge you class of 2002 to be all that you were created to be. I have a mother and father that prayed for me and have instilled a belief in me, that all things are possible. I will go on and I will have victory in my future endeavors because of my strong faith. May God bless you and keep you!" She did it. She made it through her entire inspirational speech without being cut off, and even put God right in there at the end.

The crowd in the auditorium clapped and stood up when she was finished. When her name was called to walk across that stage, we broke all rules of etiquette, screeching and whistling, standing to our feet and waving signs we'd made the night before. I know we spent at least an hour taking all different kind of shots at the podium from all angles after the ceremony was over, we got dirty looks from some of the white folk. I didn't care. I was due some graduation overindulgence, since I hadn't had a chance to attend one with Alex.

As we drove home that night from a fabulous dinner at The Cheesecake Factory, I told her that her faith would definitely be tested once she was so far from home. Anthony commented that his faith was going to be tested since he knew Mario would be right across the street at Morehouse College Majoring in Chemistry.

"I tell you what…the only Chemistry he should be studying, better be found in them books." He said at the dinner table as we discussed the fact that they would both be going to Atlanta.

"What did you tell me a few years ago?… *'All we can do is teach them the right way and pray they make the right choices'*…didn't you say that?" I knew he didn't want to hear his words thrown back at him right now, but as we now snuggled under the covers on the sofa it gave me a laugh.

"Yeah, I might have, but that was when we were talking about our boys. Girls are a whole different thing. I know these college boys got one thing on their mind. I used to be one of them." He said wiping sweat from his forehead.

"Don't get so worked up. You know Goodness, and she knows the Lord. Whatever she does when she is not around us, we can't influence, only He can." I said pulling the covers up and pointing to the ceiling.

"I know you're right but it's hard. Are you sure you don't want to move the whole family down to Atlanta? They got plenty of news for you to write about down there, and the cost of living is wonderful. We'd get three times the house down there for what we're paying up here." He was really sounding like he was serious.

"Now you didn't want to up and move to Ohio when Nick left did you?"

"No, but a certain someone…who shall remain nameless, was checking the real estate websites for available homes in the area." He said pointing to me. He was right. When Nick first left I missed him so much. He was my first-born baby boy. A momma always has a soft spot for that first baby boy.

"O.k. so now we're even. I accepted that Nick wasn't going to be close, and you have to do the same with Goodness. Don't forget we got two more in the nest."

So here we were now on the eve of her leaving for college and the two youngest were taking it pretty hard. We'd said our prayers as a family and had a meeting to discuss the move. They had been the three musketeers for all of their lives, and now one of them was leaving.

"I don't want to see any tears Shye-Shye. Marie, you know you've been wanting to move into my room for the longest time so cut the crying. This is a happy day. Look where God brought us from."

"It's just not going to be the same without you here to yell at us about absolutely nothing." Shye said half joking, half moping on the sofa beside us.

"All I know is that while I'm gone, I better not hear no bad news about ya'll giving mommy Nay a hard time. You hear me? Now give me a hug and get into bed, we got a long ride ahead of us." Goodness said gathering her brother and sister in her arm. They were both taller than her now, but she still commanded respect from them.

"For real I can have your room?" Marie said when they began making their way up stairs.

"You might want to ask the owners of the house. Maybe I wanted to rent your room out to earn some extra money." I said joking.

"Aw. Momma…why can't I have Goodness's room?" Marie said pouting again. It was good to have her back to her old self.

"You can have my old room." Shye offered. He'd moved downstairs when Alex and Morgan moved into their own apartment a few weeks ago. Alex had taken a job as a full time youth counselor at Faith Tabernacle and they were helping to pay part of his rent in addition to giving him a modest salary. Anthony helped Shye make the space into a boys' paradise. They were making sleeker models of those gargantuan screen televisions, so he was finally able to get one with surround sound, down stairs in that basement after all. He had converted one of the bedrooms to tech central with a computer and video games, and had turned the lounge area into a mini workout gym complete with free weights and a punching bag. At thirteen Shye was growing into a handsome man, and was starting to notice the looks from the young ladies in his class, so he enjoyed the time downstairs with dad pumping iron.

"Don't be smart boy, don't nobody want to sleep in that smelly room." Marie shouted.

"Alright you two, that's enough. Go to bed." I warned. They went their separate ways to their rooms with one last glare at one another.

The next morning Alex called to pray with his sister over the telephone. Ms. Carla, Traniece's mom, offered to keep Morgan so Alex could go with us, but he was still being very protective about the time she spent with the other side of her family.

Traniece had been released from prison, but went right back to her old ways. Her mother tried for a few short weeks to let her stay with her, but she was completely addicted to drugs and began using more and more frequently. It got to the point where I'd see her half-dressed walking the streets looking to score when I was out on my ride alongs with law enforcement.

Julia had thought it not robbery to point her out to me more times than I'd like to mention. A few times I pulled over to try and get her to go with me to a shelter, or program but she refused. I was working on a story recently, about the increasing number of women that where becoming addicted to the crack form of cocaine, when I stumbled over her lying on the street. At first glance I thought she was dead, but after shaking her and screaming her name, she slowly opened her eyes. I called Alex as soon as I got home.

"See mom, and she wants visitation. I can't trust her. I'm going to pray for her, but I don't want my child with her." I can't say that I blamed him.

So we went on without him, knowing he'd be praying for us the whole way. We enjoyed a few great days of orientation and got a chance to meet other wonderful families. It was nice to have the Conway's down in Atlanta getting Mario oriented to become a Morehouse Man. We went to dinner together almost every night, and attending evening inspirational services at The Martin Luther King Cultural Center. The final day came for families to leave. It was the first time I'd seen Mario cry. It might have had something to do with the little private conversation I saw him and Anthony having not too long before we all got back on the road.

"What did you say to that poor boy?" I asked him when we'd found our way to the highway.

"Just some words of encouragement for the young man…I'm not as bad as you make me out to be." He said with is eyes focused on the road.

"Yeah, right!" Marie said from the back seat.

****

Goodness promised to call at least once a week and she kept her promise. Most of the time she called two or three times a week, so I just enjoyed it, because I knew it was Freshman year and I might not get this luxury of talking to her so much once she got hip to the fact that she didn't need her old mother. We got a chance to visit her over the Thanksgiving break and she came home for a month at Christmas.

"What…they don't have washing machines at your school?" Anthony joked the last time she was here. She hadn't used one suitcase, but had all of her clothes stuffed in enormous laundry bags.

"All of these need to be washed?" I asked in disbelief, as he came and dumped one bag after the other at my feet. I'd begun a load of clothes thinking I was doing her favor, but at this rate, I'd have to have my meals delivered to the laundry room.

"Ya'll are real funny. You know how I am about my clothes. And if you just think about sharing a washing machine with a whole dorm full of girls then you wouldn't be making fun of me. Besides, don't you enjoy being a part of my college experience? Kids bringing home laundry, and loading up on home cooked meals is what it's all about…right?" She said throwing another bag on the mounting pile.

"I thought paying the tuition was enough college experience for me." Anthony joked.

"Thank you daddy." She said in that sugary sweet way that melted her dad's heart. She gave him a hug and a kiss and was off in a different direction. Most likely to see what Mario was doing, as if they didn't just spend twelve hours together driving from Atlanta to Baltimore.

In all honesty, we really didn't have that much financial obligation…God had blessed Goodness with a full academic scholarship. We were responsible for room and board, books, and making sure she had spending money. We wanted her to be able to concentrate on her studies in her freshman year, and not worry about having to work to earn extra cash. Anthony made sure she had money for food, clothing and movies.

When she turned twenty-one she'd have a substantial nest egg to supplement her financial needs. The children didn't know it, but each of them had a custodial account. I'd taken that money Antwan threw at me the last time I was in his apartment and started investing it. I just divided it three ways, prayed over it and asked God to just do a miraculous thing. The money has grown and will continue to grow if they make wise decisions after the funds are available to them.

And although, Goodness is acting completely helpless with her laundry, she really has grown into such an independent woman. The girl went down south and just began to blossom even more from those seeds God allowed us to plant while she was living with us. She'd started a Saturday academy to help tutor local teens in math and science on the weekends. She'd joined a community group that volunteered at shelters sorting clothing and serving meals to the homeless, and together she and Mario started the FIRE study group. She said Mario thought up the acronym that stood for Faithfully Inspired, Righteously Encouraged. She said the goal was to get young people to read the word, live by faith and be encouraged to be righteous in all their decision making.

I thought I'd have to stick a pin in Anthony any time after he talked to her, he'd be floating up to the ceiling so proud of her accomplishments. He was just as proud of the way Mario was turning out as well. Dare I say he may even have come to terms with the possibility that he would be a mainstay in our family for years to come?

"I'd like to think my little conversation with Mario, set him on the right path." He said laughing to himself one night, referring to his parting words, the day we left the kids for college.

"I don't know about that, he named the bible study group FIRE. You know fire can get a little hot and heavy!" I joked with him. Maybe that's the code word kids used for the other thing now-a-days.

"Well he can be hot and bothered all he wants, as long as he's on fire for God."

"I know that's right!" I said slapping him five.

"Oh...I meant to show you the flyer for Alex's party, he saved us two tickets."

"What kind of party? He's really going back to that DJ mess?" Anthony said taking the paper and reading it with a look of concern.

"It's not what you think. The couple's ministry at Faith Tabernacle is throwing a Nite On The Town fellowship, it's going to be catered and they'll even be some live entertainment. Alex is going to DJ in between sets."

"So he's a gospel DJ? What will they think of next?"

"I'm just glad that he's found a way to do something he's good at, that he loves to do, that also honors God."

"Well I can't wait for all this to turn into a sermon one of these days. I can see it Renee, when he's sitting there thinking about what to say to those young guys he counsels, he's writing stuff down, and checking it in the bible. He's on his way."

"I know…I checked the mail today, and there are brochures from two theological counseling programs. Both of them say *'thank you for your inquiry'*. That means Alex has been looking into furthering his studies." I said excited.

"Girl you know you not suppose to be reading other folks mail. That's against the law." He joked with me.

"I didn't open anything, they just happened to be lying on the table in my house, He must have given them our address." I said trying to defend my actions.

"That sounds like good news to me baby." He said kissing me and turning the light out on his bedside table. I still had some more scriptures I wanted to read, so I propped myself up on my pillows and continued to read the bible until I began to doze.

Chapter 44: Stay Ready For Battle

§

When I woke up this morning I had a stiff neck from the way I fell asleep, still sitting up in the bed, my hand was resting on the last page I could remember reading. I looked at the words interested in what God would have to say to me. I had to squint because who knew where in the world the glasses went that where on my face last night as I dozed. Uh Oh... this one is kind of deep. *And they shall fight against you, but they shall not prevail against you, for I am with you, said the Lord, to deliver you, Jeremiah one and nineteen.* I really don't feel like fighting today Lord, but nevertheless you said in your word you'd deliver me. I closed the bible and slowly creaked out of bed. Anthony had gotten up and fixed Shye and Marie their breakfasts and drove them to school. I already knew I had several stories to finish so I took a three-minute shower, threw on something comfortable and headed to work.

"Oooh, hey Renee! Girl your desk phone has been ringing off the hook, and two people called here asking for you. They sounded very official but didn't want to leave a message. What you got going on?" Marguerite asked being all in my business again.

I made her eat all of those nasty words she said to me by turning in one of the best stories I'd ever written for that station. I'd even agreed to be interviewed for part of the background video that Julia would be presenting when she did the expose she titled "The Little Secret of a Big Man: The Rise and Fall of Antwan Billows." It was a bit dramatic but she really did her thing. It was our top rated show. The station received a commendation from the police department and the federal government for our reporting that led to some house cleaning shall we say in law enforcement, not only in Baltimore, but all up the east coast. I found out Antwan even had some ties to suppliers sending him drugs from California. At the press conference, Alvin was singing my praises a bit too loudly for Marguerite who stood in the back of the room looking like she swallowed acid.

"Hello in there…did you hear me? I said what's with all the calls this morning, what you working on?" She asked again, blowing the nail polish dry on her acrylic claws.

"Nothing out of the ordinary, it was probably some leads for the stories I'm working on."

"Naw that ain't it, 'cause I asked a few times, you think it's related to all that stuff your son was in to a while back?" She was leaning forward in her seat, using her wrists to pick up her large cup of iced-coffee so she wouldn't mess up those precious talons.

"First of all, I thought you didn't take messages anymore, so why were you asking anybody about what they were calling me for?" I loved making her squirm.

"Hey I was just looking out for you. Just because you got your little recognition for that pitiful story about your sorry little poor childhood doesn't mean you can talk to me any kind of way. Believe it or not, there are other people here that want your job Renee, so shoot me for trying. Ooh, I didn't mean to mention shooting, I know that's a sore spot, with you and your little gangsta son." She said laughing and giving me a rude look.

"I don't have time to sit here and try to figure out who could have possibly called, but just for the record, we don't discuss anything my son used to be involved in because the book I read says old things are passed away and behold you are a new creation in Christ. If you want to know something about my son, then drop by his church on Sunday morning and introduce yourself." I said picking up my mail and stomping back to my cubicle.

"What's with her, I hope I'm not that nasty when I start going through the change?" I heard Marguerite comment as Harold walked up to the front desk just as I was leaving.

"Hey you o.k.? You got Ms. Gossip up there on edge." Harold laughed peeking into my work area.

"Harold, you know how I am and that woman just gets to me sometimes. I'm ready for her though, you should have seen the scripture God gave me this morning."

"Let me guess, something about warfare...'cause you two are going to really get into it one of these days. Just do like I do and ignore the woman, you can't let her get to you."

"She doesn't bother you as much as she bothers me." I complained, sorry Lord, I told myself I wasn't going to do that today.

"You keep thinking that...Marguerite is one of those people that thrives on pointing out other peoples faults. She's been having a field day with my divorce."

"Oh, yeah...listen to me complaining. I almost forgot about all you've been going through. I'm sorry things didn't work out for you and Cynthia."

"We gave it...or at least I can say I gave it my best shot. Thanks so much for the referral to the Branch's they were fantastic. I really enjoyed the sessions and it seemed like Cynthia was too on that second go-round, but we still just got two different messages. She's not ready to give up that old lifestyle we used to have, and she's not ready to accept me as a born again believer in Jesus Christ. And you know more than anybody, Renee that a marriage where the two partners are unequally yoked cannot be successful. Instead of praying for me, she wants to get on the phone to her single girlfriends." He said throwing his hand in the air in defeat.

"You know my momma used to always tell me that it wasn't nothing my single friends could tell me about how to save my marriage, because as much as I complained to them about my man, if we weren't together any more, they'd be running to get with him." I laughed trying to make him cheer up.

"You ain't lying either...I saw one of Cynthia's best friends in the grocery store the other day and she told me to call her if I ever needed to just talk. Yeah, right...I'm staying as far away from that foolishness as I can. Well...look, I won't keep you from your work any longer, I know you've got exclusives to work on. Once day when I make senior writer, I want to be just like you." He joked and gave me a pat on the shoulder.

"It's just a title...believe me, you don't want all the craziness that comes along with it." I said powering up my computer. At that same moment I could have sworn I heard Alex asking for me at the front desk. Not a moment later I received confirmation that he was indeed in the building, when he came storming into my cubicle.

"Mom, why haven't you answered your cell? I've been trying to get in touch with you all morning."

"What's wrong baby, is it Morgan?" I asked jumping up from my chair. Alex had probably been to my job three times in his whole life, there was definitely something wrong.

"No mom, she's fine. It's Shye, I got a call from his principal today…" He stopped talking and looked at Marguerite who was still standing next to him, I'm sure she was making mental notes to share with the office later, when she thought I was not in earshot.

"What about Shye?" Marguerite asked leaning into Alex.

"He's been arrested." Alex mumbled.

"He's been what! When? For what?" I could hear myself talking very loudly. I needed to get a hold of myself.

Marguerite was just enjoying this latest news. I'm sure this was better than her soap operas. "Oooh…girl, you really know how to raise 'em right don't you? What's that book you read say about that?" Her words were laced with sarcasm.

I placed myself between her and Alex with my back to her deliberately. "Ignore her…go on."

"Yeah, the principal was trying to call you before she called the police, but apparently he was going off, and they needed to call the cops. When she couldn't get a hold of you, she said Shye told her to call me at Faith Tabernacle." This poor child was out of breath, I could tell he must have been in full rush mode since he got the call, and not being able to get in touch with me…this can't be happening. Panic you can't do this to me right now.

"Oh my goodness. I can't believe I didn't get any messages." I was frantically searching my purse looking for my cell phone. I usually hear it if it's ringing or feel it when it's on vibrate.

"I tried to tell you a lot a people were calling." Marguerite chimed in with an attitude.

"Harold, I know you can hear all of this, I have to go check on my son, most of these stories are done, they just need to be cued." I said talking over the partition that divided our cubicles and doing my best to ignore Marguerite.

"Not a problem, get out of here." He said. "Let me know if there is anything else I can do."

"I appreciate it. I'll get back to you before the evening broadcast." I grabbed my cell phone, which much to my dismay had been set on silent, causing me to miss six calls this morning. As I sat in the car with Alex racing to the precinct I listened to each frantic message. It seemed like the school really was trying all they could to let me get to Shye before they had to take drastic measures. When we got to the precinct we were ushered right into a family waiting area. Most of the guys there knew me from all the stories I covered with Julia. They also got a nice thank you basket from our family for the wonderful care and protection they demonstrated for Alex when he was in the hospital.

"Mrs. Renee, I'm sorry we had to do this, your boy was completely out of control by the time we got on the scene. Believe me…me and my partner wanted to let him stay on the school premises, but he was making all kinds of threats."

Officer Shaw was trying his best to make me feel at ease, but I was boiling inside. How in the world did Shye end up getting arrested? It looked like I was going to get a chance to ask him myself. As soon as I looked up he was being led into the small room, with his hands shackled behind him. He had a swollen lip and an eye that was already starting to turn a sickening blue-black color. I'm sure I should have felt pity for him, but at this moment I was beyond angry.

"You want to tell me why I'm sitting here at the police station at 9:30 in the morning? Shye how could you?! What did you do?" I started off talking calmly, but my voice had now escalated to a yell. Shye just shrugged his shoulders and refused to look me in the eye.

"No! That's not good enough. Have you not learned anything from living under my roof the last six years! Dad dropped you off at 7:30, so what happened in less than an hour that got you so out of control?" I was standing directly in front of him with my face in his face.

"Mom, just calm down. Let me see if I can get to the bottom of this." Alex said taking me by the hand and leading me back to my seat.

He pulled a chair up in front of Shye so that their knees were touching.

"Shye man, it's me…you're big brother. Look at me…help me understand what is going on. When that principal called my phone, all I could hear was you screaming in the background."

"It's not fair! I'm not the one that started the fight. These boys at school are always trying to start stuff with me. You should hear the things they say about me. They said I was gay because I talk about God. They said you was a punk for cooperating with the police when you got shot. Man I just couldn't take it." Shye looked like he was starting to get angry again.

"Shye, how many times I got to tell you that what people say about you does not define you. Don't let words get you confused. You and I both know somebody that can fight our battles for us." Alex said placing a hand on his brother's knee.

"All that church stuff don't work at my school. Everybody wants to be a thug. I get called names because I get good grades, and because I'm on the debate team, man. When I came back from that taping of It's Academic, that was all she wrote. I was a laughingstock. You know I don't even get recognized by half the guys at school until I mess up and forget to hand my homework in…yeah, then I'm the most popular guy in class.

Everyday I walk through groups of kids cussing and smoking right on school property."

"So man you live in this world, but you ain't got to be of this world." Alex continued.

"Yeah, but today, I saw this boy making fun of Marie and her girls. Ma you know she gets with them in the morning to pray right? Goodness started that routine, so most times I just stand by to make sure nobody messes with them. Right as they got done, this kid named Jason threw a rock and it hit Marie. I just went off!" He was standing now, trying hard to retell the story, which was awkward because his hands were still behind his back.

"I just started punching him, and telling him he better say he was sorry. But he kept going, saying me and Marie were crack babies, and calling our other mom a slut. Ma you just don't know how I wanted to just kill that boy!" He was getting so worked up that he was turning red, and spit was flying out of his mouth.

"Shye! Stop it right now. I understand you being hurt by his words, and I even understand coming to the defense of your sister, but you don't have the right to make threats like that. I talked to your principal and this thing got way out of control."

"Yeah Mrs. Chase, once Shye and this kid Jason started fighting, the crowd got involved and fights starting breaking out everywhere. They were able to get Shye out of the crowd and into the principal's office, but he tore the place up, throwing things and breaking furniture." Officer Shaw interrupted my tirade, he was reading to me from his police report.

"We had no choice but to arrest him for disorderly conduct and assault with a weapon. The school is looking to expel him." He said with a grim expression on his face.

"Assault with a what! What weapon?" I asked in disbelief, this was turning into a nightmare.

"The young man Shye started the fight with somehow got stabbed in the leg and in the abdomen and none of the witnesses is talking. The only person we know that had physical contact with him was Shye."

"Ma I swear to you…I never had no weapon. I didn't even know he'd been stabbed until they told me when I got here. I had nothing to do with that. Somebody else that jumped into the fight must have stabbed him. It's plenty of rivalries up at that school. Somebody is just trying put this on me."

"We need to have a full investigation, but the fact that we can't find the weapon, and the victim can't name anybody else that he was fighting, means we have to hold Shye here."

"This can't be happening." I said slumping in my seat. I was always the first person to say never give up, but this seemed pretty insurmountable. Then I remembered my scripture from this morning.

"Ma…please don't leave me here, I honestly didn't mean to hurt anybody." Shye was crying now, and it made my heart hurt.

"Baby, they may fight against you, but they will not prevail. The Lord is with you and He will deliver you. Trust Him. Dad and I will do our best to get you out of here as quickly as possible." I gave him a kiss and hurried to leave before I lost my nerve. Once we were outside and Shye was led back to the holding area for juveniles, Officer Shaw approached Alex and I.

"Mrs. Chase, I know ya'll are praying people, so just believe that we'll find that weapon, or that somebody will start talking. I know in my heart that Shye didn't do this. I won't rest until he gets back with you where he's supposed to be."

"Thank you so much. You don't know what a blessing you are to us." I said giving him a hug.

As soon as I was back in the car with Alex I broke down. There comes a point when you feel like you've done everything right, you've prayed and tithed, and sacrificed and believed, and obeyed and...

"I want to scream! I want to go absolutely mad! I feel like I should be the one tearing stuff up and breaking furniture. How can one family endure so much?" I began to cry. I honestly was just talking to myself. I didn't expect an answer from Alex.

"Do not do that. Do not begin to feel defeated. Keep your mind on the things you know ma. You know God is with you, you said it yourself a few minutes ago to Shye." Alex's voice was firm. He was starting to get that same bass his dad had.

"What does this look like? I must seem like the biggest joke to anybody that is looking in from the outside. I profess to have this holy Christian lifestyle, and I got a brother killed that I could really care less about, two children that I was responsible for raising have been involved with the criminal justice system, my marriage nearly ended in divorce. What do I really have to offer to anyone looking for advice on how to raise children holy, or live holy?" I almost didn't recognize my own voice. This was not my style...for the last few years, the pity party was the last kind of party you'd find Renee Chase dancing at, but I'd said it. I was feeling tore down.

"Are you serious? Ma you have a testimony. Without these tests, you would not be able to tell the 'how I got over' story. Don't start doubting now. Go back to your word, find some peace, but don't let the enemy get the best of you right now." Alex had pulled over so he could look me in the eyes.

"I am here because of your faith, Goodness is where she is because of your obedience, and your marriage did not fail because of your belief in God. I won't sit here and listen to you giving up…I don't accept that ma." He said pounding the steering wheel for emphasis.

"Then help me…pray for me. I need you to pray for me." I said beginning to let the flood of tears pour down my face. And without a second thought to who may see him, or what people may think, Alex Chase went to God on behalf of his mother. Every once in a while you need to just praise Him in spite of and not because of…so God I praise you even though the enemy came against me to destroy me today, because he did not overtake me.

****

The enemy didn't overtake me, but for the next few days he was trying to undermine my faith. Something was not quite right about this whole situation with Shye. The fight managed to make the news and a special report on a rival station about school violence. Yeah, this is just what I need.

"How's my man hanging? Shye staying strong in that detention center?" Harold inquired about Shye everyday.

"He puts on a brave front, but I know he's scared. I'm sure every parent says this, but he's not supposed to be there. He's not like those kids."

"You'd be surprised Renee…he's probably a whole lot like those kids. Most of them are just as intelligent as Shye and want to succeed just as much as he does, they just don't have anyone that believes in them. I'll be down there with the men from my church this weekend. I'll make sure to give him some words of encouragement."

"Thank you." I said, powering up my computer and logging into my email. Since last night I'd gotten fifty emails from people saying they had the next big story for me to write.

"Here…these are for you." Marguerite tossed two pink message slips on my desk, with telephone numbers on them.

"I hope you didn't hurt yourself writing these numbers down." I said sarcastically.

"Now who's acting ugly? For your information, Chloe was sitting at the front desk for me while I was on break, and she took the messages, said they didn't leave no names. I was on my way to the back, so I thought I'd be nice and drop them off for you."

"Thanks, but I can't do much without a name or a reason why the person called, next time tell her just to put them through to voicemail." I had to talk to her with my back turned while I was clicking away on the computer, it's the only way I could have a conversation with her and not get drawn into her pettiness.

"That's not in my job description." She smirked and sauntered off throwing a little more hip into her step as she passed Harold's cubicle.

"Count to ten." He said with a chuckle.

Just then the telephone on the desk rang, and one of the numbers on the message slips was flashing in the caller ID window. I wanted to let it go to the message, but what was the point, if it was a silly story, I might as well get this over with, so they wouldn't keep calling.

"Renee Chase Channel two."

"Mrs. Renee…long time no hear. You probably forgot all about me by now, but me and your friend 'Lita go way back." My heart stopped, this was the voice of that stranger that had Shelita's cell phone the night she was killed.

Pick your jaw up off the ground and say something Renee. "What can I do for you?"

"It ain't what you can do, it what's you already did. I don't think Big Ant woulda been too happy 'bout how you put his business out in the street. That story got you some big ratings but you put our crew in a bad situation. We had to shut down some operation and that means I'm not making as much money as I used to make." The man was doing his best to put on his spooky voice, with the gruff raspy whisper. Almost sounded like he had the mouth piece down his throat. But see what he didn't know was that he was talking to a woman that had decided she was not going to fear evil. Now I done been through too much for this foolishness today.

"Forgive me if I don't feel sorry for you. Now if you don't have a story then I'm gonna ask you to hang up and don't call back here."

That last statement got a big laugh from him, although I don't know why, because I definitely was not doing a stand-up routine.

"I got a story for you…try this on for size. Local teen gets twenty years to life for attempted murder of a classmate."

"I don't know what you are trying to do, but your threats don't scare me."

"Oh it's more than a threat, ask Alex about how we roll? He thought he could just walk away from that raid, snitch on his boys and Big Ant and get away with it? Well we don't even want him no more, we gonna make sure that little boy of yours they got over there in juvy don't never see the outside again."

Now my head was starting to hurt. Did he just mention Alex and Antwan?

"Why are you doing this? Antwan is dead, Alex didn't snitch on anybody, and there was enough evidence in that raid to send Antwan to jail for the rest of his life. And let's not forget he was the one that came out shooting like a mad man."

"Too late to try and protect him now, there's no way you got some of that information for that story from anybody but Alex." Just listening to the harshness in his voice, made my throat hurt.

"You are wrong, we had an informant. As a matter of fact, it's somebody that's still rolling with you. Now I want you to stop whatever revenge you think you are getting right now, because you've got the facts wrong."

"Too late, I'm not the one that makes the rules. Shye has to pay for what his brother did and for Big Ant's death. Shame...we all can't get along like family."

"But he didn't do what you're saying...you have to believe me. I will not let you do this to my family."

"It's already done. You ain't gonna find nobody that will testify to what happened that day. We've made sure of that." He laughed and hung up. I sat dazed. This was a set up just like Shye said. I knew something wasn't right. Lord please help us through this one.

Chapter 45: The Past Coming Back To Haunt

§

I tried not to show how I was really feeling as I entered the doors of Faith Tabernacle, but if I didn't make it to Alex's office soon, I was going to crumble in a heap on the floor.

"Well isn't this a nice surprise! How you doin' Mrs. Chase?"

"I'm good Ms. Agnes. Is Alex in a meeting with anyone right now?" So much for the strong front, my voice was cracking with every other word I spoke.

"He ain't and even if he was, they would have to go, 'cause you looking like you just lost your best friend. Let me buzz him and tell him you're here."

Agnes, was the church secretary and like a grandmother to Alex. According to Ms. Agnes, she loved and protected him from all the 'triflin' women in the church. From where she sat at her desk outside of Pastor Bantum and Alex's door she could monitor the goings on and didn't mind saying no whenever young ladies came calling for either one of them.

"Brother Alex, your momma is out here for you. Now I'm gonna clear the rest of your afternoon, 'cause it look like ya'll gonna need to do a whole lot of prayin'." She said speaking into the intercom.

"Send her in." I heard Alex say. He opened the door before I had a chance to knock.

"What's wrong?" That simple question made me lose it. I fell into Alex's office and plopped down on the large leather sofa, crying.

The words just came tumbling out of my mouth.

"Baby, I got a disturbing call today. It's from somebody that used to hang with Antwan. They are making all kinds of threats. They said they'll make sure Shye gets charged with attempted murder, that he has to pay for Antwan's death. Look here's the number the call came from. Do you have any idea who this is?"

"Wait a minute. I'm confused, you need to slow down. You got a call from a member of Uncle Ant's crew?"

I tried to slow my breathing, and make more sense.

"Yes, and he said that they were going to see to it that Shye got charged with attempted murder for that stabbing at his school. He made it seem like this was some payback for the part he thinks you played in bringing down all those cops that were supplying Antwan with drugs and weapons."

"Payback for something I did? This is unreal. Why didn't they just try to get back at me?"

"Whoever this guy is said, they weren't worried about you, they were going after Shye to teach you and me a lesson." I said, in between sobs and blowing my nose, that was running like a faucet.

"No! They've messed with the wrong one now. I am not going to have my baby brother charged with a crime he did not commit. I'm going to go handle some business and get this straightened out." He grabbed his coat and made a move for the door.

"Wait a minute! Where are you going? Are you trying to get yourself killed? You have a baby to think about. What about Morgan? We have to do this the right way, or you could end up dead." I couldn't believe that I was the voice of reason in this situation, but I could tell Alex was fuming.

"Ma you don't understand these people. They got everybody on the block so scared, nobody will come forward to testify. If I don't go down there and handle my business, then it will seem like I'm a coward and then they really will end up pinning this thing on Shye. I plan on going down there and changing their minds." He said jamming his arms into his coat. He was so angry he was having a hard time getting the zipper to line up so he finally gave up.

"So that's it. You are just going to throw away everything that you've come to stand for, and lower yourself to their standards. Everything you try to minister to these boys about you're just going to throw that away. I came here because I wanted to talk to the Alex that had some common sense, the Alex that could remain calm and rely on his faith for a solution. I need you. Don't go to them…it's a trap." Just then we heard a very familiar sound coming from his desk…a loud beep indicating the intercom had been activated.

"Brother Alex…I ain't one to get in folks bidness, but you better listen to your momma. Them scoundrels in them streets ain't nothing to mess with. I was just buzzin' to tell you I'm on my way to lunch in case you want me to pick something up for ya."

"No Sister Agnes, I'm fine. Take your time and enjoy your lunch." Alex was trying to remain calm, he often told me that he felt like Sister Agnes was out there listening in on his conversations, but he knew she did it in love.

"Thank ya...I b'lieve I will take my time. You just remember to mind yo' momma! That comes straight from the bible." She abruptly hung up and Alex turned back to me to finish talking as if she'd never interrupted.

"But I'm the one they want. I can't let them do this to Shye when I'm the one they want." He said with tears in his eyes.

"No, Alex...I'm the one they want. Your Uncle did everything in his power while he was still alive to destroy me. Came at me from every angle, but when the devil sees that he can't touch you, he starts to infiltrate those things that mean the most to you. He's doing it now from the grave. We are going to get your brother out of that detention center, and we are going to do it legally. Now take a look at this number on this paper. The guy was calling from here. Do you recognize it?" All of my tears had dried up and I was turning into mama bear on a mission to protect her cub.

Alex looked at the paper, and closed his eyes as if trying to will something into remembrance. He opened his eyes and looked again, then squeezed them shut one more time tapping his temple with his fingers.

"Think Alex...think...think." He said to himself. He opened his eyes and looked at me for a while without saying anything.

"Let me see that paper again...yeah, that is definitely the number I remember." He picked up the telephone and dialed slowly.

"Who is it?" I asked. He put his finger to his lips to signal me to be quiet.

"Hello? Yeah, it's me...We haven't talked in a while but I was just thinking about you. Your daughter's been asking about you and I think it's time we had a little talk, don't you Traniece?" I guess Alex could tell by my expression that I wanted to take that telephone from him and go off, he held his hand up in the stop position and mouthed 'let me do this'.

"Yeah, I'm still here. Where are you staying I can come pick you up and we can get dinner tomorrow night." He scribbled an address down on a piece of paper, said his goodbyes, and hung up the receiver.

"Traniece? You've got to be kidding me!" I yelled. No this little girl didn't. Got me all frantic and worried, and she's letting somebody play on her phone.

"Don't let your guard down ma. My guess is, she's getting drugs from these guys and they are getting the kind of payment only Traniece can offer. This is still a very real threat, but maybe if I get her talking she'll tell me who is masterminding this whole thing and we can get Shye cleared."

"It still sounds dangerous. How do you know she's not setting you up? You might get to this address and be ambushed by this crazy guy that called or something."

"I want to get the police in on this, you have to report the threat and they'll be interested in knowing how Traniece is connected with all of this." Alex had placed his coat back on the hook behind his door and was sitting beside me.

"I'm just not sure about you taking Morgan to see her if she's still so involved with that lifestyle." Now it was time for the grandma in me to come out.

"Don't worry ma, I'll do it on my terms. Morgan stays in my possession at all times, I'll pick Traniece up and we'll go to the Towson Library for story time, then to get a little bite to eat at McDonalds. I don't plan on spending more than an hour with her, but that should be enough for me to get what I need."

With a plan in place, we called the detectives in charge of investigating Shye's case and passed along the recent events. Traniece was so happy to see her daughter the next day that she ran off at the mouth about everything. Alex said she mentioned that his boy Troy had been hanging with Traniece lately. She even mentioned that they'd started a relationship.

"Can you believe my best friend from back in the day is kicking it with my baby's mother?" I knew he no longer had feelings for Traniece, but he sounded heartbroken at the betrayal from his friend. He was sitting with Anthony and I in the living room recounting the events from his meeting at the library.

"Man I not only believe it, I'm not surprised. Troy is no good. I know you said he turned his life around when you saw him working at the hospital, but I think that was a front." Anthony said handing him a cold soda and a plate with a massive sub sandwich on it.

"I honestly believed he did try dad, it's just that the temptation from the streets, that high, that money, the girls…It's hard to resist if you not anchored. Ya'll don't know how I fight those dreams every night. Sometimes I wake up sweating because I've had a dream about snortin' or smoking on something that seems so real, I'd swear I could still taste it. No, I can't pass any judgment on Troy." Despite his heartache, Alex was still trying to be compassionate.

"I just wish it wasn't Traniece tempting him, I mean not too long ago, this was the woman I thought I wanted to spend the rest of my life with."

"So do you think Troy was the one making the call? The caller sounded just like the guy that called here that night Shelita was killed. I will never forget the sound of that voice. I can't believe that all those years ago, Troy was involved with Antwan and his crew, he would have been so young." I said

"He was too young, but his dad wasn't…Bam-Bam was running things even before Uncle Ant got on." Alex explained.

"Bam-Bam? That's what the man's name is?" Anthony said in disbelief.

"Yeah, it has a little something to do with the sound a gun makes." Alex said devouring his sandwich. Morgan was upstairs taking a nap. It was the only time since yesterday she had stopped talking about seeing her mother. She was in heaven to have both her parents together with her for story time.

"It sounds like a little boy from the Flintstones." I said sarcastically. I was sick of grown men renaming themselves for the sake of being considered more gangsta. It sounded like a stupid name to me, just like Man-Man or Pookie.

"The names sound silly, but trust me when I tell you, these boys ain't nothing to laugh at ma. I tried to convince Niecey to just leave that whole thing yesterday, and not even go back, but you know she was itching to get high after she'd been with us for about thirty minutes. It was all I could do to make her sit still in her seat during the story. Morgan was oblivious to all of it. She just kept saying *'mommy's cold daddy, give her hug'*. She thought that would stop the shaking." He'd paused with the sandwich in mid air, finally putting it down.

"I'm not even hungry anymore. Look, I'm going to go to the station and talk to Officer Shaw and let him know the little bit I found out today. I'm sure they have Bam-Bam in their records, they should be able to pick him up for something."

"Honey, I'm worried about you. I know that seeing Traniece hasn't been the greatest of reunions, but maybe this will be the push she needs to get her life right, if not for her own self, then for Morgan."

"I seriously doubt that mom. Well let me get my number one lady. I'll call you guys tomorrow." He gave me a kiss and hugged Anthony then took the stairs two at a time to wake Morgan and take her home.

Chapter 46: When You Feel Like Giving Up

§

"I hate to say it mom, but this is not unusual. Criminal law is not my specialty, but I have enough colleagues that tell me sometimes these investigations can drag on, despite what seems like mountains of evidence." Nick was trying to put my mind at ease. I felt like nobody was moving fast enough to get Shye out of lock down. It had been six months since the day he first stepped foot in there. You heard me, six months, one half of a year, one hundred and eighty three days and my son was still behind bars. Well really he was in a cell that was enclosed in clear Plexiglas, but he was wrongfully incarcerated no matter what the cell looked like. It broke my heart to have to leave him after visiting hours. He'd been moved to a floor for higher risk inmates almost two weeks ago, because he was fighting, so our visiting times were cut down to thirty minutes and I could no longer sit with him in a family meeting area, I had to look at him through a scratched up, cloudy, plastic partition.

"So what are you trying to prove...that you are just as ignorant and thugged out as the prosecution is trying to make you out to be? Do you want to be in jail for attempted murder, because if you do, then keep on doing what you are doing and let me go on about my business."

I said coldly looking at him in the eye, my mouth pressed to the receiver of the telephone that allowed us to talk to one another.

"I have to fight ma. You don't understand...it's bang or get banged in here...if you know what I mean." My soon-to-be-fourteen-year-old son's voice had gotten deeper, his demeanor completely changed since he'd been in here. He would be celebrating a birthday in here next weekend if we didn't hurry up and get this trial on the ball.

"Are you reporting the incidents to somebody? A security guard?"

"It's the guards you gotta watch out for sometimes in here. Look I don't mind being put in solitary, at least nobody is bothering me." He said nonchalantly, shrugging his shoulders. He even had a grin on his face that made me want to bust through that partition and put that little boy over my knee. He was not taking this seriously.

"But it doesn't help your case Shye. We are trying to show that this was out of character for you, that you know how to resolve conflict without fighting, and that you were just protecting your sister. You need to be a model prisoner. Are you still praying at night?" He didn't answer me right away, but instead looked down at the floor.

"God don't love me no more ma. I was doing everything right, even put myself out there to be ridiculed, talked about...and this is how I get rewarded. Ever since I came to live with you I ain't never lied, or stole anything like my other mom used to make me do when we went into the stores. I ain't cuss, I read the word, stopped playing those bloody video games you hated, and I thought I was doing real good." I could see his eyes getting watery, but he refused to let any tears fall.

"You are doing good. Shye don't give up because your family hasn't given up on you. We believe you.

Trust in God even in this bad time. Rev. Fowler always says that when your back in against the wall…just when you think you're going to fall, is the exact time you'll get a miracle. Think about it…you might be here to minister to other boys. Have you even considered that, or tried to tell anybody about how Christ has changed your life?" I was trying to soften my tone and make him feel some sort of comfort.

"It's kind of hard when somebody is trying to bash your head in to tell them about the goodness of Jesus." Shye answered sarcastically.

"O.k. you win. That's how you want it. You want to just discount all the blessings you've received then go right ahead. You want to fight like an animal in here…fine with me. You could have been the one that got stabbed that day. There is a testimony in this situation Shye, but you want to give up. I can't watch you do this. Dad will be by in a few days. I'll be praying for you."

I continued to hold my breath waiting for him to say something. I was waiting for him to say he'd changed his mind. I wanted him to signal to the guard that he wanted a few more minutes to talk to his mother and reassure her…but instead he hung up the phone on his side and got up early to leave me sitting there.

It took me two weeks to get up enough strength to go back to see him. He stopped talking about God all together, would just pretend I hadn't even mentioned His name when I brought up church or a scripture. He chose to ask about home, Alex, Goodness and Marie. He would ask if I could put money in the commissary for him to get food and magazines, but that was it. I didn't get the one phone call he could make every two days, now he either called Alex or Anthony. One time he called Goodness at school, but he was avoiding me like the plague. I knew he was expecting Anthony to visit him today, but I changed those plans real quick. I did not like the feeling I was getting that I was losing this child to something deep and dark. He was fading away from his beliefs, and not that we all don't do that from time to time, but he was feeling unloved. He was feeling like giving up on God and I could not have that. Imagine my surprise when he showed no hesitation in picking up the receiver of the telephone on his side of the glass.

"I knew you were coming here today." He said with a smile on his face. I hadn't seen him smile the whole time he'd been here. I can't say that I blame him for not smiling.

"How do you think you know so much? Dad was supposed to be here instead of me."

"I heard a voice tell me that I needed to make peace with you." He said still smiling and looking like a little boy.

"You hearin' voices now? Do I need to get them to send you to the psychiatrist in here." I was trying to keep my voice calm, but inside my heart was doing flips. Was my son finally listening to that inner voice of his spirit?

"You'll be happy to know I was praying. Actually I been praying for the last week. And for the first time last night, I heard this voice say '*she loves you…tell her you love her.*' So I love you ma…and I'm sorry for the way I've been acting. I just want to be out of here."

"And you will. Let me tell you something about them prayers baby…God hears them and he considers every one of them. Don't keep praying about getting out of here, just pray for His Divine will, then whatever He wants to happen will happen. Those people that are threatening you will get what they deserve…trust me. You can't mess with one of God's children."

"Well I know you got…I mean *hav*e a direct connection, so if you wouldn't mind, could you say a little prayer for me?" Now I was the one sitting in silence.

"What? I thought you'd be glad I finally wanted prayer, why are you so quiet?"

"Just thinking about how awesome God is. You are about to be blessed baby, believe me when I tell you that. Now close your eyes and just breathe in all that God has for you and blow out all the negativity that is surrounding you in here. You are getting out of here Shye." And I began praying for him.

He never once opened his eyes, but I could tell with each word he was changing. Silent tears slid down his cheeks. When I had finished he opened his eyes and said thank you, then got up and slowly left the room. But this time, he wasn't sulking and looking at the ground, shuffling along. He was walking proudly with his head held high. The very next morning I got a call from officer Shaw that he needed to see me and Anthony at the station as soon as possible. There had been an unexpected break in the investigation. Just when you need Him the most! Thank you Lord, you had me on pins and needles there for a minute.

Chapter 47: No Fear, The Real Lawyer Is Here

§

"And it is your sworn testimony that this young man initiated the attack by throwing the rock at the group of girls standing outside the school?" Officer Shaw was questioning one of Marie's friends in a private room. It had taken seven months from the day of the attack, but Marie convinced her friend's family to let her come forward and tell what she'd witnessed. There's that number again. Many of the students involved in the brawl were afraid of any consequences they would suffer as a result of coming forward, but this young woman finally agreed. Her parents were in the room with her and the officer for an hour answering some preliminary questions before we were allowed to come in.

"Yes sir." She said, nodding at the picture he was pointing too. Jason Wilkes had a juvenile record a mile long, and while I would not condone my children judging anyone by their past, this young man was definitely trouble.

"Can you just recount the story you told me so we can be sure everything is consistent." The officer said as he pressed the record button on a tiny machine sitting on the table.

"Well we were all praying as usual. Jason and some of his boys were getting so loud, a few of them even bumped into us on purpose. They kept doing it over and over. Shye told them to stop, and they said 'or what', and he said he would go in and tell Principal Geller. Well then they just laughed and made fun of him." She said looking between us and her parents for support.

"You said they began taunting him and making rude gestures?" The officer asked.

"Yes, but I don't want to repeat that part…it really was disgusting the things they were saying and the gestures they were making Mr. and Mrs. Chase so if it's o.k., we can just skip that part." She said giving us a faint smile.

"Of course sweetie, you tell us the best way you can." I said trying to sound comforting.

"Well Shye got really upset, so he moved away from us a bit. He said he needed to count to himself and cool off. Once Jason saw him walking away, he picked up a rock and said 'hey maybe your crack baby sister wants another piece of rock', and he threw it really hard at Marie. The rock hit her right above her eye and she started to bleed, that was all it took, Shye just went off."

"Did you see anybody else come in contact with Jason Wilkes?" Officer Shaw already had his answer, but was just having the witness restate facts to be sure there were no holes in the story she was telling. Anthony squeezed my hand as we waited for her response. It was barely audible, but when she finally answered we were relieved.

"Yes, I did. I don't know the kids name, but he's older. He's part of this gang of boys that hangs around in the morning before the bell rings. They don't go to our school, but Jason is part of their rival crew I think. I know for sure he had a knife because everybody was screaming they saw him with one. I hope this helps you guys. Shye was really just standing up for his sister." She ended, and reached for her mother's hand.

"This testimony will be key to us finding this suspect and getting Shye out of here." Officer Shaw said with a smile.

"But what about the weapon? Believe me I appreciate the witness account, but it would just be he said, she said, don't we need the weapon to prove it was handled by this guy and not our son?" That was just like Anthony, the man watched his fair share of Law and Order and was not quite ready to call the case solved.

"Don't worry Mr. Chase, he's been identified by this witness with a photo line up, we have his information in the database, we'll be doing our best to track him down."

"In the meantime, my son is sitting in a cell where he does not belong. Can any of this recent evidence get him released until the investigation is over? I mean I know murder suspects that's walking the streets while their trials are under investigation." He said getting a little intense.

"We'll get Shye's lawyer to make an appeal to the judge based on this recent development in the morning. Until then…if I were you, I'd get over to see him before visiting hours are over, he's been asking for you guys."

We did just that. Our poor baby was trying to put on a front and be strong, but I knew he was scared. He'd been moved back down into general population for good behavior, so we planned on spending the full hour visiting with him. Before we ended our hour-long visit, he asked if he could pray. We were able to join hands around the small table where we were seated. It felt good just to have contact with my son again.

"Dear Lord, thank you so much for my mother and father. God I am sorry to have to put them through this, but I'm glad they love me enough not to judge me. I am so thankful that you are protecting me while I am away from home, just like you did my big brother Alex. Give mom and dad some peace of mind, and let them know they didn't do anything wrong. I trust you Father that I will be home soon and all of this will be taken care of according to your will. Amen."

What can I say about you God? This is a thirteen year old praying and asking for forgiveness. This is a child who the society said did not have a chance for a successful life. I know he can do it. I know he will be all that you've said he will be. The warm hug felt good and reassured me that Shye would be alright for one more night. I was claiming his release in the morning, and he was too.

"Ma make sure you get some subs from Greek Village tomorrow, I expect to be home by lunch!" He laughed and waved as he was led back to his cell.

The next morning we got the news that the judge would release Shye to us, but he was not allowed to go to school pending the investigation. Alex stopped by each night with homework assignments he'd picked up from Shye's teachers. The two boys spent hours at the table working on the assignments and talking brother to brother. Alex made sure to arrange a baby sitter for Morgan so he could attend each day of the trial with Anthony and I. With the prayers of his family, the Faith Tabernacle and Calvary Zion Baptist families and friends from school the boy was covered. Shye did have to plead guilty for assaulting Jason after he threw the rock at Marie, but got sentenced with time served. The charges of assault with a deadly weapon and attempted murder were dropped. In a scene that seemed like deja'vu from just a few years earlier, I was leaving the court building with yet another black male involved with violence.

"That judge didn't do you like Alex's judge did, but let me just let you know little boy…I betta not ever have to come down to nobody's jail to get you ever again! Do you hear me?" Anthony had waited until all the proceedings were done and we were all sitting in the truck before he turned to Shye to give him his warning.

"Yes Sir." Shye answered looking his dad right in the eye. "You don't have to worry about me dad. I know that's not where God wants me to be. I'm making a promise today to do better."

"I still think the idea of anger management is a good idea. Alex does workshops for young men at his church and I don't think it would hurt you to sit in on a few and learn how to deal with conflict. Hey I might have to join you…I know brotha's have a hard time dealing with anger towards one another. When Alex was living with us, he'll tell you me and him got into a lot of altercations and mainly it was because I just didn't know how to say to him what I wanted, but I knew how to use this." He said making a fist and waving it in the air.

"Yeah, big-head…I never got a chance to say it, but I appreciated you coming to my defense and everything, but I would have never wished this on you. I know we grew up watching people literally fighting right in front of us over drugs or who was gonna get a chance to go in the room with our other mom, but we don't have to do that no more. Shye you got talent boy. As much as I hate to admit it you can really draw good, so use those hands for something more productive." Marie was sitting beside her brother in the back seat. As much as they fought, she missed him so much while he was gone. She prayed for him every night and cried when she thought about him.

"I'm gonna say thank you because I know I might not get another compliment from you this year." Shye said laughing and breaking the tension. He even leaned over and gave her a quick hug and a peck on the cheek.

"Yuck…didn't nobody say nothing about wanting no stinky germs. Get on your side of the car." And with that we had our family back. Alex had gone back to work and we were on our way to the Golden Corral so Shye could fill his belly.

Chapter 48: Back In Stride Again…one more time

§

It only took a few days for Shye to get back into the swing of things, and for our family to fall right back into filling every waking hour with some activity or another. One would think that with my first day off in about a month I would be sitting in a warm tub soaking my tired body. It would be nice to just enjoy the fact that Shye and Marie both are at after-school activities, Goodness and Nick are in a whole 'nother state, and Alex is working and going to school. But then you'd be forgetting about Morgan. I've got babysitting duty since Alex has an early morning Saturday class. I couldn't say no even if I wanted to. Alex was enrolled in classes in theological counseling program at Loyola College. Without telling us, he'd taken night courses to receive his GED, then went on to get his prerequisites for the theological studies program. He proudly told us he was going into the ministry of counseling. Of course Anthony and I just looked at him like…yeah and…you know this is leading to a sermon one of these days. He was doing it the way God wanted him to, so how could we be mad. He'd made such a difference as a mentor at his church, that counseling was just the next logical step. So here I sit with my Morgan girl reading for the millionth time, *The Cat In The Hat Comes Back*.

"Morgan sweetie, nana thinks it's time for a nap so you'll be nice and refreshed when daddy comes to get you after his class. You don't want sleepy eyes when he takes you to playgroup this afternoon do you?" I was begging. If I could get her to take a nap, I could close my eyes for a few minutes too. I was just so drained.

"But I'm not sleepy nana. I want to say prayers."

"Well you can always say prayers. Let's go upstairs to Marie's room and you can say prayers and get up on her bed to rest your eyes for a while until daddy comes." She seemed to agree with that all the while yawning and insisting she wasn't tired. I knew she was, because before we sat down to read, I wore her out real good running around in the back yard. Well it was more like me watching her run around because I was so short of breath lately, but it was fun nonetheless. As soon as we were on our knees she squeezed her eyes shut and put her little hands together.

"Nana close your eyes, daddy says God gonna hear us better if we gots our eyes closed." I did as I was commanded. "Lord thank you for my nana that gots a lot of grass for me to run on. And thank you for my Cat In The Hat book, and for my baby doll, and for my new dress that my daddy got for me. Thanks for my mommy 'cause she gets sick sometimes but her still love me 'cause my daddy told me. Amen"

"Amen. What a nice prayer. Let me see you get those tired bones up here and take a rest. I'm gonna make sure there is something special for you when you get up." I said kissing her forehead and pulling the covers up to her chin. Those long eyelashes were batting and I could tell she had a question behind them.

"Nana do you love my mommy too?" She asked, barely able to keep her eyes open.

"I love your mommy because she is a child of God. I don't love the way she makes herself sick, because it makes her stay away from you too long. But I know if you keep praying for her she will get better." Did that do it? I sure hope so.

"Daddy says that." She smiled.

"Well then it must be right." I said laughing and tickling her under the chin. She squirmed a bit, but turned right over on her side and closed her eyes. I'd just gotten comfortable on the sofa with my feet up when Alex came in the door.

"You're early. I just put Morgan down for a nap."

"Let her rest a bit, we had an exam so I took it and bounced." He was making his way over to the kitchen.

"There's nothing good in there, just junk food…I need to go shopping."

"See ya'll done just fell to pieces since I left. I need to get ya'll hooked up with my nutritionist. These are temples ma, temples…" He said making a sweeping motion from his head to his toe.

"Boy, don't get smart with me. Didn't Ms. Agnes tell you to 'mind me'. I don't want to have to tell her you over here getting' smart." I joked.

"No please don't do that. So how was my little lady? Did she give you any trouble with the green beans I packed for lunch?"

"She's no trouble you know that…although she did throw me for a loop asking me if I loved her mother."

"Man, she's been asking me that a whole lot too. Yeah, sorry about that. She's really missing mommy time, because at all the playgroups and gymnastics everybody is there with their moms. She hears the tension in my voice whenever Niecey's name is brought up and I'm sure she's picked up on the fact that her relationship with her mom is different than her other little friends."

"Isn't it something how these little ones can just read us? We just going along thinking they don't know anything about grown folks business." I remarked, laughing to myself. I was thinking about how Anthony and I used to spell words we didn't want the kids to know when we were having grown up talk, only to find out later that most of the time they'd figured out what we were saying.

"You ain't lyin'. I was counseling a young lady in my office the other day, and out of the blue Morgan says 'daddy you like Ms. Keisha because you always touchin' her on the hand.'. I hadn't even noticed that I did that."

"Keisha, huh? Watch yourself young man."

"Oh, it's nothing to watch. Ms. Agnes heard Morgan when she said that so Keisha hasn't been allowed into my office this whole week!" We both laughed and he went off in the direction of the kitchen as I laid my head back to try and catch up on some much needed sleep.

Chapter 49: It's Getting' Hot In Here!

§

I think it's been established that I need more sleep. I can never catch up on it and lately there just isn't enough time in the day. I'm sure if I wasn't running around like a chicken with my head cut off I wouldn't be so out of breath. I'm sure if I'd packed last night instead of the morning of my 5:00 am flight I wouldn't be so frantic. But I was up late working on stories and just didn't get around to it, despite the fact that my husband warned me that I'd be doing this very thing.

"Is there anything I can get for you Renee? I hate seeing you rush around like this, you haven't gotten any rest." Anthony said sitting on the edge of the bed watching me run back and forth from the dresser to the suitcases on the bed.

"I'll sleep on the plane, right now we gotta get going." I was just stuffing suitcases with clothes and hoping that when I unpacked I'd have something useful to wear.

"Well make sure you have something light, I hear it's going to be blazing down there the whole time you're away." I knew he was right so that gray sweater I just stuffed in my luggage would have to come out…why on earth was it still in my drawer? Anyway I was on my way to Atlanta. Goodness and Mario had driven down a few days ago, and I was gonna use my two weeks of vacation at the end of August to make sure my baby was all set up for her second year of college.

Despite the hurried beginning to my vacation, I managed to make it to the airport with time to spare, catch a few z's on the plane, and find all my luggage at the baggage claim area. I was thoroughly enjoying myself down in peach country until a few days before I was scheduled to come back home. I called myself trying to 'hang' as the young people say now-a-days. We'd toured the Coca-Cola museum and the world famous Underground Shopping Mall. I had to make a stop at the CNN building for Anthony to pick up some t-shirts, and then pick up post cards from the High Museum. I did all that while I was trying my best not to melt into a pool on the ground.

Now incase you don't know anything about August in Atlanta…it's HOT! Now when I was younger I might have meant that as a positive, as in Hotlanta, the place where the men are hot and the food is hot and the music is hot, but right now a middle-aged sista was just plain old heat hot! I needed a cool beverage before I passed out.

"Mommy come on, we have to get in on the floor or else the show will be no fun!" Goodness was shouting at me because she was easily a half-mile ahead of me. Even though I was down here about the business of getting her ready for her next semester in college, I thought it would be fun to treat her to a Kirk Franklin concert at the Georgia Convention Center.

"Baby…the spirit of the Lord will also be dwelling in the balcony, so don't break your neck. Go on in and I'll catch up with you." I said huffing behind her.

"Mrs. Chase do you want me to carry your backpack?" Mario offered. We had been out earlier at Six Flags over Georgia so I had some snacks, a bathing suit for the water rides, and some gift shop items stored in my heavy backpack. Don't ask me why I felt like I could keep up with those two. I'm sure they were walking fast on purpose so they could ditch the old lady, but I was hanging on in there. I knew I was going to be no good the next morning though. I could feel the pre-burn of the Charlie horse that was going to be wracking my left calf tonight.

"Thanks baby, the tickets are in the front pocket, just hand me one and I'll see ya'll after the show." He handed me the ticket and raced off to catch up with Goodness. As soon as he caught up to her they looped their arms together and he gave her a too-long-from-where-I'm-spying-kiss on the lips. If I had enough breath in my lungs I would have yelled for them to cut that out, but I was wheezing so I had to let that one go. Right now I needed to get some cold water and have a seat. I'd just have to *STOMP* while I was sitting in the air-conditioned concession area of the building. Besides I could feel enough of the bass jumping through my bones that I felt like I was right on stage with the band that was playing. After a few opening acts had completed their performances I decided to get a snack from the concession. I normally wouldn't waste my money, but I was famished and Mario had my backpack with my free stuff in it.

"Renee?....Renee Chase?" This cannot be who I think it is. Breathe Renee. Turn around slowly, maybe it's not...

"Matthew Redmond. Oh my goodness. It's been a long time." I said with a fake grin on my face.

"Eleven years, three months, and two days, but whose counting. You still look beautiful. What brings you to Atlanta? I hope you're not following me." Matthew said, laughing that deep slow laugh, I remember from years ago. So what he still looks like Campbell soup…mmm, mmmm good, Renee…do not get distracted.

"How's your wife?" I asked coolly.

"She left me, can you believe that? Found someone else to make her happy." He said standing a bit too close for comfort. Did this man just put his warm hand on the small of my back?

"I'm sorry to hear that. How long have you been divorced?" I asked stepping away to put a few feet between us.

"Well things are not finalized yet, but I expect within a month I'll be an eligible bachelor. Wouldn't I be lucky if you and Anthony weren't doing so well?" He had a sly smile on his face.

"We are actually doing wonderfully. Things were a little rocky, but we made it. I'm not ashamed to admit that we went to counseling, and it made all the difference, that and of course putting God in the center of our relationship." I answered proudly.

"Yes…well…I'm happy for the two of you. Where is Anthony?" He was looking around the large concession area as he stepped even further away from me. His skin still looked like velvety melt-in-your-mouth chocolate. And those lips…get a hold of yourself Renee.

"He's back home in Baltimore. Our daughter goes to Spelman and I'm getting her settled back into her dorm. We just decided to get out and have fun today." I was gulping my lukewarm bottled water, did somebody turn off the air conditioning in here?

"You can't have a college-aged daughter already. When you and I were together, it was just the boys right?" O.k. now he's stepped back toward me, and is throwing around the *when we were together line*. Renee you need to get away from this man as soon as possible.

"We adopted three of my godchildren. And Goodness was the oldest girl."

"Did you say Goodness? Wow...this has got to be some coincidence. My daughter Talia was meeting her friend Goodness here at the concert today!"

"You've got to be kidding." I said more under my breath than to him. Please be kidding, I mean I really want you to be kidding. Please let some other crazy person in the world have named their child Goodness.

"Let me call her on her cell and have her meet us. Wouldn't that be a trip?" He said flipping his cell phone open and punching in a number. Meanwhile I wanted to run. If I did not think I'd pass out from exhaustion, I would break camp right now.

"You really don't have to do..." He put his finger up to my lip to signal me to stop talking. Is this Negro touching my lip? He has really crossed the boundary lines now.

"Hello? Talia...I have someone I want you to meet. Is your friend Goodness still here? Yeah...bring her with you." He folded the phone and gave me a wink. "They are coming right out." Please, please don't be her. Please Lord please don't be...

"Mommy! Where were you, we tried to save a spot for you." Goodness said coming over to me and giving me a big hug. There was Mario with my backpack of snacks as I stood here with over priced Nachos and a half-gone bottle of water.

"I was a little winded so I needed to rest a bit. Besides I could hear the concert just as good out here where the air is circulating. So...you didn't tell me you were meeting a friend here today." I said through a smile that was hurting my cheeks.

"Yeah, mommy Talia used to live in Baltimore can you believe it? She even used to go to our church."

"My dad was a deacon at the church when Rev. Fowler first got there." Talia said stealing a sip of her father's soda.

"I know. I remember you when you were a little girl." I said.

"Wait…you guys know each other?" Goodness said pointing to Matthew and me.

"Yes…Renee and I go way back. We used to be good friends. It was hard to move away, but sometimes you just need to start over, isn't that right Renee?" Matthew said, looking directly at me and only me. Put the eyes on someone else brotha because it ain't that kind of party.

"Cool…well we're going back in. Are you coming ma?" Goodness asked, grabbing Mario by the hand and pulling him toward her. Did I just see him give her a quick little tap on the behind? I hope my mind is playing tricks on me.

"Actually we have some catching up to do…you guys go on ahead." Matthew answered for the both of us. I don't know if I was starting to have my own private summer, but something about him answering for me was making me boil.

"Look, just so you know. I don't need you to answer for me." I said once the children were out of earshot.

"Whoa. Same old feisty Renee." He said laughing, holding his hands up in an I surrender pose.

"Wrong. There is nothing the same about me and the Renee that almost ruined her life getting involved with you. I have grown and matured, not only physically, but mentally and spiritually." I corrected him. Sounded good enough Renee…repeat it three more times to yourself, spin around and touch the ground, and you might actually sound convincing.

"I didn't mean to offend you. Take it easy. You always were a little dramatic. Half the reason I didn't get on that plane with you to Jamaica was because I was afraid you'd get too emotionally attached and I'd never be able to make a clean break." Did this man just stand here and say that to me?

"So you're saying that it was not the pure guilt of committing adultery that made you change your mind? I thought when we were sitting in that airport that day, we both agreed that what we were doing was wrong before God."

I was starting to flashback to that day. The morning didn't start off with me feeling any kind of guilt. No guilt when I lied to my sons who were standing in my room asking if they could go on the fake women's retreat with me. No guilt when I bumped in to Anthony who was coming in from work late as usual, as I rushed out the door and to my car with my bag packed with lingerie he hadn't seen me in since before the children were born. No guilt as I broke all speed records getting to BWI airport to make my 7:30 am flight to paradise. But just after I passed the last security check-point and was walking up behind Matthew to surprise him with a kiss, something began to unravel. I heard a voice tell me to stop and listen quietly.

Matthew was involved in a heated conversation and I assumed he was talking to his wife trying to convince her he really did have to go on yet another unexpected business trip. So I just stopped and listened to my heart and I knew this was not the right thing to do. God was stopping me because He knew I had something to work on at home. So as soon as Matthew hung up, I approached him. His look of desire soon faded when I began to tell him that I wanted to back out and I thought we shouldn't go on the trip together. It may have been eleven years ago, but I know I distinctly remember us both crying.

Matthew rudely interrupted my thoughts. "You were the one doing all the talking. I was mad that I was going to lose all that money for those tickets. I could have taken someone else besides you."

"O.K. I can give you that one...taking your wife would have been the better alternative." I said trying to put myself in his shoes. O.k. maybe he's not as bad as I thought, I mean he was on the phone talking to her before we left. I hadn't even given Anthony a second thought on my way to the airport.

"I'm not talking about my wife that would have been a waste of a good ticket. I meant someone else like Sis. Choates. She was always willing and able." He smiled rubbing his hands together in the most sinister way.

"Sis. Choates? You cheated on your wife with Thelma Choates?" I was completely taken off guard. Thelma was the associate pastor's wife.

"Oh come on Renee? You can't have thought you were the only one. The women at that church were ripe for the picking. You weren't the first and you certainly weren't the last." He said callously, sipping on his soda, and taking one of my nachos to munch on. He really was getting a little too comfortable. Rule number one, you don't touch my nachos.

"So if you had it like that, why did you leave Baltimore? Why not just break it off with me and keep doing your dirt? It seems like you had plenty of people willing to cover for you." Renee, why are you even entertaining this fool with more questions?

"Things were getting a little hot. When Thelma found out I was taking you to Jamaica instead of her, she threatened to announce that I was the father of her baby in front of the whole church. That was the other half of the reason I didn't go. I spent most of the morning trying to calm her down. She was on her way to the airport the morning we were scheduled to leave, calling me and threatening to come do you some bodily harm. I was on my cell all morning talking her down and then you pulled your little 'I'm a Christian, this ain't right' act on me. As soon as you were done boo-hooing, I went to her house to work things out." He said coldly. He attempted to reach for another nacho, and promptly got the back of his hand slapped.

"I can't believe it! Man when they say He protects you from dangers seen and unseen. I sure didn't see that one. God sure is good. That's all I can say. I was about to ruin my life. For you! And you ain't nothing but a low down dirty dog." I was emphasizing each of those words with a tap on the seat of the bench we were sitting on.

"Hold up girl. I really did have feelings for you. I mean you were different. I could really feel an emotional connection between us. Didn't you ever wonder what if…" He said sliding closer to me.

"I have never even thought about it since we left the airport. God took that away from me. As crazy as it sounds, I told Anthony about us. That man loved me enough to stay and work on our marriage and I thank God. I guess I understand why your wife left you. I bet you just continued on cheating when you got down here." I said standing up to move away from him.

"I deserve your anger. I understand it must be hard for you to find out that I didn't really feel about you the same way you felt about me."

"Matthew are you really that selfish?! It's not about you. You have hurt a lot of people in your life. You sat up in that church and purposefully hurt whole families. Do you know how tormented Thelma was after the birth of that baby? I couldn't figure out why she was so defensive when people said the baby didn't look like Rev. Choates. She has been carrying a secret that will destroy her. Not to mention she and Sis. Gloria, who were best of friends, had a falling out as soon as you left. You were probably sleeping with her too right?" I was getting so angry I could feel my chest tightening, and the whistle of air coming out after every few words.

"Don't get yourself so worked up. Those women deserved just what they got. It was too easy. Like taking candy from a baby. They weren't like you Renee. No matter how hard I pushed, you never gave in. It almost made me want you even more. You know the thrill of the chase. Get it...Mrs. Chase." He said winking at me. Why did he think I was joking with him?

"You know what...I'm done. I've repented because regardless of whether you think I gave in or not, what I did was wrong. The only way you can truly move on and find happiness is to ask God to forgive you and change you. If not, then be careful Matthew Redmond because you reap what you sow." I said and turned to walk away from him.

"So this means we can't have dinner while you're here in Atlanta!" He called after me. I didn't even dignify that with a response.

****

I actually enjoyed the rest of the concert despite the run in with Matthew. Right now I was packing up to make my trip back home. Goodness wanted to stay in the hotel with me, despite the fact that we were paying for a dorm room that was now full of all the essentials a sophomore needed at college. She was staying in the newer Living Learning Center dorms, also known as LLC 1 and 2. The buildings were air-conditioned and came with laundry rooms on each floor. I was hoping to see a whole lot less of her dirty clothes being brought home this year. Her dad made sure to send about five pounds of quarters to school with her this time and a year's supply of detergent. I sensed that something was wrong with Goodness as she helped me fold my clothes into the suitcase. I didn't know if it was because I was leaving or if our encounter with Matthew had unnerved her.

"So you and that dude used to be boyfriend and girlfriend or what?" She asked out of the blue. How's that for getting right to the point.

"What makes you ask me that?"

"Well, he said that you and him go way back, he didn't say nothing about knowing daddy." This girl needs to be a private investigator because she picks up on all kinds of things that I don't.

"You are too smart for your own good. We did have a close relationship, but we met at the wrong time, so we didn't pursue it." How many times can I fold and refold this pink shirt in my hands? I'm not supposed to be nervous about my past. You're a new creation Renee, just remember that.

"Oh so ya'll was creepin'." She said looking directly in my eyes.

"It was not like that. Dad and I were going through some difficult times, and Matthew was just a shoulder to cry on." Put the pink shirt down, it's in a ball now. Move on to something else before little Ms. Detective picks up on these non-verbal cues you're screaming at her.

"And that's all." She said looking at me suspiciously.

"How can I have this conversation with you?" I covered my eyes. I wanted to hide under the bed.

"You always told me I could ask you anything."

"Yes, but not about your mother being trifling over some man." I said trying to chuckle and break the tension. The child would not look to the left or the right, she was just waiting for answers.

"Unfortunately, Matthew and I had some pretty intimate encounters."

"Oooh, intimate encounters. We talking baby-making encounters?"

"Goodness! Why are you doing this to me? What difference does it make? It was wrong. Look we got close enough that the man thought he could invite me to an

Island for the weekend and that I would go. Now we wasn't gonna be readin' books. Up until that point, though, no...no baby-making sessions."

"You sure, that's all?" She said smiling.

"Yes, that's all! Trust me...and I'm glad too. I found out that he was not the person I thought he was back then. God reveals things to you when He knows you can handle them. I am a stronger person now. I used to be so vulnerable."

"Why didn't you go any further with him? I understand if you don't want to talk about it." She had put the shirt down she was folding and took the pink ball from me to fold it properly. The girl scared me because she looked like she was settling in for a long heart to heart conversation and I sure wasn't in the mood to talk about Matthew Redmond any more.

"Well because honestly, I was convicted in my heart. I really loved your dad deep down, even though we were going through. We just didn't have our priorities straight. Through it all I prayed and God kept me from doing something I knew was wrong, but might have done had He not been ordering my steps. And since we're talking about giving in..."

"I knew it, here we go..." Goodness said with a little smile, playfully rolling her eyes.

"Well since you know so much...I've noticed that you and Mario are very touchy feely. Are you two having any second thoughts about your commitment to being abstinent?" My heart was racing, but since we were putting it all out there, I was just going to go for it.

"I'm not going to lie, mom. It's very difficult. Everybody here is having sex with their boyfriends. I found out some of the girls in the FIRE group are even active. I couldn't believe it! Everywhere we go, everybody is all hugged up. Me and Mario are trying mom, but I don't know. What would be so wrong with it, since we know we are going to be married?"

"Goodness, there is a lot of responsibility that comes along with being sexually active. I know you think you are in love right now, but you are young. I like Mario, he's a good person, but if he really cares about you he'll wait. Are you feeling pressure from him?"

"Not at all. We both are sort of just wondering what it would be like." She answered honestly.

"You are not ready. Trust me. Wait. Listen to God on this one. I know he'll probably kill me for having you do this, but call Alex. I think because you guys are young you'll be able to relate. But he's taken a vow of celibacy until marriage. It's a big commitment because he's had experience so he knows what he's missing. Let him talk to you and give you some scripture that he uses when he is feeling weak…sound good?" I offered with the infamous kiss on the forehead. I really am done with this one, no more answers, it's getting a bit hot in here.

"Alright ma, you can stop squirming. I won't ask any more questions." Goodness said with a smile. We zipped up my bag and she carried it to the door for me, so I'd be ready in the morning. We both knelt beside the bed for prayer and then each hopped into our separate double beds. Goodness turned on her bedside lamp and opened the bible that was on the nightstand. I rolled over and fell fast asleep.

Chapter 50: Is This The End?

§

 Note to self... never ride in a car with Goodness or Mario behind the wheel. No person under the age of thirty is driving me anywhere from here on out. The way that boy whipped around those side streets and through the crowded drop off area in front of the airport, I liked to died. Goodness wasn't any better. She called herself chauffeuring me around in her man's car while I was down here, and honey...let me tell you I wouldn't let her drive Miss Daisy...she doesn't put her brakes on soon enough for me! But I thank you Lord for putting your angels all around the car and getting me to the airport safely. I am going to miss my baby, but it's time for me to get back to my man. Seeing Matthew made me long more and more for the wonderful mate that you placed in my life.
 "Hey Lady." The familiar voice said in front of me. It never failed. Bask in some glory and the devil gets mad and shows up.
 "Why are you doing this? How did you find out when I'd be leaving?" I was looking over my huge cup of steaming coffee into the eyes of my past mistakes.

"Why are you so cold? I did a little digging, Talia told me Goodness was coming to the airport with you this morning and I checked a few flights and made an educated guess." Matthew said sitting beside me.

"That's called stalking Matthew and it's a crime." I said dryly. I was not flattered or amused by his attention.

My nostrils were burning from the smell of the cologne that he obviously bathed in this morning. And I used to think he smelled so good. What was really going on with me back then? "Where is your daughter anyway?" He was looking around as he slid closer to me in the seat.

"Not that it's your business, but she wanted to get back to register for some last minute courses." I said still pretending to read my magazine.

He reached across my lap and plucked the boarding pass out of my travel bag. He had some nerve. First of all thinking that he could violate my space like that and secondly to be so bold as to follow me and think whatever it was I was sure he was thinking.

"I'm just saying, you are all the way down here…no husband, no kids, just you and me. According to this boarding pass, your flight doesn't take off for another two hours. What do you say we just pick up a quick bite to eat, right here. We don't even have to leave the concourse."

"Then you'll leave me alone?" This could be a good thing.

"Scouts honor. It's just lunch Renee, come on…my treat." He said taking my hand and pulling me out of my seat. I'd forgotten just how warm and firm those hands were. I snatched my hand away from him immediately.

"Let's just go right here…I'm not that hungry, but if it will get you in the direction of the exit quicker, then let's do it." I said walking to a small deli, he followed closely behind.

"Ouch...I guess I deserve all the hostility. I couldn't stop thinking about you last night. I really am sorry that I hurt you. And I have to admit that I was a bit jealous that you and Anthony were able to work things out. I admire your character and your forgiving spirit. I wish Melanie could be the same way."

"If you want to admire someone it should be Anthony. He put up with my mess, knew that I'd been out with you and still staid with me. He tried to be the bigger man before we even got to the marriage counseling."

"Well I don't blame the brother. I'd try to stay on your good side too...We're ready to order." Matthew said turning to the waitress.

"What are you talking about? If anybody needed to kiss up it was me. I'm the one that stepped outside of the marriage. I'm the one that foolishly turned to someone else thinking that I could fill the missing pieces." I said quietly as the waitress approached.

"Yes, I'll have the Surf and Turf with a Corona. The lady will have a Chicken Caesar Salad and a raspberry iced tea." He had totally ignored my question, and he was speaking for me again. That burned me up.

"I hope you don't mind that I ordered you the salad, you've lost a few pounds and I want to help you keep it off. If you'd have been this tight when we were dating..."

"Don't even go there." I said interrupting him. I was not in the mood to hear any more of his stroll down memory lane.

"I'm just trying to compliment you Renee. Anthony is a lucky man. I got to call the brotha and take some notes from him. I'd never be able to get Melanie to take me back after all the dirt I did."

"What could Anthony possible have in common with you? When it comes to doing dirt, I think you have him beat?" I said crossing my arms and legs, hoping to shut off all signs of welcome he thought he saw.

"Your husband is not as perfect as you think he is Renee. You wanna know why he was so quick to forgive your relationship with me, because you weren't the only person in your marriage that was being dishonest." He was leaning back in his seat with his arms folded. Those eyes that I used to love to gaze into were now cold and black.

"You know what…I'm not going to sit here and listen to any lies you have to tell me eleven years after the fact. And even if there is some truth to whatever you think you have on him, it is in the past. There is nothing you can tell me that will make me love my husband any less."

"I'm not so sure about that." He said looking me in the eyes and smiling. I wanted to wipe that grin right off of his face.

"I know I'm going to regret this later, but I'll bite…what do you think you have on Anthony? Nine times out of ten, I already know. I know he used to smoke weed, I know he had his days in the strip clubs, I even know about when he lapsed back into drinking…but again all that has been given to God."

"Ahh…Little naïve Renee. Let me fill you in on something. When your man comes home willingly telling you about all the indecencies he's been doing, he's just trying to throw you off so you won't find out about the real stuff. Weed? Strip clubs, alcohol, baby come on…those are petty offenses."

Our plates had arrived, but at this point I was not even hungry. Everything inside of me was telling me to just get up and leave him sitting there, but I had to know. What had Anthony done?

"Aren't you going to eat?" He said digging into his food like an animal, chugging the beer and belching loudly. What a pig. How could I have not seen him for who he really was?

"I'm not hungry. I think I'm going to let you just finish this alone. I can't stand to be in your presence anymore." I got up and tossed my napkin over my food. I wanted to throw my drink on him, but that was a bit too *As The World Turns* for me.

"Walk away Renee. But when you get home ask Mr. Perfection about Lydia Anderson…yeah ask him if she still has that short yellow dress with the pink flowers on it." He was laughing a sly dark laugh now. If I had my eyes closed I would have thought Vincent Price has come back from the dead and any minute goblins and ghouls were gonna start dancing and prancing around talking about a killer, thriller, tonight!

I turned to him, this time I could not maintain my composure. The tea ended up in his face. "You are a liar and the truth is not in you! I don't know why you are doing this to me, what you think you have to gain…but I believe my husband. He doesn't even know a Lydia Anderson."

"No…Renee…you don't know Lydia Anderson. Your husband knows her all too well." He said as he continued to laugh hysterically. "Have a relaxing flight…I look forward to seeing you back in town sometime. Maybe next time we can just stop all the games and get right down to business. I know you still want me baby." He'd stood up and was in my face sneering with the tea dripping from his face like sweat. His breath was hot on my neck as he reached toward me and tried to pull me into a hug. It took all my strength to get out of his grasp.

"I hope I never see you again…you are a sick, deranged person Matthew Redmond." Thank God they began boarding calls early. I was among one of the first groups of people that was called to board, and none too soon, because I could not stand another minute with this man.

I was tortured the whole flight. Not by the annoying snoring of the man next to me, or the child kicking my seat from behind, but by my own thoughts. I thought Anthony and I had cleared the air, put everything out in the open and he neglected to tell me he was having an affair with some tramp named Lydia? How could I have been so blind? And he's just smiling up in my face like butter doesn't melt in his mouth, pointing the finger at me like I was the one to blame for the troubles we've had. Well he has another thing coming when I get home. This is the end of me being taken for a fool.

Chapter 51: United We stand, Divided We Fall

§

As soon as the plane landed I was praying that Anthony would be at the airport waiting for me. I'd made arrangements for Alex to pick me up, but knowing Anthony he'd want to surprise me with some silly flowers or candy or something. As my bags were making their way around the carousel, my lying husband did not disappoint. I could see him approaching the baggage claim area with a huge bouquet of yellow roses.

"Hey baby, I've missed you so much. These are for you." He sang loudly, kissing me and squeezing me to him with the arm that wasn't weighed down with the flowers.

"Yellow. Is that your favorite color?" I said coolly with my arms still at my side.

"You know my favorite color is red girl. What's with you? I haven't seen my woman in more than two weeks and I can't get no love?" He said putting the flowers down beside him and opening his arms for a hug. I walked toward him and gave him a short hug and kiss on the cheek. When I stepped back he had a confused look on his face.

"O.k. I'm pretty good at reading your moods, but right now I'm a little confused. You wanna tell me what's got you so bothered that you can't even greet your husband with a hug and a kiss?"

"I did give you a hug and a kiss, oh but maybe I didn't do it like Lydia Anderson."

"What in the world are you talking about?" Anthony asked, with his face so twisted up it was almost comical.

"Don't stand there and act like you never heard the name before. I said Lydia Anderson…and I want to know why I had to go all the way to Atlanta to find out about her."

"Is Lydia living in Atlanta?" Anthony asked. He looked like he'd even perked up a bit. Don't make me have to go upside his head.

"So you do know Lydia Anderson." I'm going to jail for murder. Help me Jesus!

"Of course I know Lydia, Renee. Her son and daughter went to school with our oldest boys. You don't remember Nick was going to take her daughter Precious to the prom his junior year?" Let me think. I remember some girl named Precious, I mean how many girls does one come across named Precious? He didn't go to the prom with her for some reason that escapes my mind right now…

"You remember she was in that horrible car accident with her brother about a month before the prom. A drunk driver hit them. Her brother died and she ended up in the hospital for a few months. Man, Lydia was never the same after that. That thing took a toll on her marriage. Man, everybody was talking about the fact that her and her husband didn't stay together. She kept blaming herself for what happened. It's good to know she's doing well. Where abouts is she living in Atlanta?"

"She's not living in Atlanta." I snapped at him. "I mean I don't know where she's living. I just ran into somebody that told me you two knew each other, and had been spotted in an intimate situation with each other." I was starting to feel like a fool because Anthony appeared genuinely concerned about this woman, and wasn't reacting in a way indicative of somebody trying to hide anything.

"You know you're not making any sense. Who did you see in Atlanta? An intimate situation? Wait…wait a minute."

"Well it's really not that important so let's just get my bags and go." The words were running out of my mouth. I picked up the flowers and started heading for the exit.

"No, don't try to change the subject now Renee. You came at me with venom when I approached you a few minutes ago, and I know that's because you must have been in the company of a snake. You saw Matthew while you were in Atlanta?"

"Why would you say that?" I answered. For some reason my voice had risen five octaves.

"Just answer the question." Whew if looks could kill, I'd be six feet under right now.

"It wasn't anything bad. His daughter is friends with Goodness, can you believe that? I saw him at the concert I took her to, and the next day when we were having lunch…he mentioned…"
Anthony cut me off. "Wait you had lunch with him? Unbelievable. I'm here thinking about you, can't wait until you get home…and you're out having lunch with the man that almost ruined our marriage!" It was Anthony's turn to storm off now. He'd grabbed my suitcase and was stomping through the airport toward the exit.

"I just did it to get rid of him. He was bothering me Anthony. He wouldn't leave me alone about what we used to have, and how you were doing dirt too…and I don't know I just let it get to me."

"Renee I have been nothing but honest with you. I never cheated on you I can promise you that, but you keep getting pulled in and fooled by this man. Why?"

"How come you didn't tell me about Lydia? Matthew said he saw you guys together and to ask you about her sexy yellow and pink dress." I said folding my arms. Now what do you have to say?

"You want the truth. O.k. I did go out with Lydia one night. NO I didn't say anything to you about it because there was nothing to tell. After that accident with her kids the woman went off the deep end. I was coming home from work one morning and it was pouring down rain. Who do I see standing in the middle of the street but Lydia? She's hysterical…crying, cursing, and high out her mind. She was blabbering about wanting to end it all. I made her get in my car and I took her to get some coffee. Man she was so out of it we literally stumbled into the bar…it was the only place opened at that time in the morning. And guess who I saw all hugged up in a corner?"

His voice was like acid now, I was afraid to answer so I just stood silently looking at him.

"I saw your little boyfriend Matthew with Thelma Choates. I knew you two were seeing each other before you even told me…I'm not dumb Renee. I could tell the way you guys were looking at each other in church. He saw me and thought I'd go run off and tell Rev. Choates about them being there, so he told me that if I ever mumbled a word, he'd let everybody know I was cheating on you with Lydia."

"So you didn't tell me because you were afraid of Matthew Redmond? That doesn't even sound like you Anthony…try again." I hissed. I was getting a little bolder.

"No I didn't say anything because Lydia was hurting. I wanted to get her help. She was embarrassed and didn't even want me to mention her name when I went to the church looking for some contacts for her. You can ask Rev. Fowler if you don't believe me, I went to her and got some names of therapists Lydia could see. Now because you and I were talking divorce at the time I just felt sorry for you because I knew that you were counting on Matthew to be your knight in shining armor and here he was out with the church tramp. I never thought this would come up again. I really thought that we'd matured enough to not let the enemy come in between us again…but I guess I was wrong."

At this point we'd made it to the car, even in his anger Anthony stopped and opened the door for me. He did slam it just a bit too hard once I was in, but who can blame him. When I turned to put my purse on the back seat I felt even more stupid if that's possible because there were two huge teddy bears in the back seat each holding a large bouquet of yellow roses. On the dashboard there was a card addressed to me.

"What's all this for?" I asked him once he'd gotten in and zoomed away from the curb causing the card to fall in my lap.

"Open the card." He said without taking his eyes off of the road. He was clenching his teeth so hard I could see the muscles in his cheek jumping.

My eyes watered as I read the words of the hand written note.

To my dearest Renee,
Words can not describe what a blessing you have been to me. The whole time you were gone, all I could do was think about you and what you've meant to me. Our vows say until death do we part, and for a while I was not sure we'd make it that far. But thanks be to God for your trust in me and your faithfulness. I will love you until the end of time. Welcome home!

Anthony
Way to go Renee. I let the enemy trick me again. Lord help me to make this right.

*****

The thirty-minute ride home felt like an eternity. Once we got inside, I heard Anthony calling The Chart House downtown to cancel our dinner reservations. He walked passed me and went upstairs without one word. He came back down and handed me a small black velvet box.

"This was for you." He mumbled.

"Anthony…I'm sorry for not believing in you. What can I do baby to make you talk to me?"

"Let me just have a little time upstairs to myself." He said putting his hand up to stop me from talking.

"I can make you something to eat. Are you hungry?" I said trying to sound happy.

"Not really…I'll see you in a bit, let me get changed out of these clothes." He dragged himself over to the stairs, reaching up to tear down the paper banner that had WELCOME HOME SWEETIE written in bold purple block letters. How could I have been so stupid? The man obviously had prepared a romantic evening with me as the guest of honor. I had to get busy here. I know when I'm wrong and I needed to get my husband to forgive me.

He must have been in that prayer closet for almost two hours, because I was able to whip up a delicious dish of Shrimp fettuccini Alfredo, a tossed salad, and chocolate mousse for dessert all before I heard him emerge from upstairs. I'd taken the time to set the table with the good china, light candles all over the first floor and get out a bottle of white wine. Next I jumped in the shower and washed away all that filth of distrust, and the lingering smell of Matthew's cologne. I put on a fresh white silk gown, pulled my locs up into a chignon, put the stunning diamond earrings in that my husband just gave me and glided down the stairs in my fluffy high heeled slippers. Anthony was standing at the bottom of the stairs waiting for me.

"So…trying to get on my good side huh?" He said taking my hand to help me down the last few stairs. It has been a while since I'd been up on top of these stilettos, he could see I was struggling.

I playfully leaned on him, and gave him that big hug he was looking for at the airport. "Trying. Is it working?"

"It might be…I'll let you know after dessert." He said and kissed me. It was the perfect evening to a day that started out in chaos. God I thank you for being you. For giving my husband and I the power to stand strong together in spite of the enemy's attempts to destroy us. I know we haven't seen the last of trials and tribulations, but we are going to continue the fight and prepare ourselves together for whatever may come our way.

Chapter 52: Another Journey Begins

§

In the words of Danny Glover from one of those Lethal Weapon movies, 'I'm getting' too old for this stuff.' I feel like one of those host from animal planet hovering in a bush whispering about some unsuspecting animal that's about to get a tranquilizer dart to the rear end. Julia and I are literally in some bushes behind an abandoned warehouse downtown waiting for the infamous police signal for yet another raid. Lord knows my knees are wondering why we've been crouched down here for the last forty minutes instead of sitting in the news van drinking hot coco. Everything in me is telling me that this is not going to be pretty. I told myself no more undercover mess, but Harold needed me to cover and goodness knows the man has done so much for me that I just couldn't say no. So here I sit, I mean crouch with my knees and ankles screaming for me to stand up and get the circulation flowing.

"Tell me one more time why we are doing this Steve Irwin impression behind these bushes?" I whispered tapping Julia on the shoulder. Girlfriend was putting on makeup getting ready for her close-up I guess.

"Because Renee…if we wait in the van which is all the way down the street, we'll never make it up to the action in time to get these guys on camera before they throw their jackets over their heads. I have to get the close ups."

"You ever heard of something called a zoom? They got one on every camera now. You know Jamie the camera man can get shots of stuff from blocks away, he's done it before."

"He can get the shot, but I can't get the sound byte." I could tell the girl was getting annoyed with me, by the way she was rolling her eyes up in her head with every answer.

"So why am I here with you? You're getting the sound byte, I don't have anything to write for you." I was beyond frustrated. I was tired and cranky and it wasn't even that time of the month.

"You're covering for Harold, and he gets in the trenches with me. I want to try and get as close to the building as possible so I can hear whatever is going on in there. Come on let's move a little closer." Before I knew it, she'd taken my hand and was guiding me closer to the back entrance of the building.

"I think we need to wait for the signal. I don't even see any cops back here. Are you sure they went into the building already?" At this point my heart was beating a mile a minute and that annoying whistling sound squeezing out from my lungs was about to blow our cover.

"Renee, you're not turning into a wimp on me, are you? We've done this stake out thing more times than I can count, now get your breathing under control before somebody hears us out here." Julia was trying to make light of the situation I'm sure, because she was smiling and trying to shush me quietly, but that done just made me mad.

"Look, don't forget who your elders are. I'm not trying to get hurt out here. Now I believe in my Creator's ability to get me out of any situation, but I also know that

I need to use some common sense so I don't end up in something I'm not supposed to be in. Now my question was...are you sure the cops went in that building?" I guess the fact that I was talking through a tight jaw let her know I wasn't up for no foolishness, because the smile quickly faded from her face.

"I'm not sure, so let's get closer and see if we hear anything. Renee come on, where's your sense of adventure?"

I was about to find it real quick, because as soon as she finished her question the back door burst open and suddenly there were people running everywhere. Now I don't know who was running or why they were running, but honey I tell you I took off in the opposite direction with the quickness. All of those days training for that marathon a while back came to remembrance. I was gone like a light and I would have been back to the van safely if not for two very unfortunate incidents. The first was that I was quickly beginning to notice that my chest was tightening, my lungs were burning and I was starting to wheeze even more. The second is that I lost my footing and fell hard to the ground skidding a few feet and landing with a thud up against the passenger side door of the van. I know we were trying to be covert and undercover but the moment I came to a stop I had to scream because of all the pain in my left leg, which was pinned underneath of me.

"Renee! Renee! Are you alright!" One of the engineers that was still in the van was yelling frantically at me. He got out and ran around to help me. He reached down to help me get up and I immediately collapsed back down to the ground.

"Ouch! I can't stand on it! I can't walk. I'm gonna need help!" He flipped open his phone to call 911. Meanwhile Julia was running toward us.

"What is going on? Renee why in the world did you take off like that?"

"What do you mean? You didn't see all them fools come running out of that back door?" I was yelling because of the pain and she was getting on my nerves with the stupid questions.

"Those were some of the under cover guys. They were trying to get them out of the building quickly so when the police came in from the front they wouldn't be shooting at any of their own guys!"

"Well I mean they just came busting out the door, and we hadn't gotten any signal, I didn't know what to do."

"Well if you had been listening you would have heard them say they were sending them out." Julia said throwing her hands up in the air. The girl almost sounded like she was upset with me.

"Well forgive me for being confused at two in the morning in a back alley! You could ask how I'm doing seeing as I'm being loaded in an ambulance." Since we were literally right behind Johns Hopkins Hospital the ambulance arrived in about two minutes. Julia seemed oblivious to the whole fact that I was injured.

"I'm sorry…it's just that…I can't believe I missed that one Renee. It was gonna be big. Let me see if I can get some information to go live with in the morning. Give me a call once you get back home." She sulked off in the direction of the officers who were standing around near the entrance I'd just run for my life from.

I didn't even have time to think of a good comeback to that one. Paramedics asking questions surrounded me.

"I just need something for the pain, my left leg is killing me."

****

"Girl you got to learn how to just ask for days off." Anthony said when he finally made it to the hospital. I didn't want anybody making a big deal out of what I assumed was a sprained ankle so I asked the hospital not to call him until after his shift. I should have told the kids the same thing because as soon as I got off the telephone with Marie she called her dad.

"Ha, Ha very funny. I'm in pain be nice to me." Just moving to find a comfortable position for me and my leg which was swollen to twice it's size from the knee down was pure agony.

"I love you babe, but you ain't no spring chicken, you can't be running around with these youngster and trying to do what they do." Anthony said laughing while he helped me prop the pillows behind my head.

"Look don't worry about what season chicken I am…I'm glad you're here. The nurse said the doctor wants to talk to me about my labs. And as tired as I am right now I'm liable to miss something important, so I need your alert ears." As soon as I said that the door eased open and in walked a young handsome doctor. I recognized him as one of the first doctors that greeted me at the door. He barked orders that an x-ray and CBC be done and then was on his way.

"Mr. and Mrs. Chase, I'm doctor Merick. Sorry you've had to wait so long for the results of your diagnostics, it's been kind of crazy. But listen I have some good news and some bad news." He pulled up a chair and motioned for Anthony to sit down. Not a good sign when the doctor wants you to sit down to hear news.

"What you got for us Doc? This here is Renee Chase and she can pretty much bounce back from anything." Anthony said with a bit of a chuckle. I appreciated his attempt to lighten the mood, but it wasn't doing a thing for me right now.

"Well the good news is you have two hairline fractures, right here and here. One at your distal fibula, and the other just below the proximal head of the tibia."

O.k. what does that mean? He was holding up the x-ray and pointing to stuff, but that's just like handing me a newspaper written in German and asking me what the day's headlines were all about.

"Doc, can you tell us what that means in English? I get the hairline fracture part…means it wasn't a clean break, right?"

"Yes, Mr. Chase, you are correct. This kind of fracture means there is just a tiny crack in the structure of the bone, but it certainly doesn't minimize the pain."

"Amen! I can attest to that! So let me try to get this straight. I've written enough medical stories to know that those two bones are somewhere around my lower leg."

"Absolutely correct Mrs. Chase. You basically have an ankle and a knee fracture. The way you landed on your leg caused the bones to twist just enough in opposite directions to cause the cracks."

"And that is the good news?" Anthony and I spoke the same exact words at the same time.

"It's good in that you will need to be off of your leg for a few weeks, and you won't require any surgery or even casting. We can give you an immobilizer and you can be expected to recover full function in the leg. Now about the other concern…" This time Dr. Merick was looking around for a chair to sit on. He found a stool and pulled it up close to the railing on the bed. The look on his face reminded me of the look Dr. Grander had the first time I was diagnosed with cancer. "The other concern is your white blood cell count. Your numbers are very high. I'm also not happy about your oxygen saturation levels while you're on room air. Your lungs didn't sound good on auscultation, so I've ordered respiratory therapy for you and I'm starting you on oxygen, and with your history we called your oncologist. He suggested we get a chest x-ray. He wants the results STAT…said he'd be in to talk to you himself in the morning."

"Are you thinking that my cancer has returned? You can be straight with me, you don't have to try and sugar-coat anything." Even though I said that I really didn't mean it. Right now all I wanted was sugar and lots of it. Coat it anyway you want it…powdered, crystals, roll it in melted chocolate…I don't want this thing back at all.

"The guys are right here now to do the x-ray. I won't really have answers until I can see what your lungs look like."

"My lungs…my lungs…the wheezing…the shortness of breath." I wasn't really talking to anyone in particular, just whispering to myself. But it was becoming clear to me. If I was being honest with myself I had suspicions a while back, but I didn't want to let myself believe that it could be back. I hadn't felt any lumps in my breast during my self-exams in the shower and I just refused to believe that…

"Renee, listen don't start worrying. Let's see what this test looks like." Anthony interrupted my moment when he touched my face trying to smooth out the furrow that had grown between my eyebrows.

"Listen doc, we've been trying to do all the research we can about this thing ever since Renee first got diagnosed almost six years ago. Now I thought since we got past that five-year mark we'd be o.k. Is it typical for breast cancer to spread to a lung?"

"Again, I don't want to rush to diagnose until I have more testing. We need to see your lungs. I need to be as informed as possible before I can discuss your options." I'm sure he already knew the options, but with a six-foot-three black man staring you down, daring you to tell his wife she got cancer, you kind of want to soften things up a bit.

"I already know what it's gonna be. I already know. I waited too long." I was still talking barely above a whisper. I didn't want to waste any good air I might have in my lungs. I just laid still, reclined back in the bed while they had Anthony step out of the tiny room so I could get the x-ray done.

Chapter 53: God Gives Us Courage

§

Like I said...I already knew. So it didn't really upset me when Dr. Grander came into the room about two hours later with a very grim look on his face. Apparently it was bad enough that he couldn't wait until his usual 9:00 am rounds. Here it was 7:00 am and he was walking in the door. I had to nudge Anthony awake. He'd quickly gone home to make sure the kids were up and moving so they'd be able to get out to school on time, and rushed right back without having a wink of the sleep he was used to getting in the wee hours of the morning.

"Let me guess...you have some good news and some bad news right?" I said smiling at him.

"I know, we have to come up with a better opening line don't we? Can you believe they actually teach us that in school?" Dr. Grander pulled up a chair and sat beside me, taking my hand in his. "Renee, I sure wish I didn't have to be the one to tell you this, but the cancer has returned, and it is unfortunately in your lungs. The films show a significant amount of metastasis on the left upper lobe, with some fluid infiltrates bilaterally in your lower lobes. Your lungs are just not working at full capacity. It explains lots of those symptoms you've described to the team here with the onset of wheezing, the fatigue, the difficulty breathing, those bouts of coughing. It presents like a stage III lung cancer. Your blood work indicates there are elevations in four proteins that we now know are markers for this kind of cancer."

"So what do we do now? Can't we just start some chemo again?" Anthony was still rubbing his eyes, but jumped right into the conversation.

"Yes, I actually want to get you ready to start a round as soon as possible. We want to keep you here for a few days and see if we can give you a heavy dose of tamoxifen, we'll put you on the port again and keep an eye on your red and white blood cells. Today though I want to get you started on some B12 just like we did before, your system is going to need that folic acid. I'm thinking we'll follow that up with some radiation therapy to get to that lung tissue, since surgery is not an option for you at this point. I am going to do my best to offer you as many options as possible." He never looked down, or pretended to read his papers like most doctors did. He looked Anthony and I right in our eyes as he talked to us.

"I trust that you will." Talk about awkward silence. I guess he wanted me to start crying in hysterics, but there you go again God. I have peace. I know that whatever your will is, it shall be done. Now I'm a firm believer in your healing power, so that is how I choose to deal with this recent medical news. Dr. Grander squeezed my hand and quietly got up to leave. I looked over to Anthony just in time to see him wipe away a tear. If I opened my mouth to talk, I knew that I would be crying too, so I just motioned for him to come to me. He laid his heavy head on my lap and cried like I never heard him cry before. All I could do was rub his rough cheeks and chin, where he'd let the hair grow in just to please me because I loved seeing him with facial hair. He did it even though it bothered him and made his face itch, but he loved me just that much.

"I don't want to lose you Renee." He said between loud sobs, his shoulders shaking so much it was almost making my leg hurt more.

"I'm not lost. You have me forever...remember? We will always be together. This is not the end of anything, only the beginning. I need you to be strong for me and for your family."

"I can't!" He cried.

"You can. You can and you will. I need all my energy to go through this treatment and I need your prayers. You can go on and cry sweetheart...it's so good to cry, but then you wipe those tears and listen to what God wants you to do for us." I knew that we were in for a rough road ahead, but I also knew that it was not my battle to fight. I have given so much over to you God that I can't let this be any different.

****

After the third day of treatment I was wishing I could give up the nausea and vomiting, but then I stopped to marvel because hey I could have been gone a long time ago.

"Hand me that pink thing that's shaped like a jelly bean...quick!" I yelled at Alex making him jump up from his chair and rush to my side with the emeses basin.

"Ma, I wish you didn't have to go through this. Do you want me to get the nurse?"

"Unless she can get sick for me I don't think there is much she can do. I got to ride this out...it will all be over soon. Listen you've got to thank Sis. Agnes for that huge bouquet of flowers over there, and tell your pastor I appreciate all of his prayers."

"You got that. I'm about to get out of here...Niecey wants to meet again to see Morgan. Supposedly she's been doing pretty good at the half-way house she's staying in. I told her we'd meet at the park for an hour, then I've got to get to class. I'm having a test today on spiritual gifts."

"Dad told me you were studying hard last night. Said Morgan made him read the same story over and over again while you were gone." I had to beam, Morgan turned Anthony into a big pile of soft mush whenever she was around.

"I can't tell you how much it has meant to have ya'll support with that girl. Oh, and check this out...I told dad I would show you this because I wanted to see what you'd say." He handed me a folder with what looked like a test on the inside. "The professor wanted us to take this before we came to class."

It took me a few minutes to scan the report and understand what I was reading. "And I see here that according to this test you have the gift of Shepherding or Pastoring." I just looked at him smiling.

"Well those test are wrong all the time, I might have been tired when I answered the questions. I know I'm definitely not nobody's preacher." He said backing away from the folder he just handed me like it was on fire.

"Boy you didn't have to get on the computer and take this test to know that God is calling you to a higher place. I pray that I live to see it."

"Ma don't talk like that. You still got a lot of kick left in you, besides I need you around to help me raise my little girl into a Godly woman. I want her to be just like her nana." He leaned in and gave me a kiss on the forehead.

"Baby God has equipped you with all you'll need to raise her in the right way. Now go and take that test and you don't worry about if the answer is what you want it to be, you pray that it is what God wants for you." He rushed out the door, leaving the folder with his spiritual gift inventory in my lap. I spent the rest of the day reading over it and asking God to give him the courage to step out and lead the way he was created to do.

Chapter 54: Using My Breath To Plant Seeds

§

After the first week of inpatient chemotherapy, I was back in my blue recliner getting a round of chemo two days-a-week as an outpatient. Madison from Soulful Survivors was there faithfully on Tuesdays and Thursdays to take me to my appointment since I wasn't able to drive with my bones still on the mend. The therapy had wreaked havoc on my red blood cells destroying bone marrow, and making it difficult for my little hairline fractures to heal. My leg was still just as swollen and painful as it was more than three weeks ago. The good news was there were no clots, the bad news was the fractures weren't healing. There we go with that good news and bad news again.

"Girl after I drop you off, I'm going to get us some strawberry gelatos from Rita's! I haven't had one of those in forever and you deserve one." Madison said as she helped me out of the car and into a wheelchair.

"Yuck! I can't even think about strawberry anything. It seems like this go round I have an aversion to all things citrus, just bring me back a large decaffeinated ice-tea." Just the mention of strawberries had my stomach starting to gurgle.

"Boring! I'll see you in a few sis." Madison was on her way after she dropped me off on the oncology floor.

"Hey Mrs. Renee, I got your cocktail all ready for you! Let's get this party started right! Dr. Grander just left orders that you'll be discontinued from this treatment and then start your radiation next week." Shelly said. She was still doing her thing, being the best nurse ever. I had to admit she was a little rough around the edges when she spoke, but the girl knew her stuff.

I must have dozed off for an hour or more because the next thing I knew I was being shaken awake by Madison.

"Nay?...Nay? Girl I got your iced tea. Nay girl wake up so we can talk about this fine guy I saw working in the radiation lab, he must be new because he wasn't there the last time I was here."

"I was right in the middle of a nice dream." I yawned taking the drink from her with a smile.

"Oooh, did it involve Denzel all thugged out like he was in Training Day?!" She screamed and put her hand up for me to slap her five.

"You know you are just about as crazy as they come. I was dreaming about my life and my blessed family. God has been so good to me, that it just makes me smile."

"I hear that. Listen, I've wanted to tell you this, but with all that you've had going on, I didn't know how to bring it up." She paused and was actually wringing her hands together.

"What's wrong, you look like you're scared to tell me something. Did you see Niecey on the corner again? Girl that is old news, supposedly she's in some half-way house." I said taking a sip of my tea and shooing her with my hand.

"No...I got some news from Dr. Grander and I just...well he says I'm doing real good...um...that he thinks I'm one of his success stories since I'm ten years in remission."

"So why do you look so sad, Madison that is great news! I am blessed by hearing it and you should be doing a happy dance right now. If my leg wasn't all gimped up I'd do one for you!" I screamed and motioned for her to come closer so I could give her a hug.

"It just doesn't seem fair that you're the one with the great relationship with God and always trying to set us on the right path, yet you're the one in here with the worst diagnosis out of all of us. You have so much more to live for...you have your family and your grandchildren. You have a husband that loves you and you have to go through all of this. I look at how I've been living my life since my diagnosis, and I haven't always done what I should, I haven't been in church or thanked God as much as I should, yet He saw fit to heal me completely." She said all of that with a look of bewilderment on her face.

"When you realize that it's not about you then you'll understand. I'm not in a relationship with God to try to trick Him or bribe Him into giving me a longer healthier life. I have life and I have it abundantly. Now I don't necessarily get to decide what abundantly means, but God knows what He wants it to mean in my life. I have abundant peace, I get abundant love from my family, I am abundantly proud of my son Alex and what a great father he has become. I am abundantly blessed by my friendships and the joys I get to share. Do I wish I never had cancer? Sure. Do I wish I didn't have to be back here? You bet. But it doesn't make me love God any less. This is nothing compared to what He gave up for me."

"You're faith is unbelievable Renee. Your trust is beyond anything I'm capable of." Madison said quietly shaking her head.

"That's where you are wrong. This faith I have is on the inside of everybody created by God. You just have to know how to tap into it. I want you to promise that you'll come to Calvary Zion Baptist with me this Sunday."

"Girl you know Sunday is my only day off. I've been working crazy hours. Besides I watch Creflo on TV, without fail."

"When I get up from here, I'm going upside your head for that comment." I laughed at her. "You know how I feel about folk that stay in on Sunday to rest...the bible says you must assemble together to hear the word of God. When you get home, open up that bible I gave you last year for Christmas and go to Hebrews the tenth chapter and the twenty-fifth verse...it says 'Let us not give up meeting together, as some are in the habit of doing, but let us encourage one another'...you read the whole chapter picking up where I left off." She was scribbling down the passage on the back of her Rita's napkin.

"I'm gonna do it too Renee. Of course I have to figure out where I put the bible, but as soon as I find it, I'm gonna read it." I just shook my head, the girl was a trip.

Chapter 55: What A Difference a Day Makes

§

The last few days have been good days for me. I'm eating whole meals and keeping them down. The radiation wasn't as bad this time. I was feeling relaxed because it had been almost a month since I'd been into the station. Alvin approved my extended sick leave to allow me time to fully recuperate. But it was hard for me to stay away so I started picking up bit assignments here and there that I could do from home. I really overdid it last night, which is why I was sitting in bed trying hard to keep my eyes open to catch one of the stories I'd submitted for the news at noon.

"Renee, you'll never guess who I saw today."

Anthony said, flopping onto the bed. I know he thought he was helping, taking some time off of work to be with me all day every day, but didn't somebody say absence makes the heart grow fonder? I was really trying to get my nap on since the little snippet of the piece I wrote just ended, but it was looking like I was going to have to play blast from the past with my husband. He was always running into this one or that one when he was out doing missionary work for the church. God love him.

"Boy, you know I am not good at guessing, so just tell me who it was." I said pushing myself up so I could prop against the headboard. My leg was still pretty uncomfortable, and the pain pills weren't doing anything but making me more sleepy.

"Just take one guess. It's somebody very close to you, that you haven't seen in years…girl you'll never guess!" He was so excited, I almost felt like he didn't want me to get the answer right.

"Is it somebody from school, or my old neighborhood?" I asked, barely able to keep my eyelids open.

"Yes." He responded with the silliest grin on his face.

"Yes, what Anthony? You just said yes to both questions." I was beginning to get annoyed, I wanted to go to my happy place.

"The person did go to your school, and did live in your neighborhood. In fact ya'll lived very, very close to each other." He said acting like he'd just given me a great clue.

"I have no clue, babe…the meds have me spaced out, just tell me already so I can get back to napping."

"I saw your sister Gwen."

"What! Gwen? Where was she?" I was fully awake now, and pulling on Anthony's shirt.

"Me and a couple of the guys from church were going to fellowship with the men at the shelter, when we passed a long line of sistas waiting to get into the women's shelter right next to it. Babe, when I walked up to the door and looked over, it was no mistaking who she was. Ya'll are identical especially since your hair is so silver now. She said her husband passed away a few years ago, and left her in a bad financial situation. She's been in and out of shelters for the past two years."

"Are you serious? Why didn't she contact me, why wouldn't she let me know she was in so much trouble? I mean I would have given her shelter." I would have jumped up and gotten dressed that instant if my leg wasn't throbbing.

"You know I asked her all that. She said she didn't want to be a burden. She heard through Antwan a while back that you had breast cancer, she even knew about the tussles you had with Alex while he was out on the street. She told me she was praying every night Alex would get away from Antwan."

"How did her husband die?"

"Renee, he was caught up in drugs too. Can you believe it, Antwan just about tried to destroy everybody in his family. Gwen was able to find out all this stuff about you because Antwan was her husband's supplier. Once he got real hooked, she had to sometimes go get drugs for him to keep him calm. You know Antwan was loving that. When he overdosed, your brother was still looking for her to pay him the money that her husband owed." I was in disbelief.

"So where is she now?"

"She didn't want to come home with me, but I let her know we were still at the same address, and I gave her the number again. When it's time she'll come around, Renee." He said all that, patted me on the shoulder like he didn't just come in here and turn my world around, and headed on downstairs.

Anthony wasn't lying...she did come around. The very next day. I was just patting myself on the back for successfully making it down the stairs with my crutches and getting my leg propped up on the sofa when the doorbell rang. Now normally that was not a problem because there was always somebody to get the door. Since I'd left the hospital family and friends have made sure to work in shifts at my house so that I'm never left alone. But today of all days Anthony told me there would be about a thirty minute gap between the time he left for volunteer work at the shelter and the time Sis. Agnes from Alex's church would be able to come and sit with me. Not a problem right? I mean what could I need that couldn't wait thirty minutes? I'd made a bathroom run, Anthony had snacks laid out for me by the television, and the remote was in reach. Well right now I needed somebody to open my door because I just sat down and it took me almost a half an hour to get here. And to make matters worse, the person was ringing the bell repeatedly, whoever this is when I get to this door in about ten minutes is gonna get it.

"Wait a minute! I'm coming…wait a minute!" It dawned on me that it was fundraising time at school. I had to sell pizza for both Marie and Shye, which I usually ended up buying and eating myself. If this was one of those snotty nosed kids from my neighborhood botherin' me about buying something I was gonna make sure I went off real good. The bell just kept ringing.

"I said I'm coming! What part of wait a minute don't you understand?" I managed to get to the door and stuff both the crutches under one arm so I could yank it open with my free hand. And when I did, I nearly fell in the floor. One because I'd put too much weight on my injured leg without thinking, and two because my sister was standing on my front porch with her finger poised over the doorbell ready to ring again.

"Hey beans!" My sister screamed the nickname she called me during childhood and reached to hug me. I didn't even care about my leg at that point; I dropped those crutches and pulled her into my arms.

"Oh Gwen! Gwendolyn it is so good to see you again. I missed you so much. Come on in here." I turned to hop back over to the sofa so I could sit down.

"Sissy beans, what happened to you?" Gwen said immediately reverting back to that big-sister worried voice I remembered from when we were growing up.

"Girl it's a long story, but I'll fill you in, once you get in here and tell me why you've been homeless for two years and haven't tried to contact me." Enough with the small talk. I love you, you love me, and we're all a happy family so let's get down to the nitty-gritty.

"You were always one to waste no time gettin' in my business. It's hard to even tell you why I made most of the decisions I've made in my life." She laughed and continued on. "But for real before I go giving you my life story, can a sista get something to eat...I'm starving."

Whoa. I hadn't even paused to take a look at Gwen. I don't mean to sound rude, but she looked awful. Now that I'd just stopped to look at her I noticed the deep frown lines around her mouth, the dry rough skin on her hands, the rough uneven hair that just stood out all over her head. The two teeth missing on the right side of her upper row of teeth. Her cheeks were sunken in and her clothes hung on her like she was a hanger.

"I'm sorry. Of course you can have something to eat. You must be famished...let me fix you something." I said struggling to get up from the sofa.

"Beans! I got this. You just rest. I haven't been in a home for two years, but I still know what a kitchen looks like and what to do in there, so I can fix myself something to eat." When she came back to the sofa, she had a little bit of just about everything there was in the kitchen except the soy sauce packets from the carryout that we always stuffed in the drawer. I didn't want her to feel self-conscious so I pretended to be interested in a magazine for about ten minutes while she wolfed down a sandwich, a snack bag of chips, and two slices of cold pizza.

"So where do I begin?" She started with a mouth full of food. "Life basically turned to crap after I left with Miles back when we was still on McCulloh Street. If I could tell you a day in our marriage when he wasn't high, then I can tell you that I was elected the president of the

United States on that same day. I might have had two days where I got to sleep through the night without worrying about getting woke up with a punch to the face or ribs 'cause he was pissed about not having nothing to get high on."

"Gwen…why didn't you just leave? Why didn't you come back to the house with us, or even try to get away when it got so bad?" Alright girl, stop sounding like Oprah. You know from all those stories, you've written that it's just not that easy.

"Crazy. Just plain blinded and crazy. 'Nay I was out there too. I was shootin' and snorting just like he was, it was the only way I thought I could keep him, make him love me. Then after I got so bad, I ain't think nobody else would want me. Come on look at me. Last time I went to the clinic I think I weighed 115 pounds. When I left high school I was a healthy woman, hips, chest, all that. People look at me now they see crack walking."

"You smoked crack!" I shrieked.

"No girl, but that's what the young guys yell out when they see me… 'look over there, that's crack walking right there!' or 'hey baby I can get you some more crack if you come over here and take care of me'." She said making a rude gesture with her hand, imitating the guys on the street. She was devouring her second bologna sandwich as I watched and listened in horror.

"And who am I to say my weed smoking, and heroin shootin' was any less of an offense than somebody smoking crack. I was out there hustling just like everybody else. Shoot, half the time Miles used me as payment for some of his drugs. Then one day I just woke up and wanted to be done with it all. Girl, you know I was never as much as a religious fanatic as you and mom, but I know it wasn't nobody but God that woke me up that day. It was like any other day. I was groggy, had a splitting headache and I was laid up with people I didn't even recognize from the night before. But all of a sudden a voice told me to get up, get out of there and never go back. I was scared Beans, but I can't describe it...I never even had a taste for the stuff after I left that building. Miles though....he was too deep. Antwan just laughed at me when I said I wanted him to stop selling to Miles. Miles found out and somehow I ended up just getting the stuff so I wouldn't get beat up as bad."

"Wow...wow..." I didn't know what to say. Thankfully, I was saved by the bell because Sis. Agnes had arrived as scheduled and after ringing twice, which was our little signal, she let herself in with the key hidden under the flowerpot by the front door.

"Oh...excuse me; I didn't know you had...uh...company." The woman was typically not known for being at a lost for words, but you could tell by the way she was stammering that Sis. Agnes was visibly taken aback by my sister's appearance.

"Sis. Agnes this is a blessed day for me...this is my sister Gwendolyn, she surprised me today and came to visit." I was smiling another one of those tight smiles, at the same time wishing Gwen would put the chips and salsa down long enough to shake the woman's hand.

"Well my lands!" She said squinting hard at us. "I guess if look real hard, squint and close one eye, ya'll do resemble one another. Pardon me asking but...you from 'round here?" She was still clutching her purse to her ample middle.

"As a matter of fact...as of today, she's from right here. She's going to be living with us until she can get back on her feet." I declared, while my sister sat with her mouth wide open, thankfully she'd just washed down the chips with a swig of Anthony's famous iced-tea.

"Well then, let me get on upstairs and run you some hot water child, you look like you need a good soak." Sis.

Agnes was never one to mince words. As she waddled up the stairs all Gwen and I could do was laugh.

"She means well." I said rubbing her leg.

"You know you don't have to do this right?" Gwen had put down the last bite of Alex's famous pound cake that I was saving for my midnight snack, as she looked me squarely in the eye.

"I do have to do this. It's supposed to be this way. And besides we can be a blessing to each other. You will have shelter and I will have a personal assistant. Anthony can go back to work, you can help get the kids back and forth and tend to all my needs…it will work out perfectly." I said half-joking, half hoping she'd agree to the arrangement. I was kind of tired of having so many well-intentioned, but nosy folk up in my house at all hours of the day. And as much as I love my husband, he needs to get back to work, before we drive each other crazy.

"Looka here…ya'll got plenty of time to catch up." Sis. Agnes said once she'd gotten back downstairs and saw that we were still locked in a sisterly embrace. "Gwen you need to carry yourself on up them steps and let Calgon take you away. I would say you need to get some meat on them bones, but from the looks of things here you well on your way to workin' on that situation. I'mma get this mess cleaned up and start on some dinner for you girls."

"Yes ma'am! I think I'm about ready to wash away the past, and begin a fresh new life. Yesterday if you told me I was going to be here, and that I'd get a chance to start over again, I might not have believed you, but what a difference a day makes." And with that my sister skipped up the stairs two at a time, singing and humming to herself.

Chapter 56: Even So…I Am Blessed

§

Fresh and new began to look good on Gwen. She would still get down on herself but she was slowly coming around. She started to pick up weight almost as soon as she got here. Today she was wearing a sweat suit she'd bought herself from Wal-Mart, refusing to buy anything expensive with the money I gave her each week. She was definitely earning her keep, taking Marie to soccer practice, getting Shye to baseball practice, cooking dinner for Anthony and even keeping up with her great-niece Morgan. Anthony and I prayed about it and felt led to give her a monetary compensation each week. Gwen hadn't had a bank account in years so Anthony had to go help her open it and show her how to manage it. I was helping her with her interview skills because I wanted her to eventually be able to get a job and be independent.

"Here Aunt Gwen, look at this one…it says all you need is a high school diploma, an ability to learn quickly, and have a pleasant telephone voice." Marie was looking through the classifieds with me and Gwen as was our custom now on Sundays after church.

"Yeah, but I don't have my diploma. Like a dummy I left school two months before I was gonna graduate. Girl when I tell you that you need to be strong and don't let no boy trick you out of your future...I mean it!" She said shaking a finger at Marie.

"You don't even have to say that to me. I know God wants me to be an engineer and a fashion designer, so later for some immature boy." Marie was rolling her eyes as she scanned the paper.

"Oh really? Engineer and Fashion Designer...that's quite a combination" I laughed.

"Yeah mom, I'm gonna design cars with the slickest interiors and sleekest exteriors, you'll see, the car world better get ready for Marie Chase."

"I believe it. Now Gwen, you know you can do just like Alex and get that GED...it's never too late."

"Yeah Aunt Gwen, me and Shye will help you study. By the time we're done, you'll be ready to get a college degree." Marie laughed and got up to answer her buzzing cell phone. At sixteen-years old, she'd finally gotten the phone she'd been bugging us for since she was ten. As she moved away to hold her conversation with a person that made her whole body language change I turned my attention back to my sister.

"I've been meaning to tell you that I am very proud of what you did today." Gwendolyn had a confused look on her face.

"What? Staying for two services? I really wanted to hear that second part of what Rev. Fowler was talking about making it on your broken pieces. Honey, I think that woman was talking about me."

"I'm talking about tithing. I know it's a big sacrifice for you, and you did it today." I said patting her on the back.

"Well I wouldn't have anything to tithe if it wasn't for you and Anthony, so thank you." She said looking down at her feet.

"We wouldn't have anything to give you if it wasn't for God, so thank Him." I said pointing up. She just nodded in silence. I could tell it was coming together for her and that made me feel at peace. I only wished Antwan had been able to find his faith and trust God in his life before he was killed.

****

Later that night I was awaken by Anthony, lightly shaking me as I labored to breath.

"Nay baby...I think we need to call Dr. Grander you really sound bad to me. You just got through a coughing fit, didn't you feel it?"

"I'm trying my best to keep quiet over here...do you want me to sleep in the guest room?" I slurred. I was so tired from all the coughing and my breathing exercises weren't doing a thing to help me.

"No, girl...I'm just saying, you're worrying me. This hacking cough has been getting worse each day, and your breathing is so bad here lately. Just go let him take another look at you. He said he wanted to know if there were any changes."

"And so what if there are changes Anthony? What if he says there are more spots and the treatment didn't work this time? What do we need to know for? What will it change?" I didn't mean to take out my frustration on him, but this was one of those days. I get them every once in a while.

"I want him to tell me how to make you stop coughing. I want to know how to get you back the way you were before all this happened. I want us to be able to go for walks again without you having to stop and rest every few feet." He was rubbing my back, trying to be gentle, but I could feel the tension in his hands.

"Anthony, can you accept that things may not be the way they were? Can you just right now, accept that I may not be able to do those things? I'm done asking God for things." I was fooling with the pillows wedged between my legs, and behind my back, and under my knees. Finally I just threw them all to the floor and tried to lie on my right side.

"How can you be done? God is a supplier of every need. He says you can ask him for anything and it shall be done unto you...especially because you love Him Renee and you live your life for Him." Without a word he got up from the bed and retrieved my pillows working slowly to put them back in place for me.

"Anthony, I'm done asking because I don't need anything else. Don't get me wrong, I have not given up on God by any means...but I am to the point where I just don't want to keep asking. I am so blessed. I know this hurts you to see me like this, I wish there was something I could do about it, but baby…"

"I'm calling Dr. Grander in the morning. You need more tests." Anthony said interrupting me. "I love you Renee, and I'm not going to let you leave this earth without me having tried everything in my power to keep you here with me."

What could I do? I was not in Anthony's shoes, but I have to say if it were he struggling with this thing, I'm sure I'd be the same way. Fighting tooth and nail to defy death. As we lie together I silently began to pray for his peace and his spirit, not as my husband but just as a man of God who was hurting.

And for my husband I did go see Dr. Grander the next day to get some more testing done and discuss the changes in my health status.

I was at the beginning of an important stage in my life and I knew it before I even stepped foot in that office. I heard it again last night when finally my jagged breathing slowed, and for a brief moment my lungs felt like they were clear and healthy. I was able to take beautiful deep breaths of air and exhale them without any wheezing. It was amazing. I thought I was dreaming, but I was very wide-wake. When I'd taken the deepest breath and exhaled I heard the Lord saying to me…*purpose*. Then my lungs were tight again, and I began coughing, but in that moment I knew that very soon that type of calm I'd just experienced was on its way, and it would come as soon as my purpose was fulfilled.

Chapter 57: God Is In Control

§

I'm dying. Sounds a little obvious when you say it like that. I mean aren't we all dying? No earthly vessel lives forever. From the time we are born we are gradually aging and ultimately we die. But to be told that you are dying is different then just dying from old age. When someone says you're dying it means they regret to inform you that you won't be living into the golden years. Typically it was said with a very grim look on the face, at least that's the way I'd seen it on all the soap opera's I've been fortunate or unfortunate to watch over the last few days. And to be honest when I stopped and thought about it, Dr. Grander did have a pretty sad look on his face when the words rolled out of his mouth. It must be difficult to work with patients that you know will most probably die, despite your most valiant efforts. We've had a long road of it. But when he sat with Anthony and me in his office to review my latest diagnostics I felt like I was the one that needed to provide him with comfort. He literally looked on the verge of tears.

"Mr. and Mrs. Chase…I honestly wish there was something else I could do. We have been as aggressive as we possibly can and these cells are just not being affected. Your last biopsy shows the malignancy has spread to both lungs. It explains the bouts with the severe shortness of breath and those coughing fits. Your oxygen levels are very low so I want to start you on home oxygen. It will make you much more comfortable." He paused. It looked as if he were searching for more words to say. Anthony and I just sat quietly and held hands. No one said anything for at least a minute. The silence was deafening to me, I felt like I had to say something.

"Thank you. Dr. Grander, you don't know how much you have given to me and my family. We are so appreciative of your valiant efforts, and your prayers." I whispered to him with a smile, as I reached across his large desk to touch his hand.

"I feel like we've failed you. When we saw those first spots a few months ago, I was sure we'd gotten to it in time." He said shaking his head, and rubbing his tired eyes.

"We tried. It was just not meant to be." I said, letting tears fall.

"In my line of work it is a sure thing that I'll have patients that will die at very young ages. My colleagues that are in other fields of medicine often say they could never do what I do. They wonder what joy or fulfillment I get out of treating a person that I know I can not save." He said with his elbows on his desk, head resting heavily in the palms of his hands.

"I have to tell you doc…I don't know if I'd be able to get up every morning and come in here with the joy and love you possess. It not only gives hope to the sick, but their families as well. God bless you man." Anthony said, while he was dabbing the tears that fell from my eyes.

"My faith keeps me going. I wouldn't be able to do this without direction from above. This is why this news hurts me. I often don't talk openly about this to most patients, but the two of you are a peculiar people, so I feel like I can share. I have been praying to God that this would not be the answer. I thought surely you have this one wrong God. Renee Chase is a fighter, she beat cancer once and I know she can beat it again. I have some patients that never mention God even as He heals them and delivers them from cancer. But you two always stood firm in your beliefs. I prayed the moment I took that biopsy and sent it off to the lab, and I prayed the whole time it was gone. When I opened the report I was fully expecting that you'd be walking out of here like you've done so many other times with a clean bill of health." He sat shaking his head and skimming over the report again with his finger tracing every line.

"Dr. Grander…the answer is not in that report. I have won. My tears are not of sadness, just pure joy. I have always had a certain calm in my spirit about this diagnosis. I can handle this. So I don't get to throw that birthday bash with the hundred candles, but I am still going to live my life to the fullest." I said looking alternately at Anthony and Dr. Grander who were both weeping silently.

"I've been able to ascertain the projected length of time you have to live based on the growth pattern of the cells." Dr. Grander said, wiping the tears from his eyes, and assuming a more professional tone.

"If it's alright with you, we'd rather not know." Anthony said quietly. We'd discussed the night before that if the result were not positive we didn't want to be given a dooms day deadline.

"If you're sure that is your decision then I will respect that." Dr. Grander said closing my very thick file folder and pushing it away from him on the desk.

We ended the meeting with a prayer and an appointment to follow up and get all the medicines I would need to make myself comfortable while I was home preparing to…well…go home.

****

That was two weeks ago. Respecting my hard work ethic, and my desire to keep doing what I loved to do, Alvin consented to letting me work from home for as long as I was able to do it. He told me he had every confidence in my work, and would feel honored to have me continue to turn in Emmy award wining material. Of course you know that made Marguerite just so green, but what can I say, it matched the weave she was wearing this week. So I'd set up my laptop in front of the big screen and went to work. I was still getting work in on time and making Julia look good thanks to Harold.

And speaking of Harold, something very strange was happening. Two weeks ago when he came to pick up stories from me, Gwen was wearing old sweat pants and a head scarf…today, she's got on one of my v-neck sweaters and some shape showin' jeans. Not to mention, the hair is flat ironed to perfection. She's just bouncin' and behavin' all over the place.

"You got a hot date or something?" I joked with her as she passed me on the sofa. She stepped into the powder room and primped in front of the mirror before answering me.

"Why must I have a hot date? Can't a girl just get up and put some makeup on for herself?" She answered planting her butt on the arm of the chair beside me. These folk know I don't like people sitting on the arms of my chairs.

"Gwen, now come on…the last time you wore makeup was at your junior prom…so we talking more than thirty years ago." I laughed. My sister really was a tomboy when we were growing up, she didn't even want to wear a dress to her prom. She even ended up wearing a cream-colored pantsuit to her wedding. My mother almost had a heart attack.

"Whatever. Is that guy Harold coming to get your little story you've been typing up?" She said trying to sound like she wasn't interested in the man.

"He's divorced, just turned fifty-five, lives in a super swanky condo downtown, is a strong black Christian man, and yes you have my approval to go out with him." I said totally ignoring her first question.

"What makes you think, I'm even interested in the man? I mean he's nice, but he's not my type."

"You're right, he's not triflin'. Seriously sis, he's a wonderful person. I have been watching you slowly change since he's been coming over. It's alright to want to date again; it's alright to want a companion in life. I'm not trying to be a match maker, but it would make me feel so much better to see you with him, than that jezebel Marguerite."

"Oh, is he seeing the receptionist from your station?" She asked immediately assuming a slouched posture.

"No…much to her dismay. She completely dogged the man out while he was going through his divorce and hasn't left him alone since it was finalized. He won't give her the time of day, and it is eating her up." I had to give Harold props. Old girl was throwing everything she had at him, but he was standing his ground. The doorbell made both of us jump.

"Let me get it for you." Gwen said making a beeline for the door. She paused to fix her top, tossed her hair out of her eyes and placed her hand on the knob.

"Oh…and just so you know, I can really email these reports to Harold…he requested to come pick them up. Does that answer any questions you might be having about how he feels about you?" She stood with her mouth wide open.

"Well don't leave the man waiting. Ya'll got a wedding to plan before I make my way on up to the pearly gates." I said smiling and waving my hands for her to open the door.

As soon as the door swung open three dozen red roses with two well-dressed legs greeted her.

"For the lovely lady." Harold said peeking out from behind the monstrous bouquet and extending his arms to Gwen.

"For me? Oh you shouldn't have." I joked as he came further inside the foyer. My sister was glued to her spot with a silly look on her face. "Gwen you should go get a vase to put those flowers in." I suggested, shooing her in the direction of the kitchen.

"Oh...right! A vase." She said running off to look for one.

"She really does know how to speak in full sentences with more than two words." I said to Harold loudly enough for her to hear.

"Do you think these are a bit much? I don't want to scare the woman off? It's been a while since I've been in the dating scene." He was sounding just as nervous as Gwen was acting.

"You two are a trip. That is a pretty gargantuan bunch of roses, but they are beautiful. I'm impressed." Gwen had made her way back in the room with two large vases.

"These are beautiful; you didn't have to do this, but thank you." He helped her divide the bunch in half and arrange them in the two vases. They were talking so quietly and giggling, it was cute.

"Hey speak up...for the sake of the sick woman on the sofa, I can't hear a word ya'll are saying and it sounds juicy." I joked as I clicked away on my laptop. I'd just sent all the reports to Harold's email, but I'd let him sit here for a few more minutes so the two of them could get to know each other better.

"So that settles it, then Gwen...I'll pick you up tomorrow night at 8:00." Harold put on his shoes that he'd left by the door; sorry Renee's house rule number five...this carpet is too costly to clean.

"Make sure she's back in this house by her midnight curfew." I said laughing. I handed him a folder with a single sheet of paper in it that just said 'Check Your Email'. He didn't even open the folder, or ask any questions, I swear the man was floating on air.

Gwen came over and sat beside me with a huge sigh and a smile on her face a mile wide.

"Isn't he just the cutest?" She sighed.

"Oh Lord, now you sound like somebody from the Mickey Mouse club. Yeah he's swell!" I joked with her.

"Stop it Renee...I have serious matters on my hands here. What in the world am I going to wear? I don't have any dressy outfits, what about shoes? What should I do with my hair?" She was pacing back and forth.

"Child calm down. You have two nieces that have doctorate degrees in shopping honey. Let them take you to the mall and get you hooked up. In the mean time, come over here and sit down you're making me dizzy." She finally sat beside me, being careful not to sit on the tubing from my oxygen line. "I want you to realize that you deserve someone like Harold. Somebody greater than you and me designed this moment in time. And besides all the practicing you've been getting around here, cleaning, fixing meals, chauffeuring the kids around, you'll make a great wife!" We both laughed.

Chapter 58: Working Together For The Good

§

There goes that dang doorbell again. You would think that since Gwen was getting ready for her third date with Harold this month, she'd be downstairs ready and waiting for him. But no, right now she was in the shower just a singing about 'I love me some him'. Everybody else had mysteriously disappeared from the house, so you-know-who that just dozed off on the sofa had to get up and answer the door. I didn't have enough juice in the pipes to yell out 'who is it', so I moved at a snails pace conserving my energy and hoping against hope that Gwen would get out of the shower in enough time to get the door. Needless to say the water was still running as I turned the knob to put an end to that annoying ringing. When we first got the chimes put in I loved the way it sounded, at this point I was ready to disconnect the wires myself.

"Surprise!" It wasn't Harold at all, but standing on my doorstep was Nick, Laurie, a now four-year old Nicky, and a chunky 15 month-old EJ.

"What in the world? Nick what are you doing here? Come on in!" I sang. "I don't know where dad got to, but everybody just scooted out of here about an hour ago. He's going to be so surprised to see you."

"Girl ain't nobody surprised but you." Anthony said coming through the door with two heavy bags in his hands. Goodness who was home for the summer, followed with a carry-on and one of Laurie's diaper bags, Alex hauled in a car seat and a stroller, Shye struggled with a heavy garment bag and a rolling trunk, Marie came in with a large box labeled 'kitchen tools', and Morgan bounced in carrying one of the boy's stuffed bears.

"What in the world is going on here? Ya'll look like you moving in." I was so confused.

"We are ma! Well not in here, but back to Maryland. Laurie and I wanted to keep it a surprise! I can't believe dad didn't let it slip. But we've bought a home in Owings Mills, so we'll be right around the corner." Nick said dropping his bags and squeezing me tight.

"I don't understand? What about your beautiful home…the restaurant? Why would you come all this way?"

"For you mama…you've done so much for all of us, we wanted to come back and take care of you for a while." Laurie answered.

"Don't stand there with your mouth open, sit down and let the kids tell you about how this thing is gonna work out." Anthony said gently guiding me to the sofa.

"Mom, I know you don't like anybody to make a fuss about you, but consider this a Chase family meeting and right now I'm the one leading it." Alex started, taking my hand. "I have been praying about this, and I know God has spoken very clearly that this is what His will is for the rest of the time we are blessed to have you with us. Me and Morgan will move back in here to help you and dad out for a while, Nick and Laurie are right around the corner to help with appointments, shopping, and cooking."

"But Gwen is here and she helps with all of that. I wish you guys would have told me you were doing all of this...I would have..."

"Mom, just listen...Aunt Gwen is going to be working at Faith Tabernacle as an administrative assistant."

"What! That's great when did that happen?" I momentarily forgot how angry I was with my family for not letting me in on this secret to be blessed that Gwen had a job.

"Beans, Alex just told me this morning. Isn't it exciting? So I'll be gone most mornings for a few hours, but Laurie will be able to be here." Gwen said descending the stairs with the most beautiful summer dress on that I'd ever seen. The girl was just glowing. You'd never guess she was turning fifty in a few days.

"Well...it seems like you guys have everything all figured out." I mean I knew that I was on my way out, but I didn't appreciate everybody just planning my life without consulting me. A sista does still have some breath in the lungs. True it's being pushed in with the help of an oxygen tank, but its breath nonetheless.

"Renee, don't go sounding down. It's good for everybody. We all want to be here with you. Nick and Laurie wanted to come without hesitation as soon as we got the latest news from Dr. G." Anthony piped in, trying to cheer me up.

"Please know, that we seriously prayed and considered all our options before we came. I have already set up two possible locations to open new restaurants here in Maryland. And we have a great crew back in Ohio, I'm not worried about the businesses at all. We are doing what God has told us to do. When God says move, you move even if it doesn't make sense to you at first. Our being here will have a purpose beyond what we can even imagine...I just know it." Laurie had come and was looking at me with reassurance in her eyes.

"Well...since you put it that way...I can't argue with a move of God." I laughed still feeling a little hurt and left out of the decisions.

"It's gonna be a little tight around here for a while because the house won't be ready for another few weeks so you'll have to put up with us and all of our junk." Nick said pointing to all the bags in the living room. "We had most of our stuff shipped down and put in storage, but these are the essentials."

"Well get them essentials out of the middle of the floor and on down to the basement. And everybody in this house hear me and hear me good..." I started in with a stern look on my face, which slowly gave way to a sly smile. "Thank you so much for loving me the way you do." Everybody laughed and hugged.

Gwen floated on out on cloud nine to her date with Harold, and the rest of the Chase clan just sat and watched movies and ate popcorn into the wee hours of the morning. I spent most of the time dozing in and out, but it felt good to have all the family trying to talk quietly and pretend they weren't staring at me every time I opened my eyes.

"Look, why don't we just let mom get some rest, we'll head on down to the basement with the boys." Nick whispered as he picked up Emmanuel who'd long since lost the battle with the sandman. Nicky on the other hand was wide-awake and blowing bubbles with the power-ranger bubble maker Alex had given him earlier this afternoon.

"No need to act like ya'll are whispering, I'm up." I said yawing and stretching.

"Yeah, but you don't need to be. I'm taking mom upstairs guys we'll see you in the morning, come on sweetie pie." Anthony said pulling me up gently and putting my portable oxygen bag over his shoulder. Alex and Morgan left when it was close to her bedtime…he didn't want to have to deal with a sleepy Morgan, who'd missed her nap with all the commotion earlier. It was not a pretty site. He was going to be in his apartment until the end of the month and then he and Morgan would take their place back down in the basement after Laurie and Nick moved into their new home.

Chapter 59: Living For Right Here and Now

§

Peace. Tranquility. It was definitely coming. I was on my way to a glorious place. Right now I was just meditating on the word purpose and it was giving me such great peace.

"Nana? Nana are you getting ready to go to heaven?" Nicky asked. When I opened my eyes he was standing so close to me all I could make out was one of his large brown eyes and the curly eyelashes that went with it.

"Nicky hush! I told you not to bother your nana when she was resting." Laurie scolded him and pulled him back from the sofa, where I'd permanently taken up residence. It was becoming my custom to lie here and look at the fabulous home movies we took of all the kid's special events. I had the official day that Goodness, Shye, and Marie were adopted and got our last name, Goodness' high school graduation, the road trip to Atlanta for college, Nick and Laurie's wedding, Alex and Morgan's baptism, Morgan out playing in the yard. And that was just the tip of the iceberg.

"It's o.k. He's not bothering me. Nicky, your nana sure hopes she's done enough good works and been a good enough person that she's on her way to heaven." I smiled at him.

"When you goin'? Can I come with you?" He was so innocent.

"Daddy said when you go I gotta still be good 'cause you gonna be able to see me if I'm bad." Morgan piped in from her favorite spot, sitting in her granddad's oversized chair. She was going to be spending the night because Alex had a shut-in he was leading with the youth at the church.

"Your daddy is right! I'm definitely gonna be watching you guys." I laughed softly.

"I'm gonna miss you nana banana." Morgan said poking her lip out.

"Don't miss me…remember me. I'm not going anywhere just yet, but you remember all the good things we got to do, and even the times I had to tap that bottom for things you should not do anymore."

"Oh…no I don't want no more taps nana." Morgan said shaking her head from side to side, jumping down from the chair and moving closer to me.

"Well I know somebody that's gonna get tapped if they don't get down from the arm of that sofa." Laurie warned as she made her way back into the kitchen. I mean you can't beat having a gourmet cook for a daughter-in-law. She was making very special meals for me that were easy to digest and healthy for me, and she was just spoiling the rest of the family with all kinds of specials from her menus. She'd only been here for three weeks, but already had orders to cater for two brunches at local churches. Today she had the kitchen smelling good with delectable treats for the grand opening of Chicara's Dreams, a full service hair and nail salon. She'd met the owner back in Ohio when she'd catered a hair show at the convention center in that area. They'd made promises to hook up whenever Laurie made it back to Baltimore. Just as she was packing up items to take to the salon opening, Gwen breezed through the door.

"Mmm...what smells so good? I would say I was starving, but me and my man just had lunch so I couldn't possibly eat another thing." She bent over and kissed my forehead, gently pulled Nicky off the corner of the sofa, put the cap back on the purple marker Morgan was using while sitting on my white sofa, and grabbed a tray from Laurie as she made her way to the door. Harold you are a blessed man, this woman is quite the multi-tasker.

"You and your man are sickening." I joked.

"As the kids say now-a-days...don't hate." She laughed tossing her glossy hair over her shoulders. I was absolutely loving the fact that she was finally happy and looking like the beautiful woman that God wanted her to be.

"Besides I'm surprised your man recognized you with all that extra hair you got going on up on top of your head." The girl went and got hooked up with some honey blonde tracks that hung down past her shoulders.

"I know right! Laurie, when you see Chicara, tell her Harold loves the new weave. Told me to tell her that he's got somebody that needs her services real bad." I knew she was talking about Marguerite. I think that girl was still using tracks she had from when she was in high school.

"Ya'll are a trip. I'll probably be a few hours, please make sure the boys don't stay up too late they have to sing at church in the morning. Dinner is in the oven." Laurie said shaking her head at us.

"You look like you could use a little rest, so close those eyes. I'll take the kids out back for a little while to play in the kiddie pool." She turned to her great-niece and nephew. "Ya'll go get your swim suits on."

"They are asking me about going to heaven." I said to Gwen once they were out of the room.

"They understand so much that you are not the same nana from a few years ago."

"I know. I just don't want them to be scared." I whispered quietly.

"I know I for one am not looking forward to not having you here. Renee you literally saved my life and now it just makes me so upset that I waited so long to come to you." Her eyes began to water.

"Everything in life, every time in life, every action has a reason. Gwen you are not going to blame yourself. We both made decisions in our lives that took us away from each other, from family, from God…but right now is all that counts. We are here right now, and while I have the breath I want to say that I am so proud of you. I love you. I want you to say yes when Harold asks you to marry him."

"Girl what on earth are you talking about? I've only known the guy for two months and you're talking marriage. He's not even thinking like that, and besides do you really think he'd be crazy enough to want to marry me? I have a past that is so much deeper and darker than what he sees in the smile sitting across from him when we are on our dates."

"Everybody has a past. Harold has a testimony honey, that I'll let him tell you when he is ready. But the past is just that…the past. You all have a wonderful future ahead of you, trust me."

"Thank you beans. I'm so glad that I'm here with you right now. You always say God ordains things the way He wants them and I can't help but think that the day I walked out of that apartment on Monroe, He knew I'd be right back here with you at this appointed time." She got up and headed out back to play with the children. I quietly drifted back to sleep with a smile on my face. Yes all things were coming together for the good.

****

"And do you Anthony Gordon Chase take Renee Desiree Billows to be your lawfully wedded wife, for better, for worse, for richer or poorer, in sickness and in health, to have and to hold from this day forward, 'til death do you part?"

"I Do." I heard Anthony reply from his chair beside me in the living room where he was reclined before I heard the response from the video of our wedding tape he was watching. About twenty minutes ago, I heard him quietly sneak down here while I was napping and push the tape in. It was the third time this week he was watching the tape and probably the fiftieth time this month. I felt like I was intruding on a private moment for him, but I really had to move because my leg was starting to cramp.

"Oh hey babe…did I have this up too loud? I didn't mean to wake you." He said reaching to turn down the volume.

"No…it's not too loud at all. I noticed you been watching this one a lot this week. You got tired of all of Nick's football games huh?" I said making an attempt to laugh without coughing. Anthony saw me struggling to sit up a bit, but being so weak, I was losing the battle. He got up from his seat helped me to sit up, tapping me ever so gently on the back to help loosen my cough. He sat down beside me and let me rest against his chest, with my head nestled under his chin.

"This is my favorite one to watch. You know I hate to admit it, but at the time I was saying 'I do' to all those words, I really didn't think I'd have to live through the poorer, sick or…you know…part of it. I was just so young at the time that I thought to myself I was saying 'I do' to a perfect marriage. Boy was I wrong."

"Thanks a lot!" I laughed, but I wasn't offended. I could totally relate to what he was feeling. I never in a million years could have anticipated the worse, the talk of divorce, the infidelities, and the utter dislike for one another that we had. The even more amazing thing is that you couldn't have told me that we would go through all of that and still be committed to one another. That even though my health was failing, I was not the vibrant young women my husband fell in love with and said 'I do' to, yet here he was gently stroking my hair, and loving me in what were surely my last days on this earth.

"You know what I meant girl! Look at those two young naïve kids in that video. And now look at us. Would you do it all again Renee?"

"In a heart beat." I said taking his hand from my hair and kissing the back of it.

Chapter 60: The Breath Of Purpose

§

I can literally feel my heart beat slowing down. It's a rather unusual pace. I've been so used to the instant gratification, gotta do it and have it now, no time to rest lifestyle for the last twenty or so years of my life that this seemed so strange. Everything and everyone seemed to be moving in slow motion around me. There were lots of conversations going on around me that were about me, but didn't include me.

The dayshift nurse was over there by the dining room table assuring Anthony that I was not in any pain and letting him know she'd increased the dosage on one of the medications that was being delivered to me through the IV's. Goodness was telling Marie that she could keep talking to me and telling me about her soccer games because I could still understand everything that she was saying. Laurie was scolding Nicky and EJ for making too much noise and bumping into the foot of the hospital bed that was planted squarely in the middle of the family room. I just overheard that Alex was bringing a tape by for me to hear that would make me smile, something about a sermon from Faith Tabernacle. I have enjoyed all the sermons, and gospel music he plays for me when he would come and sit at my bedside. Most of the time he comes to sit he doesn't say a word, just pops in a tape and sits next to me either holding my hand or praying silently. It felt good, his hand. It's a different type of warmth. When he touches me my spirit lights up, I am at peace.

    I feel like I have so much to say. And I have been saying a lot, just not out loud for anybody to hear. I probably haven't talked for the last few weeks, at least not since I began drifting and making my transition the night Anthony and I got finished watching our wedding video. At first I tried to fight it, I mean I tried as much as I could to come back to him because I didn't want to see him hurting. But I couldn't. This feels right. This is where I'm supposed to be right now.

    "Mom…I'm going to get Mario, he said he wanted to see you today, he has something to tell you…or rather ask you." Goodness said leaning over me and smiling.

    "What you mean ask? That boy ain't thinking about marriage is he?" Anthony asked, stopping his conversation in mid-sentence with the nurse in the other room.

    "No daddy. And even if he did want to ask me that…I'm eighteen so what's the big problem. Lot's of girls my age are getting married and having babies."

    "Lots of girls whose last name ain't Chase. You got two more years of college then graduate school so you have plenty of time before marriage and babies. What this boy gotta ask your momma about?"

    "If you must know, he wants to do a painting of momma and have that be displayed at her service. He wanted to surprise you and present it to you afterwards so you could put it up here in the living room."

    Awww. That is so sweet. I wish she could hear me screaming yes! I would be honored. Of course I don't want Anthony to feel like he has to put it up, I mean he'll be a single man and it might be creepy if he starts dating again. On second thought…whoever that woman is betta recognize that I am the first! Yeah Mario make sure that picture is floor to ceiling! Only you would think of something like that Renee…at a time like this.

"Babe I'm sure your mother would be honored. I'll get some good pictures of her that he can use to do the painting." Anthony said looking and sounding relieved that Goodness wasn't going to be getting hitched.

Later that night I enjoyed the company of the entire Conway family. Mario, his parents, and his two younger sisters. I can remember how the two girls loved Goodness and tried to dress like her and talk like her. That was when Goodness realized that her actions had consequences and that she was very much responsible for the generations that came after her. Nick and his family were over to visit, and a few of the Soulful Survivors. After there was time spent laughing and reminiscing, Mario asked if he could talk with me privately. Everyone excused themselves to the backyard to sit on the deck and enjoy the warm evening. Mario quietly whispered to me.

"Mrs. Renee, I have to say that outside of my moms, you have had the most influence on me and my walk with Christ. I wish I had said all this stuff to you when you were feeling better, but Goodness told me that she knows you are hearing us, so I figured now was as good a time as any. I bless God for you, because if it had not been for your loving heart then I would have never had Goodness in my life. I appreciate how much you love her and me enough to be on us about staying abstinent, and respecting ourselves, and having a personal relationship with Christ. I love you and I would be honored to do a portrait of you if that's o.k.?"

I was about to burst. I was so touched by his words. That somehow without even knowing, I had influenced this young man with the way that I lived my life. It took all the strength I had, but I reached out to squeeze his hand. The look on his face was truly one of shock.

"Did you just say yes to me? Mrs. Renee, can you squeeze my hand again?" I did it and he nearly fell out of his chair.

"Goodness! Goodness come here for a minute. Mr. Anthony! Mom, Dad!" Everybody came running back in the room.

"Boy what is all the yelling for? Are you o.k.?" Anthony said breathless as he came in and immediately went to checking IV lines and monitors.

"Mrs. Renee just squeezed my hand. I asked her a question and she squeezed my hand." Mario was so excited it made me giggle only nobody was able to hear it, but my heart was glad. My heart that had been slowing was actually glad and skipping all kind of beats. This was it, my time to shine. All my family and friends were here. I wanted to do more than squeeze hands. I wanted to say my final peace, I wanted to fulfill my purpose. I held my hand up to beckon Nick and Laurie to the bedside. Everyone was so shocked it took them a moment to realize that I wanted them to come closer. It took an agonizing few minutes to form the words, but eventually they came, just as clear as God wanted them to come.

"You...love each other always." I said in a cracked voice.

"Yes momma. We promise to do that, to always keep God first and to love each other unconditionally." Nick said kissing me on my forehead and moving aside so Laurie could hug me. They pulled the kids up onto the bed and let me nuzzle them with my nose. Goodness came to the bedside, holding Shye and Marie up on either side of her. My rock...what a dynamic woman she had become. Thank you Lord that I was responsible for them for just a little while. After they'd stood for a while with Marie quietly repeating the words 'thank you Lord', I was able to give them the words God had for them.

"You all...be greater."

"Mommy...I don't want you to go, but when you are looking down on me...I want you to be proud of me. I wouldn't have a chance to become greater if you hadn't been there for me." If he hadn't been standing right in front of me so that I could see his face, I would not have recognized the smooth deep voice coming from Shye's mouth. He leaned in to kiss me and I felt the brush of the soft whiskers that were over his lips and even smelled aftershave. Shye...shaving? Wow...a few years ago I wouldn't have trusted that hyper kid with a razor if you gave me a million dollars. Now here he was at fifteen, strong...intelligent...handsome...and most importantly trusting God with his life. I know Marie wanted to say more, but she just couldn't make the words come. Instead she wiped a few tears that were slowly rolling from my eyes. Then she turned to her sister for a comforting hug.

"Mom, you know there is nothing I could say to you and dad that would even come close to how grateful I am for you. I thank God that Shelita knew enough to place us in your care. It wasn't nothing but God. I am so blessed because you are going to a place that we all can only dream about. Be blessed mommy and fly so high." She broke down and began to sob laying her head right in the middle of my chest. Come on now guys...no sad faces. This is a good thing. After a few minutes Alex gathered his sister in his arms and took her to the sofa where she was joined by a host of other friends that surrounded her with hugs and warm words of encouragement.

"Alex?" I managed to whisper.

"I'm right here ma. I'm right here." He said patting my hand.

"You...preach." He just nodded his head, got up from the bedside and was out of my sight. That was quick...That boy, still running from his calling I guess. Anthony came into my view. My love. My strong black man. Still so handsome even with the gray sprinkling his beard and the hair growing finer on the top of his head. He'd sacrificed so much for me in the last few months. Taking family leave from his job, waiting on me hand and foot, and not letting the nurses do their jobs. What am I saying…this isn't a new thing, he spent our whole marriage making sacrifices.

"Hey babe…I love you." He said, showering me with soft kisses on my face and hands. He's still got that touch. The kind that makes you all tingly.

"'Til death…right?" I said with what felt like the last bit of air in my lungs.

"I do." Anthony said calmly, taking his hands and brushing them over my eyelids so that I could close them and complete my journey. From that point on there was no more talking. For a long time I didn't even sense any movement and then a light rush of warm air seemed to suddenly fill my lungs. I could hear hushed voices that sounded so far away.

"Make sure it's not too loud." That was Alex, yes I can still recognize that voice, he must have returned to the room. "I want her to hear it, but I don't want to disturb her transition. I wish I could have gotten this to her earlier." He was always my little worrier.

"Sorry man, I didn't mean to leave it in my car. I saw it on the kitchen counter the last time I was here and I had to put it in…that word really spoke to me." Nick…yes that is my oldest boy. Sounds like he was listening to one of Alex's Faith Tabernacle tapes. Well I sure don't think there is anything wrong with a little word while I'm on my way to glory. I was able to hear the faint click of the cassette door to the boom box being closed and then the spoken word began…and I drifted, just kept drifting…so peaceful…so calm….just drifting.

"You were right. Look at that smile on her face. You said that word would make her smile and she did." Nick said. And why wouldn't I. As I was quietly floating the last words I was hearing were from the tape of Alex's trial sermon at Faith Tabernacle. He was preaching! Thank you God that I was here long enough at least to hear your plan for him fulfilled if I could not physically be there to see it. All I can say now family is that God has so many great things in store. That's it…I did it.

What? I know you're thinking where's the lighting and the fire works…right? What was the purpose she's been talking my ear off about you ask? The answer: To speak life. It took me so many years to figure out that I had the power to speak life. To speak healing into the brokenness and distrust that my marriage had become. To speak awards for essay contests and debate teams to a boy born drug addicted with a speech impediment that society had labeled as dumb. To speak college education and honor roll to a young woman who'd witnessed her mother abusing drugs and being abused by so many men. To speak soccer scholarships and respect to a young lady who thought she had to use her street toughness to get ahead. And what can I say about Nick and Alex? The children that God placed in my womb. Look what they have become…and it does not yet appear. So don't be disappointed. The ending is not always what we want, but it's always what God planned.

Oh well it's time. Where are the smiles people? It's not the end of old Renee. I got children's lives to run from the great beyond. But I do know this…my living was not in vain. My breath had purpose.

The Breath of Purpose: Discussion Questions

1. Renee is obviously frustrated with the state of her life at the beginning of the story. Why do you think she is able to hear from God at this point in her life about purpose? Have you ever been in a situation where you've received a word from the Lord that seems like it is at the wrong time?
2. This story deals with painful relationships, and the idea of forgiveness. Discuss the relationship Renee had with her brother. Why did he harbor so much animosity towards her?
3. Renee kept a lot of emotion bottled inside of her. The past with her brother, her friend Shelita, and Matthew Redmond. How do you think each of these things contributed to or where affected by her faith?
4. Despite "raising her son's right", Alex has chosen a life in the streets. Do you think Renee and Anthony are responsible for this turn because they put him out? What would you have done in their same situation with your teenaged child?
5. It seems as though after Renee began to accept God's will for her life, her world turned upside down. What three things stand out to you, the reader, as events ordained by God that will directly relate to Renee's purpose at the end of the story.
6. Although it may seem insignificant, half-way through the story, one of Renee's adopted daughters' changes her name. What are the biblical implications of a name change? Why was this a big deal for her daughter?
7. At the very end of the story we know that Alex has preached his trial sermon. What do you think will happen with him as he continues on this journey without his mother?

8. What was Renee's purpose? Do you think it was fulfilled? Do you know what God has purposed for your life?

My Purpose is:_____
_____
_____
_____
_____
_____
_____
_____
_____

Turn the page for a sneak peek of the next novel in The Anointed Breath Series:

Taking Deep Breaths

Prologue

§

I took a deep breath in and held it for what seemed like an eternity. As I slowly let the smoke curl out of my lips and float out of my nostrils I closed my eyes and put my head back. I'd been waiting for this all day. I'd heard enough sob stories, prayed enough prayers for one day. Saved enough lives. I was getting good at playing the role of preacher. I can't even tell you when the act of faith stopped being my everyday walk not even knowing where God was taking me, and turned into just that…an act. A whole bunch of talk and a lot less walk.

This was not where I was supposed to be. This was not what my mother prayed for me. My heart was pounding, but I knew it would slow down in a minute. My head didn't even feel like it was connected to my body. It felt like it was somewhere up in the ceiling. But that was my body. I could look down and see me. How did I get here? Who am I kidding, I'm not lost. I came here of my own free will. And my will wanted more.

"Let me get that again shorty." I didn't recognize my own voice. Raspy and low from smokin' too much, and not talking for a while I guess. A thick brown hand was extended in my direction pinching my desire between the first finger and the thumb.

"Dat's all you son. Finish that up, I got another bag upstairs." The dull male voice said to me somewhere in the distance. I put the delicate paper up to my mouth and took the deepest breath I could take. My right eye was closed tight and my brows furrowed. This wasn't the breath of purpose my mother talked about. It was the deep breath I swore to my wife I wasn't "cheatin'" on her with. It was the deep breath I promised my daughter I would never take again, the one that could take me away from her for a long time. And after I'd taken that breath, I knew I was in hell, because when I exhaled I saw him, the tall dark figure of Antwan Billows. He was standing right there in front of me. That's it. It's over. There's no way I'm making it out of here alive as high as I am, with Satan standing just inches way. So I closed my eyes and prepared for the worst. The last thing I remember was his two large hands coming toward me.

Chapter 1: Never Let 'Em See You Sweat

§

I need air. I'm suffocating in this room and I can't get any air in my lungs. All I can think about is breathing right now. *Come on Alex…just keep taking deep breaths.* My office was supposed to be a place of great peace and solitude. Right now though, I couldn't control the sweat pouring down my face and the loud pulse of my heart beating in my ears. I want the privacy and protection of my safe four walls. To be able to hide behind the heavy wooden door with my crazy thoughts and not have anyone even know how truly r-rated those thoughts could be at times. I wanted my darkness, my solitude that I could push deep down in the core of me so far down that to the naked eye I appeared pure and free from any ill-thinking. It scared me to have this kind of emotion bubble back to the surface. It meant I wasn't in as much control as I pretended to be. I've been clean for five years. I'm not talking about zestfully clean like from soap and water. I'm talking about no alcohol, drugs, needles, cigarettes, pornography, gossiping, back biting, lying, overeating…oh you started to separate yourself from me when I first started rattling off my sins, but you see that anything can become addictive.

Trust…I'm not one to condemn. I believe in that whole "let He who is without sin" adage. But I'm getting scared right now. I'm distracted in my prayer closet. That hasn't happened for a year. I used to be able to spit that "when-I-was-in-the-street" phrase to the young boys around here that I mentor and it would seem like such a far off time, but lately my mind remembers that it was not so long ago that I can't visualize what it is I'd like to be doing right about now.

Breathe Alex. Breathe. Breathe. One day at a time, man. Nobody's perfect. See my mind is jumbled right now. And this room usually gets me calm. But it wasn't always that way. I had to do a lot of work in here to transform the space into something that worked.

Before I even stepped foot in here I was warned that I'd need to have an open mind in order to make the space feel like my own. I understood what all the fuss was about the day I walked in to set up shop, because I could tell the space previously belonged to a woman whose favorite color must have been pink. I'm talking rugs, wallpaper, sofas and chairs…all in some shade of pink or another.

I had the room redecorated in warm masculine colors and the words *"relax, restore, and renew"* stenciled in gold calligraphy on the wall behind the sofa that sat across from my desk. I don't like to brag, but the richness of the room was taken to a whole 'nother level with the suede technique of the rustic copper-toned olive paint, done by yours truly. These is where I usually come to shut the door and have some peace, to work in solitude, or let's just be honest; just enjoy a game or two. As a matter of fact about an hour ago I was locked in here secretly enjoying ESPN on my forty-seven inch, flat screen and kicking back with my Kenneth Cole's propped up on my desk. But at the present moment, I feel like I'm choking. No joke…I'm not getting any air and the last time I checked air was essential for survival. Who turned off the central AC? It's burning hot up in here. I bet it feels just like this in hell. If I don't take it easy I'm gonna start hyperventilating. *That's it Alex...take it slowly inhale and exhale and whatever you do man, don't open your eyes.*

I can't tell if the pep talk I'm giving myself is working because sweat is still running down my back and making wet dark spots grow in the armpits of this shirt I just picked up from the dry cleaners. *Alex, if you know what's good for you just pretend like the smell of this woman is not driving you absolutely insane and just get on with the prayer!*

God help me this is so hard. Lord please bring some words to my remembrance to help this sista out. See I'm talking to myself again and once I start talking to myself I know I'm in trouble. It runs in the family...I used to catch my mom talking to herself all the time. God rest her soul. Come on Lord do it!

"*And won't you just stop by here Lord, you said that where two or three are gathered in your name, that if we just touch and agree...you would be in the midst. This sister comes today Lord asking for prayer, that you heal her body and help her to be the daughter and woman you would have her to be. We are believing God that you'll take away the confusion of the flesh and renew a right spirit in her Lord. I ask all these things in your son Jesus name. Amen!*"

I opened my eyes against my better judgment and yes...there they were. I mean there she was, Lakeisha Bantum the reason I predict that I'll be on my face before God all night tonight. Lakeisha is running some serious game on me. The sista is fine, I'm not gonna even deny that. Look like somebody I would have stepped to in a minute if I was who I used to be, but who I am right now makes everything I think about her just a shameful sin. This is the third time this week she's been in my office for special prayer. Each time she walks through that door, the blouses get tighter and the skirts get shorter. This is the kind of stuff I called myself running away from when I came to this church a little over five years ago.

I was young, and fresh off of a six month house arrest. Still had eighteen months of probation to go for my involvement in a drug raid that almost took my life. My mother was actually there when it happened. Of course she didn't know that morning when she was called into work to cover the story for the Channel 2 news that she'd be watching her son get gunned down doing something he knew better than to do. But in spite of all that, she loved me and I know it was her prayers that saved my life.

Yeah I got a testimony. The whole time I was in rehab, she encouraged me to read the bible and to pray even though I was sitting up in a hospital unable to walk because of a bullet that was still lodged in my spine. See I know it wasn't nobody but God that had me stuck in the house with that ankle monitor on. I was reading that Word and I began to notice a change on the inside of me.

But the minute I got a little freedom, my flesh started to become weak again. To be honest I came here to the church looking to hook up with my physical therapist from the rehabilitation hospital I was in for almost three months. She was a fine Egyptian sista that invited me to hear a sermon from this pastor she couldn't stop talking about. I initially was bummed out to discover she had a fiancé and was really trying to invite me to hear a word and not trying to secretly get with me using church as an excuse.

When I got here though I was excited to find out that the singles' ministry was on and poppin'! Even after all this time my mind wanders back to the good old days. Let me stop. There wasn't anything good about them.

Before the life altering night of the raid, I was known as Big G. I told my mother it was because my middle name was Graham, but really it was because I was making that serious paper out on the street. Yeah, North Avenue from Greenmount to Dukeland I was handling my business, making an easy thousand in less than twenty minutes. My Uncle Antwan was my boss at the time and my hustle impressed him so he gave me the nickname G and it stuck. I added the 'Big' part because I was desperately trying to make myself seem larger than life.

  I wouldn't ever admit it to my boys, but because of how my parent's raised me, before I chose a life out on the streets I hadn't had much experience with women at all. But oh boy! A brotha got out on them corners and after a few weeks of really smelling myself, let's just say I knew my way around a woman's body too. The people I used to hang around, would never believe me if I told them what I did now, and more importantly what I'm making a vow not to do until I get married. I'm gonna have to get this girl out of here soon because all I can hear in my head is the tune to Nelly's song *Hot in Herre*. You know it's gettin' hot in here, so take off all your clothes.

  "Whew! I am getting' so hot I need to get home and get out of these clothes. Would you look at me, I'm just a mess." Lakeisha said fanning herself after she finally let my hands go. I was just sitting stunned in silence. It's like she was reading my mind. Nobody told me the AC was malfunctioning? When I was in here by myself I wasn't this hot. What is really going on? *Come on Alex, those are not her eyes, look up brotha.*

  Lakeisha is really about to put the act on. I've come to know her body language. She's slowly working herself into a cry complete with sudden trembling and shaking and dabbing her dry eyes with a tissue. The devil is a liar. I'm am not going to get up from this desk to give her a comforting hug if that's what she's expecting, I fell into that trap last week and almost got myself in trouble. It definitely wasn't a 'holy hug' as Pastor always tells us to greet each other with.

"Minister Alex I know you must think I'm pitiful. I just can't help it. I know God is going to work for me, but I just feel so confused. I want to be a good Christian woman, who is virtuous, but I'm growing from a little girl into a woman and I just get these crazy feelings. There is so much pressure out there to…to…you know. I mean I cry myself to sleep at night because I can't explain the feelings I have for a certain person. I feel so lonely and you are the only one that understands me." She said, batting her eyelashes a million times a minute, still dabbing eyes that were as dry as the desert.

I jumped up from my desk chair to open the office door. "Well Sister Bantum…"

"I told you to call me Keisha…that's what all my friends call me." I was doing my best to get her out of my site, but she interrupted finding a reason to rub my arm with her fingers ever so gently while she did her Tyra Banks supermodel walk to the door. My mother would say she walked like her feet hurt, but when I was doing my thing out in the world…if I'd have ran up on her and that walk; it would have gotten her a lot of expensive gifts and attention.

"I will of course be praying for you. I know that at your age, relationships and desire can be confusing. Why don't you make sure you come to the Youth Conference in the next few weeks, we'll be discussing all kinds of issues that teens are dealing with in our community?" I was doing my best to talk in my concerned parent, mentor, and minister voice right now. While she stood there with a smirk on her face just staring at my mouth as I was talking. I was pressed against the wall trying to avoid physical contact with her at all cost. She knew what she was doing…more than I wanted to admit that I might have liked it. All the lines that I used to say to women were popping into my head at lighting speed. If I wasn't careful I might have had to ask her if she was tired from running through my mind all day.

"Well Minister Alex, I'm not exactly a teenager. I'll be turning twenty very soon, so I consider myself a full-grown woman. And I have been attending meetings with the twenty-something ministry already." Lakeisha corrected me and just to add insult to injury she placed a hand on one of those healthy hips of hers. Good God Almighty!

"Yes, I can certainly see that you have grown into a beautiful woman since I attended your sweet sixteen almost four years ago. I know your father is so proud of you. And because you are maturing in Christ, you'll be the perfect role model for our teens, so make sure you see Sister Agnes or Sister Gwen on your way out to sign up to speak for one of the workshops." There that did it. Just mention her father, and signing up for work in the church and her whole attitude changes. All of the sunshine left her face as she brushed by me to leave with a loud sigh.

Hallelujah! That was close. I almost got caught up that time. I'm gonna have to let my Aunt Gwen, who was one of the church's administrative assistants; know that she can't let Lakeisha in my office for the rest of the week. She was getting to me and I could not have that. My heart was racing, but just one look at the framed picture of my one and only lady was all it took to bring a smile to my face and calm my spirit. The loud buzzer from the intercom on my phone startled me from my daydream. I quickly snatched the receiver from the phone.

"Yes Sister Agnes."

"Which workshop did you want Pastor Bantum's daughter to sign up for, she's standing right in front of me?"

"Oh...put her on the list for the *Waiting for True Love: Abstinence* workshop."

"She'll love that." Sister Agnes replied giggling to herself. She was our senior administrative assistant. She was here to welcome me when I first accepted the position to mentor the young men of the church. And she became a mother figure for me when my own mother passed a few years ago.

Sister Agnes don't take no mess. She's had to run interference for me many a Sunday after service when Lakeisha and her crew tried to bum rush me. She always says '*it ain't right for men pastors to be entertainin' women congregants for too long in their offices*', so she sits outside of my office and Rev. Bantum's office just turning ladies away left and right. She likes to tell me that all of them that don't got husbands and even some of them that do, have an ulterior motive for coming to see me. What can I say, I feel like the R. Kelly of Youth Ministers. You know...my minds telling me no, but my body be saying something totally different. I mean I'm not trying to do anything, but live a life according to God's will and these young girls will not leave a brotha alone.

****

"Man you keep this up, you gonna be so swollen you won't be able to put your arms down to your side." My brother Nick said laughing, as he watched me struggle through my third set of bench presses like a madman. I was on a mission. I called him as soon as I left the church while I was driving. The remedy for keeping my mind stayed on Jesus was in the basement of my oldest brother's spacious home. It was getting so bad, that practically every other day, I needed to go to his house and directly to the basement to workout. Cold showers did nothing for me; I needed to get my sweat on.

"It sure beats the alternative. Man it just seems that the closer I get to where God wants me to be, the more temptation there is." I whined, feeling sorry for myself.

"I could have told you that a few years ago, and saved you a few workouts! At the rate you're going, you're liable to give yourself a hernia." He continued to laugh at my expense.

"I'm glad you think this is so funny. But you're not in my shoes. You are married to a beautiful, saved, black woman, with two great kids, and one on the way. You got a house better than anything I've seen on MTV Cribs, and the whips in the garage. All you need is a dog and The Cosby's wouldn't have nothing on ya'll. I mean you are truly blessed."

"I know I'm blessed man, can't even tell you how I thank God every day. But come on man. You think I don't get tempted. I'm a Chase. You know woman can't resist the charm of a Chase man. And besides I think I have it worse, because I'm married. Man you are single; you can date all the women you want."

"No I can't either. I'm a minister man. Being single and a minister is harder than being married. My wife is God and the church."

"It can't be any tougher than being married to Laurie, that woman can be a beast sometimes." He said lowering his voice.

"I heard that!" Laurie yelled from the top of the stairs.

"See what I mean, all seeing, and all hearing…just like God." Nick said shaking his head while he picked up some free weights to work off some of his own tension.

"You're going to be in the doghouse for that last comment." I said, poking him in the chest. Now it was my turn to joke.

"I'll just have to turn on the charm and break out the hot oil. Laurie can't resist my massages." Nick winked, confident that he'd be getting back into good graces with my feisty sister-in-law.

"I have a headache!" She yelled again from the top of the stairs.

Chapter 2: Sometimes Being In The Closet Is Good!

§

It was well after dinner by the time I got home, but I knew my baby would be waiting for me. The girl loves me with all her heart, and I was in the mood for a hug and a kiss.

"Hey dad," I yelled from the front door. I could still smell the fantastic dinner he'd prepared. Ever since my mother died two years ago, he's been slowly getting into a routine of cooking, cleaning, and washing clothes. All the things he relied on her to do. My older brother and his family initially moved back to Baltimore from Ohio a few months before my mom died just to help dad with the transition. Nobody wanted dad to be alone. They decided to make the move permanent when Nick found a job with a law firm downtown. Laurie, who owned two restaurants back in Ohio, opened an event planning/catering business called Heavenly Delights and God blessed them with a beautiful home in Owings Mills. I moved in with dad after they got settled in their own home. It's a long story, but this was my third time moving back into the house where I'd grown up. It has turned out to be a blessing for me to save money and hear wonderful stories about my mom and dad's relationship. I pray that God grants me a helpmate that makes me feel the way my dad feels about my mom.

"Where's my baby girl? I thought she'd be waiting for me?" I asked. I was a little disappointed that she hadn't waited up for me. I didn't realize the time had gotten away from me. I'm even more upset with myself that Lakeisha was the reason that I missed spending family time, with the one person that means the world to me.

"You just missed her…cleaned her plate and went on upstairs to bed. I told you that girl could eat when ya'll first moved in here. I might have to increase your half of the grocery bill, just to cover her food." He said laughing.

"Could you fix me one of those food-so-good-it-puts-you-to-bed plates, while I go up and check in on my baby?"

I ran up the stairs two at a time and burst through the door that used to be my sister Goodness's room. My mom and dad adopted my three younger siblings when their mother, a close friend to my mom, was tragically murdered. In an instant we went from calling each other god-brothers and god-sisters to just plain brothers and sisters. For the last ten years Goodness and Marie my 20 and 18-year-old sisters, and Shye my 17-year-old brother have been a part of the Chase family.

"Where's my sugar! I want some sugar! I'm the sugar bear and I need sugar!" I playfully growled and pulled the covers back.

"Daddy! Daddy!" Squeals of laughter where all I heard as my beautiful daughter jumped into my arms and showered me with kisses.

"How's my princess Morgan doing? Daddy missed dinner, I'm sorry." I said pretending to be sad by poking out my bottom lip.

"And you missed story, but Pop-pop read me *Good Morning Brown Butterfly* and one about bears and honey, so next time daddy you have to say you are a honey bear, not a sugar bear. Ok?" She said shaking her finger at me, scolding me and looking just like her nana doing it too.

"I stand corrected." I laughed. This girl was so smart. God knows she's seen a lot in her short six and-a-half years, but she has a wisdom that is beyond explanation. The Wonderfully Made series by Lisa McNeill that included the story about the brown butterfly has been a lifesaver to me many a night. Morgan loves the books, and I love that they show her such positive images of good Christian girls. Humph, maybe I needed to read Lakeisha one of these books. But then that would mean she'd have to be in my office. See there you go again Alex.

"My eyes are getting sleepy, but can you still say my bedtime prayer with me?"

"Of course angel. Get down here on your knees with me; you know daddy likes to say prayers down here."

"Does it get to God better this way?" She asked so innocently, settling in beside me and resting her head on my arm.

"Your nana Renee always told me it did. I just believe baby that when you make yourself humble and get down a little lower, that you can hear from God a little better. Now close your eyes."

"I'm gonna go first daddy, ok? Umm…Jesus thank you so much for the beautiful day, and for Pop-pop's fried chicken, and for my daddy giving me hugs and kisses…and…um for my own princess bed…and for my mommy to get better. Amen!"

"And Lord just continue to cover this angel of mine named Morgan. I pray for peace for her mother and a special blessing over her entire household. I ask that you continue to keep our family in your will and direct our paths. Show us who we can be a blessing to each day. Keep watch over us tonight as we sleep and grant us new mercies in the morning. Amen!"

"That was good daddy. You the best prayer sayer in the world. Is that why God made you a special person in the church?"

"Honey I can't tell you why God called me, but He did. So I have to live my life so He'll be pleased with me."

"That's why you say good things about mommy and try to help her be a good person?"

"That is right. Now shut those eyes tight, really squeeze 'em and don't open them until morning time. Good night Morgan." I gave her one last kiss on the forehead, switched on her Brown Butterfly nightlight, and left the room.

I got downstairs just as the timer was signaling that my plate was piping hot in the microwave. And yes there was fried chicken! My dad can throw down on the chicken. KFC ain't got nothing on Anthony Chase. I grabbed my plate and headed into the living room to watch the big screen with my dad. I remember when he first got the television; my mother was so upset because it wouldn't fit downstairs in the basement where dad had set up a "man room". He had to leave it right in the middle of her cream color themed living room; we all dubbed "The Museum" because she didn't want anybody really sitting in there. Eventually she grew to love the television, and relied on it for comfort. I remember as she grew weaker and weaker from her cancer, she would lie on the sofa and watch home movies until she fell asleep, always with a peaceful smile on her face.

"Thanks dad. Morgan was raving about your dinner. I appreciate you keeping an eye on her."

"You know I don't mind. How was Nick?"

"His usual self, trying to stay in the good graces of his wife."

"And getting in trouble doing it right?" My dad said laughing.

"The two of them remind me of your mother and me. Man when I think about the fights we got into…can you believe we both even threatened to leave each other a time or two?" He said shaking his head and looking at the large portrait he kept of mom hanging over the sofa.

"See I know ya'll had disagreements here and there, but I would have never guessed that you would have ever considered divorce."

"I don't think neither one of us would have guessed it, and to tell you the truth I probably can speak for your mom when I say it was all just talk. I loved your mother even after…well I mean we went through a lot of stuff, but God got us straightened out. I tell you we worked on our marriage. Ya'll hip hoppers today just take it for granted. Every time you get in a fight, you hollerin' divorce. Your generation get married one week and call it off the next. We had rough patches, but it wasn't anything too hard for God." He reminisced, placing his arms behind his head and closing his eyes.

"Yeah, I remember hearing some of those rough patches. It got a little fiery from time to time. Ya'll must have forgot the walls where kinda thin and I was right next door."

"Well I was hot headed…" My dad said as if he was telling me something I didn't already know.

"You don't have to tell me, I was on the receiving end of a lot of that heat!" I interrupted, thinking about the tough love my dad showed me, as I was growing up in this very house. It got so bad when I was eighteen that he just up and put me out one day. Well since God is ruling my life, let me be honest and say I deserved it. I was coming in late, drinking and doing drugs, right under his roof. And it sure wasn't like I didn't know any better. My parents put their trust in me, to make the decisions I was raised to make, and time after time I betrayed that trust. It just got to the point where my father decided he wasn't going to enable me by providing a nice warm, safe place to come back to after I'd been out whore-mongering, drugging, and drinking.

"Boy please, you lucky your mother had your back or you woulda had a permanent third degree burn on your behind…now that's how hot it could have got in here"

"But God!" We both yelled as if on cue. And it was God that saved the relationship between me and my dad, and saved me from the certain death I was headed toward. I was not only involved in using drugs, but I was selling. Yeah after my folks put me out, I didn't waste any time getting hooked up with my Uncle Ant, better known as Big Ant around the way. If I knew then, what I know now, I would have seen him for the devil he was…seeking to destroy and kill by any means necessary. But with a heavy dose of I-think-I'm-grown clouding my vision I walked right into the trap. He was just someone I wanted to emulate. I wanted his cars, his money, even his gold and diamond studded teeth! I almost truly lost my life trying to be something I was not. Just as I was beginning to lose my appetite thinking about what I almost became, my dad's voice brought me back to the present.

"Yeah, I could get heated, but your mom knew how to cool me down. She'd love to hear me say this now, but about 99.9 percent of the time, she was right. And that other .1 percent she just let me *think* I was right!"

"I hear you. I can't wait to be married."

"Correction son, you can wait. You can wait until God gives you clear direction. You can't just make any decision; because whoever God gives you has got to also be a mother to that little one upstairs. And trust me; you are going to see so many available women, just falling in your path, especially now that you are a minister. Be careful. Just like you looking for a wife, the devil is looking to send you somebody to trip you up."

"You ain't lying dad. I think the devil has sent somebody to my office three times already this week." I said attacking the food on my plate.

"Oh…so that's why you had the impromptu workout session at Nick's. Reverend Bantum's daughter got you all messed up again? What's her name, La…La something?"

"Her name is Lakeisha dad. And I know the thoughts I have for her are wrong. It hasn't really even gotten that bad, but dad the girl smells so good, and she's so fine, and her…" I didn't realize I had closed my eyes and was making a not so Christian gesture with my two hands until I looked over to see a very unpleasant look on my dad's face. I was twenty-six, but my dad could still scare me straight with just a stern look.

"Now you just stop right there. Go on up to your prayer closet and read that word boy. You preached many times to those young people that sin is not only actions and words but thoughts. Now all those thoughts you over there contemplatin' are carnal and are a sin." When he didn't turn his eyes away, I took that as my cue to get to stepping to my sacred room upstairs.

When we were growing up my parents had an area of the loft on the second floor designated for prayer and meditation. It was holy ground and not to be disrespected. I was finding that I really needed some private space because a brotha could get to moaning and crying and scare somebody half to death. So my prayer room was literally the walk-in closet in my bedroom which used to be my parents master bedroom suite. After my mother died my father said there were too many memories in there for him to ever go back and feel comfortable so he moved down to one of the smaller rooms and let me move in so I'd have plenty of room to write sermons at the desk by the window, and read my word in the small sitting area. He helped me convert one of two of the walk-in closets to a private sanctuary for meditation, taking care to build shelves for my countless books, candles, and pictures. From time to time I'd hear him in there talking to God about my mom and how she was doing up there with Him. But tonight, was gonna be a long night. I had a lot of praying and meditating to do to get my mind right. I knew as soon as I saw her walk into my office that Lakeisha Bantum was going to have me on my face before God.

Made in the USA
Lexington, KY
16 December 2011